Critical Acclaim for Ross E. Lockhart's *The Book of Cthulhu I & II*

"The enduring allure of H. P. Lovecraft's Cthulhu Mythos, now nearly a century old, is evident in this representative anthology of modern tales, most of which were written in the last decade."

—*Publishers Weekly* (Starred Review)

"Gathering Cthulhu-inspired stories from both 20th and 21st-century authors, this collection provides such a huge scope of styles and takes on the mythology that there are sure to be a handful that surprise and inspire horror in even the most jaded reader."

—Josh Vogt, *Examiner.com*

"There are no weak stories here—every single one of the 27 entries is a potential standout reading experience. *The Book of Cthulhu* is nothing short of pure Lovecraftian gold. If fans of H. P. Lovecraft's Cthulhu mythos don't seek out and read this anthology, they're not really fans—it's that simple."

—Paul Goat Allen, *BN.com*

"*The Book of Cthulhu* is one hell of a tome."

—Brian Sammons, *HorrorWorld.org*

"…a stunning collection of Lovecraft inspired tales all centered around the infamous Cthulhu myth."

—Drake Llywelyn, *Dark Shadows Book Reviews*

"…thanks to the wide variety of contributing authors, as well as Lockhart's keen understanding of horror fiction and Lovecraft in particular, [*The Book of Cthulhu*] is the best of such anthologies out there."

—Alan Cranis, *Bookgasm.com*

"As he did for his previous anthology, Lockhart has cast his net far and wide to haul in outstanding stories from publications both well-known and obscure, none sampled more than once. He has also commissioned four new stories, several so good that they are likely to be selected for reprint anthologies in the future."

—Stefan Dziemianowicz, *Locus*

"The second volume of *The Book of Cthulhu* exemplifies the richness of Lovecraft's legacy: gloomy terror, mystery, thrills, vivid action, chilling visions, satire, science fiction, humor—all of that, and then some, is crammed into more than 400 pages awaiting readers eager for some apocalyptic horror."

—Dejan Ognjanovic, *Rue Morgue*

"…any fan of Lovecraft can't afford to miss out on this one."

—Justin Steele, *The Arkham Digest*

THE
CHILDREN
OF OLD
LEECH

Also by Ross E. Lockhart

Anthologies:

The Book of Cthulhu
The Book of Cthulhu II
Tales of Jack the Ripper
Giallo Fantastique (forthcoming)

Novels:

Chick Bassist

Also by Justin Steele

The Best of Arkham Digest: Writings on Weird Fiction (forthcoming)

THE CHILDREN OF OLD LEECH

A Tribute to the Carnivorous Cosmos of Laird Barron
Edited by Ross E. Lockhart & Justin Steele

WORD HORDE
PETALUMA, CA

First Edition

ISBN: 978-1-939905-02-4

A Word Horde Book
www.wordhorde.com

TABLE OF CONTENTS

For Laird

INTRODUCTION: OF WHISKY AND DOPPELGÄNGERS

Justin Steele

If you value your health, sanity, and general sense of well-being, then you should stop reading this book right now. Close the cover, put it back on the shelf, and head on over to the non-fiction section. Pick up a book on fishing, or pottery, something safe. Anything but this book.

If you're still reading you must be damaged goods, nothing to lose. Maybe you saw that I started with a warning and felt the need to prove me wrong, to prove that you like to live life on the edge, laugh in the face of danger, shit like that. Maybe the warning tugged at your curiosity, intrigued you enough to carry on. Just remember what happened to the cat.

I'm supposed to be writing an introduction. That's what Ross wanted me to do anyway, but I owe some responsibility to my fellow man, and what we did with this here book, what we unleashed, well, it's just *wrong*. I'm sitting here at my desk, a near empty glass of Lagavulin on the desk edge, the bottle in easy reach. Three feet from me, propped in the corner of the room, is a 12-gauge pump-loaded with double-aught buckshot. If that's not enough I have two .45s and a recently sharpened hunting knife within reach, so no matter how it goes down, it won't go down easy. But who am I kidding. *THEY* want me to write this. It's part of the project. Until my part's done I'm safe. At least I think so.

I should probably start from the beginning. Tell you how I first discovered this Lovecraft guy, and how reading his fiction kicked me off onto this whole "weird fiction" thing, but I'm sure you've heard that one time and time again so I'll skip ahead a little bit. A few Cthulhu Mythos anthologies into my tentacle binge, I picked up Ellen Datlow's *Lovecraft Unbound*, and was pleased to see an anthology striving to avoid falling into pastiche territory. It was during my late night readings that I discovered my first Laird Barron tale. "Catch Hell" did something to me that only a few special stories managed to do: upon finishing I reflected on the story for a minute or two, and then turned back to the first page and immediately reread it. After the second read I walked over to my computer and ordered *The Imago Sequence* and pre-ordered *Occultation*. There was no question that I had stumbled upon something special, something dangerous. Who was this Laird Barron guy? He looked like a pirate, or a grizzled Viking warrior. His writing was a blend of genres that I loved. One part pulp, one part noir, two parts pure cosmic terror, blended smooth and seasoned with a literary skill that few possessed. I had found weird fiction for the connoisseur. If I had only known what I was getting into.

Flash forward a few years later, and I'm sitting here in my dimly lit office space, gulping scotch and wondering how I ever let myself get drawn into this mess. The light from my lamp is reflecting off my tin poster of *The Good, the Bad, and the Ugly*. I let Clint Eastwood's stoic squint and Lee Van Cleef's predatory glare serve as reminders that I have to be tough, finish this up. The wind is whipping at the window and I find myself eyeing the 12-gauge once every few seconds.

In September or so I had a conversation with Ross Lockhart, the other man responsible for what we've done here. We were both huge fans of Laird's fiction, recognized its power. By the end of our talk, the wheels were in motion. We were so excited, completely oblivious as to what the actual significance of the anthology would be.

Finding the authors to take part actually proved to be the easy part. Laird's work is highly respected, and offers authors much to work with. Ross and I wanted to find some of the best writers of weird fiction and offer them a chance to play in Laird's playground. They could use the more literal elements of Laird's growing "Pacific Northwest Mythos" or utilize his themes. Pastiche was not welcome. We wanted the authors to use their own unique talents and voices in order to do Laird justice, yet not by simple mimicry.

The thing is, Laird's fiction is powerful, and not just in the literary sense. Some theorize that there exists some fiction that has the ability to bleed into reality. The words serve a higher function, act as a sort of formula. When these words are read they open a gate to somewhere else, allow *them* to come over. What Ross and I have done is complete the formula, see? Laird's works were the base, the true source of the power. With these stories we amplified it, radio towers strengthening the signal.

Ross experienced it first. He'd be out walking his dog in sunny California, or out at his local bookstore when he would see *him*. Only it wasn't actually him? Ross would catch a glimpse, just enough for him to realize he'd seen Laird. When he looked back he would see Laird standing there, at the mouth of an alley, or the end of a row of bookshelves. And it was definitely Laird, his mug isn't the kind you mistake for someone else. Ross was perplexed, he told me later, because he was sure he was seeing Laird. He looked long enough for the imposter's face to split into a black grin, and then with a wink the not-Laird would duck into the alley or step away from the aisle of books. Ross thought Laird must have been playing some kind of elaborate prank on him, until I pointed him to one of Laird's blog posts. Apparently some of Laird's friends have seen this doppelgänger before, but never more than once. I know this spooked Ross, and he hasn't been the same since. I often ask him if it's happened again, but whenever I bring it up he goes pale, changes the subject. If I push, he firmly denies anymore sightings, but I have my doubts.

I figured it out. Ross thinks we are just putting together a good group of stories, tries to justify his weird sightings with lack of sleep and too much reading for the project. But I know better, the dots are all there, easy to connect. Several of our authors have confided in me that during the writing process they were fraught with night terrors, and even a few cases of sleepwalking. One author turned in his story in a daze, and swore to me that he doesn't have a single memory of writing it. One could chalk all this up to writer's stress, working in overdrive to meet the deadline, but that doesn't explain what happened with our foreword. A certain big-shot author sent us a foreword, before disappearing. Nobody has heard from him since. Ross and I debated on using the foreword regardless, only to find that it had somehow been erased from both of our computers. Strange coincidence considering we both reside on opposite sides of the country.

And then there's me. Being woken up in the middle of the night by whispers from friends long departed. Easy enough to pass off as echoes from dreams, but that doesn't explain why I would find the dog cowering under the bed whimpering. Or the black, sticky foot-prints left across my kitchen floor, cellar door ajar although I always check the latch before heading to bed.

If you're still reading this you must now know that it's too late for you, too. You've started to twist the handle, and the opening of the door is soon to follow. You're going to meet the dwellers on the other side. The Children of Old Leech will soon be whispering in your ear, and they will whisper the same thing they whispered to me: *"There are frightful things. We who crawl in the dark love you."*

THE HARROW

Gemma Files

*T*he earth is old and full of holes, Lydie Massenet's mother used
to say, at least once a day, back when she was still Lydie Pell.

*Its crust is thin, and underneath there's nothing but darkness.
A rind, that's all we live on; just thin ice, waiting for it to thaw and
crack. No need to dig, really—if they want to find you, they will. Never
trust anything that comes out of a hole.*

And: *Okay, Mom,* Lydie would say, the way her father had taught
her to. *That's good. That's fine.* Then just smile and nod, all the time
staring off at nothing much, something invisible—contemplating
Mars, he called it—until her mother finally stopped talking.

You have to know this, Lydie, if nothing else, her mother told her.
*Darkness shifts, darkness conceals; it's impossible to know what's hiding
inside it, no matter how hard you try. But if history teaches anything,
it's that what we don't understand, we fear... and what we fear, eventually, we come to worship, if only to keep it in its rightful place. To
make sure it doesn't come after us.*

Yes, Mom. Okay. Sure.

'Til, one day: *Stop saying that, goddamnit!* her mother yelled, and
slapped Lydie across the face, so hard her glasses cracked in half.
That was the day her father brought Doctor Russ home, the day
before her mother went somewhere else—first for a rest, and then,

5

after everything they did to her while she was there had utterly failed to make her well enough to come home again, to stay.

What's wrong with her, Daddy? Lydie asked her father, at last, to which he only shook his head and sniffed, trying to pretend he hadn't been crying.

Honey, I wish to God I knew, was all he said, in return. And hugged her a little too long, a little too tight.

***

By April, Lydie couldn't stand it anymore. "I have to learn how to drive," she said to her husband, Ethan.

"Told you," he replied.

Thing was, in Toronto proper, you just didn't need to have a car, let alone a license—*she* certainly hadn't, her first twenty-one years of life. Lydie had vague memories of having passed the Young Drivers of Canada exam's written portion, once upon a time, but more as a personal challenge; to go further required money she was loath to spare, at the time, and after that there was always the subway, or streetcars, buses, even taxis. Living in the downtown core, where she and Ethan first met, meant you could speed-walk almost anywhere you needed to in an hour or less.

Five anniversaries in, however, the powers that be decided Toronto proper was too expensive a place to rent offices, relocating wholesale to Mississauga. No big deal for Ethan, who'd grown up there. But to Lydie, it was the ends of the earth—"suburbs" squared, with no sidewalks, no easy-access stores. For a few seconds, the day they'd arrived, she'd fantasized about dragging her shopping cart the equivalent of five blocks to the local GO Train station, then investing in a four-hour/twelve-dollar return trip just to pick up enough food for the week from her previous neighbourhood's supermarket.

"Oh, no need," her mother-in-law had offered, helpfully, when she voiced this idea. "There's a mall, just twenty minutes northeast."

"Can I walk it?"

An odd look. "I... really wouldn't, dear."

In the morning, she saw for herself just why: the sole connecting road was a highway turned freeway, overpass after overpass looping sharply up, around and down, like J. G. Ballard porn brought to life. Standing there in shock, she couldn't keep from asking Ethan: "People *live* like this?"

"Well, yeah, Lyd, apparently so. And most of them manage just fine."

"How?"

He shot her a pitying look. "They have *cars*."

That morning, she woke with a headache-seed lodged right between her brows, hard and sharp as Bosch's Stone of Folly. Google gave her a list of numbers to call, trying to line up an appointment with an Adult Drivers instructor. By noon she was still on her cellphone, out in the back yard—another unfamiliar Mississauga oddity, weird combination of luxurious and annoying—when she came across what she'd eventually call the artifact: felt something uneven shift under her foot as she stepped back, almost tripping her, then squatted to squint at the ground, regardless of how high her skirt might hike. There, just protruding out of the earth with its uppermost portion wreathed in grass (a tiny crown, promise-green and fertile), a rough-carved, triangular little face peeped up at her, framed by a pair of short horns or antennae—one broken off jaggedly, almost at the root.

Black rock, lighter than it looked, and warm to the touch once she'd scratched it free, ruining Monday's manicure. Her fingers curled 'round it instinctively, an almost sensual grip, to find it fit the hollow shaped between thumb, forefinger and palm, as if made for it.

Some sort of insect on top, yes, carapaced and six-limbed. But in the centre, where its thorax should be, something else sat instead: the sketch of a human skull, empty-socketed and noseless, grinning wide. With a neat little hole placed just where its brow-ridge should be, for no apparently obvious reason.

"What's that?" Ethan asked when he came home to find her sitting at the kitchen table, dinner not even slightly started, still staring at it. And: "I don't know," Lydie answered, barely looking up; just kept on studying the bug-skull-thing in her hand, 'til at last he sighed, and called out for pizza.

Later, she took pictures with her phone and googled the resulting images. A trail of links (*insect totems, catal huyuk, gobekli tepe, lbk culture, tallheim death-pit, herxheim*) led her to something recognizable: prehistoric trepanning, the procedure of cutting a hole in the skull to relieve cranial pressure, as of a subdural haematoma. Sometimes done for ritual purposes, or so various archaeologists claimed... but in Mesoamerica, at least, those waters had been muddied by the fact that prisoners' and sacrificial victims' skulls were often routinely pierced to facilitate the creation of skull-racks: rows on rows of severed heads, hung up on pegs, or hooks.

The hole goes at the back, usually, she thought, tapping a finger against her teeth. *Or on top. Never in front.*

Between the brows, though, or slightly higher—there was a symbolism there, right? The pineal gland. The third eye.

Around two, she lay down next to Ethan with her eyes open, contemplating the ceiling while he snored. Thinking: *I wonder if there's more.*

***

When she and Lydie's father were kids, there'd been a girl, Lydie's mother used to tell her. And one day, when they were all out in the woods playing, this girl had somehow stepped... wrong, laid her foot on the one place she shouldn't have, and broke through, opening up a hole. Had tumbled down into what later proved to be a cave that went straight down, too deep to see the bottom, and with no earthly way of ever getting back out, once you were in.

A story grew up amongst the group of children Lydie's mother ran with, afterwards, that if you were to go to that hole, that cave, and hang your head out over the edge—if you did that, and whispered your greatest fear or wish or dream down into the black pit below, while clinging on for dear life with both hands—then if you only waited long enough, a voice would answer. And that voice would tell you if your dream, or wish, or fear would... if it *should*... come true.

Whose voice, Mom?

No one knows.

Didn't anyone ever ask?

Oh, no. No. That would be...

Here Lydie's mother had trailed away into silence, one so long Lydie had thought at the time it might signify the conversation was over, before finally adding, minutes later—

...never, no, never. No one would dare.

Lydie studied her hands for another few beats of her pulse, letting the moment stretch on. Then asked: *Did* you *ever do that?*

Lydie's mother swallowed.

Once, yes, she said, reluctantly. *Only once. And that was a mistake.*

Why? No reply. *But... did it answer you, Mom?*

And: *No,* her mother replied, with a sad, angry sort of hunger. *But that's just as well, isn't it? Because you can't trust such things, I've told you that already... those sorts of places, the earth's open holes. The dark, and the ones who live there.*

Why not?

Because... they lie.

***

"What is it you're digging, dear, exactly?" her mother-in-law asked, on Friday, when she turned up to take Lydie shopping. Lydie smiled and drew her gardening gloves off, pausing to thwack them clean against the stake she'd sunk to mark her initial excavation; dirt fell in clumps, dusting her boots. "Flowerbed," she replied, without blinking.

"Ah. Eh—isn't that one already, over there?"

"Sure. I just... wanted more."

"A little project, to keep you busy 'til driving school?"

"You got it."

Ethan never even bothered to ask what she was doing out there, all day, every day—not after that first night. Not so long as she got her cooking done in the morning, and made sure there was something for him to eat when he came home.

"Boss might want to come for dinner," he told her, skimming headlines on his iPad, as she catalogued her latest finds: more insects, some mammals, even a figure or two. Through the window, the tarp she'd thrown over the hole caught her eye, dun and dull, flat as a cataract. Without prompting, her mind went to those other things she'd uncovered, the ones she'd never bring inside: some locked in the shed, others still underground, concealed by the dig's lip. Down in the dark with the worms, where no one would see, unless—one day soon, perhaps—she decided she wanted them to.

"Better to take her out, don't you think?" she suggested, smoothly. "That place with the steak, maybe—the Korean banquet-house. You remember."

"Oh yeah, that's right. Where we took Mom and Dad, for their fiftieth."

"That's the one."

"Mmm, good call, hon. She'd like that."

"There you go."

***

Some people say God turned the world upside down, once, Lydie's mother whispered, into the close, hot air of her small, dim hospital room. *Just for fun. And many strange things came up out of the earth, then, things trapped down there for a hundred thousand years, ever since the world was made... just like the Flood, but different. And many bad people joined with these things, and flourished, and many good people died screaming. Until finally, when he didn't find it quite as funny anymore, God flipped it all back over again, and made everything the way it was. Like when you lift up a rock to see the bugs crawling underneath, and when you're bored, you just drop it again, and squash them; you don't have to care what happens, because they're just bugs, after all. And better yet, it's not like you have to* see *it.*

But some people say he never did flip it back again at all, God, Lydie's mother whispered, later. *That's why things are so bad up here, even though God made us, and everything around us. Because this world, all we see, was never meant to be on top at all. It was meant to be hidden, kept down, trapped. Because where we live, right now... we live in hell. What* was *meant* to *be hell.*

Shush, Irma. For Christ's sake, shush.

(But: Where did the people who were meant to be in hell live, then? Lydie used to wonder. And the things down there in the dark, the people who weren't people, the ones her mother kept on warning her about... who were they? Was that meant to be *heaven*, down there?)

What happened to that girl, anyways? Lydie was finally unable to keep from asking her father, one night, as he stroked her mother's hair back from her rigid, sweating face. *The one from the story. The one who fell into the hole.*

Oh, well... they never did find her, honey, though they looked a good long time, all the time your mom and me were at school together. And that's why you should stay away from places like that—in the woods, under the ground. To stay safe.

But: *Karl, why would you lie to her that way, our own daughter?* her mother broke in, suddenly. *You know as well as I do that she did come back, eventually... all cold and wet and naked, knocking on her family's door and crying, in the middle of the night. But they knew they shouldn't let her in, because they were old now, and she—she was the same, just a kid. Just like the last time they saw her.*

Irma, please, be quiet. My God, why won't you ever keep quiet? You'll frighten her to death.

At this, Lydie's mother's lips drew back; you couldn't call it a smile, not quite, for all it involved was lips turning upwards. Not after you'd spent some time alone with it.

Oh no, she said. *No, she's not frightened—are you, darling? Don't listen to him, Lydie; go where you want, do what you want. Go dig. Go whisper in every hole you see, for all anybody cares.*

See what you get, then.

***

In agriculture, a harrow (often called a set of harrows, in a plurale tantum *sense) is an implement for breaking up and smoothing out the surface of the soil, distinct from the plough, which is used for deeper tillage. Harrowing is often carried out on fields to follow the rougher finish left by ploughing operations. The purpose of harrowing is to break up clods of soil and provide a finer finish, a good tilth or soil structure, suitable for seedbed use.*

In Christian mythology we speak of "the harrowing of hell," Jesus's descent into the underworld during his three days of death. In this case, the word "harrow" derives from the Old English hergian, *meaning to harry or despoil—the idea that Christ invaded and triumphed over hell, releasing all those kept captive there, including redeeming Adam and Eve, the fount of all original sin.*

"Excuse me," a voice said, from behind the back fence.

Lydie bookmarked her page and set the iPad aside. Someone was looking in at her through the narrow mesh of the gate next to the shed, so dense it barely suggested their eyes, like the facial grille of an Afghan *chadri*—female by the voice, Lydie could only assume, which was husky, flute-y. Though the level of the shadow "she" threw did suggest a fairly unusual height.

"I'm sorry," Lydie said, automatically. "Can I help you?"

"I hope so, yes," the voice said. "Could I come in and talk to you, just for a minute?" Quickly adding, a moment later, as Lydie hesitated: "Boy, that *does* sound sinister, doesn't it? Better to come back later, maybe, when you're not all alone. I'll bring pamphlets."

"Oh, no, no, no," Lydie found herself protesting, hand already on the latch. "I'm—it's fine, really. I just… wasn't expecting anybody."

As she opened the gate, the woman—it *was* a woman, now Lydie saw her up close; she was almost sure—smiled, lips canting sidelong like a slow-typed emoticon (back-slash, then semi-colon plus an apostrophe, to mark where that dimple formed closed-quotes punctuation), and stepped inside. Her skin was aggressively tanned, hair bleached at the top and brown at the tips as though she'd been out in the sun for weeks somewhere far hotter than here, let alone today, and held back with a tight-wound bandana so low it brushed the tops of her equally pale eyebrows.

"Paula Neath," she announced. "From the Society for Ecological Rebalance."

While: *1. in or to a lower position;* Lydie's brain filled in, automatically. *Below. 2. underneath, prep. 3. under. 4. farther down than. 5. lower…*

She shook her head, scattering words, and held out her hand, smiling too. "Lydie Massenet. I don't think I've ever heard of you."

"Well, we're a fairly recently formed project. Most of us were doing other things before we got the call… I was in Turkey, for example, tracking genetic variation in honeybees, locust migration patterns, that sort of thing. But actually, what I'm here to talk about is bats."

"That's an interesting subject-shift."

"Not really. All part of the same ecosystem." Paula jogged her head towards the yard's back left corner. "Now, the reason I wanted a word is that as it so happens, your property corners onto this block's drainage ditch—do you know where that is?"

Lydie nodded. "Runs under the mouths of all the driveways on the south side, then dips down under the street. Tell you the truth, I hate that thing: when it rains, it's a stream; the rest of the time, it's a sump, stagnant. It stinks."

"Exactly—perfect for breeding mosquitos, which spread West

Nile disease. Previously, the city's plan to deal with that involved spraying, but we're seeing some very alarming fallout from that… denuded bee population, for one, which affects pollination, which cuts down on new growth generally. So we'd like to put up a grouping of bat-houses in various areas, including right here."

"Like a birdhouse, but for bats."

"Exactly." That smile again. "I'll be honest, Mrs Massenet—"

"Lydie."

"—a lot of people seem to think the idea of opening their arms to flying mice is a bit of a deal-breaker. One lady was convinced they spread rabies, for example; that sort of stereotype. Old wives' tales, to put it frankly."

"Didn't want guano in their hair?"

"Didn't want *bats* in their hair." They both chuckled. "Foolish, I know. Bats are nocturnal, far more interested in insects and nectar than anybody's follicles. You'd barely see them, except at dusk."

"Sounds sort of nice, to me. Do they make noise?"

"Not within the hearing-range of most humans."

Lydie shrugged. "Okay, then. I'm sold."

"Wonderful! You won't regret it—we'll be in and out, no muss, no fuss. And the public health benefits will be striking, once the bats have had a bit of time to do their work."

"I don't doubt it. So… you must be from the university, right? Did they bus you in?"

"Most of us, yes; some of us live here, in the area."

"Nice to work where you live."

"Yes." Paula's sharp eyes—an odd non-colour, neither grey nor blue, almost clear when glimpsed straight-on—shifted from Lydie's, focusing instead on the tarp, as well as the earth piled neatly next to it. "You've been doing some work of your own, by the look of it."

"Oh, uh… not officially. I mean—"

"May I see?"

"Well…"

…why not?

Surprising, in its way, the idea that she would *want* to show Paula, a complete stranger, what she'd so carefully managed to keep from everyone else—her loved ones, supposedly. The people who loved her. And yet, that did seem to be what that usually silent voice deep inside her was suggesting… that midnight whisper, sexless and dark, ambiguous as Paula's own throaty purr.

(*Don't listen, Lydie. They* lie.)

So—

"Yes," Lydie replied, and moved the tarp aside, allowing Paula to see: the hole, and what it concealed. A gaping, sod-lipped mouth which never quite promised answers, for everything else it delivered; oddities, rarities, the strange, the unique. Something you could hold in your hand and study, but never fully understand, except perhaps in dreams.

The dig went ten feet in, these days, much of it almost straight down—a ladder she'd found in the shed providing access, tall enough to reach the roof when unfurled—and with an odd little trailing twist at the bottom, brief sloping sketch of further possibilities. Ethan would be horrified; Lydie couldn't even venture a guess at what her mother-in-law would think. They were such sweet people, really, it seemed only *right* to hide the truth where it couldn't hurt them… kinder, in its way, than the alternative.

If Mom'd only done that, she found herself thinking, sometimes, as she hadn't let herself for years, *then things would've—might've been—very different.*

Paula took in everything Lydie'd spent the last two months doing, then hiding—the open wound of her craziness, at long last laid bare—with one swift, shrewd, searching glance. Then turned her back, stepping down into darkness, sinking 'til all Lydie could see of her was the top of her head; her voice seeped back up, dirt-magnified, made hollow at the bone. "Fascinating," she said. "This is… Neolithic, would you say?"

"Older, maybe. I think it got folded under when the glaciers shifted."

"Yes, very likely. You're extremely perceptive, Mrs Massenet."

Lydie shrugged, embarrassed. "Hardly. I mean—it's weird to think about, something like *this* under our feet, just hidden away… still so perfect after so many years, with all this suburban crap slapped on top. But there you go."

"It is odd," Paula agreed, words deepening further as she bent to rummage through the slick bottom of the shaft, picking and choosing. "But no more so than anything, really. The earth is older than any of us care to acknowledge, and *everywhere* was somewhere else, once. Most people simply don't bother to look any closer than they have to at what they already think they know, unless…"

"…unless something *makes* them."

"Exactly."

(*Old, and full of holes. But do not put your hand down to see, because…*)

Lydie took a small, shallow breath. There was something—she wasn't sure what. A kind of wobble, at the corner of her eyes; black spots hovering, blinking. Was she going to pass out?

A few moments later, however, Paula had made her way back up the ladder in two massive steps, and was standing once more on the lip's moustache-like rut of trodden grass. Extending one huge, muck-filled hand, she scoured free an entirely new type of totem between her thumb and forefinger, with swift, almost brutal strokes: a squat, oval thing, bulgy at both ends like a toad, and small enough even Lydie might've mistaken it for a mere clot of mud-wrapped rock… except for the fact that she knew where to look, and what for.

"Beautiful," Paula named it, reverently. "How many have you found, so far?"

"Oh, more and more, usually five, eight a day… sometimes ten, if I can dig uninterrupted 'til my husband comes home. They don't ever seem to stop. I'm thinking votive objects, a whole cache of them, brought here on pilgrimage and buried, as some sort of— prayer, or sacrifice. Some sort of payment."

"You've done your research." As Lydie shook her head: "No? Then your instincts are *very* good, considering. Nice work, either way."

"I took archaeology in university," Lydie offered. "Just one course a year, but I kept it up all the way through my degree; I'd've liked to go back, to specialize, but…"

"Things happen, yes—sadly, almost always. We move away from our dreams, or they move away from us; seem to, at any rate. But sometimes, the universe provides a second chance." Here Paula closed her hand, tucking the totem away, and watching as Lydie couldn't stop herself from flinching. "May I keep this? Not forever, believe me… just for a few days. I'd like to show it to my supervisor."

"Um… all right, sure, okay. You do that."

"I promise I'll bring it back soon, after the bathouse goes up. Would that be acceptable?"

"…yes."

That smile again, a little wider. "Then it's a deal."

Gone, moments later, as though she'd never been. Only the tarp, peeled back like a lid, gave any evidence of her passage. Lydie stood there looking at it for a few more breaths, thinking: *You need a break, food, a minute. Go inside. No more today.*

But the sun was hot and bright, the cool, dark hole inviting. A minute more, therefore, and she was already halfway down—far enough inside to glance back up, just for a second, and almost think she saw the hole itself blink shut, grass-fringed rim knitting like eyelashes, to shutter away her from the harsh surface world forever.

So nice, she thought, happily, going down on both knees to grub in the mud some more. *So very nice, always, to come home.*

***

The bathouse went up both fast and easy, as advertised. A week on, Lydie watched its inhabitants fly up at twilight, scattering like thoughts into the night as they chased their food, the next echo, each other. By bedtime, undressing in front of the window that looked down onto the back yard, she felt as though could still hear them twittering, even though she knew they probably weren't there. Beneath its tarp-lid, the hole gaped open, its presence always a slightly painful, slightly pleasurable ache; she lay there trying not to think about it, but enjoying when she failed.

"Today wasn't your first class, was it?" Ethan asked, sleepily, from beside her.

"What?"

"Well, you said six weeks..." No reply. "You missed it, didn't you? Oh, honey."

"I can make it up."

"Yeah, hope so."

Annoyed, Lydie turned over, scoffing. "C'mon, Ethan, they want our money, don't they—*your* money. Of course I can."

The next day, however, she was back down in the hole (cellphone still charging on the bedside table, blissfully forgotten) when Paula's long shadow fell over her, making her look up. And: "Hey!" Lydie called. "So you *did* come back, after all."

"I said I would."

"Uh huh. Your supervisor... he like the artifact?"

"Very much. I've got it, if you want it back."

"Just give me a sec."

More like thirty to finish up, thirty more to clamber free, wiping the sweat from her eyes. Paula stood there, toad-rock already extended, offered up; Lydie put out her hand as Paula dropped it, fisting the totem gratefully, as if reclaiming a lost piece of herself. She gave a cave-deep sigh.

"That feels good," she'd said out loud, before she could think to stop herself.

Paula smiled. "I thought it would. Now—if you don't mind me disturbing you just a *little* bit further, might I possibly be able to see what's in the shed?"

***

No actual rack, just a long, low trio of shelves which had once held flowerpots, before Lydie relocated them. She'd cleaned the skulls off carefully, one by one—each so muddy they'd initially looked like they were sculpted from clay—by first letting them dry before going at them with a variety of unofficial fine-cleaning tools, paring away dirt and grime with brushes meant for paints or makeup, scaling the eye-sockets with wire loops to remove as much detritus as possible before breaking out the sand, the bleach soaks, the polyurethane sprays. Now they grinned in welcome, display-organized left to right, until Paula gingerly picked up the first on the uppermost row, raising it towards the light.

Each came with a hole just above where the bridge of the nose would be, if there was a nose, mirroring the totems, and on each the hole at first seemed differently shaped, though careful examination revealed another, more subtle pattern of variation. For in those holes, so seamlessly fitted they almost appeared to have been individually made *for* the space it now occupied, Lydie had laid each of the totems she'd dug up carefully to rest: insect, bird, snake, bat, toad, plus some sort of low, broad thing with long claws, squat legs and a blunt, blind head, like a mole or badger. A catalogue of every crawling and creeping thing which ever forced itself through some crack in the earth and hid itself inside, trading light for dark, at the urging of some hidden, hollow voice.

"Thought they were signs of trepanning, at first," Lydie heard herself explain, her own tone thinning, flattening, words tumbling out in a breathy, secretive rush, as though she feared being stopped before she could finish. "Even though they were in the wrong place. I didn't even think to match them up for… must've been weeks, a month. A happy accident."

"Often the way," Paula murmured. "And then what?"

"I started thinking about why. The point of the exercise." Lydie

paused, feeling her way, waiting for the words to suggest themselves. "What you could hope to—extract, that way. From the same
place people used to think visions came from, or dreams… the seat
of enlightenment."

"The *ajna*, or brow chakra. Where things open up."

"Yeah, but not if something's blocking it—fear, maybe. Desire,
Some kind of… lower instinct. Like an animal."

"And you think that's what they were removing."

"Metaphorically, it makes a certain kind of sense—I mean, no
sense at all, really. But still… that *is* what it looks like, to me: like
they were trying to create a completely new way of seeing. A totem
for every hole, a congealed bit of nightmare, a filter that needs to
be removed, before you can see clearly. The plug that keeps us all
from letting something out—"

"—or in."

"Or in, yes. The light…"

(*the dark*)

Unable to keep from connecting the dots, now it'd finally been
said—from seeing the hole, the place left empty for an answer, and
being therefore driven to fill it. To keep from wondering whether
that had perhaps been her mother's problem all along, solution
inherent in its own equation: *Could* she have been cured all along,
and this easily? A single, fairly simple operation, just one; cut a
hole, take out what you find there and throw it away, down into
the dark. Just offer it up to whatever wants it, and find the courage
to finally accept things *as they really goddamn are,* without having
to be afraid. And then…

…and then.

Standing there wound down, sunk inside herself, no longer able
to tell whether or not she was saying any of this out loud, or what.
Then something at the corner of her gaze again, a black flicker; she
looked up. Just in time to see Paula put down the skull (carefully,
gently, *reverently*) and reach up, behind her head, to flick open
some sort of knot or clip, slackening her headband until it was

loose enough to unwind. Which she began to do, one long fold at a time, without haste or worry—slow and careful, the very same way she told Lydie, still smiling—

"I *knew* we were right about you, Mrs Massenet… Lydie. Though of course, I haven't been as entirely honest, from the beginning, as I might have hoped to be; I knew you already, you see, that first day I came here. *Of* you, at any rate."

Lydie swallowed, dryly. "Oh?" she managed, eventually.

"Yes… as Lydie Pell, to be exact. Through your mother."

One twist, then another, then another—just one more, the final one. Leaving Paula's forehead bare at last, high and broad and smooth, yet pitted centrally with a perfect shell of scar tissue, cracked just a hint at its core: the very same place where Lydie could feel that intermittent migraine-seed of hers re-forming, bone-planted but pushing upwards and out, threatening to bloom. Because here she was at last, arrived, like she'd always somehow known she one day would be: this place, this very moment, teetering on the brink and wondering just what might be lurking under there, waiting, in the dark. A naked pineal bud, eyelid-furled, waiting to breach the scar's tissue-plated embrace, sip at the air, twitch and blink?

But: *Does it matter, Lydie?* her mother replied, wearily, memory-locked. *The hole has its own reasons, always. Do you really want to know what they are?*

Inside the bathouse, the sleeping bats cooed and scrabbled, shrilling sleepily.

"I fell in a hole once, a long time ago," Paula went on, stroking down along the ridge that threatened to bisect her open, guileless gaze with one pinkie delicately lifted, as though she were about to serve tea. "Just like this one. And it was scary, at first: so dark, so deep. But after a while, once my eyes adjusted, I found that I didn't want to get out again at all, let alone go home. Because there were *so* many wonderful things down there, to see, and do, and be. Wouldn't you like to know what?"

"Do I have a choice?"

"Always. You always have a choice."

Which sounded plausible, and not, both at the same time—a truth, thinly disguised as a lie. Or vice versa.

Tongue leather, head swimming. Migraine between her eyes, turning in a tightening spiral, like a screw. Like the coin-shaped burr hole a trephine leaves behind, after the flesh has been cut away and the skull pierced, to show the sweet grey-pink beneath.

Thinking: *So the first harrowing was me breaking up the earth and sifting it for traces, exposing more and more of this buried ruin. But the second harrowing will be a descent into the underworld, a sort of anti-transfiguration... instead of rising into the sky, sinking into the earth and burrowing down, fertilizing it with yourself, a hole inside a hole. Become, at last, the mulch from which something new will grow.*

Lydie looked down, then up again, meeting Paula's gaze with her own. Felt herself nod.

"I thought so," Paula said, happily. "Now—hold still."

And Lydie did, drawing herself taut, rigid, eyes wide. Trying not to flinch as the wickedly curved black stone blade Paula pulled from behind her back made its necessarily painful mark, x-signing the spot where her Folly-stone hid, first one way, then the other. 'Til it radish-rosed a great peel of skin, parting the bloody petals key-into-lock smooth, to lay the slick white bone bare at last and open her up in one swift punch, digging the hole to set her final nightmare free.

Then down, always down, curve after curve, counterclockwise— following the signs which marked her path 'til she could go no more: markings, so luminous and many-layered, on stone which had seemed empty under light, lit up like stars now darkness led the way. Until the surface disappeared. Until Ethan and the rest fell away. Until there was nothing left but one step and the next, over and over: the signs, the path, its eventual end.

(*Lydie, don't*)

The mouth of the cave, whispering in her blood. Her question, and its answer.

(*don't trust it*)

Like you never did, Mother? Lydie thought, unsympathetic. Remembering Paula, whose family had cast her out instead of welcoming her back; Paula, who took the gifts they spurned, and grew to fit them. Paula, her three eyes shining, beckoning to Lydie from the very, very bottom of the hole, the once-top of some inverted mountain huge enough to dwarf Chomolungma.

Here at the bottom, where she finally had worth, and truth, and purpose. Where in led out, and out back in. Where no one mattered more than she did, at least for task at hand.

I walk the harrow, downwards-tending, Lydie Massenet Pell thought, wiping her own blood from her pitifully weak, light-dependent lower set of eyes, while concentrating hard enough to let the uppermost of all three show her the way. *Dragging my blades, ploughing 'til there is no more left to plow, waiting below 'til harvest comes, and we all ascend. 'Til the pale sun shrinks so far it becomes nothing more than just another star in a half-forgotten sky.*

Above her, the rock, like choirs. Below her, the dirt, like flesh, and blood, and food. The great, uprooted currents of the earth, pulling her towards its burning, pulsing, molten heart.

Home.

PALE APOSTLE

J. T. Glover & Jesse Bullington

Wah Sung replaced the box on the shelf and made another mark on the tally sheet, shivering all the while. The February cold of Seattle had nothing on the blizzards that roared down from the Chiung-lai Mountains and blasted across the Red Basin, but something about the cold here chilled her in a way it never had back in Ch'eng-tu. Her father didn't heat the stock room, claiming that it saved the potency of the various herbs, dried insects, and animal parts they imported for the local apothecaries... to say nothing of the tea!

Privately, Wah suspected this decision only preserved the potency of their coalscuttle, but considering the sorry state of their ledgers, fuel might soon become as rare as bear bile. Running a shaky hand over her loosely tied-back hair, she scowled at the obstinate numbers on the sheet, wishing so much were different.

Her father had crossed the Pacific even before the Revolution, paid back every debt accrued in setting up the import/export business, and survived all the random cruelties his adopted country heaped upon him. He'd gone without seeing a single family member for a decade, and had used up most of his carefully saved money to send for Wah just before Congress banned any further immigration from their homeland. Wah had barely recognized the haggard old man who retrieved her from the squalid detention center. Only when they stepped outside and he embraced her right there on Union Street, tears mixing with the drizzle, could she see past the wrinkles to the smiling father she remembered from her childhood.

"Oh Wah Sung," he'd murmured. "You're as lovely as your mother was at your age."

Here was a man who had sacrificed everything, and his reward? Steadily decreasing sales, steadily climbing bills. Even dry goods could go bad, in a place as wet as this, and each order Wah placed reflected their shrinking budget. Before, her father had done well exporting smoked salmon to Canton, but the state had outlawed Chinese from selling locally caught fish years ago.

"I never wanted to be a fish monger, anyway," her father said, shrugging when she asked.

Wah sighed as her eyes passed over the sacks of rice crowding the bottom shelves. Great clay jugs of moutai and yellow wine had once occupied that space, but when the federal government outlawed alcohol, her father had insisted on obeying the law.

"I never wanted to be a wine merchant, anyway," he had told her as they gently argued the point over sweet dew tea. "And I certainly don't intend to become a smuggler. They treat us bad enough when we follow the rules."

Yet rice didn't cover the overhead the way booze had—or fish, or any of the other mundane stock they were forbidden from moving. She'd joked about converting the basement into an opium den, but her father had replied that thieves had once broken through the walls below and trashed his shop, presumably in search of the precious dragon. The whole city was apparently riddled with abandoned tunnels, and many a basement in the business districts abutted them. As if Wah needed another reason for disliking that mildewed hole, where the walls seemed to breathe softly whenever she descended to retrieve a crate of crockery or tools…

The bell at the front of the shop tinkled, and Wah clicked her teeth—she hadn't heard his key in the lock, which meant he'd left the door open again. It was bad enough he insisted on making deliveries to all the family associations himself, but his forgetting to lock up was simply unsafe. Ducking through the curtain, her slippers whisking against the boards, she saw his familiar silhouette across the dark shop. He'd turned and was locking the door.

"It doesn't do much good, now," she said, trying to keep the chiding tone from her voice. "When I'm in the back, though, try to remember to—oh!"

The white man smiling at her across the shadowed bins and shelves was not her father.

"I sorry, honorable sir, but we closed right now," she said, speaking with deliberate fresh-off-the-boat awkwardness even as her mind raced.

Her father was probably talking over old times at some association by now, and might not return for hours. It wasn't late enough yet for the police to be rattling doorknobs, and they rarely took much notice of crime in the Chinatown anyway. Who would hear if she screamed? Mr. Dong next door, perhaps, but perhaps not...

Top shelf, middle aisle. As she stepped around the counter, she studiously kept her eyes on the intruder, instead of the modest display of cutlery. If she could just—

"How excellent," the stranger said, speaking in perfectly unaccented Szechuanese as he glided toward her, past the knives. "That means we shall not be disturbed."

The smile he gave her stretched his strangely ageless face into a rictus—like most white men, his exotic features somehow coalesced into a bland, nondescript whole. His black coat and broadbrimmed hat were wet with the night's rain, leaving puddles on the floor, but his skin looked parched as scrolls from a temple. He reached inside his coat, and Wah flinched, wondering if it would be a weapon, or worse, handcuffs—given the choice between a stickup man or a plainclothes Seattle policeman, she would take the lesser villain. Instead, he held out an envelope to her, as dry as the withered hand that held it.

"My name is Clarence Kernochan, and I have a business proposition to discuss with you."

"My father—" Wah began, but he cut her off in the rude fashion of Americans, waggling the envelope.

"I trust you will surely find this to the advantage of both yourself *and* your father, Miss Sung."

Wah looked back at his face, and in the instant before she saw him straight-on, she could have sworn that his black pupils seemed to undulate, as if something wriggled behind them.

***

A quarter of an hour later, the fragrance of green tea flooded Wah's nostrils as she calmly poured some into Mr. Kernochan's cup. Having heard the man out, there seemed to be no immediate danger beyond arousing her father's annoyance, if he returned to find her entertaining a stranger in their back room.

"Thank you," Mr. Kernochan said, leaning forward and inhaling. "It is a cold night, I appreciate the hospitality."

"It's nothing," said Wah. "But your proposal is… unusual. We do business for ourselves. There are other ways to transport packages."

"Indeed," he said politely. "But safely, without undue inspection, and without their couriers taking an interest in the scrolls' contents? I would prefer to avoid the more, ah, *rigorously* lawful channels, as it were."

"We are not criminals," she said, her irritation causing the chipped pot to shake slightly in her hand as she poured for herself. "There are plenty of others who would—"

"I apologize. There was no offense intended. These scrolls are family records, precious to my colleague up at the University, but nothing that should trouble the authorities. You know what can happen when overzealous customs agents get their hands on such things."

She winced, remembering the hard expression on the face of the official at the docks when he handed her the packet of letters that her aging uncle Bao had naively entrusted to the shipping company. Torn and smelling of piss, they were practically illegible, nor did they contain the locket that the letter had mentioned.

"I am willing to pay well for your services," Mr. Kernochan said, opening the envelope he had initially tempted her with and casually dropping more cash on the table than Wah had seen grace their cash register for three long months. "An advance. Shall we say ten times that, when I receive my scrolls?"

Wah did not reply, couldn't have, even if she had wanted to. This was it, the answer to prayers she had never voiced. Yet even as the relief swelled, her common sense was quick to resurface, freeing her vocal chords.

"And?" she asked him, taking a sip of tea to wash down her initial foolishness.

"And?" Mr. Kernochan did not seem surprised by the question. If anything, his sparkling eyes seemed amused.

"And when we import these scrolls for you, Mr. Kernochan, what else will we find in the box?" Wah set down her cup and crossed her arms. "A false bottom, perhaps, containing opium?"

Mr. Kernochan's chuckle did little to put Wah at ease. "Oh, no no no, no secret compartments, no opium. Just the scrolls, nothing more—you have my word."

His word. Most of the words Wah heard from white men had to do with her eyes, dress, or what they expected her to acquiesce to, so it was not that Wah took him on such a shaky thing. Rather, his word gave her all the permission she needed to focus on the money before her, instead of unduly concerning herself with the contents of yet another crate arriving at their shop.

Clearing her throat, Wah asked, "So how does this work, Mr. Kernochan? I write to your contact in Wuhan and request these... *Chin-ts'an Scrolls?*"

"The Gold Silkworm Scrolls are already on their way to your shop, as part of your next shipment." Mr. Kernochan said this last in English, setting his empty cup back on the lacquered tray. "I was confident we could come to an arrangement."

The affront of his presumption barely registered to Wah, for her ears had begun ringing as soon as he said "gold silkworm." The tannins in the tea turned bitter on her tongue, and as Mr. Kernochan stood and retrieved his coat and hat from the peg, Wah found herself unable to rise from her chair. She felt as though the slightest movement would upend her onto the floor…

Golden-hued silkworms, a countless number, sliding over-under-around-through one another, packed tight into her skull, threatening to burst from her eyes, nose, mouth, ears…

"Shall we shake on it, Miss Sung?" asked Mr. Kernochan, and, just like that, Wah was herself again, the ringing in her ears fading to a distant echo. Getting shakily to her feet, she accepted his dry palm in her damp one, and found surprisingly soft fingers yielding beneath her firm grip. Tucking the money into her pocket, she showed him to the door, praying that her father would not return at just that moment. "Good night, Miss Sung."

"Mr. Kernochan," Wah said as he stepped out onto the slick boards, having almost forgotten to ask. "How did you learn Szechuanese? Over here even most Chinese don't speak it."

"I was a missionary," he said, smiling blandly. "Still am, in fact."

Then the rainy night took him, and Wah hurried back inside to clear the teacups away before her father returned.

***

Wah's father was gone so long, she finally asked the milky-coated horse that helped her in the storeroom to go find the old man.

"Bring me the scrolls," the black-eyed equine said in immaculate Szechuanese, and Wah nodded her assent.

When the beast returned a short time later with her father, she snatched a cleaver from the top shelf of the middle aisle and hacked its ear off. It tried to flee, but her father took up a hatchet and helped her. The dead-dying-deathless creature stared at them with enormous eyes as they flayed it. A pile of red-stained skin gradually rose up next to the carcass.

"I never wanted to be a horse thief, anyway," her father told her as they worked, both wet as new arrivals slouching down Union Street, already wishing for umbrellas. "In Mongolia they have horses that sweat blood."

Wah had to go down to the basement some time later, though the very thought of it filled her with the blackest, oiliest dread. If she didn't go down the creaky steps, though, her father would find out she had taken Mr. Kernochan's money, so she went. Pausing on the dark stairs, she realized that she wasn't entering the basement, but a tunnel.

A cave.

Turning back, she fled from the darkness, slipped on the slick moss and stone. Tumbled. Skidded to a stop in the resinous pine needles carpeting the forest floor. For the first time since coming to Seattle, it seemed, the sun shone from a clear sky, warming her face. Warming the heap of horse skin that sat beside her in the clearing.

The bundled skin shifted the slightest bit. Maggots, no different from those boiling all over the dead cat she'd found in the alley a couple weeks back. Just worms, lending the semblance of movement, of impossible life.

No.

The hollow head of the horse reared up from the coiling, roiling mass of skin, poising to strike like a centipede or a snake. She tried to flee, but the horse skin exploded from its bower of dripping and sun-dappled pinewood. The membranous hide enveloped her, lifting her off the ground as it tightened, wrapping tighter and tighter—

***

Wah tried to sit up, but the clammy sheets swaddled her tight, and her aching limbs lacked the strength to extricate herself. Even before the back room came into focus and she saw the worried faces of her father and Dr. Yam, the apothecary, she knew it was a fever. Before her mother had died, Wah had fallen victim to the same pox. She had been the one to bring it home.

Lying there, waves of heat and cold sweeping over her body, Wah remembered looking up at her mother. The woman's graying hair pulled back into a loose bun, features tight as she'd sponged the sweat from her daughter's face. Then as now, Wah felt like a child all over again. Usually she was as hardy as any peasant's daughter, but in the shadows of the lantern-lit room, all manner of *yaoguai* had laughed and capered, the demons mocking her suffering.

The worst of that fever had come toward the end, as she shivered on the raised, heated platform where the family slept—her mother had kept the *kang* warm even as Wah roasted alive. She'd dreamed of a pinch-faced crone at the edge of the bedding, tall as an old gingko tree, with joints like knots, whispering blasphemies that Wah could no longer remember. Even with her mother's hard, knobby hands wiping away the sweats and residues of sickness, she had flickered in and out of view. Wah remembered convulsing with the last wave of chills as the limbless, needle-mouthed flukes circled her bed in a wave, rearing up to caress her toes with their slick cheeks.

"What are you dreaming of, Wah?" her mother asked.

"I'm not," Wah panted. "Nothing."

"Miss Sung, I asked if you ate or drank something peculiar," the apothecary said.

Her pox-killed mother's face melted into that of Dr. Yam, the old apothecary's tobacco-stained teeth something that she could fix on, cling to as a jetty of reality emerging from the tumultuous fever.

"Tea," she said, shocked at how much effort it cost her to speak.

A hand in hers, warm and familiar. She flicked her eyes left, and behind the calm set of her father's face, she saw all the things she knew he feared.

"Did you have any customers?" Dr. Yam asked. "I haven't seen any sickness like this."

"What do you think…?" her father couldn't finish, squeezing her left hand.

Dr. Yam frowned, holding up Wah's right arm. Even half-delirious, she could see the red splotches on her hand, and the squiggly red lines that stretched up toward her elbow. The patchwork seemed almost to writhe beneath her skin.

"It presents as an infection of the blood, but you have the chills and delirium of a fever, or poison. You saw no one?"

Wah squinted backward, through the shadows congealing in her mind. There were the dreams, of course: a skull-faced man, fracturing into a million horses that galloped in clouds around the world. And there was…

"Golden silkworms," she muttered.

"What's that?" the apothecary said, leaning forward.

"We have a shipment," she said.

Her father and Dr. Yam looked at each other and shook their heads. She wanted to tell them that a rider was coming, but when she opened her mouth, she started coughing, and then she was falling. The cave yawned and swallowed her whole.

***

Wah woke in darkness. She didn't know where she was, or when. The sound of raindrops on the roof brought her further awake, and the dank chill in the air spoke of Seattle. In another room, her father's voice, low. The memory of her last period of wakefulness came back, Dr. Yam's concerned expression. She tried to look at her arm, but it was too dark. There was a dull heat under the skin of her arm and shoulder. Pain when she tried to think back further, but it didn't seem important.

The distant murmur of her father's voice reminded her of something else, the faintest memory. Pine trees, a lantern? She shivered, and that did the trick.

"You must understand," Mama Sung said, "this is an honor for her. She becomes a goddess by the end of the legend."

The wind whispered through the trees outside of the old house. Somewhere in the distance, the laughter of other children, her cousins playing amongst themselves. But Wah loved her grandmother, in no small part for the tales she told, full of magicians and monsters, and so she did not resent sitting with her on the bench while her mother talked with her sisters.

"I don't like it," Wah said, shuddering uncontrollably. "I don't want to hear any more."

"Liar," Mama Sung said, not unkindly, and when Wah returned with more tea for her grandmother the old woman continued her story. "As I was saying, before a scared little girl interrupted me..."

"I'm not scared," Wah said sulkily.

"Liar." Mama Sung sipped her tea. "Ah, that's better. So yes, the horse hide came to life, and fell upon the bratty girl. It wrapped her up tight and carried her off, away into the forest. And when her friends went looking for her, they found the skin hanging from a high tree branch, bulging down like a sack full of wet rice. One of the girls was bold enough to climb up for a look, and do you know what she saw?"

Wah shook her head, feeling dizzy.

"The hide was transparent, like that of an onion, and so through the horse skin she saw her friend, curled up inside. But the girl had changed, her head growing heavy and long like a horse, her body stretching out oh so thin, and that's when she realized what had happened."

"What?" Wah asked, breathless.

"She realized the horse skin was a cocoon, and when her friend emerged she would be a beautiful silkworm. And so she did, and although her family wept to lose their daughter, they rejoiced to welcome a new goddess to the heavens. Now isn't that nice?"

"No, it's not nice at all. It's a nasty story." Wah looked up past the lantern that wavered from a pine bough in the breeze. She was peering into the darkness of the treetop, trying to see if a cocoon hung somewhere over their heads…

"Birth is never pretty," said Mama Sung, lifting Wah up so that she could reach the lower branches and begin to climb. "The worst sorcery comes from feeding one poison worm to another. It concentrates the essence, the dog to the viper, the viper to the spider, the spider to the centipede, the centipede to the worm. This gold silkworm she mentioned…"

Looking back down to the empty bench far below, Wah realized the memory had become a dream. Dr. Yam's voice swirled down out of the pungent pine, the scent not from her childhood in Ch'eng-tu but her new life in America, and she clung to the sap-oozing bark, listening. Her father reached through the sticky boughs and patted her forehead dry, and blinking, she drifted up toward the shining heavens. One by one, the stars were blotted out as the horse skin stretched itself wider and wider, filling the night sky with its embrace.

"Thank you, Dr. Yam," her father said. "You've saved my daughter's life."

The pain had actually risen, but as Wah returned to herself, the fever seemed to be slackening. The cot felt wet and rumpled beneath her as she blinked and the old apothecary swam back into focus. Dr. Yam was scowling at her with an expression that made her wonder if he was altogether happy about her recovery.

***

By the following afternoon Wah was able to leave her bed, and by the end of the week she felt as though nothing had ever been amiss. Quite the contrary, she felt better than she ever had in her life. Other than the dreams, at least, but dreams were just that, nothing more. As the nightmares worsened, she awoke from them feeling strange and high, almost invigorated.

Her father insisted she check in with Dr. Yam to see if she should keep drinking the foul tea he had prescribed. She would have thought her rapid recovery would have pleased Dr. Yam, but he seemed downright grouchy when she called on him. Being made to wait while he served the men in his shop was bad enough, but when the last of them left, he had her lock the door behind them.

"I told you, I'm fine," said Wah, scratching absentmindedly at her arm. She spoke English, since her Cantonese was even worse than his Szechuanese. "I had the fever before, back home."

"You have a fever, to be sure," said Dr. Yam, returning to his counter and reaching beneath it. He retrieved a small brown paper bag, the kind he used to fill his prescriptions. This one was already weighted down by something. "You must be very careful, Wah Sung."

Taking the bag, Wah's eyes widened and her hand shook as she looked inside. "Apparently so! What are you trying to—"

"You can fool your father, but you can't fool me." Dr. Yam leaned across his counter. "You brought this on yourself, Wah, and for your father's sake I hope you put an end to it before it grows worse. And it *will* grow worse."

"Are you saying I should…" Wah imagined the taste of metal mixing with her own blood, but instead of revolting her it sent a delicious shiver up her spine. She rocked on her heels, paralyzed by the unexpected sensation. Then came the fear and disgust his suggestion should have conjured from the first, and she shivered, picturing her father all alone in the shop. "What would he do without me? I feel fine, why should I…"

Dr. Yam offered her a wan smile. "This cure is not for you, child. It's for the sorcerer who poisoned you. He will return, and when he does… well. Now you have the medicine."

Wah gulped, wrapped the bag tightly around its cargo, and shoved it into the pocket of her trousers. Hurrying out of the shop and into the hubbub that was an unseasonably warm and sunny weekend on King Street, she was glad for once that she could not afford the tight-fitting dresses that were becoming popular. Rounding the corner to their shop, Wah stopped short at the sight of Jim Sasaki and Sam Lee tying their team to the post. Somewhere in the wagonload of precariously stacked barrels and crates, she knew, was an ordinary-looking box with far-from-ordinary contents.

A pall fell over the sunny street so quickly that Wah found herself glancing up to see if something unnatural had obscured the sky. Dark clouds were racing in from the coast, and rain began to patter against the shingles and perpetually soft streets, but she took no further notice, other than to pull her damask jacket closer around her. She looked around the intersection, gaze restlessly roving over faces familiar and not, but nothing seemed out of order.

Even so, she knew Mr. Kernochan was nearby. Watching. She scratched at her arm, wishing for the hundredth time that the rash would just go away.

The skies opened, releasing the pressure she hadn't noticed in the air. She went to greet Jim, and his smile was a familiar comfort. She busied herself with the delivery, helping unload the wagon, checking the order forms against the manifest, and trying not to think of the weight in her pocket.

***

"I won't be gone long," her father said, adjusting his hat. "But don't wait up."

Wah nodded, grateful for once that the Chans' pai gow game had come around again. Her father was careful with money, and he rarely gambled, but every few years, it appeared, his will weakened.

And what of it? He's only flesh, only food for the worm.

She blinked.

That wasn't the first time in the past few days that she'd heard the cold voice in her head, whispering cold, cold things. They horrified, and yet, something about what the voice whispered seemed *right*.

"...do you say?"

"I'm sorry, Father. My mind was an ocean away."

"That's all right, my dear. You are the best daughter a father could have, and wherever else it wanders, I know your mind is also on the shop."

He headed off into the gathering night, and even though Wah was still on the floor, he paused to lock the door behind him. He always locked up now, ever since the night of the fever. She went to make tea in the back room, setting out two cups as the water boiled. Within the folds of her dress, Dr. Yam's prescription dangled pregnantly, the pull of its weight concealed by her skirts' flaps and folds.

What will it take to keep him safe? she thought.

Two days ago, when she'd returned from Dr. Yam's to find the delivery wagon at their shop, she had expected Mr. Kernochan to materialize by closing time. He never arrived. She could not find sleep until the wee hours, and when she did, she dreamed of dragging a slippery horse hide up Beacon Hill and scaling a red cedar, building herself a cocoon from skin and sap…

When she had awoken, the rash on her arm no longer itched, but it had spread overnight to cover most of her body. She'd stood in her room, naked, tracing the red, squirmy lines everywhere they ran, from the crook of her elbow to the folds of her eyelids.

And then, as she watched, they had visibly paled—weakened— fled. They'd sunk into her without a trace.

Could there ever be a cure? she'd asked herself, staring into the mirror.

The end of the world, the cold voice said, echoing in her skull. In that moment, she understood everything.

Now, listening to the tick and ping of metal expanding under heat as the water warmed, she gave thanks that her father was gone. Whatever was to come, it wasn't for his eyes.

Even as steam began to leak from the pot, Wah heard a soft, slidey thump from below. She looked at the pot with mild regret, set it aside. She toweled her hands dry and lifted a small crate from among those piled nearby.

She navigated the back room easily in the dim light, familiar with the layout from years of stocking. The scarred, unpainted door to the basement stood open just a crack, conjuring a smile on her lips—she was sure it had been latched.

Wah lifted and lit the lantern next to it, then threw the door wide and began to descend. Something inside of her spoke slyly, urging her to douse the lantern and experience the dark in its full glory, but she tamped it down.

The basement looked ancient by lamplight, though it was barely half a century old. Cobwebs festooned the pillars that supported the shop, and the dank lay like a heavy film on her skin. There were a few window frames left intact, from back before the Great Fire had lifted the city up and turned ground floors into basements, but for all the shadows and spiders, it might never have seen daylight. After a break-in several years before, her father had barred the doors that led to what had once been the sidewalk. Now both stood open, leading… she knew not where, save that it was dark.

"So good to see you again, Miss Sung," Mr. Kernochan said, stepping out of the shadows.

"And you, Mr. Kernochan." His face looked more waxen than ever in the lamplight. He came for her, then, but before he took two steps she tossed him the box. He caught it almost as an afterthought, his black eyes never looking away from Wah's, and she set the lantern on the stair—she needed both hands free. "It's not a scroll, and it's damn sure not a genealogy, so what is it?"

"You peeked?" Mr. Kernochan's eyebrows beetled together as he inspected the box, as though noticing it for the first time. Digging fingernails into wood, he tore it open. A splinter drew dark liquid from his thumb that dripped and trickled into the shadows. Unwrapping the small black book from its padding, he sighed with satisfaction. "Well, I may have fudged some details, but I spoke true when I said it was a family record. Of sorts. I'm surprised you're giving it back, having stolen a taste for yourself."

"Maybe the flavor didn't agree with me." In truth it had, and packing it back up to turn over to him had taken more strength than she'd known she possessed. Wah sat down on the stair beside the lantern, casually resting a hand on her bunched-up skirts to prevent Dr. Yam's prescription from knocking against the step. "It's not Chinese, so what was it doing in China?"

"The same thing I was," Mr. Kernochan said, tucking the book into the hip pocket of his suit. "Spreading the good word."

"Uh-huh," said Wah, snaking her fingers into her skirts but never taking her eyes from his. "Your word's not all you spread, is it, Mr. Kernochan? Something in my tea, last time you called?"

"So that's what he told you." Mr. Kernochan took a step toward her, and the lantern's flame wavered and dimmed, recoiling from his advance. At the same time, Mr. Kernochan's silhouette seemed to undulate, and Wah felt the heavy pulsing of the silkworms behind her eyes. "That Chinaman doctor of yours wouldn't know his ass from an aspirin, Miss Sung. Whatever potion or poison he gave you won't work, not on me."

"Why did you come here?" Wah demanded, rolling the larva around on her tongue as Mr. Kernochan came closer. He could reach up and touch her slipper now, if he wished. "Why me? I don't think you needed us to recover your book."

"Maybe, maybe not," said the pale man, his face rippling as he spoke, as though his skin were coming loose from his jawbones. "It's all a question of potency, Miss Sung. In Old Cathay, sorcerers believed the strongest toxin came from shutting up several venomous creatures in a jug or box. They devoured one another in the dark, and whichever one remained in the end would have the combined strength of all. The concentrated poison of such an animal could have all sorts of applications."

"If I go with you, you'll leave my father alone," Wah said, tightening her hand on the medicine secreted in her skirts. "You hear me? You leave him alone."

"Don't worry on that account." Mr. Kernochan smiled, his yellow teeth squirming like pupae. He rested a long-fingered hand on the banister, set a foot on the bottom step. It was bare, his toes even paler than the rest of him. "Your father will never be alone again, Miss Sung."

Dr. Yam's prescription came free of her skirts, but her elbow knocked the lantern over, its already pitiful light snuffed out as it fell. In the blackness she could hear Mr. Kernochan panting, her own heart pounding, and the silkworms squirming, but not the lantern landing on the next step. It seemed to be falling forever. Just like Wah.

"What do you have there?" Mr. Kernochan's voice blew warm and wet against her exposed ankles, stirring the edge of her skirts. "Whatever herbs that quack gave you won't help."

"No herbs," she said, steadying one hand with the other, focusing on the spot where his rich, earthy breath emanated from the inky basement.

"Taoist witchcraft, then? Or wushu?" Fingers that felt like worms brushed against her ankle, leaving a tacky trail as they pushed up her calf. "Some other ancient Chinese secret?"

"Something like that," said Wah, the iron digging into her thumb as she levered the hammer back.

"Wait," he said, perhaps recognizing the tell-tale click, but she didn't stop. The first muzzle flash illuminated something quite different from what she expected, and it filled her stomach with warmth... warmth and eagerness for what lay ahead. The next shot filled the basement with white light, and he was only Mr. Kernochan again, his body flopping like a landed carp as the second bullet struck. The breast of his black suit flapped wetly with the third shot.

And the fourth.

And the fifth.

Then it was quiet in the basement for a very long time.

Wah groped her way up the stairs and stumbled into the dim shop. She steadied herself against a shelf and looked longingly toward the table where she and her father had drunk so many cups of tea. It wasn't too late. The only voice she now heard drumming in her head was her own. It wasn't too late...

Then she went to the third aisle, inspecting the knives on the top shelf. Wah Sung took her time selecting one that seemed ideal for skinning, and then she went back down into the sweet and silken darkness.

WALPURGISNACHT

Orrin Grey

O n the train, Nicky told me about the Brocken Spectre. "It's a sort of optical illusion," he said, leaning forward, his elbows on his knees. Nicky was younger than me, and prettier, and his dark hair fell in front of his face whenever he slouched, which was often. "The sun casts a giant shadow of you on the clouds below, right, and your head gets this prismatic halo. Like an angel."

"I hear the sun only shines here like sixty days a year," I said. "Besides, it's night." I was only half-listening anyway, my head lolling against the cool glass of the window. I'd had more than a few drinks at the airport bar, and I could feel a headache trying to force its way out past my eyes. Outside, I could see our destination looming up out of the darkness, the two towers of the *Sender Brocken*, old and new. Like Tolkien's Minas Morgul and Orthanc. The sun was still going down, and the towers stood out like shadows against the gloaming, their lights already on. Gleaming yellow ones in the windows of the old tower, now the Brocken Hotel, and blinking red ones to warn planes away from the new tower, a candy-cane-striped lance that jutted skyward from the peak.

"It doesn't look terribly inviting," Nicky said, noticing my inattentiveness and nodding at the towers.

"Now to the Brocken the witches ride." I intoned, and then, without bothering to glance and see his puzzled expression, explained, "It's Goethe. From *Faust*."

That was why we were going, of course. It was Walpurgisnacht, the night when the witches and devils gathered on the crown of the bald mountain to welcome the spring. Nicky and I, and whoever else was on the train with us, were the witches in this equation, and we were all gathering on the Brocken to kiss the ass of a black goat.

***

We met Henri at the Steadman Gallery. Nicky had some of his photographs there, as part of a show called "The New Decadence." From his "Conqueror Worm" cycle—my name—all graveyards and ossuaries, done in lots of blues and greens with the occasional splash of red or yellow. A leaf, a salamander. They were good pictures, some of Nicky's best, in my opinion, and I guess Henri thought so, too.

I don't remember the other stuff in the show, but I remember Henri. Tall, old-fashioned handsome, Van Dyke beard, clothes like a Vincent Price villain. He carried a cane that was pure affectation, black wood with an amethyst top. He was a regular in the galleries, though word was that he spent more time in Europe than the States. Why he was in New York that year, I never learned, just as I never learned his real name. DuPlante was the most common surname associated with him, but how accurate it was, I can't say. Henri kept as much about himself veiled in mystery as he could, kept himself interesting.

Even before we'd met, I'd heard about him. Rich, listless, a Decadent of the old school. He was known for throwing wild parties with strange themes, and for occasionally throwing large wads of money at young artists who caught his fancy, which meant that Nicky and I were of course very happy to make his acquaintance, to catch his eye.

Where exactly all his money came from was the subject of some speculation. One story went that his father was a lord, another that he was heir to a fortune in pornography. Some said that he'd been some kind of *wunderkind* and had invented some patent as a child and still lived off the dividends.

There were lots of stories about Henri, many of them contradictory, but he seemed to welcome all of them. There was only one that I had ever known him to actively refute. Supposedly he had an older sister, one whose tastes made Henri's seem positively Puritan by comparison. Some people claimed to have met her, though never in his company. They always described her the same way, which was odd. Tall, dark hair, stylishly dressed. Always named Alexandria. I was so bold as to ask Henri about it once, but he replied, with uncharacteristic clarity, "I'm an only child."

"Maybe she was an old lover," Nicky hypothesized once. "Somebody who just pretended to be his sister." It was certainly kinky enough.

Real or imagined, Henri didn't like to talk about her. The subject made him visibly uncomfortable, was maybe the only subject I'd ever come across that did.

Luckily for him, I was less concerned with stories about where Henri's money came from, and more concerned with where it went. The fact was, he spent it like water and never wanted for more, and Nicky and I had expensive tastes and no inclination to a hard day's work, so men like Henri were bread and butter for us.

At the Steadman Gallery, he kissed Nicky's hand but shook mine. He struck me then as I would continue to think of him throughout our acquaintance: as a spoiled dandy who enjoyed playing the beast because it amused him, more than because there was much actual beast in him.

Aside from his money and his interest in the arts, he was known mostly for what he called his "revels." "Party," he said to me once, "is far too small a word." I don't remember how many of them Nicky and I attended in the years that we knew Henri. Nicky always brought his camera, and he got a couple of decent series out of them, neither of them half as good as the work he was doing when we met, but then, booze and drugs and other temptations flowed freely at the revels, and Nicky was no less susceptible to them than I, and they took their toll on both of us, in different ways.

How to describe one of Henri's revels? He once told a reporter, "I take intent, and marry it with time and place." Which isn't really very helpful, either. I guess that fundamentally they *were* just parties, on a grand scale, complete with the kinds of party games that would have shocked and titillated Victorians, but Henri saw them—or maybe he just *sold* them—as something more like performance art. A séance held at midnight in a haunted hotel. A black mass in the catacombs under Paris. Diversions for the bored and the rich and the morbid. Nicky and I were two of those, and Henri was rich enough for everybody.

This one, though, the one atop the Brocken, on Walpurgisnacht, was supposed to be different. More intimate, more personal, and his last. That's what the invitations had said. Henri had supposedly discovered a rare film print by Eadweard Muybridge, something suitably infernal, not just studies of animals in motion, and he was going to screen it for a few dozen of his closest friends at midnight, "in its native habitat." There was to be a small chamber orchestra, and Henri had reserved the entire hotel, so we wouldn't be disturbed. "Unless of course some other witches decide to drop in."

***

When the train pulled up to the station, Nicky and I got out, along with a few others that I recognized from Henri's inner circle, and still more that I didn't. Maybe new additions, maybe lapsed recruits pulled back in for one last hurrah. I helped Nicky shoulder one of his camera bags, and we all walked down to the cars that were waiting to take us the rest of the way to the top of the mountain.

We shared our car with a girl who looked young, and too thin for my tastes. She was wearing a black dress, with diamonds glittering at her wrists and neck, and silver hair that was probably a wig but might have been some impressive dye job. Nicky pulled out his camera and held it up, giving her a quizzical look to which he received a nod and giggle. He snapped several photos on the car ride up, flattering her, I'm sure, but I knew that he was just warming up, getting ready for the main event.

Would I have accepted Henri's invitation, if it hadn't been for Nicky? I don't know. We'd not had the best time at the last of his revels that we attended, in some hunting lodge in some godforsaken part of Washington state, and it had left a bad taste in my mouth. I couldn't really remember why, too much booze turning the filmstrip of my memory into a series of disassociated snapshots. Something about sitting in the dark by the fire, after the meat of the party was over, playing some idiotic child's game called "Something Scary." I'd never heard of it, but apparently Nicky played it when he was a kid, with his abusive father, the one he never talked about. He told me so afterward, on the car ride home, and he cried and shook in his sleep that night, and didn't say why.

Everything else was blurred, just a bad, sick feeling in the pit of my stomach, but enough that I might have thrown the overwrought bit of paper—with its wax seals and calligraphic script—in the trash, had it not been for the mention of Muybridge. The old photographer fascinated Nicky, and I was happy for anything that got Nicky's attention onto something I found interesting.

The cars deposited us on the foot of the steps leading up to the Brocken Hotel. The building had once been a TV tower, maybe the oldest one in the world, built before World War II. It had transmitted the first live broadcast of the Summer Olympics in Berlin. The war didn't do it any favors, and when the new tower was built they converted the old one into a hotel. The only thing left to mark its former function was the golf-ball-like radome that crouched on the roof and held air traffic control equipment.

The lights that had looked so tiny from the train were dazzling up close, but the tower that rose above us, with its tiny windows and the radome on top, reminded me of something from a futuristic prison. Not terribly inviting, as Nicky had said.

Inside, however, the hotel proved to be as luxurious as it had appeared Spartan from without. Red carpets, crystal chandeliers, gilt everything else. We were shown into an enormous ballroom where a projector and screen were set up in pride of place, with couches and divans arrayed for our viewing pleasure. The artwork that normally hung along the walls had been removed, and in its place were easels draped in black cloth. All part of the night's festivities, I assumed.

I knew that Henri himself had dabbled in painting once, when he was younger. I'd never seen the results, but I'd heard that at his best he'd mostly just knocked off Goya. At Henri's one and only gallery opening a critic was apparently overheard to remark, "If you've seen everything Goya ever did, and you still want more, then Henri's the man to talk to," though whether that was intended as condemnation or praise, I couldn't say. By the time Nicky and I met him, he'd already given it up, but his passion for the arts remained a constant throughout his life, so I wasn't exactly surprised to see the easels there.

The man himself was there too, playing the good host and glad-handing his guests as they entered. He looked much as he had the last time I'd seen him, which was also much as he had the *first* time I'd seen him, though now his hair and beard were grayer, and the tiredness that was supposedly driving his retirement could be seen in the corners of his eyes, even as they sparkled as ever with his smile. The years had made him seem distinguished, rather than old, as they were kind enough to do for some people, and he wore his age well.

He kissed Nicky's hand, shook mine, and then he and Nicky were flirting again—Nicky always was flirtatious, Henri always shameless—and then Henri had drifted away to talk to one of the other guests. "It'll be some time before the festivities start," he said over his shoulder as he departed. "The witching hour, and all that. One of the servants can show you to your room, if you'd like to freshen up."

The "servants" were men in coats-and-tails, wearing shapeless *papier mâché* masks that made them look a bit like disfigured corpses. I knew from previous revels that under the masks I would find invariably young, attractive men, paid well for their forbearance and their discretion.

One of these broke off to escort Nicky and me to our rooms, which were next to each other and connected by an adjoining door. Henri, gracious and accommodating to the last. The rooms were as sumptuously appointed as one might expect, except for the narrow, slit-like windows that were the lasting testament of the building's former function. "There's an observation deck on the roof," the faceless "servant" told me when he saw that I was eyeing the window with some distaste. "It provides a much better view."

I sat down on the bed and kicked off my shoes. The clock on the desk said that I still had almost two hours until midnight, and I was suddenly very tired. The headache from the train was back, and I just wanted to lay down in the dark.

Nicky came from the adjoining room. "I'm going up to the observation deck before the party starts," he said, patting his camera bag. "You want to come?"

I shook my head and laid backward into the softness of the bed. "I think I'm going to take a nap," I said. "Wake me before you go downstairs."

***

He left then, and I slept, or I must have, because I dreamed. In my dream, I had gone with Nicky to the roof. He was standing near the railing, trying to see a Brocken Spectre in the mist that had grown up around the hotel. There was a blindingly white light coming from behind us, maybe from the radome, throwing our shadows out like expressionistic paintings on the rooftop, and across the clouds.

I wanted to turn around, to look for the source of the light, but I couldn't. I was staring across the clouds, watching keenly as Nicky tried to position himself to create the halo effect that he was looking for, his camera held up to his face. For some reason, the camera made me uncomfortable. I wanted him to take it down. I had the irrational feeling that he couldn't, that it was welded there. I saw him as some kind of cybernetic Cyclops, staring out through the camera's lens at his own shadow.

I couldn't speak, and there was a distant roaring in my ears, so that I didn't hear Nicky, even as I saw his lips moving. We were not alone on the observation deck. There was a third shadow leaping out across the roof of the clouds, one that didn't seem to shift and move, to jump around as ours did. I tried to turn my head, to see who was standing beside us, but I could only catch a glimpse. It was a woman, straight dark hair, wearing a fur coat, and I knew that it was Alexandria, Henri's older sister, though in the dream she couldn't have been much older than Nicky.

I tried to turn my head, to catch her eye. She was standing behind Nicky, her eyes were dark, holes in a mask that was her face, and her finger was coming up to her lips, shushing me, as though we were sharing a secret. Her shadow and Nicky's shadow were the same, stretching long and dark across the clouds, and he was smiling, the halo appearing around the shadow's head, and the camera snapping and whirring again and again.

***

I sat up in bed. Though the clock said that only a few minutes had passed, a strong wind had come up outside. I could hear it howling against the walls of the building. I turned to look out the window, but the black slit was a mirror against the lights in the room. Still, something was hurtling past through the darkness, something like sparks or embers from a great bonfire, whirled up into the sky in a cyclone.

I got out of bed and walked over to the window, pressing my face against the cold glass and peering out through cupped hands. The night outside was a black maelstrom. The lights of the hotel were gone, and the red warning lights of the opposite tower were lost in the darkness. The only illumination came from the burning shapes that I had originally taken to be sparks but that I saw now were lanterns, lanterns made from human skulls and hollowed gourds. They were carried aloft by figures, some nude, others shrouded in tattered garments whipped by the wind. Some were young, their flesh milky and smooth, while others were impossibly old, their skin puckered, their breasts withered and pendulous. All rode through that swirling darkness, some astride goats and pigs and cats the size of ponies, some on brooms and benches, some carried by owls and vultures and ravens tied on strings.

A woman's voice spoke in my ear, husky and somehow familiar, "*Now to the Brocken the witches ride,*" and then I woke on the bed, still dressed, my face and hands beaded in cold sweat. Again the clock averred that only a few minutes had passed, and I had a moment of lurching terror, the feeling of being trapped in a hallway that you know you have just walked down before. Outside the window the night was merely dark, the wind only a whisper that played along the eaves, the red lights of the *Sender Brocken* blinking their warning.

***

I splashed water on my face, had a drink from the mini bar, and then another. In spite of my earlier instructions to Nicky, I couldn't stay in the room, and I didn't feel like navigating the blind, empty hallways that would take me up to the observation deck, a prospect which left me sick with indefinable horror. Instead I left him a note and went in search of the elevator, which didn't seem like it could possibly be too difficult to locate since I remembered riding it up. Still, I took two wrong turns in the red-and-gold halls trying to find it, and at the second turn I thought I saw someone from the party up ahead, just going around a corner. A flash of silver and fur, a glimpse of a leg, and then she was gone. My first thought was of the girl that had ridden up with us in the car, and I opened my mouth to shout, but then I remembered the woman from my dream, and my voice died in my throat.

By the time I found the elevator and got down to the main floor, it was only twenty minutes to midnight. Buffet tables had been set up in the entryway, covered in brie and strawberries and other delicacies. I passed them by without a second look, because even though I hadn't had a bite since the airport, the very thought of food made my stomach turn.

Inside the ballroom, the black drapes had been removed from the easels. The paintings they revealed must have been Henri's own. They could have passed for Goya in bad light, or at a distance, but their colors were more garish, their subjects more universally grotesque or occult in character. Goya's entire oeuvre, rendered into nothing but Black Paintings. In the largest painting, sitting in a dominant spot along the far wall, warped figures crouched around the form of a massive black goat, an obvious and blatant copy of Goya's *Witches' Sabbath*. More the 1798 one than the 1820s. I walked over to it, and found that there was a title hand-written on a piece of paper and affixed to the easel: "Chernobog."

"Chernobog was a Slavic god, represented by a black he-goat," Henri's voice suddenly said from over my shoulder. "Of course, when the Christians came, he got turned into the devil, like so many others."

"Subtle," I said with a forced smile, turning around and reaching for his hand, not wanting to let him see that he'd startled me.

He smiled himself—his more genuine than mine—and shrugged. "Subtlety, like painting, never really was my strongest suit."

We were momentarily isolated from the noise and bustle of the room, caught in a bubble of quiet and stillness near the big painting, under the golden eyes of the black goat, and I was still shaken from my dreams, which seemed to lurch about in my head like wheeled carts on the deck of a ship. That's probably why I didn't banter with Henri as I normally might have, and just asked him straight, "Are you really giving it up? Retiring?"

He nodded, and though his smile didn't falter, his eyes looked sad. More than just tired, as they had before. Exhausted, spent. "I'm afraid so," he said. "My time has come. One last revel, and then it's out, out brief candle."

As he spoke, I saw Nicky come into the gallery out of the corner of my eye, and at the same time Henri looked down at his wrist, though he didn't wear a watch that I could see. "Speaking of which, the time is almost upon us. You'll excuse me?"

I nodded and he was gone, lost to the crowd. I started to walk toward Nicky, but then Henri reappeared, standing near the projector in the center of the room, and everyone was muttering into silence and Nicky was raising his camera to his eye, and so I froze where I was.

I can't remember what Henri said, standing there next to the projector. There was a ringing in my ears, and my headache had come back full force. I thought I could see someone over his shoulder, a familiar shape in fur and silver and long, dark hair. No matter how I moved, though, I couldn't get a clear look.

Henri thanked everyone for coming, and started to talk about why we were there, about Muybridge and his films. First the stuff that you could find in the history books—studies of animals in motion, his murder of his wife's lover and subsequent acquittal—but no one in the crowd was there for so mundane a scandal, so then Henri talked about Muybridge's *other* films. Short topics of occult interest, all of them lost to rumor and speculation and myth. Some said he'd even caught the Devil Himself on celluloid.

My head was splitting, and I needed to get out of the gallery, find a drink, hair of the dog. I was pushing past the other revelers, who all had their gazes fixed forward, on Henri, while my eyes were only for the door. Maybe that's why I saw her there, standing just inside the entrance. Long, dark hair, dark eyes, fur coat. Her hand on the light switch.

The lights went down, and the gallery filled with the whirring sound of the projector. In the flickering silver glow that came from the screen, I could see the faces of the people around me, all of them transformed into pallid, disfigured masks by the play of light and shadow, the "servants" now indistinguishable from the guests. All their eyes were black pits, all staring up at the screen. Reluctantly, I turned to see what they were seeing.

Twenty feet tall, on the wall of the ballroom, three figures wearing conical hats danced in a circle. Their arms were interlocked, their heads down, the points of their hats nearly meeting in the middle as they turned, slowly, rhythmically, like figures on a German clock. Intercut with them were other frames, more animal studies, but wrong this time, donkeys up on their hind legs, turning in a circle. It was just a few frames, figures and donkeys, repeated again and again. Turning and turning, in a dance that would never end.

There was a flicker, then, and the scene changed. A grove, somewhere, in a black forest, dark and thick as the Doré-inspired jungles of Skull Island, but a real place. Fires burned in the background, out of focus, and cloaked figures watched as a young girl, not more than sixteen, coupled with a black goat the size of a bison. Her eyes and mouth were black holes burned in the film. The images moved with the stuttering, shuddering jerkiness of a zoetrope. Just a few frames, turning on an endless loop. A dance that would never end.

The blemish began at the place where the girl met the goat. A rip in the film, a hole that gaped wider and wider as the film burned through, with that familiar sound of bubbling and tearing. For a moment the screen was white, and then there was a crack as glass shattered under extreme heat, and the room was plunged into complete darkness.

It's hard to remember what happened next. The mind almost certainly played tricks at the time, the memory just as surely has played them since. I know that there was a moment of stillness, as the white light burned on the wall of the gallery. I turned in that moment, my eyes searching for the woman I'd seen inside the doorway, but all I saw were our shadows transformed into giants on the walls behind us.

When the light went out completely, there was a sound like a rising tide, as dozens of voices all spoke at once, whether to calm or panic, and dozens of bodies all started to move in different directions. The ringing in my ears seemed to have left my head and spread out into the room itself, and underneath it I would have sworn that I could hear the orchestra playing. Others would later say that they heard it too, some wild, discordant melody that none of us could identify but that we all thought sounded very familiar. Then the whole room tilted, or at least that's how it felt, like the hotel was just a model sitting on a tabletop that somebody had stumbled into.

I felt bodies slamming against me, elbows jamming into my sides, my face. I felt my lip split against bone, I felt myself stumble over someone or something in the dark. Bright strobes of light were going off, and at the time I couldn't account for them, thinking maybe they were going off inside my own head, though now I know that they were the flashbulb of Nicky's camera as he desperately sought to catalogue something of the disaster.

In the flashes, I remember feeling like I had stumbled somehow into one of Henri's paintings. The faces of the people around me seemed bloated and dead, seemed to float up from out of the darkness to assail me. Like I was drowning in a black river, with only corpses to keep me company. The "servants," I told myself later, in their grotesque masks.

I have no clear recollection of making my way outside, but that's where I found myself, my hands on my knees, Nicky trying to staunch the flow of blood from my face. The bright lights of the hotel were on, making our shadows long on the gravel in front of us, turning the night sky into a black dome above our heads. I turned around, and saw that the hotel was on fire. Flames licked out of the doors and windows of the first floor, sending embers spiraling up into the darkness, like lanterns carried aloft.

***

I talked about it later, with the other survivors, with Nicky, with the police. I told them what I had seen, what I could remember, though it didn't seem like much. A few people had been killed in the blaze, many others suffered from burns, smoke inhalation, injuries acquired in the panicked rout. Once the fire was out, the authorities sifted the ruins for bodies, identified the charred remains, sent them back to their families to be buried. Henri wasn't among them. He was never seen again.

When Nicky went to develop his photographs from that night, he told me that none of them came out, from any of the cameras. He said that not even the pictures he'd taken earlier, at the airport and on the train, had returned anything but black squares. He blamed a bad batch of film. He should have been devastated, but he didn't seem to be. After that evening, it was like something turned over inside Nicky. He started photographing again, and turning out good work. The best he'd done in years, but I didn't like them. They reminded me of things I'd seen that night. He'd go to the zoo and take pictures of the animals; kangaroos and donkeys and goats, yellow eyes staring out of darkened paddocks.

I believed him, about the photographs, though I wondered about the explanation. I had crazy thoughts, that maybe there was nothing wrong with his film, but instead something wrong with that night. Then I found two of the photographs that supposedly hadn't come out. They were under the grate in our fireplace, scorched at the edges. One was a blurry shot taken up on the observation deck. It seemed to be one he'd snapped by accident, with the camera in motion so that most of the picture was a smudge, the stars falling like embers, the radome an enormous white blot consuming one entire side of the image. Right at the edge of the picture, though, was a woman, standing near the railing. Only part of her was visible, the edge of a fur coat, long, dark hair.

The other photograph was obviously one that he'd captured with the flash after the lights had all gone out. In the foreground were the fleshy shapes of panicked guests running in front of the camera, pushing and falling over each other in the darkness, but in the background was Henri, the focus on him perfect so that you could see the defeated expression on his unsmiling face. He stood in front of his "Chernobog" painting, looking out at the rioting crowd as though he could see them, his eyes vacant. Worse, though, than anything about his expression was something that I tried to tell myself was an optical illusion created by the effect of the flash and the angle. The hoof of the painting's black goat, resting on Henri's shoulder, beckoning him to turn and follow.

I kept the pictures, thumbed through them relentlessly, obsessively, wearing smeared fingerprints into the edges. I meant to confront Nicky with them, throw them down on the table, demand to know why he hadn't shown them to me, why he'd lied to me, burned the evidence. But instead I watched him, his new confidence, his new photographs. He made friends that I didn't know, went to parties and gallery openings that I declined to attend, staying home with a bottle in my hand. When he was gone I would take out the pictures, look at them again and again.

Finally, I waited for him to leave the apartment one night and I followed him. Watched him walk down the street, his head up, not slouching, not anymore, and saw him go to the corner and get into a cab with someone. A woman with long dark hair, wearing a fur coat.

LEARN TO KILL

Michael Cisco

I glance up; there's a pale young girl, a stranger, standing in the doorway, her dark eyes on me, her set lips motionless, sealed, telling me:

"Michael—learn to kill."

...and gone, in a blink. There might have been some movement back there; a little girl, having somehow wandered into this silent house without being heard by me, might have been able to get out of sight again in the time it took my eyes to close and open.

I struggle to my feet and cross the bare boards, over to the doorway. I peer the length of the empty hall beyond it. I shuffle the length of the hall, looking around, not looking very closely, not caring, not really, going through the motions. What would I do if she were there?

No one is there. Not a sound. I can hear the trees on the slope outside, not making sounds. Somewhere, far off, I hear a familiar noise I can't name. The sound of a motor, I guess. A groan, getting louder, going higher.

Now what shall I do?

I go back to my chair and sit down again, as before. Without intending to, I find that I have even reproduced the same posture, like the cast-off coat that keeps the wearer's shape for a while.

Perhaps this sameness will induce her to return; but I don't think so. It doesn't work that way, is that what I'm thinking, is that what I am foolishly presuming to know? It doesn't fail that way, could that be what I mean?

I already know how to kill. I killed Dad. He would have killed me, if I hadn't gotten him. No doubt. Little did he ever dream he'd be the first among equals—is that the right phrase? First among my actual, all-withstanding family, taking pride of place, I think, as well he should, and forever in his prime and vigorous as he was the day he died. In protest, I forget at what, I slipped out the front door in the night and pissed on the house. I sprayed everything in sight. It froze, and the next morning I recall the noises of the hinges—the whine of the door hinges with the gasp of the screen door just after—and the usual bang followed by another report I soon learned was the sound his neck made as it broke against the edge of the top step. The slipperiness of frozen urine. So much for him.

His sister had never liked me and didn't want me; she disliked children. There was ice everywhere that morning. She didn't know I'd killed him, no one did. Melted, all of it, before noon. Perhaps there was an odor of urine about the front steps, but a man with a broken neck is liable to let loose, I suppose they thought. No one said a word about it. Angela, Dad's sister, resented my indifference to his death and, since there was nothing I could do about it, my indifference to my own fate. I felt as if my life were over, too. The end of my life there, with him, and nothing to begin. Nothing else. I had no future, only getting up and going to bed, neverending meals, neverending shittings, neverending conversations with Mom about the same things.

My mother—baffled. A baffled woman. Even after I killed my Dad she was always buried in who knows what fantasies. She and Dad's sister made a feint of fighting over me, but without managing to be convincing. I wasn't convinced, anyway. Mom had a way of forgetting all about me; every least fraction of her attention I ever received I wrung from her by trespassing on her dreams.

"What do you want now?" she would ask me, as if I'd been hectoring her, even when I hadn't exchanged a word with her for two or three days.

Early one afternoon I woke up and found her gone. She'd taken nearly everything worth having, which wasn't much, as there was never much in the house. I'd overslept so long that I had no mind to speak of, as I remember. She normally woke me up. I could get one thought to appear, but not to tumble over into another. Nearly a week, she was away, and when she came back, I was gone. Angela had tried to call and found the phone was out, then came by one evening and took me, plunked me down on the sofa between Brian and Stephanie.

I know how to kill, already, but I suppose something new is meant.—Kill Brian.—And kill Stephanie. Just the one or the other won't be enough. Each is nothing without the other, they're a team, hateful word, a team and the one I leave behind will kill me.

I'm old enough, why not let them kill me? It would make them happy, it would mean they could do more of what they always wanted to do. Death doesn't scare me.

I am old because I have never wanted to die, have always been careful—careful, and determined not to give up my life for nothing, and not alone. That's no premonition. It's a desire, with some of the externalities of a premonition, that's what it is. If I go, I go sledding on your corpse, there's too much of me to go alone.

Is that the meaning of this little girl? At seventy-seven I have a lot left to learn, or does she mean at last, at last I am ready for the final lesson?

***

Nodded off! How long was that? Everything looks the same. My boots, bony knees, knuckly hands. My chair. The window. Bare boards.

Lessons from Dad. When I was about eight or nine, I decided, I forget why, to provoke my father. I was very contrary and then, I remember standing stock still shouting

"FUCK YOU! FUCK YOU!"

at him. He smiled at me, queerly. Then he went and shut himself up in his room. That was his sanctum. He padlocked it when he wasn't in it. I wracked my brains for a way to get in, and I never did. With all my ingenuity, my genius for trouble, my intuitive sense of escape routes and infiltrations, when there was no hillside full of dense foliage I couldn't wriggle inside somehow, to think, I never managed it. I never saw the inside of it, even after I killed him.

That night, the night following the day on which I shouted fuck you, I dreamt about him. He was "going off to work in the morning." In my dream, this entailed his putting on his jacket and tie and going over to a post beside the front door. The dream supplied the post, which was blackish, scarred, splintery. My father picked up a sledgehammer and began slamming it against the side of the post with a heavy crash that shook the whole house each time. This was his dream-work, hitting the same spot on the post with clockwork regularity. Tooth-rattling. In the dream. There was a dent he hit at, scarred white, where the post was more like metal than wood.

I woke up screaming, flying through the air, and there was another scream, louder and deeper than mine, and angry. Dad had crept into my room as I slept, snatched me out of bed, roaring, and flung me up into the air. He caught me and began swinging me by one arm and one foot around the room, throwing me up at the ceiling and catching me, spinning and twirling me, bellowing at the top of his lungs, and I was sobbing. Then he suddenly let me fall onto my bed and left the room, chuckling to himself. That was how he paid me back for "fuck you! fuck you!"

"You could kill him, you know," my mother would say to him sometimes. He liked pouncing on me, whipping me off my feet and hurling me all around the room with sudden barks and cries that made him sound like he'd gone wild. Then he'd right me and put me down on my two feet and go on about his business. Whistling. He didn't really whistle, but it was like that, nonchalant. When my mother complained, he would chuckle. But once I overheard him say, raising his voice and laughing through his words:

"I know, I know… we need him, I haven't forgotten…"

I wasn't supposed to hear that, or to know that my parents had some special reason to keep me alive—a reason that I sensed at once had nothing to do with nurturing feelings. I knew, too, that there were unusual practices in my family, and things taken for granted that were anything but in the families of the other children I knew. It did not take me a great while to learn that I could not speak freely about what went on at home. My parents never told me to keep any secrets, although more than once, come to think of it, my mother did ask me if the other kids were curious about us. We lived far enough away, though, on the other side and beneath the hills, so that it was taken for granted we would be different. Hicky hillbillies.

Dad was not a squeamish man. He took to hunting, in particular, with gusto, and he loved cleaning fish or the carcass of a bigger animal, liked flicking blood on us for a laugh. He was always up to his elbows in some carcass and the house stank like a butcher shop. He taunted me and frightened me out of my wits when he could, but he never struck me. A man like that and he never struck me once. Something restrained him, and it wasn't love.

His only friend was his cousin, Tyler. Tyler's son Amos was a little ahead of me in age, and we played together whenever Tyler came over. I got the feeling that Amos did not always want to come with Tyler, that he was brought along to keep me distracted, and perhaps to keep him out of something too. Tyler had a locked room, too, but Amos was handier than I was.

During these visits, Tyler would vanish with Dad behind the door to the room and I would hear the snap an instant after it was drawn to, which meant they were locked in together. An ear to the door—nothing. Silence. No window to peek through. I asked Amos if Tyler ever hit him. He said no, never.

"Not ever?"

"No," he said. Wonderingly.

"Dad never hits me either."

"Huh."

"He grabs me and throws me around the room, up in the air."

"You mean he swings you around?"

I nod.

"Mine does that to me," Amos told me.

At the time I supposed it was family taboo. Tyler had never said anything in Amos' hearing about needing him for anything.

After I killed Dad, then, away we—

That sound again. The motor. Up and then down. Only the one road. They back already? How long has it been?

"Michael," the voice says behind me. "Learn to kill."

I turn. Nothing. Violent pain in my back. There is nothing behind me but the outer wall of the house. A window, though. Coming on to dusk outside. Wind. Just now starting. It rustles up and dies away.

All quiet again. No sound but me, the creaks of the chair as I return to my position, facing the door. Stephanie and Brian aren't back yet, but they will be back soon. When they come back, it will be them or me. I don't know how I know, but I know. Today.

A brief flurry of nausea. Must have been the turning. A rib scraping something, squeezing. And there's a pain in my back, too. Incipient cramp.

No sound at all. Only the breath in my nostrils, and tinnitus. Big nostrils. Dad's were huge and stiff in his coffin. They take the brain out through the nostrils, and shellac them. No motor. Nothing.

He hated me enough. Why didn't he beat me? Why didn't Tyler beat Amos? He struck his wife. Amos told me. Dad hit Mom. They weren't peaceful men.

After I killed Dad, away we went, Mom and I, then Angela, and so on. They did not quite fight over me like two people who wanted nothing more to do with each other. They fought over me like two people who were going to have to go on with each other. I noticed that. They obviously despised each other, but something bigger made them set hate aside.

It was all very mysterious, but not interesting. Amos and I attended the same miserable high school, and wasted our time with the same pack of beer-mad wretches, beer conspirators, brigands of the cheapest, the very worst liquor imaginable. The day came when, drunk, Amos was challenged, on pain of ritual thrashing, to shoot a can out of another boy's hand with a rifle. We had always been forbidden even to touch a gun. Dad kept his guns locked up like art treasures, and so did Tyler. I couldn't have picked my father's rifle out of a group of three, I saw so little of it.

Amos was given three chances and missed each time, somehow managing not to hit the boy who gingerly held out the can. As punishment, he would have to hold the can for someone else to shoot at. An older boy, a good shot and a bit less drunk, took the shots, but Amos couldn't help himself. He flinched and winced, kept drawing the can back in again with a look of abject defeat on his face.

The boy who would administer the whipping was a wet-lipped pale fellow named Curtis. He always wore a heavy belt, and now he slipped it loose and began assailing Amos with it, chasing him around, smacking at him. Amos ran off and hid. Curtis went after him. When I next saw them, Amos had Curtis up against a wall in the shadows and was ramming his fists into Curtis' stomach as regular as pistons and with such force that Curtis bounced against the wall. The bigger boys tried to pull Amos away—couldn't budge him. His face was dead calm, it was a corpse's face. Those punches struck, one, and again, and again, regular. Regular. Punching. Curtis rebounding from the wall. Sagging over the fist.

Amos stopped of his own accord. Curtis collapsed. The blows had been all that held him up. Blood poured from his nose and mouth in a steady stream. We all watched. Curtis was dead. Amos looked down at him, grey and calm. Then he turned away.

Amos told me what had happened, years later. He was out—how? Parole?

Curtis had found him in the cabin and started drubbing him with the belt. Amos, smarting and confused, could only ball himself up and wait for it to be over. He said it was awful, not because it hurt, but because he had no idea what to do.

I saw a flame, he said.

I went numb, he said.

I felt nothing. I knew he was still hitting because I swayed, but I couldn't feel it any more. There was a flame right in front of me, but nothing was on fire—I couldn't see what was burning it, it was just one light like a candle, straight up and down in space ahead of me, well back. Well back in the room. And there was no flickering or anything, it was so still. Even in the air from the belt—nothing. Straight. I didn't look away, but I was sort of taking it all in, and when I looked again, then there was a ring of them around the first one. I could see the first one up through the ring. They were just standing there in space. Then they came toward me, all in the same formation. The moment before that happened, though, I saw a face beneath the first one. I couldn't see it quick enough. It was too faint, I wasn't sure, but there was something there. Then they all came at me, in the same formation, not too fast. They swooped over to me and I saw the fires around me, around my head. Not like a crown. They were out around chin level. Maybe chin level.

The next thing I knew, Curtis was on the floor. And I was... looking down.

His father never beat him because he knew what would happen if he did. That's why. What did that mean about me? That was why Amos told me. Neither of us told all he knew, or suspected. But we knew and suspected the same things. That we were reserved for some purpose known to our parents and not to us. But Amos killed Curtis and was taken away, away from Tyler, and I killed Dad.

Tyler never asked about me, so apparently a cousin wasn't the same thing as a son. I guess he just left. I don't where he went.

Sometimes, I would be home, thinking I was alone, and I would hear Dad, his voice raised to a weak falsetto, calling "Archy… Archy…" in a drawn-out voice. I think he did it to frighten me. He never burst the bubble, though, to laugh at me. I would see him later, poker faced. I never met any "Archy." It might have only sounded like "Archy," through the locked door.

Brian and Stephanie are Amos' kids and some family outlier got to them. They killed Amos. I couldn't prove it. If I could, I'd be next. I am next, anyway, unless I kill Brian and Stephanie. Just the one or the other won't do it. Both.

We were not guest-hosting people, but people, neighbors I think, used to come around anyway, once in a while. To ask if we still had power, or water, or if we could spare any gas for a generator. Things of that nature. Mom handled the talk. I remember the knowing look my Dad exchanged with Tyler when one of our visitors said—

"Pray Jesus the rain'll stop!"

The faint curl of the lip, relaxed again at once. A smug little transport of contempt. Witches. I never saw any plain proof of it, but I knew it was there. And that it was being kept from me for some reason. And that reason could not have had less to do with love, or pity. I was confused to discover that it didn't have much to do with caution, either. What did they ever do that was illegal? It seemed to me that my family were exemplary citizens. My father drove the speed limit religiously and never failed to come to a complete stop at a crosswalk. With a snicker.

They were saving me—us—for something. And they didn't dare strike us nor hurt us. Amos had not just gotten mad; that wasn't anger that punched Curtis in the stomach to death. So, no killing in store for us, after all. No Isaac-to-completion-this-time. But if Amos or I were killed at a stroke?

The Harvester, damn it I remember now, thinking Dad and Tyler had been talking about a harvester, although neither of them had anything to harvest, and it was *the* harvester they were talking about, not *a* harvester. I had left them together and come back a moment later to get something I'd forgotten—a knife, or something, I forget—and I overheard them talking about "the harvester," and they hushed up about it the moment they knew I was there, and they did know, even though I'd made no sound, all at once their voices stopped. Dad called to me, then. I was observed closely in the little chat that followed. What had I heard? they were wondering.

"What harvester? You goin' to plant something? You goin' to plant crops, Daddy?"

I didn't tell them everything.

I hadn't heard anything about any harvester, because, after some careful remembering, I decided the word they'd used wasn't harvester but a word I didn't know, which was "evester," a word I stored away, in case I ever heard it again. I knew better than to ask them what it meant.

Then, years later, the garage, me trying to get open a jammed drawer in the workbench and noticed the corner of the book peeping out from behind the work table, where it had fallen unheeded some time ago—a spiral notebook, Dad's of course. I peeled it open and saw—

"The Evester is a thing like a shadow on the wall."

The top of the page had PARACELSUS: THREE BOOKS OF PHILOSOPHY WRITTEN TO THE ATHENIANS.

"The Evester is a thing like a shadow on the wall," the page said.

"The shadow riseth and waxeth greater as the body doth, and continueth with it even unto its last matter…" the page said.

"So when one is ready to die, death seizeth not on him till the Evester hath first past sentence, either by blow, bruise, or fall, or some such other kind of example; by which if a man perceive the Evester, he may see a signe of his approaching death," it said, and also, "…a mans Evester remaineth in the earth after his death…"

And it said, "the dead mans Evester… departeth not hence till the

last minute when all things shall come together. This Evester wor-
keth strange things. Holy men wrought miracles by their Evester
onely."

Amos died alone, in his car. Instantaneous. Hence, no driving for
me. No car. No where else to go. No money.

The passage is vague about something important—can someone
do strange things with someone else's Evester, once that person is
dead? Did they wait, Tyler and my Dad, for the Evesters to grow
with our bodies? My body stopped waxing and started waning
again a long time ago. Perhaps the Evester grows younger again, as
the body withers?

The stillness is thickening out there. In here, there is the noise of
my breathing, the chair's complaints. Out there it is getting stiller
and stiller and stiller. The trees, the waning day, are turning to
church pews. I don't know what I mean. There's an expectancy
around the house. It will come fully to life when Brian and Stephanie get back, try to kill me. If they can. I think they think I'm
passed due. But no one ever told me anything. Amos did say to me,
once, that he thought his Dad was watching for something bad,
and sudden. It struck me because it seemed like my parents were
fugitives from something worse than the law. They never talked
about the past. They had set pieces about the past, but they were all
lies, they never talked about—

The motor—

Nothing. Did I—?

There!

Coming. Do I know it will be today?

I'm afraid. I'm sweating. My hands are shaking. Shaking more.
Why did I stay?

I get up. Can barely breathe, I'm breathing so hard. My back is
killing me.

To the back door, back porch. Then out. Away, anywhere. Throw
myself into the woods, crawl if I have to. I can't get my breath. Sick
to my stomach. I reach to steady myself and I tear something in my

arm. I can't stand up straight. My knees keep folding.

The motor sounds clear, coming around the bend. A blast of wind drives me back toward the door. The wind... thrashing... shoving at me... My arm... Splintering pain in my knees as I drop onto the back porch. Screaming in my arm—the muscle torn in half—impaling in my back, gouging its way up into my neck— —I didn't tear anything in my arm it's a heart attack.

I hear a chuckle, like Dad's.

Coming from my open mouth.

Stop laughing!

I can't help it...

Car door.

You're a bit late! My dears!

Agony—nausea, and pain, my neck ripping.

"He-ey!"

Brian's voice.

What is that? A silence? Something went silent? I look up.

—I see it! I see it! A flame! There! It's there! Standing in space, the wind lashing the trees behind it and it burning straight up and down! Not a flicker! Not a waver! Not a glimmer! I see it, Amos! I see them! The ring of lights! Tears—what a time for them, choking on them—The face is there too, Amos—oh God it's me! It's me. Young! The flame burns from the crown! I still feel it ripping—

Why don't I go numb?

"To me!" I groan. "To me!"

There! I see what it is now! It's a *reflection!*

It begins to come nearer. I go numb.

***

The after-silence. The last vestiges of a terrible noise fading, like the last of a ripple, the barest trace of an echo, wailing off into the trees. Whose voice? More than one voice, mingled. A hoarse shout, and a fraying, high-pitched cry... a drawn-out, despairing cry, mingled.

The face of that little girl who spoke to me is there on the wall, relaxing into a smile. The cabin around me. The woods around that. The sky above. The earth, briefly, below, and then void.

I am standing upright, weightless. I can't tell if I am still numb.

No, I don't tell you everything.

GOOD LORD, SHOW ME THE WAY

Molly Tanzer

To: Anu Dhawan, Michael Crater, Mel Fong
Subject: Altman's pre-defense reminder

As you know, last month Jennifer handed in her dissertation prospectus, "Who Shall Wear the Robe and Crown? Secret Leaders: Reimaging the Role of Women in Three Western United States Cults." I trust you have all had ample time to read and digest her argument concerning the sacred feminine, Foucaultian pseudo-patriarchies and sub-matriarchies, and the "distended womb" as status symbol. Her pre-defense is scheduled for <u>Thursday, February 13th.</u> See you all there.

Lee Hudson
Chair, Department of Anthropology
Freglanton University
@lee_hudson_prof

History is, strictly speaking, the study of questions; the study of answers belongs to anthropology and sociology —W. H. Auden

***

To: Lee Hudson
CC: Anu Dhawan, Michael Crater
Subject: Altman's pre-defense reminder

I seem to have misplaced the file... would you please resend? Sorry!

Mel Fong
Associate Professor of Sociology
Freglanton University

***

To: Mel Fong
CC: Anu Dhawan, Michael Crater
Subject: Altman's pre-defense reminder

Mel, I've attached the file.

Lee Hudson
Chair, Department of Anthropology
Freglanton University
@lee_hudson_prof

History is, strictly speaking, the study of questions; the study of answers belongs to anthropology and sociology —W. H. Auden

attachment preview: altmanprospectus-1.docx

[Preview]
Who Shall Wear the Robe and Crown?
Secret Leaders:
Reimaging Perceptions of the Role of Women in
Three Western United States Cults

Summary: Page 1 of 15

Sensationalist news stories often cast cults such as Angel's Children and The Citizens of the Shattered Star in a certain light: compounds full of sex-charged lunatics, whose orgiastic furor is fueled by one charismatic personality. This leader is always male, and compels his followers to live debauched lifestyles while feeding them bunk theology to justify sating his own lustful appetites—appetites for flesh, but also for power over the minds and bodies of his followers, who are literally bred for the purpose in many cases, as birth control is largely unknown inside the above cults. Similarly, The Church of the Broken Circle, while far less in the public eye, has also been accused of sexual depravity and using women as "brood stock," i.e. keeping them continuously pregnant from menarche to menopause (or death) in order to expand the ranks of the faithful.

Interestingly, in recent years, several women have "escaped" the compounds of Angel's Children and The Citizens of the Shattered Star, and have, either in interviews or in written narratives, revealed their experiences living within these communities. To my knowledge, no one has yet collected these stories and analyzed their content via a critical and anthropological framework. Yet what is revealed by these accounts is astonishing. My research has shown that while there is without question a patriarchal structure within these cults—men are, by and large, the sole possessors of positions of power, such as allocators of resources, leaders of worship, and regulators of who has sexual congress with whom—within these patriarchies, women have created their own internal matriarchies. As all three groups view menstruation, pregnancy, and childbirth as the sole province of women, within the patriarchal systems of the cult a sub-culture exists where women rule women, and men are not allowed to intrude. This internal matriarchy—a sub-matriarchy, as I have termed it—both provides relief from the constant sense of observation these escapees expressed feeling while inside the cult, and allows women to "rule from below." I shall demonstrate that as women and children play the most major role in sustaining the viability of these cults, those who produce those children are the "secret leaders" of these communities, thus making the cults pseudo-patriarchies.

This is not to say these sub-matriarchies are utopian spaces within a larger dystopia; instead, the escaped women express feeling even greater pressures within female-only spaces. The womb is God within these societies, so barren, pre- or post-menopausal women, lesbian women, and women who express exhaustion with the process of childbearing or a disinclination to accept the embraces of fertile men are ostracized, and sometimes physically compelled to submit to the needs of the group.

With my work, I wish to shed light on common misperceptions of cult life while providing a broader picture of sub-matriarchies. Via analyzing existing accounts, conducting interviews when possible, and using Foucaultian panoptic theory and cross-cultural analysis to demonstrate cultural universals, I will draw a picture of the similarities and differences between these three cults, one in New Mexico, one located in Pacific Northwest, and one in Southern California, where

[continues on p2]

***

To: Lee Hudson
CC: Anu Dhawan, Michael Crater
Subject: Altman's pre-defense reminder

Whoa now; hold up there, pilgrim. Maybe it's that I'm coming at this from outside the department, but you signed off on this, Lee? The last time I talked to Jenny, this wasn't exactly the direction she was going with her research.

How is Angel's Children a pseudo-patriarchy (a term which I feel Jennifer fails to adequately define)? And I looked up this "Church of the Broken Circle" but there is zero information on it, even online. In her sources, Jenny cites some news article about a "mysterious tree" but the newspaper folded years ago, and has no online archive. And the guidebook she's using as her only secondary source on this cult (also a problem!) isn't in our library. Actually went down the rabbit hole and looked to see if I could ILL it, but no deal. I guess we'll be able to ask Jennifer questions next Thursday but I must say I have quite a few concerns re: her moving forward with this…

Mel Fong
Associate Professor of Sociology
Freglanton University

* * *

To: Mel Fong
CC: Lee Hudson, Anu Dhawan
Subject: Altman's pre-defense reminder

I already spoke to Jennifer about this "Church of the Broken Circle" as I had similar concerns about her sources and the viability of her research on such a reclusive, unknown group, but she's from some town outside Olympia, and they're apparently located in and around that area. She spoke convincingly and at length about her knowledge of the community… they seem to live similarly to the Amish but are even more reclusive, and dedicated to their ideals—no hitching posts at the local Wal-Mart—hence the lack of information on them. She did show me the copy of the newspaper article. I've attached the scan. Hope it clarifies things:

——————— Forwarded message ———————
From: Jennifer Altman <j.altman@fru.edu>
Date: Mon, Dec 16, 2013 at 7:32 AM
Subject: kitsap county register article
To: Michael Crater <m.crater@fru.edu>

Hi Professor Crater,

Here's the article I mentioned. This all happened not far from my house; I was acquainted with Mr. Fines as a girl. He's the one who told me about the Church of the Broken Circle. He was a shut-in, so I used to come by with baskets from the church—our church, not the other one—and even if it wasn't raining he would open a jar of jam or something and make tea and we would sit and chat. I felt it was my duty, as he was elderly and alone, but I also liked his company. My family wasn't much for scary stories, but I loved them.

At first, I thought his telling me not to go too far into the deep forest, to stay out of caves and how I should never ever stick my hand into the hollow of a tree were for my safety, but when I got a little older he told me more. He said that some people around the area believed that trees weren't trees and caves weren't really caves, and he had seen some things that made him cautious. I asked him to explain, but he shushed me and said just to listen and do what he said. Then, just before all this stuff happened he drew an image for me, of a ring with a chunk cut out of it. He said if I ever saw this, I should run back the way I came. He said he'd gone into the woods and seen it himself, marked on trees and rocks close to where "they" lived. He gave me a page torn from an old guidebook with areas circled in black, and told me to keep it as long as I lived in the area, and to stay away from those places. I was nine years old. It spooked me out, and I told my father, who forbade me to go near Mr. Fines again. Not long after, he set that fire. What the paper doesn't say is he died in ICU just after some relative of his came and visited him. There was no funeral, as the man took Mr. Fines' body, but we held a service at the church.

I know this sounds wild, but I've asked questions here and there and confirmed what he said about that church and its beliefs, and once my friends and I thought it would be fun to see if the lake on Mr. Fines' map was real. It was; we camped there, and early that morning in the pre-dawn quiet I saw two women dressed like Little House on the Prairie or something getting water from the far edge. I had my field glasses (I was a girl scout) and watched them, but when my friend blundered out of her tent they noticed our camp and scurried off. It started raining, hard, so we packed up and left after that. Never went back.

This is just the way it is where I grew up, it's hard to explain the farther afield I've moved… but the people around our little town understood. It's strange growing up somewhere and knowing there is a whole community full of people you've never seen, much less met, far away in the deep forest, and they're living their lives in some way long obsolete, worshiping some way weirder idea of God than you've ever heard of in your life.

—

Jenny Altman
Graduate Student in Anthropology
Freglanton University

attachment: kitsapregister.pdf

Gasoline Fire Burns Olalla Man; Destroys Home
By Jim Warren

April 27th, 1992—Early Tuesday morning, Burton Wulla Fines was admitted to Tacoma General Hospital with severe burns covering the left side of his face and body, and a mangled left hand, also burned.

Sally Wallings, a neighbor, called 911 at 1:18 AM when she spotted flames reaching above the trees between their properties, alerting local authorities to "a powerful inferno" on the premises. When firefighters arrived they found Mr. Fines' home ablaze, along with several adjacent trees. Fines himself was discovered wandering around one particularly large spruce, throwing gasoline on it from a can from time to time, and "ranting" according to volunteer firefighter Glenn Woodworth.

"We tried to get him away from the tree," said Woodworth, "but he wouldn't come along. He kept shaking his fist at it and accusing it of being 'infested' and that he 'wouldn't submit' to the will of its 'agents.' He claimed it had 'whispered to him for the last time,' that he would burn out the Great Satan within, and be done with the business."

"Brent had always hated that tree," confirmed Wallings.

Woodworth and the rest of the firefighters entrusted Fines to the paramedics who had arrived on the scene in order to fight the fire consuming his house. Soon after, all present reported hearing an "explosion" and returned to find Fines scorched along the face, body, and hand. With the help of the paramedics, Fines' clothes were extinguished and he was taken to Tacoma General. Sadly, this blast resulted in the burning to the ground of Fines' home.

When asked why the paramedics had not removed Fines from the site of the burning tree, they replied he became "belligerent and abusive" when they tried. At the time he tossed the can of gasoline onto the tree, causing the explosion that burned him, the paramedics had been discussing methods of restraining or sedating him.

"He accused us of conspiring with 'vassals of The Great Satan,' whatever that is; that we were there to 'bind him' or something like that. He was pretty incoherent by then," reported Jim Baker, an EMT.

Fines remains in critical condition at Tacoma General.

Michael Crater
Assistant Professor of Anthropology
Kristoff-Wright Fellow
Freglanton University

***

To: Michael Crater
CC: Lee Hudson, Anu Dhawan
Subject: Altman's pre-defense reminder

Thanks, Mike, but I fail to see how this article sheds light on any of my stated concerns. It proves nothing—she could have just as easily based her description of the cult's terminology ("Great Satan," etc.) on this as used it as evidence of such. There is nothing here that even implies the presence of a cult. Hell, to be fair, despite her allegation that the tree was "mysterious" it seems more as if this Fines character was the queer one—so I fail to see how she can reasonably present it as a primary source without substantial additional support.

It seems to me Jenny hasn't considered the possibility that her charming memories of Old Man Fines telling tales when she was just a girl he could dandle on his knee in his steamy shack during a rainstorm may have colored her interpretation of, you know, the facts of the matter.

Mel Fong
Associate Professor of Sociology
Freglanton University

***

To: Mel Fong
CC: Lee Hudson, Anu Dhawan
Subject: Altman's pre-defense reminder

Sorry Mel. You're right, I should have mentioned that in a follow-up email, Jenny told me that when the homestead was investigated by the police after the fire, the initial report indicated the tree had not burned completely. There was a stump full of some unidentifiable, liquefied organic matter, in which, when they investigated further, was found a silver ring with a chunk missing—the sigil of this cult.

Michael Crater
Assistant Professor of Anthropology
Kristoff-Wright Fellow
Freglanton University

***

To: Michael Crater
CC: Anu Dhawan, Lee Hudson
Subject: Altman's pre-defense reminder

No offense, but did you read over what you just wrote? If this is true, where are the lab reports on this "unidentifiable" matter? Where is the ring? This is sounding more like a bad episode of the X-Files than a dissertation proposal.

Do you believe the truth is out there, Mike?

Mel Fong
Associate Professor of Sociology
Freglanton University

***

To: Mel Fong
CC: Lee Hudson, Michael Crater
Subject: Altman's pre-defense reminder

Let us not get personal with this. Jenny's pre-defense is a week from tomorrow; perhaps we should wait to hear what she has to say.

To be fair, however, I too had questions regarding her proposal, as well as additional concerns about methods. Her ability to successfully obtain an SSRC grant to secure funding to travel is of paramount importance, as she has made it clear she is unable to pay out of pocket to go anywhere but back to Olympia, as it is within driving distance. And yet, while she has the most access to the area where this Broken Circle cult exists, she has not listed any potential interviewees; she appears to have made no personal contacts with ex-cult members of that group as of yet.

But even more concerning than that (as I will be suggesting she cut the Broken Circle and replace it with a better-known group), her assurances that she has secured verbal agreements with several women from the other cults for personal interviews seems dubious in terms of her ability to fulfill it. In my experience, ex-cult members are reclusive, and even ones who agree to be interviewed back out at the last minute.

We shall have to wait and see!

Anu Dhawan
Assistant Professor of Anthropology
Freglanton University

Please print this email only if necessary. Paper is made of trees!

***

To: Anu Dhawan, Michael Crater, Mel Fong
Subject: Altman's pre-defense reminder

Hi all,

You've raised some valid points. I've compiled them and sent an email regarding what you've expressed to Jennifer. Hopefully she will allay our concerns at her pre-defense.

I was thinking of bringing a dozen doughnuts—is anyone gluten free? Pollock's has gluten free, I think.

Lee Hudson
Chair, Department of Anthropology
Freglanton University
@lee_hudson_prof

History is, strictly speaking, the study of questions; the study of answers belongs to anthropology and sociology —W. H. Auden

***

To: Lee Hudson
CC: Anu Dhawan, Mel Fong
Subject: Altman's pre-defense reminder

I don't do dairy... think they have anything without milk?

Michael Crater
Assistant Professor of Anthropology
Kristoff-Wright Fellow
Freglanton University

***

To: Michael Crater
CC: Anu Dhawan, Lee Hudson
Subject: Altman's pre-defense reminder

God, why am I not surprised. What is it—milk is rape, or is it some conspiracy theory about mind-control drugs in Bovine Growth Hormone?

Mel Fong
Associate Professor of Sociology
Freglanton University

***

To: Michael Crater
CC: Anu Dhawan, Lee Hudson
Subject: Altman's pre-defense reminder

Uncalled for. I'm lactose intolerant, all right?

Michael Crater
Assistant Professor of Anthropology
Kristoff-Wright Fellow
Freglanton University

***

To: Michael Crater
CC: Anu Dhawan, Lee Hudson
Subject: Altman's pre-defense reminder

Suuuuuuuure you are.

Mel Fong
Associate Professor of Sociology
Freglanton University

***

To: Michael Crater
CC: Anu Dhawan, Mel Fong
Subject: Altman's pre-defense reminder

I had no idea doughnuts would be so contentious. Anyways, Mike,
I'll check on dairy-free options.

Lee Hudson
Chair, Department of Anthropology
Freglanton University
@lee_hudson_prof

History is, strictly speaking, the study of questions; the study of answers
belongs to anthropology and sociology —W. H. Auden

***

To: Lee Hudson
CC: Mel Fong, Michael Crater
Subject: Altman's pre-defense reminder

I know this is strange, but anyone seen Jennifer? She missed my seminar, and then didn't reply to my email asking if she was ill. That's not like her...

Anu Dhawan
Assistant Professor of Anthropology
Freglanton University

Please print this email only if necessary. Paper is made of trees!

***

To: Anu Dhawan
CC: Mel Fong, Lee Hudson
Subject: Altman's pre-defense reminder

That is odd. Odder: I asked her friend Penelope this morning what might be going on. She said Jenny went home unexpectedly; that Jenny seemed upset, and it was regarding her defense. She mentioned she seemed distracted, and had insisted on a need to prove something with evidence she wanted to gather right away. Penelope said she encouraged Jenny to put it off until after her pre-defense, to just answer our questions about her proposal before getting carried away with research, but Jenny refused, insisting whatever she was doing had to be taken care of immediately and could only be done in person.

Lee, did you hear any of this? Did she run this by you? Our meeting is in four days!

Michael Crater
Assistant Professor of Anthropology
Kristoff-Wright Fellow
Freglanton University

***

To: Anu Dhawan, Michael Crater, Mel Fong
Subject: Altman's pre-defense reminder

I did not receive a response to the message I sent Jennifer re: the committee's questions, which is strange for her but not unheard of. People get busy. But I am troubled if she has left town so close to the date of her pre-defense... I stressed she did not need to have 100% of her research completed by the 13th, just allay our worries with whatever she had dug up already.

Lee Hudson
Chair, Department of Anthropology
Freglanton University
@lee_hudson_prof

History is, strictly speaking, the study of questions; the study of answers belongs to anthropology and sociology —W. H. Auden

***

To: Lee Hudson
CC: Anu Dhawan, Michael Crater
Subject: Altman's pre-defense reminder

The Chronicle of Higher Ed just posted an article last summer saying something like 50% of doctoral students these days are leaving their programs without completing their Ph.D. It's possible the stress got to her. Happens all the time.

Mel Fong
Associate Professor of Sociology
Freglanton University

***

To: Mel Fong
CC: Lee Hudson, Michael Crater
Subject: Altman's pre-defense reminder

I certainly hope that is not the case! I'll try to call her, I have her number.

Anu Dhawan
Assistant Professor of Anthropology
Freglanton University

Please print this email only if necessary. Paper is made of trees!

***

To: Anu Dhawan
CC: Mel Fong, Lee Hudson
Subject: Altman's pre-defense reminder

I just got this from Jenny. Not sure what to think:

——————— Forwarded message ———————
From: Jennifer Altman <j.altman@fru.edu>

Date: Mon, Feb 10, 2014 at 3:47 AM
Subject: police report
To: Michael Crater <m.crater@fru.edu>

I don't have much time, but I wanted to let you know I've returned home. I've already obtained the police report on the incident with the tree, so that's good. I've known the sheriff my whole life, so I also asked him to see if he could dig up that ring, so I could take a picture of it. Haven't heard back yet. I know this will sound extreme, but it seems my committee, who I perceived as being enthusiastic about my research, has decided that I have no idea what I'm talking about. So I'll do what I need to do not to get shot down before I can even begin writing.

Obviously I could have just emailed the Sheriff's Office to get the report, but I figured a personal touch might tip the scales in my favor for getting it in time, and the picture of the ring.

While I wait I'll also be taking a trip up past Olalla to the lake where I saw those women as a kid. I'm hoping to snap some photos of them, too. And if I can't, well, a nice long hike before my pre-defense might be just what I need to clear my mind and present my case. I'm telling you all this, since of everyone you seem the most inclined to believe me. I'll prove your confidence was warranted and show everyone else, as well.

—

Jenny Altman
Graduate Student in Anthropology
Freglanton University

Michael Crater
Assistant Professor of Anthropology
Kristoff-Wright Fellow
Freglanton University

***

To: Mel Fong
CC: Lee Hudson, Michael Crater
Subject: Altman's pre-defense reminder

This is highly worrisome behavior in my opinion. I called her again last night, and could not get through—perhaps the reception? But I called again this morning, to find that her number has been disconnected. Has anyone had any further contact from her? I hope she is merely traveling, but the disconnected line has me scratching my head.

Anu Dhawan
Assistant Professor of Anthropology
Freglanton University

Please print this email only if necessary. Paper is made of trees!

***

To: Anu Dhawan
CC: Lee Hudson, Michael Crater
Subject: Altman's pre-defense reminder

Sounds like a hot story to cover up cold feet. Ah, sweet mystery of attrition!

Lee, are you still bringing doughnuts tomorrow even if Jennifer's a no-show?

Mel Fong
Associate Professor of Sociology
Freglanton University

***

To: Anu Dhawan, Michael Crater, Mel Fong
Subject: Altman's pre-defense reminder

Sadly, it seems Mel's suspicions were right on the money. I just received this from our program assistant:

———————— Forwarded message ————————
From: Marcia Owlrey <m.owlrey@fru.edu>
Date: Thurs, Feb 13, 2014 at 10:18 AM
Subject: Jennifer Altman withdrawing
To: Lee Hudson <l.hudson@fru.edu>

Hi Lee, I know this is unexpected for everyone in the program, but Jenny's uncle just came by this morning to turn in all her paper-work—she's withdrawn from Freglanton University, effective im-mediately. Usually I'd require some direct contact from the student, but all the documents have been signed and everything seems to be in order. Her uncle implied this is some sort of medical situation… he used the phrase "delicate condition" which to me means some-thing very specific, and he was an old-fashioned sort of gentleman. Draw your own conclusions. I asked if she had any plans to return, but he said she'd made it "quite clear" she was finished with aca-demia forever. Such a shame! She seemed so dedicated.

Marcia Owlrey
Program Assistant, Department of Anthropology

"You miss 100% of the shots you don't take." —Wayne Gretzky
Make sure today's the day you take that shot!!!!!

Not everyone can hack it. If she is indeed pregnant it seems like an elaborate cover story for leaving our program, but stranger things have happened.

Lee Hudson
Chair, Department of Anthropology
Freglanton University
@lee_hudson_prof

History is, strictly speaking, the study of questions; the study of answers belongs to anthropology and sociology —W. H. Auden

***

To: Lee Hudson
CC: Anu Dhawan, Michael Crater
Subject: Altman's pre-defense reminder

At the risk of sounding cold... did you bring those doughnuts or not?

Mel Fong
Associate Professor of Sociology
Freglanton University

SNAKE WINE

Jeffrey Thomas

G orch wasn't sure which source of pain had awakened him: the headache that felt like his skull was ready to give birth to a full-term baby, or the throbbing of his left hand, which was black in a glove of caked blood and missing its index finger.

He blurted muddled curses, sat up too quickly on the edge of his bed and nearly blacked out for his trouble. He shut his eyes to will the elevator of his stomach not to rise up and disgorge its contents. With his eyes clamped shut, sizzling phosphorescent blobs swam on the insides of his lids like amoebas on a microscope slide.

When he cracked his eyes again, his innards under a semblance of control, he raised his hand in front of his face. He hadn't imagined it, dreamed it, misinterpreted what he'd glimpsed upon awakening. His left hand's index finger had been removed at the base. A glance at his bed showed no severed finger lying there, but the sheet was soaked thoroughly with drying blood. How long had he been passed out? How long would it take for blood to dry to that extent?

Gorch's apartment was on the third floor above his bar. The second floor was where his bargirls, called *bia om* in Vietnam, took amorous customers for more than the hugs that *om* alluded to.

95

A sliding glass door gave access to a balcony. Through the door's sheer curtain he could see that the sun had risen, an orange ball buoyed on the sea.

He remembered the woman then.

She had come into the bar with another man, a British tourist in his sixties, his formidable belly like a cask and his sweating and wheezing head like a fat clenched fist. He boasted of having been a professional wrestler in younger days, but Gorch didn't volunteer his own past as a fighter. He hadn't fled to this country—as a result of some paid fist work outside of the ring—only to draw attention to his bloody past now.

The big man was already drunk as he raucously ordered a round of Saigon beer for himself, his lady friend, and a number of other white tourists and ex-pats seated at the bar or clustered around the billiard table.

Himself an ex-pat from Melbourne, now four years in Vietnam, Gorch had opened a bar catering primarily to the many Australians who visited the seaside city of Vung Tau. The bar looked across the coastal road toward the South China Sea, where the surf was iridescent from the Russian oil ships punctuating the horizon. Despite this pollution, along the coast there were strips of beach where swimmers could wade far out into the water, or lounge on the sand eating crabs while clouds of dragonflies hovered above them.

The Australian tourists found the *Down Under Pub* a welcome oasis when they tired of the indigenous fare. As if the bar's name left any doubt, live rugby played on the TV and boomerangs hung on the walls along with photos of boxing kangaroos (Gorch's private joke) and a large painting of Ned Kelly in his bizarre armor and helmet, firing his revolver rifle from the hip.

The British tourist became enamored of one of Gorch's girls, No, and the drunker he got the more he seemed to forget the one he had come in with. Rather than act jealous or insulted, however, his companion appeared to take it in stride and cheerfully switched her own attention to Gorch as he tended the bar. Her English proved more than adequate. She told him her name was Hong.

Gorch thought the old man was a fool for neglecting her. Hong was more beautiful than No and probably a few years younger, he guessed between nineteen and twenty-one, but he supposed it had to do with the old man being jaded and gluttonous. Dolled up for their date, Hong wore a clingy red silk dress with a high Chinese-style collar, cut to the tops of her thighs, her hair falling to the small round posterior her dress so artfully encased.

No took the ex-wrestler upstairs to "nap" for a bit and recover from imbibing too much. Gorch hoped No didn't try to support him if he lost his balance on the stairs, lest she be crushed in the avalanche. Hong didn't bat an eye. Instead she asked Gorch where he was from. He swept his arm around the bar. "Uh, Australia," he said. She asked him what it was like there and he spoke in generalities, told her about Sydney—where he had also lived for a time—instead of Melbourne.

Atop the bar, she took his left hand and held it in both her much smaller hands, turning it over and examining it as if to read his future. "You have strong hands," she observed. "You have worked hard with them."

"At times," he admitted, uncomfortable. Then he asked himself why he was always so wary. Did he think she was a spy hired by vengeful enemies back in the city he had exiled himself from?

She didn't let go of his hand, and that was when he was certain they were going to fuck. Which was fine by him; he had already slept with every one of his *bia om*, repeatedly. Gluttony and all that.

He invited her upstairs to see his apartment. "Do you have photos of your country?" she asked him with shiny-eyed interest, though he suspected what really interested her was the money he'd doubtless have to pay her.

"No," he answered. "But I have a camera. Maybe I could take some photos of you."

"Ahh," she said, smiling. "But I don't like people taking pictures of me... I'm sorry."

"Okay, so we'll skip that part."

Gorch got one of his girls to take over behind the bar, but before he could show Hong to the stairs she said, "My motorbike is outside. In the seat I have a gift I bought today for my father, but I think I'd like to give it to you."

"Really? I wouldn't want to deny your father his gift."

"Oh, I can get him another. Please wait a moment, will you? I will go get it."

***

In his flat on the third floor of the narrow building he had bought with all his savings, ill-gotten and otherwise, Hong pulled a bottle out of the plastic shopping bag she had fetched from her Honda's seat compartment. "My father likes to drink this sometimes," she told Gorch. Smiling with charming if unconvincing coyness, she further explained, "It's good for a man's baby."

"Baby?"

"You know," she said. She pointed toward his crotch and giggled.

"Ah, I see. Makes baby grow up big and strong, yeah?"

"Yesss."

"Let's have a look." He held out his hand. "I've seen these things a million times here but I've never really wanted to try it before."

"Oh, but you will drink this one, won't you? Because it is from me?" She passed him the bottle.

"For you, and for my baby, I'll do it."

It was a bottle of *ruou*, or rice wine, and he had drunk that on its own. But this type of *ruou*, which he'd seen sold at gift shops such as those at the Cu Chi Tunnels and the Saigon National Museum, had conspicuous extras stuffed into the bottle. Usually it was a cobra, preserved in the yellowish wine as if pickled in formaldehyde, maybe with a huge black scorpion or a fistful of smaller snakes and some herbs added for good measure. Hong's gift did have some blanched-looking herbs at the bottom, but no scorpion, and the snake coiled inside wasn't a cobra, unless its hood was closed.

Gorch turned the bottle around slowly to see it from all angles, and held it up in front of the fluorescent ceiling light. His brows tightened. Definitely not a cobra. And maybe it was a result of the animal's saturated tissues being distorted, but he almost questioned whether it was even a snake. He was reminded of the animal called a worm lizard, an amphisbaenian, which possessed a long pinkish body that looked segmented like an earthworm, with only a rudimentary pair of forelegs. It almost seemed this creature had such forelimbs, if withered, unless those were just bits of sloughing skin. Its eyes were bleached dull gray. It was looped in on itself within the glass, coiled around and around in a spiral as if chasing itself unto infinity.

"A dragon fetus, perhaps? Ace." He handed her back the bottle to open. He took down a shot glass. "Are you going to drink it with me?"

"It's a drink for men," she told him. "I don't have a baby." Her smile was a mixture of carnality and passable innocence that made his stomach squirm with hunger, as if he had his own dragon fetus coiled inside him.

She filled his shot glass, and he took a tentative sip. He tried not to show his disgust lest he insult her. After all, her father had unknowingly sacrificed this elixir for his benefit. It tasted just as he had expected: crude rice wine mixed with the essence of a reptile terrarium.

"Do you like it?"

Gorch didn't think he'd be stocking this beverage in his pub anytime soon, but he said, "A fine vintage. Cheers." He took another sip.

***

He and the woman Hong were naked and stood waist deep in the sea. It was high tide, and it was perpetual dusk, the bloody fleeces of clouds strewn upon a sky like magma.

The horizon was punctuated by a number of silhouetted metal ships—or the resonance of ships that had occupied those spots eons ago, or would occupy those spots in some far future epoch—in this realm where Gorch sensed steel was as transient as shadow. Hordes of dragonflies dangled above their heads, their wings a chorus of low humming.

His left arm lay limp at his side, submerged to the elbow in the lapping water. Hong held his right hand in both of hers, to her breast. Gorch felt her brown nipples pressing erect against his forearm. She was smiling up at his face, but he was looking down at the water, if it was water. It was yellowish, a color like piss, with a tang that was sour and rotten. Not so much polluted as venomous.

A whispery touch brushed repeatedly against his submerged left hand, along with the subtlest tugging, which might only be the movement of the yellow fluid itself. Gorch was reminded of the Dai Nam Van Hien amusement park, when he had taken one of his new bargirls there as a prelude to seduction. For a fee, the park's visitors could slip their bare feet into tubs in which fish would gently nibble away dead skin. He had tried it, though his date had been too squeamish. It had felt like this... an almost nonexistent sensation, unnerving all the same.

Hong squeezed his right hand tighter, and he raised his eyes to her slowly, as if he'd been stunned by a blow in the ring. She said, "That fat man has brought pain and drawn blood, but your hands have taken life. I can feel it."

Fat man? Gorch blearily managed to conjure the image of a British tourist in his sixties, with a belly like a cask and a head like a clenched fist. The man had boasted of having been a wrestler in his younger days.

Hong went on, "You are still young and strong. You can spare a little of your youth and strength, can't you?"

"I'm not so young," he slurred.

"Compared to my father you are." She tilted her face downward suddenly, and looked around them at the yellow sea rocking against their torsos. Gorch saw her gold skin turn pebbled with gooseflesh, like tiny hard scales. "He is here," she said.

Then the tide went out, but not gradually; it was sucked back violently like a bed sheet torn away, with a roar of rushing water. At the same time, the swarms of dragonflies churning above them were all swept back as if a powerful wind had come along, though there was no powerful wind.

His lower body unveiled, Gorch lifted his left arm to find that his index finger was missing, blood sluicing from the base and diluting with the water on his skin. He contemplated his hand almost calmly, detached, turning it over and back to view it from different angles. But his gaze came to focus on something else, beyond his hand, and he looked instead to his feet and the wet sand beneath them.

Turning slowly in a circle, Hong turning with him obligingly, he saw that there was a wide groove or channel imprinted in the sand, surrounding them in a giant C. But whatever had dragged itself through the sand, coiled itself around the spot where they stood, had gone out with the tide.

**

Because No was the most accomplished of his *bia om* at English, Gorch had her accompany him in the taxi and stay at his side, in the nondescript little hospital he chose, to translate. The young doctor who saw to his hand was pleasant and barefoot, having left his sandals outside his examination room. Various tools like instruments of torture soaked in a pan of what looked simply to be water, on the floor in a corner of the room. A gecko was stuck to the wall near the ceiling. Gorch instructed No to tell the man he'd lost his finger in an accident, though he knew it looked too neatly severed for that. The doctor was too polite and shy to express any doubts. Gorch had to repress his curiosity about how his wounding had been accomplished: knife, shears? The word *bitten* bobbed up in his mind, but that would have been too messy a result, he was sure.

Talking to No past the attentive doctor's shoulder, as he bandaged his hand into a mitt bulky as one of his old boxing gloves, Gorch said, "I should have known something was off when she didn't bring up money. She took what was in my wallet, but it was like an afterthought. What she wanted was to mutilate me. Got to be someone I pissed off back home, reaching out to me. I haven't made any enemies here that I know of."

"Mm," was all No could contribute.

He considered his list of old enemies, and how to interpret this message from any one of them. But the dream, or vision, he'd experienced under the effects of the rice wine came back to him, not so much in a clarity of detail but as an overall impression. For no reason he was conscious of, if he had to sum up what had transpired in the vision in one word, it would be *ritual*. He asked No, "There isn't any rite in Buddhism I'm unaware of, where you might take someone's finger?"

No looked horrified by the suggestion. "No," she said emphatically. "Not Buddhism."

He pocketed the baggies of antibiotics and painkillers the doctor gave him, though he had no intention of taking any of the latter until he found out why this woman had taken a part of his body. He wanted his head clear. Pain he was used to working around.

Back in the reception area—a dotted trail of someone else's dried blood leading them toward the front desk, where their waiting taxi driver flirted with a nurse—Gorch said to No, "All right, then, did that big British guy happen to mention where he was staying, when you had him upstairs?"

"Oh!" No replied. "Yes… yes… he told me!"

Gorch didn't recognize the place's name, but No appeared familiar with it, as she was no doubt intimate with many of Vung Tau's innumerable hotels, from before she had come to work for him. The frugal tourist had decided against one of the bigger establishments like the Sammy or the Imperial, opting instead for one of those narrow, pastel-colored structures of a half-dozen floors or more, looking all the more elongated for being crushed cheek-to-jowl in the side streets off the main drag, where for under ten US dollars a night one could get a clean room and HBO with a minimum of ants.

Gorch gestured roughly for the taxi driver's attention, surly from pain, and said to No, "Tell him that's where we're going. If that Brit's still there, maybe he can tell us where to find this woman."

No asked him warily, "Are you sure you don't want to tell the police what she did?"

"Why would I want to do that, if I might have to kill this little sheila when I find her?"

No's eyes widened, but she nodded quickly. "Oh. Okay."

***

Crowded beside No in the back of the toy-like taxi, Gorch was almost tempted to dull himself with some of those painkillers. The doctor's numbing injections had already worn off, and steady waves of pain were telegraphed up the lines of his nerves. In addition, he realized he was experiencing phantom signals from his absent index finger. At least, that's what he took it to be, this whispery sensation of brushing caresses, and an odd subtle tugging, as if he had inserted his missing finger through a hole in a wall, and on the other side little fish were nibbling at it.

He even dozed, for what was probably only several minutes, but long enough for him to find himself standing on a damp beach, though the ocean itself had drawn back so far that the water might as well have all poured off the curve of the world. Above him he heard a chorus of low humming, and he looked up expecting to see swarms of dragonflies. Instead, dangling overhead—suspended upside-down by their feet, via ropes that vanished into the fiery sky—were countless young girls in virgin white *ao dai* costumes like students, their arms crossed on their chests. Their long hair hung down in black flags, their eyes closed and mouths gaping wide—from which came the humming chorus, a wordless chanting, lips unmoving. Gorch saw what appeared to be a pinkish tentacle emerge from the mouth of a girl in the far distance, whip around searchingly as if probing the air, then withdraw into the girl's throat out of sight. Transfixed with fear, Gorch continued watching as the single limb reappeared from the mouth of another girl in the middle distance, closer now, again thrashing in the air for a moment before it was sucked back inside its host. This time he had noticed that the thing appeared vaguely segmented, like an earthworm. And then, in a flash, the appendage or rubbery body shot from the mouth of a girl hanging directly above him, seeming to lash around for him blindly. Gorch held up a four-fingered hand to shield his face, and cried out.

He opened his eyes to find No shaking his shoulder. Her expression told him she wished she was anywhere right now but beside him, even working the cheap hotels again. "Are you all right, *anh*?" she asked him.

Gorch sat up straighter. "How much longer?"

"We're almost there."

***

Just as the taxi was about to turn into the mouth of a shadowed corridor of interchangeable hotels, they came to a snarl in traffic. Pedestrians had gathered on the broad sidewalk, craning their necks, chattering and pointing. Diligently nudging his way through, palming his horn to urge onlookers aside, the taxi driver said something over his shoulder to No.

Gorch began to ask what was happening, but when he gazed out his passenger's window he understood. The first thing he saw was a pool of blood on the pavement, standing as thick and tacky as a bucket of spilled nail polish, already congealing under the sun. As they continued to crawl forward, he saw the source of the blood. A motorbike, now lying on its side in the gutter, had been struck by a truck overloaded with red bricks, apparently as the bike rider had been turning out of this side street to join the main road's traffic. Gorch had seen other accidents in his time living in Vietnam; they were inevitable in a country choked with motorbikes. The recent law requiring riders to wear helmets hadn't saved this victim: the truck had run directly across her head, splitting her helmet into hinged halves, and her skull identically inside it. In contrast, her body was mostly untouched, her schoolgirl's white *ao dai* almost pristine. The young girl lay on her back with her head in the wide corona of blood. Someone, maybe one of the city's many Catholics, had crossed the student's arms onto her chest.

A hard shiver went through Gorch. The dream he had snapped awake from only a few minutes earlier came back to him like a punch to the stomach that he hadn't tightened up in time to lessen. He looked away from the poor girl, resisting a deep down yawn of nausea, and the taxi managed to get the knot of chaos behind it and enter the chasm of hotels.

They pulled up in front of a tall, oblong hotel with its ground floor open to the street, at the top of a flight of steps. Gorch and No disembarked, while the taxi driver settled back to wait for them. No must have seen Gorch was feeling queasy, either from his careful step or his grayish complexion, because she put a hand on his arm. "You okay, *anh*?" she asked him again.

He nodded brusquely, gestured for her to climb the stairs. They did so, stepping into a little reception area that from the street had appeared as dark as a grotto. Now that its contents came clear, it presented them with another knot of chaos.

Heavy wooden chairs, ornate and lacquered, were arrayed along the side walls, the reception desk at the far end of the room. A wall-mounted TV played a Chinese costume drama, *Journey to the West*, dubbed into Vietnamese, with an actor in makeup as Sun Wukong the Monkey King. A granite staircase swept up in a curve to the second floor. And at the foot of these stairs, a group of people had gathered, speaking noisily all at once in agitation. They stood around a bulky white mass heaped on the floor.

When the people—the couple who owned the hotel, their grown son, and several hotel guests—noticed Gorch and No, they whipped around looking nervous, as if they might be blamed for what had occurred. The hotel owners pointed at the hulk on the floor and babbled to No.

Gorch stepped past them all and stood directly over the dead man. As if overseeing the scene with celestial amusement, the trickster Monkey King let out a wild cackle.

It was the British tourist in his sixties, the former wrestler. Staring up past Gorch, he lay on his back naked, his immense hard belly a white-haired boulder. Vomit was slick on his jowls and the front of his chest. The vomit smelled like the venomous yellow sea in Gorch's vision.

The index finger of his left hand was missing. Lifting his eyes, Gorch saw drops of blood on the granite stairs, blood smears on the banister. He turned to face No. "Did he fall down the stairs, or was it a heart attack?"

No relayed this question to the hotel owners. The couple spoke simultaneously, both of them dramatically gesticulating. Facing her boss again, No explained, "He fell down the last steps. Maybe it was a heart attack, but maybe he hit his head. He was chasing a girl who ran down the steps before him."

"Yeah. The little witch should've used more of her potion than she gave me, to subdue this big pommy." Then Gorch jerked around to face out the open front of the hotel toward the street. He heard the continuous drone of motorbikes from the long, sinuous coastal road. "I'll be stuffed," he hissed. Then, despite his lingering queasiness, he was bolting across the reception area, down the hotel's front steps, past the tiny waiting taxi, and down the shadowy side street toward the sunny and open main drag.

When he reached the mouth of the narrow street, huffing, the dead girl was on a litter being loaded into the back of a truck. Gorch caught a glimpse of her lolling head, the red gape of her face. She didn't need a face for Gorch to know her. Either Hong had been even younger than he'd guessed, or had dressed as a student to excite the old lecher, or had donned her snowy *ao dai* as a disguise to fade into the masses.

Policemen in green uniforms and military caps had appeared on the scene, talking to witnesses. So far, the Honda still lay neglected against the curb. Gorch skidded to a stop beside it, intending to crouch down and open the seat compartment, but he found that it already lay open.

Several articles that had been stored inside the compartment had spilled into the street. A plastic poncho, for those sudden drilling rainstorms that came out of nowhere, and a student's book bag that had in turn spilled some of its contents. Glass shards sparkled wetly.

Gorch snatched up the bag and dumped its remaining contents onto the street. Having noticed his actions, a policeman called out. Gorch ignored him. In a stream of rice wine, at his feet tumbled more shards, a few blanched herbs, and two bloodless index fingers looking like some kind of wrinkled worm, glistening from having been submerged in *ruou*.

Gorch peered into the bag again, but found nothing more. He hunkered by the bike, leaned in low to peek under it, didn't see anything there. The policeman had come close, speaking to him sharply, but Gorch still acted as though he were deaf.

Finally he spotted something. A thin wet smear like a snail trail. It led from where the book bag had been ejected from the bike, to an opening in the curb for draining rainwater into the sewer.

Straightening up, but finding himself unsteady on his feet—close to blacking out from pain and blood loss and more than that—Gorch experienced a renewal of those phantom signals from his absent index finger. A whispery sensation of brushing caresses, and an odd subtle tugging, as if he had inserted his missing finger through a hole in a wall, and on the other side little fish were nibbling at it.

LOVE SONGS FROM THE HYDROGEN JUKEBOX

T.E. Grau

D oyle had only been back on the Hill for two days when he already planned his next escape.

He disappeared three weeks ago from a reading at City Lights, hitching to SFO and flying twenty-three hours to scratch an itch in some Indonesian shithole. Screaming through the jungle, devouring the local medicine, taking full advantage of lax prohibitions on deviant behavior. He always went alone, and came back looking like he had grown an inch, with a couple of new scars, a bag full of bizarre trinkets, and enough stories to tide us all over until his next disappearance. I didn't blame him for skating, at least not that night. The poet was garbage, mixing tenses and mushing up metaphors without knowing exactly why. Must have sucked down his scoop of melted Ferlinghetti back in Boise through a game of telephone. The girls thought he was sharp, but I suspect only because he looked like Tab Hunter. He could have looked like Borgnine and the birds still would have been chirping, just because he was standing a few feet above the rest of us, shadowed on the illuminated roof. Everyone's supposed to be beautiful when heated by the spotlight. I thought he belonged further down the coast, where blond hair and a football chin earned you a paycheck and the pros write all the lines for you. Still, he scored pretty sweet that night, saving his best verse for after the show.

In Doyle's absence, North Beach seemed to hold its breath, more out of anticipation of his return than the government spooks who were poking around the filthy dives and unheated squats that cloistered together on Telegraph Hill, hoping the rest of the tourist world would pass on by and head to the Golden Gate. The feds made their best attempt to blend in, wearing Hawaiian button ups and dungarees, trying to score a lid or making conversation with the street corner glamour boys, rummies, and shirtless Negro kids who cross-stitched the streets on their modified Schwinns. But we knew what these deadbeats were up to, combing the area for reds or fags, or the nightmare scenario for every Betty Crocker American—the homosexual communist. We could spot the stiffs as soon as they arrived, even before the whoops from the street told us there were fleas on the dog. Because no matter how deep their cover, how much research they did on the Vagabond Tribe, those Washington Joes couldn't help tucking in their costume shirts, and their footwear was always showroom clean. A square can't fake an octagon no matter how many angles they play. Not enough degrees.

We told Doyle about the Hoovers when he got back, but he brushed it off as he launched into a mad tale of getting bent on shots of deep bush nutmeg stirred into Coca Cola while a Sumatran mountain witch unfolded from a steamer trunk and pulled seven rusty nails out of the spine of some crippled child. It was wild, like all of Doyle's stories, and no one knew where the facts ended and the ball of yarn began. No one cared, either. He was our Shaman, even to those who didn't know what that title meant. He cured us with his words, wiping away the disease of home and the poison of memory. We were all going to make a new go of it on Telegraph Hill, so we naturally needed a gathering point. That point was Doyle, who seemed to be here before any of the rest of us arrived.

As he told the story of the mountain witch, Doyle passed around one of the spikes to the group gathered in front of him like a prayer circle, settling in between the roaches that disbanded their three-week circus and skittered back into the walls. This was holy time, and no one—not Jack or Allen or any street corner messiah—could touch him as he spun his silk into day-glo tapestry, hovering a full six inches off the floor. Still, earlier in the day, I saw something in his eyes when the agents were mentioned. A flash of rage that cut rare in his wide, placid face that always danced on the verge of a private wink. He knew things that we didn't, even about ourselves, and that seemed to include why the government was sniffing around the Hill. But after that day, it was never mentioned again.

His homecoming shindig was a real blowout. Everyone in North Beach knew Doyle, and held him up as their golden calf, molded in the desert under the gaze of a fickle God to give them something tangible to trust. No one knew exactly where he came from, but he had an air of Back East breeding, tempered with something carved raw boned in the wilderness. The symmetrical features, the aristocratic nose. Hair that woke up better than your entire newly pressed outfit. He obviously had money, as his frequent jags to Peru and Afghanistan and a hundred other obscure destinations showed, but he lived like a pauper, dressing in worn-out trousers and a navy t-shirt. And he never wore shoes. "I like to feel the earth moving beneath me," he explained to me the day after I first arrived while we blew through some choice Hawaiian Tai stick. He was a strange cat, Doyle, but that was why we all loved him. "Hero of the outcasts," a junkhead we all called Raggedy Man croaked one night before vomiting into a bucket on the porch. The beat-down tramp, who lost his real name in a bloody cow pasture in eastern France twelve years back, just wiped his mouth, smiled, and nodded out, knowing no one would hassle him until he ventured back into the streets. We were the Outcasts, every dancing one of us, and we were all under Doyle's protection from whatever wars haunted the outside world. Just as long as you were within his circle, and so many of us were. We'd fight to stay within the insulating glow that leaked out from behind his eyes, and probably do other things, too. Everyone needs a family, and we were all Doyle's.

At the party, the girls whipped up some mean sandwiches with fresh sourdough and end cuts of Italian dry from Molinari's, while the fellas mixed a batch of jungle juice in a bathtub half buried in the back yard. Doyle owned the house, a sweet three-story Queen Anne Victorian just off Columbus Ave, but not a car. Said he didn't like to squirm through life inside a greasy fish tin. The sidewalks told the best stories anyway, and the love songs playing from the cracks held the sweetest harmonies. Six inches off the ground, no matter where he went.

"*Nellll*-son," Doyle called out in a singsong voice. I turned and found him reclining on the cinder block retaining wall next to the alley, staring up into the murky night sky. The bricks must have only been a foot wide, but he made them seem like a king-size mattress. "Nelson Barnacles," he mused, as if tasting the words. My last name was Barnes, but I was thrilled that Doyle finally gave me something new. Something that came from him. He gave lots of people nicknames, and now that included me. The glow around me suddenly grew brighter. I felt protected in a way Raggedy Man never could, especially because Raggedy Man ended up with his head caved in and missing both eyes and his left arm when he was fished up from under the wharf last week. Dumb bastard ventured too far out of the radius and ended up behind enemy lines. Just like in that cow pasture in eastern France. "Come check this out, Barnacles."

I downed my glass and walked over to Doyle, drying my hands on my pants like a school kid called to the front of the class to receive a ribbon. I always hoped that Doyle liked me because I was interesting or special in some way, but deep down I knew it was most likely because I slept in my '48 Buick Roadmaster, which was the last working ride on the block. Never mind that it was the only home I had on earth. I probably could have crashed at Doyle's pad, but I didn't want to intrude. Anyway, I had wheels, which meant Doyle did too.

He gestured to the sky. I looked up, and couldn't see anything through the incoming fog that reflected the light from the city back down upon itself like a golden canopy. "You see what I see?" Doyle asked, more to himself.

"Yeah... Yeah, I think I do." I saw nothing, but it was very important for Doyle to think I was on his level at all times, even though I couldn't find his floor if you built me a golden elevator.

Doyle exhaled a perfectly shaped nimbus cloud of spicy smoke that he was holding in the entire time. It didn't smell like grass. It didn't smell like anything I'd ever come across. His voice dropped an octave. "Nelson, we need to find the hydrogen jukebox." He turned his electric blue eyes on me. "We need a cleansing."

I paused, then nodded slowly. "We sure do."

He stubbed out the narrow joint on his tongue and swallowed the roach. "Fire up the sled and let's burn."

I waited, expecting him to continue, but Doyle just stared at me, looking stone-cold sober, like a professor waiting for an answer. "N-now?" I stammered.

"If not now, then when?"

I thought for a minute, climbing through the gauze that spread from my stomach until I discovered that his question was rhetorical.

Doyle waited for me to say what I was supposed to say, what anyone would say, but I didn't, so he smiled and hopped down off the ledge, landing lightly on his bare feet. "Meet me out front in thirty," he said as he disappeared, taking the light with him.

I stood in the dark for several seconds. "Where're you going?"

"Provisions!"

***

Thirty-two minutes later, we were rumbling down the Hill like a dull spear thrust into the slow rising sun, just as the city was shaking off the regret of the night before.

Sugarboy rode shotgun, rolling an Atomic Fireball across his stunted teeth and awkwardly jerking his head to the Kay Starr song on the radio, a gut full of bennies beating a hole in his heart. Doyle was in back, sitting between Cincinnati and some cat I'd never seen before. He called himself Escofet, which could have been a first or last name. Didn't matter, really. Just another punter riding the carousel. I took him for a queer, with his sweat-stained silk shirt open to the waist and long lashes that fluttered over black eyes that looked perpetually on the verge of tears, and presently seemed to be locked into watching me in the rearview mirror. A lurid tattoo of something ripe and naked peeked out from behind the row of pearl buttons. Doyle brought new faces and names in and out of the group almost daily, and it never mattered the color or persuasion. He had an interest in all of it, and tried every inch of it on for size.

In between sips of Old Fitzgerald and necking pretty heavy with Cincinnati, Doyle called out directions just as each turn was almost behind us. I yanked and careened, lurching the Buick through three lanes of traffic and a hailstorm of curses, finally catching the I-80 out of the city. My dad would have had a heart attack with the way I was beating this car. Doyle howled above each tire squeal, instructing every disgruntled commuter in turn to sodomize various family members in a variety of creative ways. Cincinnati giggled like she was seven instead of twenty-four and nowhere and drunk, while Escofet kept watching me in the mirror. Sugarboy popped another handful and lit up a joint, lost in the world just outside his window as he ground his nubs further into his gums.

We crossed the Red Bridge and invaded darktown Oakland like roaring barbarians, waving to the mothers heading to the salon and nodding to the hard-eyed neighborhood toughs manning their posts under the eaves of shadowed stoops. By this time, I was dipping into the road whiskey, and after a few slugs stopped wondering where we were going and focused on how capital it was that we were getting there. "Tapping in and letting go," as Doyle so often called it. Tapping into the lizard brain to learn the secrets of the reptiles, and letting go of the ego of the sapien. It wasn't easy for a boy raised between hay bails.

The row houses ceded ground to rugged hill and Spanish fir, and we soon made our way onto the 24, passing Emeryville and Upper Rockridge as time seemed to speed up while the fish cans around us slowed like unwound toys.

***

The highway thinned out, the energy in the car plateaued, and an unspoken silence crouched just below the radio backbeat and the roar of the pavement. I watched the painted signs pass above us, looking for clues. No one said a word for a long time, going through what they were going through. Escofet's eyes made the minutes into hours.

"Where're we headed, anyway?" Sugarboy asked as he turned to the back seat, his bloodshot pinpoints darting from Escofet to the creep of Cincinnati's dirndl skirt that showed just a hint of rounded cotton. He had finally pulled himself back together long enough to ask the question I had been meaning to bring up back on the Hill, but didn't have the guts. I wanted to seem the bold adventurer, tearing off in the pre-dawn slate without a destination in mind or a care in my soul. I wanted to be Dean Moriarty. But I was just Nelson Barnes, all smooth hull without texture, and what I was most concerned about was the five-body wear on my wheezing shocks.

Doyle took another belt from the bottle and grinned, squirting a rivulet of warm liquid between his teeth onto the back of my neck like a spitting cobra.

"Up into the rim. Forehead of the Western world… We gotta get a better view of things, you know?"

I had no idea what he was talking about, and neither did Sugarboy. The back seat, on the other hand, seemed drenched in understanding. The unifying power of liquor and forgotten modesty. Finally, I tried to join in with a chuckle. "We going mountain climbing? I didn't bring my boots."

Doyle started humming, or gurgling, deep in his throat. It was a terrible sound. *"The songbiiiird waits, at'er top o' Deeeevil's Mountain, openin' them brown arms wiiiide,"* he sang in an off-kilter voice, then hit the bottle again.

Sugarboy knitted his brow and cut his eyes to me. I just shrugged. We didn't know each other well, as he ran with the Night to Day crew in the house while my hours were more in line with a college professor. But on this trip, it seemed like the dividing line between camps was separated by pale blue vinyl seats. Escofet and Cincinnati just grinned knowingly. "We are about to be enlightened," Doyle pronounced before throwing on some grandma shades and leaning back in his seat.

My copilot twitched a few times, casting lassos through his orbiting brain, then turned back around and popped a Tootsie Roll into his mouth.

I swallowed a few times. The whiskey was wearing off and left something hungry and hollow in its place. "But what does that mean?"

There were a few moments of silence. I couldn't see Doyle's eyes behind his dark lenses, but I could feel Escofet's latching onto mine, as if he was watching for the man next to him. "How's that, Barnacles?"

I cleared my throat, wishing the bottle would make its way back up front, but Escofet was holding it with two hands, blowing into it like a jug player. Licking the opening. "Enlightenment, I mean. What are you getting at?"

Doyle lowered his sunglasses and looked at me with an expression I'd never seen before. Finally, he broke into a smile, then a laugh. His backseat chorus joined in, cackling like they were watching Jack Benny.

"Do I need to break it down for you? Our brothers are dying in the streets, bodies chewed raw from the filth of Korean rice paddies. Our sisters are locked in cages by husbands turned bosses.... *sla-*

vers, while the rest of us stare at our glowing squares, worshipping Cronkite and Lucy. Laughing inside the flames." Doyle grabbed the back of my seat, wrenching it back toward him, his eyes flaring. He was strong. "What we think we know is BULLSHIT, and what we don't know is our salvation. The West ain't the best. The West is a gerbil wheel. Knowledge from the older places is what we need right now. I'll be good goddamned if we scorch ourselves off this marble and leave only a black smudge with nothing underneath. I want to go deeper, find out how to rise above."

"Right on, big daddy!" Cincinnati hooted and lit up a cigarette, pushing her limp blonde hair behind her ears. She was such a brown noser, made worse when her underwear was warm.

"We're going to see the man with the plan." Before I could ask, Doyle sat back in his seat, as if exhausted. "Take the first exit."

I drove for five more miles, and was about to turn around, when I saw the small green sign on the side of the highway. Mount Diablo State Park.

The Buick veered onto the 680 South. That was the path to Devil's Mountain, where an angel awaited.

***

After sliding through the foothills, we began to carve up the mountain on a fib of a road that degenerated into the truth of a barely paved switchback. I had to sit up straight and man the wheel like a Clipper captain amid a furious gale, lest we split open on the rocks below that waited at the bottom of a thousand-foot gorge, grasping at the tires just inches from the edge of the spotty asphalt marking the trail like flattened, black popcorn balls.

Within minutes, we were totally disconnected from civilization, as the sequoias closed in like colossal spires around us, eating the sun with arms a thousand feet high. The radio had faded to static, and Doyle started to hum again. That hideous, tuneless sound, as if intentionally missing notes. I wondered if we'd ever be able to turn around and head back down. Forward or die.

The road finally straightened and leveled off, ruts smoothed by wear and some level of primitive upkeep. I rolled down the window, and in between gusts of Cincinnati's cigarettes, I could smell a dedicated wall of pine and ancient soil, worn down from the mountains to birth a million wooden titans. This was a different sort of smell than Nebraska loam, which had a damp odor of retreated ice, shallow streams, and clumsy agriculture. Up here lay the bite of primal dust, clinging to the backs of slumbering giants, full of wisdom born way down deep.

I looked into the rearview, hoping to catch Doyle's gaze but expecting to find another's, but I saw nothing. I pivoted in my seat, and found Doyle whispering into Escofet's ear. He was leaning into the side of the car, eyes closed. Cincinnati pouted and picked at her nails, flushed ears poking through straw.

"Watch the road, man!" Sugarboy screamed, grabbing the wheel and wrenched it to the left as the right tire nearly slipped off the edge of the trail. The car found the road again. "You almost *killed* us!"

My face drained and my ears pounded. I was terrified of heights, and here I was, piloting a crew of hopped-up ragtags to the rim of the world on a broken spider web. Doyle just laughed behind me.

***

Further up the mountain, the asphalt degenerated to a dirt path. A pair of figures stood on the edge of the tree line, holding hands. It would have been hard to tell if they were male or female, as they wore matching plastic Wanda the Witch masks. But they were both naked, both male, and totally erect. Their heads turned as we passed, hollowed out eyeholes pouring darkness into the car.

Sugarboy jammed his hands to the side of his head, wagged his fingers and made a face at them through the window. They slowly imitated his hand movements in unison.

I looked at Doyle, who frowned at the naked pair like a disapproving parent. I had never taken him for a prude. Maybe he objected to their cheap costuming. "Is this some sort of orgy?" I asked jokingly, mildly disturbed by what I had just seen.

Doyle just shrugged. "It'll be what you want it to be. But it'll be something, that's for sure."

"I'm ready for anything!" Cincinnati squealed, hugging Doyle, who had craned his neck to watch the two men run back into the forest as if being chased.

Mismatched automobiles and campers were parked on either side of the road, stretching as far as the eye could see into the shadowed depths of the forest ahead of us.

"Pull in behind the last car," Doyle said.

"So many people," Sugarboy said through clenched teeth, scratching his neck raw as the car squeaked to a halt.

"Grab the tent," Doyle said to Sugarboy, who was about to protest when Doyle tossed him a baggie full of pills. His mouth cracked into a jack-o'-lantern grin, and he threw open the door and hustled to the back of the car.

The rest of us piled out into the unnatural dusk, accept for Escofet, who was sleeping in the back seat. "What about him?" I asked, half hoping he had overdosed on a noxious stowaway Doyle secreted back from the jungle.

"Leave him. He'll catch up later."

"What's he on?"

"I don't know, but I wish I had some." Doyle put his ropey arm around my neck and grinned, projecting that glow out of his mouth and eyes like a blanket. "We'll have to ask him later."

***

We walked nearly a mile on a gentle upward incline, joining a procession of travelers from all stations of life and what looked like a hundred countries across the globe. Many of them spotted Doyle and offered greetings of various sorts. He responded in turn, like some sort of pilgrimage ambassador. This was Doyle's Christmas card list come to life and congregating on one California mountain. An advert for international brotherhood right out of central casting. His mystery deepened, if that was possible. Between multilingual salutations, we all trudged toward the locus of light dead ahead that would lead us out of the forest and back into the sun.

We finally breached the womb of trees and emerged into a vast clearing, and I could have sworn we stepped into a medieval carnival. Thousands of people clad in outlandish garb or some far-flung native dress danced, spun, and congregated in tight groups on the tamped-down grass. A tent city was set up at the far end of the glade, while gaily festooned vendor booths fronted the trees to the right. Lording over it all was a massive central structure built out of a mountain cliff that rose up into the mist-shrouded peaks. It was a hundred feet high and a football field wide, erected from mortared stone and thick wooden planks, topped with an onion dome that could have been ripped from eldest Siam or reddest Moscow. Narrow windows dotted the sides, giving the impression of a church, or perhaps a fort. By the weathering and veins of creepers crawling up the sides, whatever this place was, it must have been here for a while.

"Crazy, man…" I breathed, soon realizing that Doyle was waiting for my reaction. "What is this place?"

"This is the Listening Place," Doyle said, taking all of it in with the appraising eye of a construction foreman. He glanced at me and winked. "One of them, anyway."

A smiling woman with striking yellow eyes and skin tanned from a faraway sun skipped over and hugged Doyle before handing Cincinnati a flower. It looked lush and tropical, shining as if made of wax. Just like the woman who gave it. "Power to the children," she said in a dreamy voice.

Cincinnati brought the flower to her nose and gasped. "Wow… It smells like… like… My grandmother's farm." She giggled and cooed, and I saw a glimpse of the little freckle-faced girl from

Ohio, before she traded everything certain and safe for a chance to chase kicks and wild boys in the weird hothouse of San Francisco.

Sugarboy was eying vendors' row, which was insulated by a coterie of patiently waiting customers. "Y'all sell candy around here?" he asked the woman without facing her. She handed him an identical flower before padding away, liming the magic hour sky with the serpentine curls of her black hair. Sugarboy glanced around sheepishly, then inhaled the glistening petals. A wince escaped his lips and he staggered. Swallowing a wave of emotion, he threw the flower to the ground and stomped it flat, before skulking away with that hitched, agitated gate of his.

"What did it smell like?" Cincinnati called after him.

"Aftershave," Sugarboy murmured, as his mind tumbled backwards to those places he had tried to leave buried in the west Texas sand of east Lubbock. *My stepfather's aftershave*, he thought, hoping his mouth didn't move as he worked the words across his swollen tongue.

I watched Sugarboy melt into the crowd. "We're gonna lose him."

"Probably," Doyle said. "He'll get what he needs here, or he'll go home."

I stood back and marveled at the scene, again noting the smiles and bows shot Doyle's way. This wasn't like Telegraph Hill. This was an international procession of young and old. Mostly old. Yet all of them respectful, and often near reverent. "Why does it seem like everyone knows you up here?"

"Not everyone," Doyle replied cagily, eying a pretty girl with red hair twirling like a Dervish on an open patch of ground nearby, her bare feet tamping down a perfect circle in the grass and her beatific face aimed up at the sky.

"How'd you find this place? It doesn't seem real. It's like… like a play, or something."

Doyle took me by the arm and we walked like country gentlemen, Cincinnati falling in behind us, still holding the flower to her nose, grazing her thin lips as she inhaled deeply, eyes lidded heavy.

A little girl again, almost beautiful. Almost.

"Have you ever traveled, Barnacles?"

"Me? Yeah, of course. I ended up out here, didn't I? I mean, in the city."

"I don't mean *moving*, I'm talking about *traveling*. From this plane, to the next, and the next, and to the billion billion beyond."

I felt silly, small-minded, as I often did around Doyle. Like a child trying to hang out with the older, cool kid. "No, I guess I haven't."

"You should give it a shot sometime. You'll be surprised by what you find."

"But what is this place?"

"It's... *here*. It's now. But it isn't, you know?"

My silence told him that I didn't.

Doyle took in the scene, eyes coming to rest on the snow-capped mountaintops. "The Indian tribes shunned this place like the plague. Called it The Place of Too Many Secrets. The Armenians who arrived here after the genocide named it *Hetch Hetchi*. Nothing of Nothing. The white-bread mapmakers, hearing a few of the watered down legends, labeled it Devil's Mountain, which is a fucking joke on so many levels. But I guess they didn't know how else to describe what goes on up here, and other places like this."

"What goes on?" I asked with a bit of trepidation, remembering the two naked men standing in the forest. Masked and pale.

Doyle gestured with his chin to a bearded man wearing only a loincloth, blowing soap bubbles at a group of children who jumped and laughed, snatching the bubbles from the sky. Catching rounded rainbows. "You see that guy? That's Randy, an ex-Marine from your government's army. He killed three men and two women outside Pusan, then raped the ten-year-old daughter of the mother he brained with the butt of his rifle two minutes before."

I reacted with horror, feeling my stomach tighten with nausea. "What a monster."

"Yes, he was. A monster not born, but made by the territorial army of the United States of America. Transformed from lamb to lion in the space of one tour."

"What the fuck is he doing up here?" I said, my voice rising. "Around all this? Around *them*?" I pointed at the children.

"He's transforming back," Doyle said. "On that day in Korea, in that burning slaughterhouse, he stared into the void, and found himself alone. He didn't see what was really there, waiting for him, watching him, encouraging him. Randy was blinded by programming, which only exists to take away the true eye, and make us blind to the Father." I never took Doyle for a religious man, but what he was laying down sounded like the Sunday sermons I'd heard as a kid. "He came up here, traveled counterclockwise down the spiral of what we call the mind and what hides there underneath, and found what he was looking for. His eyes were opened to the truth, within and without. He's become a child again."

Once again, I didn't understand what Doyle was talking about, and this time, I didn't try to hide it. Instead, I shook my head and collapsed onto the grass, burying my head in my hands. "I don't know what's going on," I said, embarrassed, figuring that this was the end. Maybe it was that weird stuff Doyle smoked, giving me a contact high that I couldn't shake. Whatever it was, I knew I didn't have the ingredients to stand with Doyle, so I figured I'd end the charade on my ass.

He sat down across from me, crossing his legs and sticking a blade of grass into his mouth. After almost a minute of him not saying anything, I looked up, and found him gazing up at the huge structure across the meadow, that grew out of the mountain like a distended belly. "When I was rolling through the Hindu Kush, looking for prospects," Doyle began, taking on a practiced tone, as if he had told this story before, although I'd never hard it. "I caught whispers from the local Sufis of this bizarre medicine man who sat on the summit of the highest mountain in Kashmir, in search of this empty state of mind called 'nirvana' that waited for us all behind the illusion of this meat suit we call The Self. Didn't eat for thirty years. Thirty fucking years, can you believe that, Barnacles?"

"No," I answered.

Doyle's grin dropped. "Well, it's the fucking truth. The body can be told lots of crazy things if the mind knows how to say it."

"Yeah," I said. "I get that."

Doyle looked closely at me, probing behind my eyes, waiting for a spark of something akin to understanding. Finally, he went on. "So anyway, while this cat was up there, communing and listening and not eating or thinking about anything other than what could lay beyond the roof of the world, a strand of Knowledge happened across the mountaintop, pouring into him like a lightning bolt finding a key on the kite. Flesh made antennae. ZIIIPPP!" Doyle snapped his fingers and laughed, but there was no music it in. "Old man didn't find nirvana, he found something DIFFERENT. Something older than Allah or Shiva or Yahweh or any of those bullshit cartoons. Waiting out there in the dark, with so many secrets to share. And shared they were... Now, our Punjabi friend is passing on what he learned, one person at a time. He's a cosmic guru, this one. Fully legit, and I've checked out a few. He's got the sight."

"Guru?"

"Holy man. Shaman. Professor of the Divine. Whatever you want to call it, it's the goddamn same. Always *has* been. We just put new labels on it that we recognize, like a can of fucking soup. Same soup, same can. Different packaging. So we eat it like good hungry Christians, you dig?" Doyle lit up one of those strange cigarettes of his. "This guru—The Nightjar, they call him, after some Indian bird that nests on the ground but flies in the air—climbed down from his high-altitude perch like Jesus fucking Christ himself— who spent time in India, by the way. The perverts in power won't tell you that, Barnacles. No fucking way. Too *Eeeastern*..." He drew out the last word in the flat accent of a disgusted Middle American, took another drag and exhaled, the smoke twisting into ghostly sera- phim around us. "So anyway, cat starts to wander, talking about the REAL deal. News spreads across the north, and in a matter of weeks he's tearing the country sideways, pissing on religious hierarchy and giving the finger to madrassas and false holy places, gathering his followers around new ones, carving away at the status quo from the inside, like a life-giving cancer. The Hindus hated him, and the peace-loving Buddhists weren't much kinder. The police in Uttar Pradesh put a bounty on his head. But the villagers *dug* him, all the way through Nepal and into China. They remembered the stories of the elders, the ones told around cave fires after the dinosaurs died. This guy was telling them again. Everything old is new again..."

Doyle handed me the smoke, but I waved him off. He took another drag and went on: "Finally, the heat got so bad, with the police roundups at gatherings and death threats, his disciples had to sneak him into Pakistan, wrapped him in a shroud and hid him among the Muslims, hoping to get him to the sea at the port of Karachi. Instead, he disappeared and visited eight villages in four nights. Local Imams burned down each one after he left, once they heard what had happened." Doyle's eyes burned, and not with that normal protective glow. This was something more intense, much more private. "When the Nightjar opens his mouth, opens his *arms*, what flows out of him is righteousness from the way, *way* back. This is wisdom from the Beyond, the House of the Old Father, and what he's teaching is cutting the nuts from everyone who bleeds humanity dry with threats of eternal damnation in fairytale land. He's read the poetry of the universe, listened to the music of dead stars, and took in everything that was out there waiting, his body serving as a vessel. Writing a song. A love song from dear old dad. Once he came down from the mountain, hollowed out and filled up again, he gifted us all by sharing this solitary thing with everyone he met."

"What's that?" I asked quietly, realizing I hadn't swallowed since he began his story. Maybe I believed more than my mind would allow.

"The embrace." His dilated pupils danced above his white, perfectly straight teeth like two black dimes ringed in blue.

"I don't get it."

"Don't you ever get tired of saying that?"

"Yes," I said, and meant it.

"Then stick around, and you won't ever say that again."

The low register peel of a great bell rang through the valley, issuing from somewhere deep inside the onion dome. It repeated, shaking through me like the vibration of a bass string as big around as my arm.

Doyle sat up straight and cocked an ear to the repeating sound, seeming to find new things in each chime. He grinned over at me. "Time for the service."

***

Thousands of people stood patiently in a queue that spiraled around the structure, looking inside the doorway, hoping to get a glimpse of what lay beyond. As they waited to reach the door, men and women, nearly indistinguishable from each other due to the lack of facial and cranial hair, walked up and down the line holding bins labeled "DONATIONS TO THE FATHER" in pink, bouncy letters. As each pilgrim walked past, they dropped in wallets, watches, jewelry. Some even tossed in their clothes, returning to the line in various stages of undress as the shadows of trees and peaks cut slowly across the clearing.

I walked past the line with Doyle, heading toward the entrance. Just like with every joint on the Hill, Doyle never stood in line. VIP all the way, regardless of the geography. "Why are they doing that?" I asked, motioning to the rapidly filling bins, trying to avoid the sporadic nakedness, as my blush would surely out me as a prude.

"You can't enter the temple burdened by the outside world," Doyle said. "Cuts down on the transmission, like lead between an X-ray. But aside from all that," he added, shooting me a mischievous grin, "everything's better when you're naked."

I looked around at the variety of mostly unclothed flesh, noting the variety in shape and size and skin tone and hair density. "I don't know about that."

Doyle laughed and threw his arm around my shoulders, kissing me on the side of the head. "You're a real peach, you know that, Barnacles? If I didn't like pussy so much I'd marry you tomorrow."

We walked to the front of the line and passed through the wide doorway. The side of my head where Doyle's lips touched it throbbed with a liquid warmth. Neither of us had removed any clothing, but I felt more naked than I'd ever felt in my life.

Inside, people were seated on a dirt floor in evenly spaced lines, just inches apart from each other, like a mosaic of humanity. The air was heavy with burning incense that billowed from giant copper braziers hanging from thick chains bolted to the vaulted ceiling of the dome, that wasn't as naturally sloping as one would expect from the outside, but possessed a hyperboloid geometry that made me dizzy. Or maybe it was the smoke, which smelled just like Doyle's strange little cigarettes.

The hushed congregation was facing a low stage built at the front of the cavernous space, backed by heavy curtains of a thick and lustrous fabric. Doyle led me to the far end of the room, just in front of the rise, and squeezed my shoulder. "Wait here," he said into my ear, "and don't get on stage, no matter what I say."

The bell chimed again, startling me, mostly because it seemed to be coming from directly underneath the room, somewhere deep under the mountain, and not from a hidden steeple. *This is the church, this is the steeple, open the door, and see all the people...* I realized after a few fuzzy moments that I was staring down at my waggling, intertwined fingers. Perhaps I was becoming a child again, as well. I looked up to show Doyle, but he was gone. The recessed lights hidden in a gutter circling the high walls dimmed at that moment, and the tolling of the bell abruptly stopped. I could hear the beating of my heart in my ears. It was a slow, syrupy rhythm. The sound of an organ in mid-dream.

In the heavy silence emerged the creak of rusted wheels. All heads turned in unison to the right, as another of the hairless men pulled a rope attached to a rough wooden cart, atop which was seated a small, gnarled figure dressed in thick, simple robes the color of clotted cream, a hood covering its head. That cart was led in a narrowing spiral around the stage, then brought to a rest in the center, facing the crowd. The hairless man walked to the backing curtain and pulled it aside, revealing Doyle, now changed into a ceremonial robe of rich burgundy brocade. The crowd moaned softly, a thousand strong mouthing the sound "*oooooo*" which grew in subdued strength, compressed volume amplified by the identical pitch of so many vibrating throats.

Doyle strode forward, raising his arms, as he did just before story time on Telegraph Hill, but this time without a Mason jar of Jungle Juice in his hand. A circle stitched in shiny black silk adorned his chest. No, not a complete circle. It was broken, lacking a finishing piece on one rounded side. The corrupted symmetry somehow unnerved me, and I suddenly grew nostalgic for the small crescent of Regular Family that gathered around in a complete circle on the dirty cement of the old Victorian. That seemed like a simpler, quainter time of a long gone nostalgic past, even though it only happened twenty-four hours prior.

The crowd gathered here gave off a different vibe than the one living on the Hill. This group, although similar on the outside, was infused with a frantic yearning buried shallow, just under their whimpers and supplications. Doyle strode to the cart and unceremoniously pulled back the cowl covering the crouching figure's head, revealing folds of leathery bronze skin heaped over the skull and face of a tiny man. He resembled a rotten potato, or a deflated balloon wrapped over a doll.

The man raised his chin from his chest and regarded the crowd through eyes pressed shut by deep wrinkles. One of his sockets pulsated, then opened like sliced flesh, as a sticky orb the size and consistency of a martini onion bulged from his face. Hazy, pus yellow and grown over with cataracts, it seemed totally sightless, but it moved across the crowd hungrily, his wasted body turning with great effort.

Doyle placed a microphone stand in front of the seated man and turned it on hot. Feedback squealed through the room, fading to a low drone.

The shriveled man began to hum along with it. The audience took up the vibration, and the whole vaulted structure filled up as the strength of the thrumming increased in texture, creating an invisible mass in the air that pressed against everyone. The acoustics of the building were perfect, absorbing the sound and amplifying it back without echo. The ground beneath my feet felt as if it was coming unmoored from the foundation and rising from the hardened skin of the mountain. And still the braziers smoked…

The sound of tablas began in some hidden place, pounding sharp and fast, interspersed with a metallic keening. The shrill piping of disjointed flutes joined the backbeat, bringing a frantic, zigzagging melody to the rhythm. A song was building, coalescing into something tangible, but no less chaotic, hitting the inner ear at an odd angle, unbalancing the brain. All that remained were the lyrics.

"Who among you will sing?" the shriveled man rasped into the microphone, his lips barely moving. The voice sounded like the shifting of sand, the scrape of great boulders. The accent was strange, undercut with a clipped hesitancy. Not exactly central Asian. Not exactly from anywhere.

"I WILL," a voice shouted from the crowd.

"Your father loves you," the man said. No speakers were present on the stage or dangling from the arched ceiling, but his words boomed out into the room.

"AND WE LOVE OUR FATHER!" the congregation replied as one.

"Your father waits for you."

"AND WE WAIT FOR OUR FATHER!"

"The father is a child to his father, and to his father before him. We are all the children."

"WE ARE ALL THE CHILDREN!"

"Who will enter the holiest of holies?" the man barked through rubbery lips. Doyle was nowhere to be seen. "Who will be baptized and born new, ready the truth of paradise?"

"WE WILL! WE WILL!" The crowd was rising to their feet, reaching their hands to the stage.

"Who will feel the embrace, the hug of the servant?"

"WE WILL! WE WILL!"

"Who will be first? Who will be first to be last?"

The drumming and the piping and the ping of metal stopped. I felt a hand on my shoulder. I turned, expecting to find Doyle, but it was the shaved man from the stage.

"My brothers will!"

It was Doyle's voice, cutting through the sudden stillness of the room. He stood now on the ground with the rest of us in front of the stage. Escofet and Sugarboy were at his side, both stripped naked, both standing stiffly at attention. The acne on Sugarboy's back seemed to wink like tiny, diseased eyes in the weird light of the room.

"They've come to learn the song," Doyle said, gripping them tightly by the shoulder with each hand. "They've come to feel the embrace. They are the children waiting for their father's arms."

"Approach," the man croaked, his one open eye fixed greedily on the two men.

Doyle led both to the stage and climbed the low stairs, walking them to the seated man, who slowly raised his arms, holding them out wide. "The father seeks to provide the attention and care we all should have received as children," the old man said. "The father seeks to right the wrongs. Restore the balance."

The crowd moaned again, a sound of longing, expectation. Sugarboy and Escofet got to their knees and nuzzled in close to the man's torso, clinging to him like two kittens pawing at the teats of their mother's belly. Sugarboy shook, sobs wracking his body, undulating under his jutting ribcage. Escofet just smiled, like he was finally home. The wrinkled man's arms emerged from their cloaking and wrapped around both, enveloping them in his embrace. His wingspan seemed too wide for someone of his stature, his fingers too long and knuckled in too many places. He hugged Sugarboy and Escofet firmly, drawing them into the parted section of his garment, into the wrinkled skin of his chest and stomach.

His grip tightened, the sinews of his distended arms bulging taut, and the men slowly disappeared inside the man's robes without a sound. First the faces and heads, then torsos, hips, and finally two sets of bare feet were drawn inside the seated man like pouring melted butter through a sieve.

The hidden bell tolled. The crowd gasped, clutched at each other.

"The children have gone home," the tiny man said. His eye closed, and his head lowered once again to his chest.

Doyle walked to the front of the stage and bent to the microphone, his eyes shining like sparking embers. "Thus concludes tonight's service."

The crowd began chattering at once, breaking the silence with an explosion of confused noise and animating a thousand formerly sleeping corpses. Many of them rocked back and forth. Several more shot to their feet and thrashed in some violent dance, before falling to the ground, speaking in gibberish like an old revival tent meeting. Some joined the dance, others heading quickly for the doors, expressions ranging from dreamy wonder to masks of horror. Many of them cried and held each other. I wasn't sure if this was out of disappointment or trauma. Possibly both.

I couldn't wrap my mind around what had just happened, if I was just witness to a magician's trick or something much deeper. My brain felt funny. I had a difficult time remembering yesterday, how we had arrived at this place. I just remembered locomotion, travel. A gray jumble of freeway concrete that led to this place high above the regular world. There seemed to be no going back, because forward was the only thing that made sense, and wasn't shrouded in an anxious mystery.

"Nelson."

Somehow I heard Doyle's voice above the din, the slap of bodies and weird chanting. Doyle was standing on the stage, the microphone gone. *"Nelson,"* he said again, his lips not moving over a curious grin that lit up his face. Did I imagine it? He held out his hand. The full force of that glow enveloped me, and instead of heading toward the door, I walked towards him, the crowd parting in front of me. Pleading, envious faces looked up at me, and I couldn't help but feel special. Blessed. He had called me by my first name. Not my name from the Hill, but my real name. He knew me.

That name climbed inside of me, just as we climbed the stairs to the stage, hand in hand, and followed the man on the cart through the opening in the curtain. I didn't care what anyone else in the room believed. Doyle was my guru, and I'd follow him to the ends of the earth, and probably beyond.

***

The light slowly faded with the sound of the crowd behind us until we were in total darkness. All I could hear was the squeak of the cart wheels, and the pounding of my own heart. I couldn't feel Doyle's hand in mine anymore. I couldn't feel my feet touching the spongy ground, and yet I had the sensation of moving downward in a tight corkscrew, although I never brushed up against a wall or ceiling. I was adrift inside the throat of some great beast perched on the lip of the outer void, moving toward the culmination of all of my wandering. I was about to travel.

The sound of the wheels ceased and I felt the air change, growing more damp and cold and constricting, pressing in on me as would the steam in an overheated room. There was a sensation of the material world reconstituting around me, and then I felt the ground under my shoes. It was uneven, ridged, and I had to readjust my weight to stay on my feet as my brain seemed to find my body underneath it again.

"Bring us some light," I heard Doyle say. I couldn't tell where he was. His voice sounded clear, but muffled, as if he spoke directly into acoustic tile.

"As you wish, Mr. Wolverton," someone said.

Torches flared to life one by one and started to move, as more of the shaved men emerged from alcoves in what the flickering firelight in their hands showed to be an enormous cavern with craggy walls, twice the size of the room we had just left, roughly hollowed out by tectonic shifts or some other blind elemental force that found rock to be nothing but deluded clay.

As the torches grew in number and the light brighter, I realized that the walls weren't jagged cave rock, but a tapestry of bones. Millions and millions of bones, in various shapes and sizes and species, from a dozen eras of planetary history, fused together from floor to ceiling with the mortar of time and glacial ooze of living rock. And although the bones were scattered and the body structures vague, it was clear that whatever living things they had once been, they were all individually facing—*paying eternal homage to*—one singular object: a wide sheet of raised, jet-black stone in the center of the cavern, which jutted at a 45 degree angle from the cave floor, like an insect display, and held in stasis a half-exposed fossilized spine of what looked to be a giant snake, but topped with a massive skull that more closely resembled a Tyrannosaur. Or a dragon. It had died in a loose, nearly perfect circle, open mouth and teeth facing its tail, but not quite reaching it… The broken circle pattern on Doyle's robe, here calcified and memorialized by an innumerable pattern of dead pilgrims… Ouroboros before it could complete its mad autosarcophagy… Failure of the Eternal Return, frozen for all eternity in a half layer of volcanic rock that must have been a billion years old. This was the elephant graveyard for every vertebrate creature that slithered, walked, swam, and flew across this planet since the cooling of the primordial soup.

I stood, mouth agape and mind spiraling, still somehow rooted to the bones under my feet, while the shaved men busied them-selves around me, paying me no mind as they sorted through the donation bins, grouping, counting and labeling each item down to the last sock and faded penny. Others packed up documents and took down draperies that had formed impromptu tents within this hollow in the earth—basically moving house, if one's house was a traveling circus of the damned.

"I'm sure you have a few questions," Doyle said, suddenly at my side. He shook out a stiff, leathery suit as one does after pulling a wet blanket from the wash. He began to fold it carefully, trying to smooth out what wrinkles he could in more of a nervous habit than anything actually effective. It then dawned on me what it was in his hands, but I couldn't bring myself to believe it. But, just moments later, I was taking it for granted and speaking around it, as if it could have happened, and *does* happen. A man holding the flesh suit of another man, in a cave made of bones. The surreal had become reality. Nightmares more tangible than the outside world, which seemed so far distant from where I was standing at that mo-ment.

"What happened to him? The Nightjar," I said, my voice feel-ing as if it came from someone else and I was listening to it as one would a stranger. I gestured to the suit as Doyle fussed with a zipper, digging skin out of the teeth so it would glide properly and find purchase.

He glanced up at the ceiling, which was pocked with openings that could easily accommodate a person. Or something the size of a person. "Oh, he's around here somewhere."

"What *is* he?" The stranger with my voice spoke again.

"A servant. Just like me. And just like—" A tittering hiss filtered down from the warren of holes in the ceiling of the cavern, and Doyle just grinned, laying the haphazardly folded skin suit to the side, which was quickly and solemnly picked up by one of the hair-less men and ferreted away to one of the quickly filling wooden storage boxes. "Well, okay, he's a LOT different than any of us, but lets just say he plays for the same team."

My jaw worked without sound. I needed water. I needed to drink every gallon of goddamn Lake Ogallala, where my family went camping every July 4th. The fireworks looked so beautiful reflected in the lake. Like cosmic spiders, revealing themselves in an explosion of terrifying light and sound for only a few seconds, before burrowing back into the dark. Nebraska was so far away now. Everything was. "What happened to Sugarboy and... that other guy?" I said, feeling my voice return to my throat. "Your friend."

"Now *that* I can't tell you. I mean, I would tell you if I knew, you dig? But I don't, so I can't."

The inclusion of the *"you dig"*—something the old Doyle would have said, the Doyle who wasn't some pseudo Eastern religious leader—set my already chattering teeth on edge, and seemed to focus me, ripping me away from the saw-blade edge of awe and possibly insanity at the existence of such a place, of such things, and dropping me closer to a more rational state of mind tethered to reality by the familiar nudge of irritation. It was blasphemous, the new mouth saying these old words. More so than anything that was said out on that stage, than what was buried here under this mountain.

"Why did you bring me up here?"

"I wanted you to see," Doyle said, reclining against the hipbone of some great forgotten beast. "And then I wanted you to decide."

"See what? A buried museum? Some space-case, bourgeois religion? A cheap magic trick?" Even though I said the words, I didn't believe them, not in the dismissive way they came out. I was embroiled in something huge, and way beyond my comprehension. But I wanted to insult him for lying to me, thinking me a dupe. I probably wouldn't make it out of this cave, but I wouldn't go out like a chump.

Doyle couldn't believe my words either, judging by the expression on his face. "Magic trick? *Magic* trick?" he snarled, air expelling from his lungs in shock. "Do you think what you saw up there was a fucking parlor game?"

"I don't know," I said quietly, crouching down, trying to get small. "I don't know what I saw. I don't know what any of this is."

His face became deathly calm. "Let me clarify it for you."

Doyle nodded his head, and one of the shaved men walked forward and stopped, still as stone. Doyle then snapped his fingers, and something large landed with a heavy thud behind the man. There was a ripping sound, followed by a gentle lapping. The man's face held its concentrated expression as sweat beaded his forehead, then poured down his face. His body shook, then started to writhe, as his skin expanded outwards like a stretched, veined sausage, facial features and muscles popping, before every inch of him burst, showering a twenty-foot radius with a spray of blood and meat. What bone and chunks remained were choked down in segmented jerks by a massive, squirming worm the general shape and color of a garden grub but the size of a jersey heifer, cross-mated with a jungle-variety centipede.

"The fuck!" I screamed, wiping gore from my eyes and scrambling up the wall as far as my worthless feet would take me, which wasn't very far.

Once it finished eating, the slug emitted a shrill scream like the folding of metal and slithered its way back up the wall to escape the light in a hitched, coiling motion, evidencing a total disconnect with movement on land, or possibly three dimensions.

"What is that thing!" I cried, ducking down and shielding my head as the worm disappeared back into one of the holes in the ceiling, yowling in a rising, halting pitch that sounded like madhouse laughter as it buried itself deeper into the primeval granite behind the skeletal arabesque.

My mind swam, the pattern of bones all around me twisting and diving in a stuttering pattern that made me nauseous. I dropped to my knees and vomited. I wanted to expel everything I had seen and now knew. I was sure this was all the result of something Doyle had given me. This was all a hallucinatory dream. It *had* to be. Oh fucking yes, I needed this to be true, or else I'd bash my fucking brains out with a rock. With a dragon bone. "What is that thing?" I asked quietly, playing the role in my waking dream, this inverse déjà vu, bile dripping from my quivering lips.

"A Servitor," Doyle said, gazing up with a smile of pride at the now populated tunnel in the ribcage of the world. "A Pure One sent here as a missionary to spread the ballad of Old Leech." I stared up at Doyle, not understanding. "You know, the song that gave us speech, taught us math, physics, how to split the atom."

"I don't—This doesn't…"

"Okay, call him the choir. Or maybe the A&R rep. Our tiny Punjabi friend here, or…" Doyle looked around, not finding the skin suit. He shrugged. "Wherever he is, climbed the antennae of our planet looking to hear something, *anything*, reaching WAY OUT from his mortal shell to hear the truth amid the dead silence of the universe, and OL found his frequency." Doyle looked at the circular arrangement on the black stone slab and smiled. "He called, dialing the right number, and someone answered. The rest is history, or soon will be. He's just one of many."

"Then what are you?"

Doyle cocked his head to the side, as if he had never considered this question before. "A fundraiser, I guess. Bandleader, maybe." He laughed. "With pedigree, of course."

"I've never heard of this… leech. Is he your god?"

"No and yes. If he is a god, he's yours, too. You just don't know it yet. Not knowing the truth won't stop it from existing, or doing what the truth does."

"Which is?"

"Finding its way to the light. In this case, Old Leech isn't too keen on all that illumination, so it's going to do a little major redecorating around this corner of the multiverse, make it a little more cozy for when he stops by for a visit."

I looked around the room with eyes opened just a little bit wider, finally taking in the gravity of the eons of animal and human bones stacked on top of each other, showing a devotion stretching back so far my brain couldn't comprehend it all. The hidden god of the mountains, worshipped in secret under the mountain. Humanity didn't know a goddamn thing, maybe didn't want to. Ignorance is bliss, bliss in ignorance, my crown for just one more second of ignorance. "Your god is coming...? Here?"

"Oh yes," Doyle said, his eyes gleaming in the dusky torchlight. "That's always been the plan. My family, and a few others, have made it a point to roll out the red carpet when he arrives."

I curled up into a ball, dislodging a femur of some early homi-nid in my hand and bringing it close to my chest like a little girl's dolly. Fetal position, longing for the womb. Lord, birth me again, far away from here. Or shoot me out stillborn, slimy and blue. Anything but this.

"I want to die," I moaned, fighting back another wave of nausea.

Doyle walked over and crouched down in front of my face. "Like hell you do," he said, breathing into the side of my head. "We're just getting to the good part." He stood up suddenly. "The time of the Arrival is upon us, and you could help lead the charge, my brother! We need good people, good men." Doyle fixed his gaze on the circular skeleton across the cavern. "Old Leech is patient, but he's also an impulsive motherfucker."

"I don't underst—"

He dropped to his knees again and took my by the shoulders. "Of course you don't, you fucking barnacle!" Doyle's face looked feverish, sweating madness. "I don't either, really. This is a birth-right, and who can gauge the history of a family that stretches back to the time of the first mastodon? The first tribe? Back when the play of the universe and the earth were more closely connected. Back when the Dark walked, or slithered, on our planet each and every night? What I *do* know is that a brigade is being assembled. The foot soldiers are housed in the barracks all around us." Doyle swept his hands to the tunnels dotting the ceiling. "And in a dozen other outposts scattered across the planet. I've dropped in on them all, and everyone—everything—is ready and waiting. Now we need the generals." Doyle took my face in his hands, tossing that lasso again. This time, the rope was on fire. "I know that you know that I know what creeps deep inside of you. That thirst for *experience*, the taste of the edge. For the command of things that have no name. You and I are the same, Barnacles. We want to exterminate the status quo, and kick the doors in on a new era of enlightenment that will move our species from the apes we are to the earthly gods we are destined to become!"

He was squeezing my face now, and I ripped my head away from his grip, bringing fingers to my bruised cheek. "You're... insane."

His face fell, eyes becoming cold as a reptile as he stood up. Even their shape seemed to change. "Sink or swim. Song or meat. It's your choice." He held out his hand. I just looked at it. "It's going to be everyone's choice soon, so consider yourself getting in on the ground floor."

After several moments, I sat up, looked him in the eye, grinned ruefully, and took Doyle's hand. He gripped it and brought me to my feet, pulling me in for an embrace. I leaned in close to his ear, smelling that clean sweat of his and strange incense clinging to the nape of his neck. That intoxicating aroma of my former guru... In my mind, I saw myself running through the woods. I was followed, above and below, but I didn't turn around, because I knew if I did I'd want them to catch me. To kill me, because what was following me was worse than what I had seen inside the mountain. There were worse monsters still that hadn't yet been revealed, and I wanted to live in ignorance lest I die from the knowledge. The drums. The flutes. The song. In my mind, I ran...

"Meat," I whispered into Doyle's ear, before burying the bone into his neck like a dagger, driving it so hard it poked out the other side with a crimson blurt. He jerked away from me, pawing at the bone lodged just under his jaw, stumbled backwards and fell on his ass, blood spurting out from between his fingers, his teeth.

"You did it, Barnacles," he gurgled, fixing a horrible smile outlined with dark red. "You… really did it…"

I staggered backward, horrified and proud of my action in equal measure, completely unaware of where my motivation to murder my friend, my teacher, my everything, had come from.

As Doyle fell to the floor, his life draining out of his grinning mouth, the black stone slab rippled like ink, or maybe flesh, and a sound—a voice—arose from inside all that endless black. It howled, it roared, it yammered in a language I couldn't possibly understand that nearly split my eardrums and fried my brain like an egg.

And then it sang, and I stood there, listening. Song or meat. Both Doyle and I had our role now, and I dragged his body toward the pulsating slab of rippling black that lapped up and over the bones. Shrill barks and clicks came from the holes in the mountain. Things emerged from the openings, and watched the procession on the ossuary floor below. The song from the black slab grew louder, and I started to hum, as it started to make sense. Vibrations became words, stitched together into stanzas. New real estate in my brain began to map itself out. New synaptic connections were made. New notes discovered in a sonar range I never knew existed.

The first verse in this psalm I already knew. It was born inside me, in my lizard DNA, and I just needed to be swallowed and reborn to remember:

For one to transcend, one must kill their heroes. This is the way of Old Leech.

Thus concludes tonight's service.

THE OLD PAGEANT

Richard Gavin

He didn't want her to know how physically taxing he'd found the long drive to the woods, how tedious the prospect of unpacking seemed, or how repugnantly primitive he found their accommodations to be upon their arrival. The holiday had the potential to be far too special an occasion for him to sour it by sulking.

The cabin had been in her family for decades, though the moment he spied it—an oblong box slumped between leprous-looking birch trees—he wondered why she didn't regard the cabin as a skeleton from her family's closet instead of a prideful heirloom.

After an anxious struggle to fit the copper key inside the ancient lock, the door gave, allowing the pair of them to be assaulted by the stench of long-trapped air. The dark had evidently grown so accustomed to the cabin's interior that it stubbornly refused to part for the sunbeams that the man and woman ushered in.

Shutters were peeled back, windows were pried ajar. She stripped the ancient white sheets from the beds and took them outside and hung them from the birch limbs so that the breezes might push out their mustiness.

They cleaned and unpacked and traded off-colour wisecracks. The supper they cooked together was hearty and its aroma managed to mask a bit of the cabin's cloying staleness.

After eating he delighted her by finding the detached footboard that had once braced the lower bunk bed she'd slept on as a girl. It had been wound in a shower drape of translucent plastic and stored behind her grandmother's dormant sewing desk.

Her grandfather had carved (with visible skill and obvious love) an inscription into the footboard:

Here lies Donna Hammill
Each and every summer
Dreaming...

She cried and ran her fingers along the grooved words as though they were Braille.

—I have another gift for you, he told her in a voice whose shakiness surprised him.

He was almost fearful of producing the ring case from his pocket.

Ultimately he opened the case and he asked her.

She accepted and they both began to shed fresh tears, but ones of happiness.

He uncorked the bottle of pinot noir. She stole a sip from the brimming glass he handed her.

She set it on the windowsill and told him not to move a muscle. Her purring tone thrilled him.

Leaning against the deep washbasin with its antiquated hand pump, he watched with increasing anticipation as she pushed together a pair of slender cots, draped a quilt across their bare mattresses, and stripped the dusty clothing from her body.

She giggled at his suggestion that they shut the door and windows, assuring him that they were all alone, no one within earshot. In fact, no one within walking distance.

He went to her.

The ferocity of her climax proved to him just how isolated they were, for she had always been painfully aware of the neighbours.

Birds actually rustled free from a nearby tree, startled by her passionate cries.

Buoyed by his petit mal, he lay back in the humidity and hoped that the encroaching dusk would cool him.

—Well, we've officially christened this place, she beamed.

She held up her left hand to admire the glinting star that now ringed her finger.

He asked her if she was happy.

—Very, she told him.

—When was the last time you were up here?

—Not since I was eleven, the summer before my grandma died.

—How come your family never sold it? If the cabin wasn't being used, I mean.

She shrugged.

—It had been in the family for so long, no one ever thought of getting rid of it. My great-grandfather built this cabin with my great-grandmother. They actually lived here for a few years. Eventually they moved to Olympia where my great-grandfather had landed a job doing... something, I can't remember what it was. They used to spend their summers up here with their kids. Then my grandparents vacationed here with *their* kids, then on to my parents with my sister and me. And now us.

She pecked his cheek and he smiled and tipped back the bottle of pinot noir.

—Did you like coming up here when you were a girl?

—I loved it.

Her tone was richly sincere, if a shade melancholic.

He placed his head against her breast and asked her to tell him about what it was like. He was city-born, city-bred. Nature was to him as it should be to all: utterly bewildering, daunting in its autonomy.

—My grandmother used to take my sister and me on these marathon hikes where she'd point out all the different plant types. Or she'd try to teach us how to identify a bird by its call, things like that.

She began to chew her plump lower lip and he asked her what was wrong.

—Nothing.

His bladder had been throbbing for several minutes. He rose and muttered some euphemism for relieving himself which she did not find as funny as he'd hoped. He excused himself from the cabin.

Without, the countless boughs were garlanded in fine shadows, ones that linked oak to ash to sycamore to yew as though it was some kind of dark ligament. Mosquitoes formed a buzzing fogbank and the temperature seemed to have jumped from humid to chilly with no temperate phase between.

He moved a respectable distance away and relieved himself on some spiky foliage. He experienced a sense of being not just isolated, but marooned.

Something skittered out from one thicket and was almost immediately subsumed by another. The cracking of twigs and the hushing spasms of leaves turned threatening.

He turned and ran back to the cabin, catching himself just before he came thundering through the front door. After regaining his composure, he crossed the threshold with artificial nonchalance.

She was cross-legged on the cots, her torso now covered in one of his loose t-shirts.

—You sick?

She shook her head.

—You look pale.

He uncapped a bottle of water and handed it to her. She took it but did not drink.

He nudged her sardonically.

—What's going on? I step out for a moment and when I come back inside it's like you're a million miles away.

—I'm sorry.

She entwined her fingers with his and kissed the back of his hand, then said:

—I guess this place has more memories than I realized.

—Bad ones? (Wisely, he was treading lightly.)

—I think seeing the night beginning to fall outside reminded me of this stupid game my older sister invented called *Something Scary*.

—Um... okay...

They both laughed a little bit.

—It sounds so stupid now, I know, but at the time that game really got to me.

—What's the goal of *Something Scary*?

—To scare the piss out of whomever else you're playing with, what else? I said it was stupid.

—No, don't say that. Given that you were both kids at the time and stuck out in the boonies, I can see how a game like that would have worked.

—Oh it did, believe me. But... *Something Scary* wasn't what got me upset just now. It was remembering something my grandmother introduced us to, another game.

—Oh?

—See, *Something Scary* was just a typical kids' game. My sister and I would sit in the dark here and whisper little ghost stories to one another. Mine were never that good at all because I spooked really easily so I always played it timid. My sister, she was good at it though. I mean *really* good. The funny thing is, later on I learned that most of her stories were just retellings of *Tales from the Darkside* episodes that she used to watch after my parents had gone to bed. Sometimes they were just old urban legends. Still, she knew how to tell a story.

—That seems to run in your family.

She rolled her eyes.

—No, really! I've told you that your life sounds so much more interesting than mine. You've got storyteller's instincts.

—Regardless, I remember one game of *Something Scary* where my sister said there was a decrepit hermit who lived in these woods. According to her story, the man's wife had gone out to fetch water one night many years ago but she never came back again. So every night the man still went out searching for his lost love. But of course after so many years the man had lost his mind, so if he saw any woman in the woods he would *make her* his wife. He'd just drag her away into the trees and she'd never be seen again. Any female had to fear being in these woods after sunset. And I had to try and *sleep* with that in my head! God, I *hated* that story.

—That is pretty creepy. But what about the game your grandmother taught you?

She bit her lip.

—Almost every summer night we played *Something Scary*. My sister insisted on it. Until the summer I turned eleven.

—What happened that year? Did you outgrow being afraid?

—You can't outgrow that. At least I know I can't… but not because of *Something Scary*; because of *The Old Pageant*.

—*The Old Pageant*?

—That was the so-called game my grandmother introduced to my sister and me. We'd been playing *Something Scary*, whispering quietly, or what we believed was quietly, to ourselves. There was a rustling of cotton that terrified us, but it was only our grandmother rising out of her and grandfather's bed at the other end of this room. She shuffled over to us. I remember how her white cotton nightgown and her long white hair both seemed to gleam in the dark. Without so much as a word she carefully unbolted the cabin door, pulled it open, then waved for my sister and me to come with her. We went out with her and I admit I was pretty excited at first. You know, being out at night, it was like an adventure. But the more we walked the more it soured. I asked my grandmother how far we were going to walk. I remember that none of us were wearing shoes and that my feet were freezing from all the dew we'd traipsed through. I kept asking my sister if she knew where we were going but she wouldn't answer me. Finally my grandmother stopped us.

He'd forgotten to breathe for so long his lungs actually started to ache. After gasping he asked where they'd been led.

—It was a really thick part of the woods, well off any of the marked trails. My grandma gestured for us to be very quiet. I could hear crickets and bullfrogs. My grandma pointed above her head and told my sister and me to listen closely.

—What did you hear?

—Creaking, a very low creaking. At first I thought it was the thicker boughs of the trees being rubbed together by the wind. You hear that kind of noise all the time out here. But this was actually my grandmother. She was making this low creaking sound in her throat, but it was *perfect*. You'd swear it was the sound of wood grinding in the wind. My sister laughed, I remember that because it was the only time I ever saw my grandma get angry. She grabbed my sister's face and told her to be very careful because the three of us were tempting fate being out there in the dead of night. She said that if we weren't careful there would be things from the woods that would take our place in the world. When we came to learn *The Old Pageant* we had to treat it with respect. By then I couldn't get that awful creaking sound out of my head. I put my hands against my ears. I probably started to cry. My grandma put her arm around my shoulder and took my sister and me back to the cabin.

He could feel his brow knitting in confusion, and quite possibly in anger.

—Why on earth would your grandmother have done that to you two?

She lifted her hand.

—I know, I know. But what amazes me is that I truly hadn't even *thought* about that night until we got up here. But that night wasn't what scared me earlier tonight. It was something that happened the next night, or a few nights later. Hell, I might have only dreamt it.

He gripped her hand and kissed the back of it, giving the engagement ring a playful twist to remind her that this was a happy occasion.

—We don't have to talk about this anymore. I didn't mean to upset you, he told her.

—No, I need to get this out. That other night... my grandma

woke only me. When we got outside the cabin she told me that my sister didn't understand. *Only you felt it, my Donna*, was how she put it. We went walking, the two of us, even further into the woods.

—And did you hear the creaking?

—I didn't hear anything; no crickets, no wind, nothing. It was perfectly still. My grandma took my hand and led me down to this old tree. And she told me to watch while she imitated this tree. She started that horrible creaking sound again, only this time she began to twist her arms and her fingers until her shadow was exactly like that of the tree. And I mean *exactly.* She seemed to be getting taller too. I know that sounds insane, believe me, but I felt dwarfed by her...

—Shadow-play, he assured her.

—Sure, but....

—But what?

—Then a sound came from the tree beside my grandmother: it was a newborn baby crying.

He felt his skin constrict and go cold against his spine. His eyes were watering.

—A what?

—A newborn baby. I swear to Christ. It was coming from the tree and then when I turned around to face it, the tree's bark was all swollen and pink. And then my grandmother stopped that creaking noise and all I could hear was that awful, shrill crying. It echoed through the trees. My grandmother whispered to me not to be afraid, that this was just the tree taking part in *The Old Pageant.* We mimic them, they mimic us. She went over to the tree and actually started singing to it... a lullaby... Oh fuck, why did I have to remember this tonight of all nights? After all these years...

—You were a *kid!* You were dreaming or sick. And I don't mean to speak ill of the dead, but it sounds as though your grandmother might have been a little touched in the head.

He hated himself for prodding further but he needed to know

what happened next, for he felt oddly cheated.

—Nothing, she told him. I don't even remember our walk back to the cabin. The next day was just like any other as far as I can recall; swimming at the lake, colouring books, Go Fish, the usual. That autumn my grandfather got sick. My sister and I never came back to the cabin.

—Until now?

—Right.

They drank the rest of the wine and did everything they could to pretend Donna's memory hadn't driven a spike through the heart of their holiday. He wondered about being amorous again but it somehow felt improper.

She drifted off.

Though exhausted, sleep evaded him.

A grave moon illumed her old footboard. Its inscription, coupled with the way it was propped against the basin, made the slab of polished cedar look more like a headstone than a footboard.

Here lies Donna Hammill

He looked over at her. She was breathing shallowly. Not wishing to disturb her, he slipped out onto the porch.

The night was still but, mercifully, not as silent as the one she'd described to him. He could hear the crickets and bullfrogs.

He also heard the groan of wind-bullied wood.

Something stark flitted in his peripheral vision. Something scary.

He craned his head to the left, and for a beat all was right with the world again, for he was assured that what he'd glimpsed was merely the white sheets trembling upon the limbs of the birch tree with its equally spectral-looking bark.

But then he realized that the rest of the forest was motionless.

It was not wind that stirred the trunk, or the sheet that billowed like a crown of crone's hair, like a bridal train.

He backed up until he hit the cabin wall. He turned to call Donna's name, but the figure that he viewed through a pane sullied with moonlight and grime was not one that would have recognized him.

Fabric licked the side of his face. It was now near enough to touch him.

One of its limbs was brightened by a distinct and concentrated glint. Was it wearing the engagement ring to mock or punish him?

His eyes squinted shut instinctively. He raised his boneless arms and held them in mimicry of ancient boughs. He prayed his novice pageantry would fool it.

NOTES FOR "THE BARN IN THE WILD"

Paul Tremblay

A brief note from the editors:

In transcribing the following handwritten notebook pages, notes written in the margins and between the lines are represented as footnotes. Italics represents a clear change in handwriting. Everything else has been transcribed as written, including crossouts, grammar, and underlines.

If found please return to Nick Brach, _____ Nederland, CO, 46926, email: n.brach@gmail.com

Can I be frank with you, Ms/Mr. Finders Keepers? If this notebook is lost, it means I'm lost. I am not overstating this. Please save me.[1]

---

1 *editors' note* Name, address (partially redacted), and passage was written on the inside cover of the notebook.

BLUE notebook. Notes for (working title) <u>The Barn in the Wild</u>.

Here's hoping that BLUE brings better luck than the RED note-book did on Everest[2].

Twenty-five-year-old Thomas "Tommy" Hovsepian was a gifted mathematics student. He left his graduate program at the University of Vermont March 5th, 2013: two weeks before he was to take his oral exams. He told no one of his plans[3] including his friends and family. His parents (and the university) thought that Tommy was going to continue on to the PhD program. Tommy was not your stereotypical mathematics PhD candidate. From a small town (Ryder, PA, population 8,450), he was an undersized but tenacious star on the high school basketball team. As an undergrad, he tried walking on the team at the University of Vermont but didn't make the cut. He grew his dirty blond hair long, was a serious Dead Head, worked as a bartender at the popular bar/music club called the Metronome, and grew small marijuana plants in his apartment in downtown Burlington. Tommy was gregarious, outgoing, char-ismatic. His roommate (Rob Poodiack) told me Tommy could've run for mayor of Burlington and won[4]. Instead of thumbing across the continental United States (which is what most twenty-some-thing, self-ascribed free spirits do, right? I did it when I was his age—Christ, I sound like my father), Tommy traveled north into Canada. Why Canada? And ultimately, why end up in freaking Labrador of all places? What paperback romantic hitches out his thumb and says, "Alright, screw the sunny shores of California and the wild-wild-northwest of Jack London's Alaska, the tundra of Labrador it is." Tommy took some odd jobs, living out of cheap hotels as he made his way up north through the Quebec province. <u>On May 4th he</u> landed in Happy Valley-Goose Bay.

2 When will I learn to keep my big trap shut?

3 What were his plans? Backpacking? Living off the grid? Disappearing?

4 Why leave Burlington? And choose to leave in the manner he chose to leave?

to do: Travel expense report, make contact/set up interviews with co-workers, follow up with Royal Newfoundland Constabulary, local wilderness guide?, ~~explain to Scott that I'm not really going off into the wild by myself again~~[5]

june 30

Hello from Happy Valley-Goose Bay's library! Subarctic climate, but it's sunny and pushing into tee shirt weather. Town sits at the southwestern end of Lake Melville (a town/lake only a Calvinist would love) and at the mouth of Churchill River. It's not much of a city with a population equivalent to Tommy's hometown of Ryder. A WWII boomtown, founded by sticking an air force base out here. Runway is long enough to have once served as an alternate landing spot for NASA's space shuttles. First non-military settlers were led by a Rev. Lawrence B. Klein, who was appointed as the first resident United Church of Canada, minister (1953–1954). Reverend Klein and his wife Johanna organized non-denominational community meetings that eventually led to Happy Valley being officially registered as a municipality in 1953. There were 106 charter families: 45 United Church, 24 Anglican, 21 Moravian, 12 Pentecostal, 4 Catholic. Metis and Inuit now make up close to 40% of the town's population.

july 1

Jeffrey Stephens, Royal Newfoundland Constabulary: Tall, rail thin, ruddy complexion, strong man contest handshake. Dark blue dress shirt pressed to within an inch of its life with light blue Constabulary crest patch on left arm. Big window overlooks the bay behind him and his desk. Pleasant enough. Chitchatted. Stammered through saying he enjoyed my book on Everest, well, not that he

5 That didn't go well, did it?

enjoyed the parts where so many others in my party died: "Jeeze, must've been rough. When all hell broke loose and you trip over the dead climber in the snow on your way down to camp, man, that's something that stuck with me." I told him it was rough and thanked him for reading the book. To ease the mood, I point at the pic of his young wife and baby and tell him he has a beautiful family. He doesn't ask about my family and he clearly doesn't want to be talking to me about Tommy. Maybe reading too much into vibe and his clearly defensive posture (Scott[6] says it's one of my less endearing features but I'm a journalist and can't help that).

Tommy's body was found by Antoine and Brandon LaForge (father and son snowmobilers) on March 24th. Stephens presented me a photo of the body. Tommy's all curled up in a tight ball, lost inside his puffy anorak. Adjacent to him are the dead coals and black ash of a spent fire pit. Tommy likely died of starvation sometime during the previous fall. Five fingers on his right hand were missing. The coroner was unable to determine if fingers were removed by critters post-mortem because of the advanced state of decay of the body.

<u>Were any other body parts missing?</u>
"No."
<u>Isn't it odd that animals didn't take anything else?</u>
"Who knows why animals do anything they do?"

Tommy's hands look to be hidden tight into that ball of rigor mortis. Stephens agreed. There was evidence of frostbite in Tommy's toes and Stephens suggested (admitted it wasn't likely), that perhaps Tommy cut his fingers off himself after suffering from severe frostbite[7]. Next an itemized list of the meager supplies found

6 He hasn't responded to my "Wish you were here" texts.

7 I've had frostbite, and I've had it at 20,000 feet, but didn't cut off my fingers. I'm partial to them. Do people do that? Apparently yes: see, Sir Ranulph Fiennes.

in Tommy's possession, including a camera. They were only able to produce a handful of pictures from the film in his pack and in his camera, the rest were washouts: one photo of a woman in a small apartment kitchen, hiding her face behind a dish towel[8]; three photos of woods, the hiking trails nearly indecipherable in the brush; an open field with the barn as a dot in the far background; the last picture is a self-portrait of Tommy sitting up against the barn, his hair wild, baby face tufted with facial hair, gaunt and emaciated, facial fat and muscles melting away, replaced by the hard angles of what lies beneath[9], but he doesn't look like he's suffering or in pain, but with the content, wild, ecstatic look of a zealot. He sits with his back up against the side of the barn but toward the front. Above his head, and in the upper right hand corner protruding out from the front of the barn, is an ornamental structure, like a deer's head in profile, and I do think it's some sort of animalistic avatar or totem, only the neck is elongated, but the head has no antlers, or ears, or much of a snout, it's oval, tapers to a rounded point at the bottom, human?

<u>What's that supposed to be on the front of the barn?</u>
"Not sure. The wood at the end has been all chewed up by woodpeckers."

Early town records are a bit murky on who first built the Barn ~~and cleared the area to farm it~~, but one of the town founders[10] took it over and used it to host weekend retreats in the summer. The property was abandoned in the mid-'80s by the family trust, officially condemned, but has been left standing so lost hunters/hikers/snowmobilers can use it for shelter if they get in trouble, and frankly, it's too deep in the woods, the road/trail out to it long <u>overgrown, to</u> bring out wrecking equipment.

8 Nadia?

9 Unfortunately, I've seen that face before. *You will see it again.*

10 Lawrence B. Klein again

"We get kids like Tommy up here all the time looking for free-dom, adventure, something to fill the hole in their lives. Many walk into the woods. Some don't walk out." (subtext: don't know what makes Tommy so special that a famous writer would be writing his story).

Do you think Tommy knew the barn was there?[11]
"I doubt it."

—Lunch at the Silvertop Diner[12]. Tommy washed dishes here for a little over a month, alternated crashing with a co-worker and stay-ing in a motel[13]. I sit at the counter and ask locals about Tommy. Some remember him as a friendly, smiling kid with an infectious laugh. The owner, Garrett Langan (thick glasses and thicker fore-arms), didn't have too much to say other than, "Nice kid. Wasn't afraid of hard work. Knew he wouldn't stick long. A little squirrelly."

Meeting with cook Nadia Bulkin at 6 pm tonight. Another co-worker, Steve Strantzas (unclear if he's a cook or washer or waiter),

11 *It was waiting for you*

12 Shepard's Pie with lamb and buffalo meat… Scott still isn't answering my texts. I don't call him. Let him stew

13 Same hotel I'm staying at. Serviceable. Damp and dark, smelling of never-ending winter, carpeting and wallpaper that seem older than the town itself. (a second note) 2:23 am, nightmare, Tommy curled up in the dark corner of my room, I called out to him, he stood, his bones creaked and the tendons strained like climb ropes, he staggered to my bed, walking like flipbook animation, and held up his right hand, no fingers, the skin was smooth, marble, white, eye sock-ets empty, mouth was a round, dark hole, and then it wasn't him, it was him in my dream but his face belonged to someone else, I'm forgetting (third note: *lies you can never forget and will you always remember*) who it was, I can't remember, and my fingers screamed and burned with sharp cold, then Tommy who wasn't Tommy said *cross out, illegible* we've always been waiting

refuses to meet with me[14]. "What's there to say? Seemed like a nice enough guy, but had no idea what he was getting into and died because of it. Oldest story in the book."[15] Pressed him for more, told me he was tired and hung up. (subtext: go fuck yourself, Nick.)

Nadia: Beers with Nadia at the Tavern on the Green. She was the last to see Tommy alive. He left her apartment on the morning of June 14th and hiked into the woods by himself. She's a 34-year-old outdoor sports enthusiast (cross country skiing, kayaking, and mountain climbing mainly). Sunburned face. Wary smile. She's a weird combination of chin-up/chest-out confidence and nervous twitchiness. Says she's thinking of moving to Vancouver next spring, which is the first thing she told me after shaking hands and telling me she's been stuck here for four years. She met Tommy the first night he showed up in the diner. He looked "as scraggly as a wayward dog and twice as skittish." He drank three cups of coffee and ate two steaks. Didn't take her bait in attempts at chitchat but asked about the dishwashing job. He was much more pleasant the next morning when he showed up to work, and over the next month he wowed everyone with his tales from the road and his boasts about going to live in the woods by himself for one year, just to prove that he could do it. Such a genuinely kind, enthusiastic, earnest kid, though haunted. "There was something there, behind the curtain, you know?" Nadia knew he was low on cash and she let him crash at her apartment.

She stopped there and swirled the last sip of her porter around the bottom of her glass.
<u>You and Tommy got close?</u>
"Yeah. Yeah, you could say that."
I tell her I'm sorry. <u>I know it's hard.</u>
"It is. Did I tell you I'm going to Vancouver next spring? Goddamn it, I am. I am."

14 Sounds like a real douche on the phone.

15 *Oh there are older stories*

Nadia's apartment: One bedroom. Kitchen/living room combo.
Clean, but run down. Skis, boots, weather gear, clips, piled by the
front door.

"I wanted him to stay. I think he almost did. I'm not just lying
to myself, you know. I could sense that he wanted to. That in some
ways it would've been easy to, but there was something else there,
making him not stay. Making him go to the woods."

What was it?

"He wanted to be alone. He needed to be alone. When he first
got to the Bay, you could see him filling up with all the people
around him again, a battery recharging. He was manic during those
first few weeks. But then you could see him dimming again, losing
the juice. We all weren't enough to sustain him, keep him going."

Did he want you to go with him?

"He asked me to go, but he didn't really mean it. And I didn't
want to. It didn't feel right. I'm not much of a trust-your-gut kind
of person, but this time, I could feel it." I finessed through a question about her being surprised Tommy was found in some abandoned barn only a few days hike from civilization. "I knew where
he was going."

Where? To the barn? How?

"He had this book with him. This stupid book."

Do you have it?[16]

"Yes."

Can I see it?

"Only if you take it with you when you leave."

Tommy told her he had purchased the obscure book in a used
bookstore back in Burlington, VT. He never came out and said as
much but his obsession with the book was the motivation behind

16 Stephens made no mention of a book to me. Nadia didn't answer me for a long
time. I mean a long time. Glacial

his trip. **The Black Guide** (Morderor de Caliginis)[17] is a guidebook. Thin paper, small newspaper kind of font. Table of Contents
divided the entire east coast of North America into sections. There
are occasional grainy black and white photographs, rough illustra-
tions, hand-drawn maps, but the meat of the book is comprised of
colorful/colloquial descriptions/histories of regional oddities, "hidden places of arcana" (sic), and areas of interest for the "discerning
tourist." Despite my many travels (including hiking the Appala-
chian Trail from start to finish) in the region, none of the places
in the TOC are familiar to me. There's an entry titled "Labrador:
Klein's Barn."

You didn't give this to the Constabulary?
"No."
Why?
She shrugged, said that she "sort of" told them about it. Said that
Tommy talked about how he'd read about the barn in a guidebook
as an emergency shelter if you get stuck out there in weather. "They
didn't ask me if I still had the book, either."[18]
I ask if I could borrow the book for a few days.[19]
"Like I said, I want you to take it."

"Tommy promised me the night before he left. He promised me[20]

17 Copyright 1909, with a seventh edition printed in 1986. Book attributed to
Divers Hands, no publisher listed, pocket-sized, bound in black leather, broken
red ring on the cover. Call Tracy and ask her to get more info on it.
18 What???? They most certainly should've.
19 Go back to Stephens to ask if he knows about the book and the Barn entry?
20 Do I weave my weird personal parallels into the story (blending of memoir and
reporting)? Scott finally answered the phone. He didn't say hello. "You promised
that you wouldn't do this again." I never promised I'd stop working. "No, that you
wouldn't go off by yourself…" I'm not climbing a mountain or doing anything
dangerous. I swear. I'll just be roughing it for a week in a barn just a two-day hike
out into the woods. "Why do you keep doing this again and again?" This isn't the

that he was going to stay with me, that he wouldn't go out there by himself. I wanted to believe him when he said it. He seemed relieved, like that weight was gone. We went to bed. He woke in the middle of the night, screaming from some nightmare. And I mean he was full-on screaming. It took me forever to wake him up. He wouldn't tell me what the dream was about, only that it was awful but it wasn't a big deal, that he'd had the same nightmare before and he'd be fine. He spent the next hour in the bathroom with the light on, sink water running on and off. I couldn't sleep and just watched his shadow filling the crack of light under the bathroom door. He didn't say anything when he came back to bed. I wanted to talk but he said he didn't want to talk about it, just wanted to sleep. When we got up the next morning we silently ate breakfast and in the middle of his coffee he just said that he had to go. That's what he said. 'I have to go, Nadia. I'm sorry.' He got up and packed his gear. I ran out of the apartment and jogged two miles in my bare feet. He shouted after me, 'I'll be back in the spring.' He was gone when I got back. He left the book on the counter."

<u>After he left, did you consider going out to try and find him, find the barn?</u>

"No. I was angry at him, that whole summer, tried to forget him. This was what he wanted and I'm not a survivalist type. What was I going to do out there with him? And he wasn't going to come back here with me."

(Back at the Hotel):

Cursory web search turns up only one copy of **The Black Guide** on eBay. No publisher information forthcoming. Waiting to hear back from Tracy with more deets. Most of the entries in **The Black Guide** hint at the occult.

---

same as Everest. You know it's not. And I'm not the same. "You promised." Scott hung up. (second note: *promises are kept with blood and bone*)

The Black Guide entry, "Labrador: Klein's Barn"

Klein's Barn was built in spring/summer 1955, two years after Reverend Lawrence B. Klein and his fellow United Church of Canada followers registered Happy Valley as an official municipality. They wanted to hold religious retreats in the heart of nature and away from the prying eyes of the military stationed in and around Goose Bay. During a brief but eye-opening trip to France in the winter of 1956, Klein became obsessed with the Grand Guignol Theater in Paris. The theatre's popularity was beginning to wane, but its history intrigued Klein; particularly the work of André de Lorde, who collaborated with an experimental psychologist Alfred Binet to write almost 100 plays, a handful of which featured a formless, nameless, and rapacious ancient deity whose fervent followers devolved into grotesqueries remade in its likeness. Klein admitted to being absolutely terrified by the plays, but became intrigued with the idea of crossing the lurid aesthetics of Grand Guignol with the ecstasy of old-time religion, of good old hellfire and brimstone. Upon his return from France, Klein wrote morality plays that always ended with the gory tortures of hell and with Satan portrayed as an insatiable, wormlike creature. How many of these plays were performed is not known. Whatever run they enjoyed was short, and his plays morphed into bizarre ceremonies and rites devoted to the nameless deity. The odd, long-necked carving that hangs above the entrance to the barn was apparently carved in its likeness. Klein's wife Johanna along with other players were seriously injured with a fire stunt and shortly thereafter relocated to Europe and promptly disappeared.

Drank ~~one two~~ three scotches after talking with Scott. Sorry. To do list: drink more scotch, fuck waiting around, call publisher, arrange a drop and pick up, supplies supplies supplies, more scotch[21]

---

21 more scotch was achieved, much to my detriment

july 3

Stephens dropped me at the bush line on a stretch of the Trans-Labrador Highway at one of the many snowmobile/ATV trails. I set the GPS for my rendezvous point with Stephens in seven days. Two-days hike in, two-days out, three at the Barn. Left a message for Scott (he wouldn't answer his phone) and told him that I'd have a guide with me in the bush. It's not full on lie. I have **The Black Guide**[22]. Supplies enough for more than a week. The weather is supposed to be good (always subject to change in these parts, so I'm told). Feels good having a pack on my back again. I think Tommy and I probably had a lot in common. Maybe Tommy shares my pop-psych byline: overachieving and overbearing father who had mapped out his life for him from birth, and after reading Vonnegut, the beats, and Hunter S. Thompson, he rebelled. Right? Scott asks why do I keep doing this. This: dropping out of college to backpack in the US, Europe, South America, collecting friends and experiences and stories, and then all the mountains, collecting craggy peaks like coins, each more dangerous and extreme than the last, falling into a crevasse at McKinley and being airlifted out didn't stop me, then there was Everest and everyone who died around me. I'm 45 and that was supposed to be the last adventure for me[23].

Night. Tent. Another nightmare. Still shaking. In the barn with Tommy. He was all curled up around a weak fire. Tried to help him, brushed snow off his face, and it was the dead Everest climber, German, from another party, met him briefly at base camp, I said his

---

22 No word from Tracy on the book. She usually works quick too. Showed Stephens the book. Didn't tell him it was Tommy's or that Nadia had it. "I've lived here seven years, never heard any stories about the barn like that."

23 This hike to the barn is a just a stroll down the street to the market by comparison, but I can feel it starting again. That need, that emptiness that knows no other way to be filled.

name, Karl Sidenberg[24], kept saying it until his name sounded like something else, it was something else, couldn't control my tongue, horrible sounds, hard and then slithery, his frozen mouth opened and kept opening until it was as wide as the world.

july 4

Where are all the fireworks? Dreary morning. Trouble shaking off the night before. Mood improved after I found the clearing of yellowing grass, prickly weeds, and dandelions as tall as corn stalks. The clearing pitches up a small hill and the barn is on the top with more hills behind it. It's bigger than I expected. Strange to find such a large building out in the middle of the bush. I approached from its side. Had to resist the urge to call out "hello," make sure I wasn't trespassing on someone's property. The wooden planks are a bleached-out gray but it's in damn good shape given the number of Northern Canadian winters it has endured. The roof has a few dips and waves in it, like ripples in a lazy pond, but from what I can see, there are only a handful of slate shingles cracked or missing. The barn is beautiful except for the carving over the front double doors. The carving is a monstrosity. The v-shaped head has a deep in-dentation that could be a mouth, but whatever else might've been its original features have been obliterated by woodpecker holes. A long, girthy, and frankly lewd wooden neck holds the head out away from the barn.

Inside: As much evident care went into a sturdy, weather-proof exterior, it's bare bones on the inside. No loft. No stalls. No rooms. Just a vast enclosed space. Looking up at the roof with all its beams it looks like a chest cavity, belly of the beast. White Whale and Melville again, right? Is my life becoming that obviously a literary trope? Fuck. Thick support posts line the perimeter. ~~Fells~~ Feels like a big top, a circus tent, less a barn. The floor is hard-packed dirt

24 *he is so hungry*

with only the occasional dry weed poking through. Evidence of the barn being used as a temporary shelter abounds. Empty coolers and beer cans, tarps, bags, rusted traps, shotgun shell casings, torn up blankets and socks. Evidence of its last occupant: the rock outline of Tommy's campfire in the middle of the floor, a black stain, a hole.

Back wall is covered in graffiti and names and dates gouged into the wood. The older markings look like gibberish, a combination of swooping marks and hard slashes, fist-sized circles dot the walls everywhere, some of them colored in or gouged out so they look like holes in the walls, and there are broken rings that look like the one on the cover of **The Black Guide**. Quotes from Vonnegut ("so it goes"), Hemmingway, Plath, an ode to Jack London[25], this bit from the book of Job: "Can you pull in Leviathan… tie down its tongue with a rope? Will it keep beging you for mercy? Will it speak to you with gentel words?" (sic)

In big block letters: "Tommy H. walked into the wild, June 2013 and forever."

Fire started. Tired. An hour of sunlight left. Hopefully sleep will follow. Will explore the surrounding area more fully tomorrow. I'll search for wild edibles Tommy might've eaten (or non-edibles), try to think like Tommy instead of dwelling on all my stuff. Keep busy. When alone like this, the trick is to not get hopelessly lost in your own headspace. Find another place. Looks like the BLUE notebook[26] has turned into a diary too…. Man, I'm such a pathetic, angsty teenager still. FUCK THE MAN! DON'T TRUST ANYONE OLDER THAN 30 50! Cooler night than anticipated. Outside is a symphony of insect calls. It's beautiful. It's always been <u>beautiful to me.</u>

25 "Jack London is king! All Hail his Dominant Primordial Beast"
26 Like the RED one and the GREEN one and the YELLOW one before it.

july 5

Up with the sun. Done the rounds on the grounds. Cool and cloudy. Nothing out of the ordinary. No trouble finding wild edibles, but it's July. Finding food a few months from now would be a vastly different story.

intro paragraph? Tommy Hovsepian and I both made promises to our loved ones. We were not lying and we both meant them with all of our hearts and souls at the time we said them. How could I know that? All promises of "I'm staying" are the same and are made to be broken. We've already been promised to (illegible)

Probably should knock this shit off. Publisher won't be happy with memoir/non-fiction hybrid.

Considered setting up some small game traps, trip wires and the like, if for nothing else to keep my mind occupied. But I have enough food. No need to kill any critters just for the hell of it. Spent afternoon reading **The Black Guide** instead. As one of my favorite foul-mouthed lit professors used to say, "Man, that's some fucked up shit right there." Looking forward to hearing from Tracy when I get back, see what she dug up on this crazy book.

Okay. Fuck. I'm spooked and rattled. Last light fading and I flipped through old BLUE here and found a bunch of notes that I didn't write. They're not mine. Not my handwriting. Fuck. Can't remember leaving my notebook out lying around in Happy Valley. Hotel maid with a weird sense of humor? No. No, there's some of those same fucked up symbols, dark circles, broken rings from the barn's back wall, and "he's so hungry" is written between the lines of the July 3rd entry. I wrote that entry in the tent. Out here. I mean, what, I'm writing shit in my sleep now? Creepy ass shit too. Has to be what it is. No one's out here, no one's following me. Right? I'm sleep writing, or something. Using my left hand, even? *This is my left hand.* Looks like the other notes, yeah? It does. It does. Fuck! Scott was right. Shouldn't be out here by myself anymore. I thought I could still do this. Will pack up and leave a day early. If I can't get Stephens to come out a day early, I'll thumb it back to Happy Valley. Fuck fuck fuck.

Asleep next to the fire, and those slithery sounds from earlier dreams woke me up, they filled the barn. Wet things wiggling and dragging through the dirt. Filled my head. Puked on myself. I pulled my little camper's hatchet out of my pack and called out. Movement. Shadows were alive. I circled around the fire, trying to see what was out there and where I could run. I could always run. I ran at Everest. I crouched down next to my pack, started emptying it out, keeping only what I'd need after making a break for the doors. Two thick, albino white appendages wrapped around my ankles and pulled me off my feet, dragged me away from the fire. Light and heat were gone and I was so cold, I was on the white mountain again. I thrashed and punched, then my arms were pinned down too. I couldn't move. The dying fire threw flickering images, albino white monsters writhing all around me, their arms, legs, necks, intertwined, a mass of worms. Tommy's melted rounded distorted transformed face hovered over my legs. My right hand was held out above my chest and close to my face, and another face telescoped from the writhing mass to me, and the face was no longer a face. The face, it was stupidly blind and all mouth, a wide, black hole that would never be filled. The face, it once belonged to the dead climber I left on Everest. I screamed I said his name Karl I said that I was sorry that I left him there all alone to die I was sorry that I didn't help him when he asked for help his frozen lips couldn't really move but he asked me for help. He put my fingers in his mouth slowly, fingertips passed through an impossibly cold membrane. I screamed I was sorry again and that if I'd stopped and tried to help him both us of would've died that he was too far gone I wasn't strong enough to help him down there was no way he could've made it no way he could've survived I had no choice. The mouth slid over my fingers down to the knuckle and then suddenly in the soft, wet, cold mouth, there were teeth, and it was wonderful.

july 25

At Labrador Grenfell-Health[27].

Rescue team led by Stephens came out to the barn two days after we missed our rendezvous date. I was airlifted out. Vaguely remember bright sunlight, the sound of rotors, and their mechanical wind on my face. Don't remember anything else of the rescue. Stephens said he found me with my right hand badly burnt, so badly burnt that my fingers were blackened stubs, smoking embers, like I'd fallen asleep with my hand in the fire all night long. Infection was already raging, so was a fever, and I spoke nothing but gibberish. The doctors had to amputate the hand at the wrist. I still feel the hand that isn't there.

*I didn't answer Stephens' or anyone else's questions. Told them I couldn't remember what happened or how I burnt myself, and I certainly don't remember writing that last entry in the BLUE notebook. I don't think Stephens and friends believed me and I don't care. They finally gave me back my BLUE notebook this morning. Stephens claimed he didn't find **The Black Guide** in my belongings. I think Stephens pocketed it. I do.*

No matter. My old book, the one about Tommy and me is dead. I'm not going to write it. This BLUE notebook will now become something else. A new kind of guide perhaps.

My lovely Scott is asleep in the chair next to my hospital bed. He

27 *Writing with my left hand really sucks*

looks ten years older than he did when I left him in June. I've promised Scott that I'll never leave him again. Planning a new backyard project to keep me home. We'll use it to host parties, local author readings, spoken word, folk artists, maybe even some off-off-off Broadway-style performances.

(note from the editors: The notebook ends with a rough map of Nick Brach's home and expansive land, and includes a schematic/ outline of a rectangular building that would be twenty feet wide, fifty feet long. It is labeled, simply, BARN.)

FIREDANCING

Michael Griffin

1.

Bay wakes on the living room floor amid mounded clothing pulled from the bedroom closet. The house stripped of furniture, the kitchen lacks food. Even after a night spent endlessly slow-falling through black tar, Bay aches to retreat into sleep, to face the intolerable panic moment before death.

The new reality won't be blinked away. Sunlight blazes through bare windows, reflects on glossy hardwoods. Everything Bay owns, aside from the pile of shirts and jeans on which he slept, leans against the wall. Twenty large canvases, tortured visions in black, umber and gray. Bins of crushed and depleted tubes of oil paint. Jars of solvent, thinner, a few brushes. The room in which he painted, until yesterday, stands empty as the rest.

He contemplates a fresh canvas, mixing pigments, trying to organize color into some sort of clarification. Lately his painting's been work-for-hire, no time left for himself. The job's finished. Annie's gone. His future is nothing, a vacant expanse.

Taking everything, shutting off power, that's Annie's message. He hears her voice.

All you need is art, so I'll take the rest. See how you do, just you, your ratty jeans and boots, and your fucking art.

She's right. He's stuck. A house he can't pay for, a wardrobe more suited to a college kid than a man almost forty, and a pile of what Annie calls *your primal scream paintings*. The only thing left is her note.

Just go. Our accounts are all closed. I'm with him now.

Art always trumped everything, an all-important matter of depth and complexity amid life's shallower trivialities. Now Bay feels embarrassment at this self-indulgent conceit. Art, a child's game. What's it ever gotten him? Three gallery shows, twelve canvasses sold. No options, no hirable skills, no money for a new place. Nothing to eat. Worse than hunger is the shame. Even if he had somewhere to land, he can't drive. Collecting the money owed him by the theater would mean facing the man who took his wife.

Bay sees her point now. A man's able to take care of himself, his wife. If he can't do those things, he's just a child. Worse, a joke.

Hopelessness, a gaping chasm. Recognition of his future, a dawning chill. Like blood slow-trickling from a vein, life's warm pulse replaced by icy fear. Bay envisions the bridges of Northeast Portland, questioning his own seriousness even as the thoughts occur. Would he really go there?

The bridges aren't high enough. He laughs. So lame, predictable. What options are left? He shivers.

From his pocket, the cell phone rings. He's forgotten it, assuming she'd cancel the service. The only numbers programmed in are the last two people he'd ever call. The incoming number seems familiar. 541, somewhere south.

Bay presses a button. "Hello?"

"Hi ho, Buckaroo. Been a while."

"Petersson…" Bay trails off, calculating years. Wondering, *Why now?*

"Bad time?" Petersson sounds like he's anticipating a joke. "Sorry it's been so long. You know the grind, buying wood, selling wood. Thing is, Minerva called out of the blue, told me to invite you—"

"Called you? Did I miss—"

"Divorced, yeah. Both of us traveling. One time, she didn't come back. Anyway, hill party's this weekend. Minerva says, make sure you come."

"Shit, my wife too. She just…" Bay stops, changes his mind.

"What?"

How to say the words? If Minerva left, Petersson will understand. "What's the hill party?"

"Shit, Minerva said something's up with you." Petersson's tone shifts. "She always said, if just once I'd believe… Anyway, listen, I'm driving up. You still at that bungalow in Irvington? Get your ass ready."

"When?"

"Right now, Hoss. Fucking Hill Party, capital H, capital P."

"I heard, but what's the Hill Party?"

"You visited Roseburg how many times, you missed every Mallard Hill Party? I'll be there in three hours."

The call disconnects. Petersson's coming.

Bay's hands tremble, as if in recognition of something averted.

2.

"Thoughtful of you." Bay tips back the Jim Beam fifth. The bottle knocks the ceiling inside Petersson's posh gentleman's pickup. "I was gone just a few hours. She managed to empty the place. Must've hired—"

"I said, don't talk about that. Don't think about that." Petersson's driving, I5 South. Three hours to Roseburg. "Lesson I learned after Minerva skipped. Obsessively sifting back, through everything, that ain't what you need."

"What do I need?"

"Mental reboot." He grins. "Puke your troubles away at a two-day party."

"So this Mallard Hill place, it's where Erik and Minerva grew up?"

"Mmm. Fifteen miles outside Roseburg."

"Speaking of Minerva."

Petersson's grip flexes on the wheel.

Bay tries again. "The worst thing about Annie leaving, I finally did what she wanted. Took a commission, murals for Cinema 21, that's an art theater in Northwest."

"I know, dummy. Film major, remember? You took us there." He exhales. "*Seven Samurai*. Me and Minerva."

"Lumber baron with a film degree, that's funny. Most of us liberal arts guys…" Bay stops. Another swig. "Annie set it up, knew the owner. They kept showing up, checking on me. Arrive together, leave together."

"We weren't going to talk about that."

Bay thinks, *What else?* "So Erik grew up on this hill, but won't attend the big drunk-fest?"

"Nah, he stopped that recovery shit. After he withdrew from us, his sponsor tried to make him cut off Minerva." Petersson shrugs. "Erik only drinks beer now. Lives on the edge of the Mallard tract, a cabin overlooking the South Umpqua. Started some river guide thing. Fishing, rafting." His face clouds. "Minerva's in the main house. Stopover from the endless touring."

"So much land, Erik gets his own corner." Bay resists redirecting toward Minerva. Petersson's breakup makes him feel less awful.

"Might be the most impressive parcel in Douglas County. Everyone thinks Old Mallard got rich in lumber, but Minerva let slip he returned from the Merchant Marines, World War II, a millionaire at nineteen."

"Merchant Marines, is that still a thing? Maybe they'd let me—"

"He climbs aboard the post-war lumber boom, builds Mallard Hill. Meets a woman up in Washington, on business near Olympic Forest. This first wife starts him jetting around, blowing millions in Mexico. Spends the sixties and seventies financing films, legendary stuff by Buñuel and Jodorowsky."

"Lest I forget that film degree."

Petersson makes an undignified snort. "Always trekking the wilds of Mexico, South America, Antarctica, returning rejuvenated, trailing new wives to replace ones who die of typhus or malaria. Finally disappears, the Chilean Andes. Erik and Minerva, living under Old Mallard's tutors and housekeepers, assume they're orphaned a second time. Everyone gives up hope."

"But…"

"He reappears, head shaved, silent as a mystic. No explanation where he's been ten months, what happened to wife number six, seven, whatever. Thereafter, no more film production or travel. Grabs another wife to replace the one rumored frozen to death. Further expands the house. His only indulgences are these parties, and the visiting artists, visionaries and occult weirdos. Some remain months, years at a time. Old Mallard, he's like fucking Tom Bombadil. Erik grew up thinking the man's his grandfather, later learns, no, it's *great*-grandfather."

Bay stifles envy at such a life. "One part Dos Equis' Most Interesting Man in the World, one part Kwai Chang Caine."

3.

The lower hillside is dotted with stainless RVs, psychedelic busses, cars, trucks, motorcycles. Tents fill the slope nearest the towering house. The ground floor sprawls, annexed with rock-walled gardens, greenhouse, picnic areas with fire pits, and a concert stage beneath a log pavilion. The upper levels narrow like a mountain coming to a peak. Windowed surfaces reflect afternoon sun.

"You never said…" Bay marvels. "What a structure!"

"We've got motorcycle stunts, costumed freaks, and topless hippie girl volleyball." Petersson points. "But you, you're into architecture."

"Boys!" Erik approaches, grinning and newly bearded, carrying a belled half-yard glass of mealy brown beer. "You staying all weekend? Let's kayak the Umpqua Sunday. I've got kayaks."

Bay indicates Erik's beer. "I'm just glad our friendship's no longer *regrettably over.*"

Erik smacks Bay's shoulder, leads them toward the pavilion. "We all gotta be stupid sometimes. Anyway, there's no sober at the Hill party." He offers a taste.

Bay sips. "What the hell is it? Mead, or something?"

"Belgian dark. Minerva's friend makes it. Nuts, chocolate, who knows what. Like eating a slice of cake."

Under the pavilion stand six old refrigerators with taps through the doors. Erik fills plastic cups. "So, you want to meet Old Mallard before things get ridiculous?"

The atmosphere beyond the door is rustic as a lodge, and smells of smoking game meat. A black walnut stairway climbs.

Imagining glass-walled brightness above, Bay starts toward the stairs.

Erik pulls him back. "Sorry, off limits. Old Mallard's rules."

"Such incredible design," Bay says. "Unbelievable, something like this hidden out in the trees. I'd pay to go up—"

The stairs creak under the barefoot descent of a silver-stubbled man in black robes, followed by two older men and three women, all in black outfits of striking expense and formality, considering the setting. Each carries identical luggage, glossy black leather and chrome.

Bay, Erik and Petersson stand aside.

The six, despite lined skin and silver or gray hair, are all tan, vigorous and trim. Watching their goodbye embraces, Bay wonders at identities, connections. The last, an Asian man younger than the rest and standing apart, bows and turns to depart.

"Here, Toshi." The robed one, certainly Old Mallard, pulls Toshi into a warm hug.

Old Mallard closes the door behind the others, turns with the stable grace of a judoka, and places a familiar hand on Bay's shoulder. "One party ends, another begins. Members of my circle. Octobers we gather to hunt Roosevelt elk, have done since..." His gesture suggests many repetitions. "This fall, they'll expedition six months in Chile, so we hunted early. Splendid success."

"Expedition, those…" Bay stops.

"You mean, at their age?" Old Mallard assesses Bay, turns to Erik. "Finally, you bring someone who appreciates my architecture."

Erik smirks. "You never let anybody upstairs."

"Or downstairs," Old Mallard allows. "This main floor, called Earthwide, it's for everyone. A few see the second floor. If you do, I tell you its name."

"Each level has a name?" Bay asks.

"Why not? Blackshard, Subterrain, Earthwide, Attainment, Lightpulse. Now I've told." Old Mallard smiles. "You crave a look upstairs?"

"I didn't mean…" Bay stammers. "I'm just intrigued. I studied architecture briefly, before changing to a more lucrative major."

Old Mallard turns to Erik, questioning.

"Bayard's joking," Erik explains. "Fine art degree. Financially, he's fucked."

Old Mallard laughs, touches Bay's arm. "Bayard Lane, Minerva mentioned you. If you're still upright later, come. I'll show you Attainment."

Petersson shoots Erik a look.

4.

Bay and Petersson emerge, confronted by sunlight, and a cluster of bikers speed-drinking Jack Daniel's, swigging and passing. Another group of bikinied girls and shirtless boys smoke pungent weed from punctured beer cans and kick hacky-sacks.

Petersson heads uphill. "Let's dodge the crowds a bit."

Bay sees something's wrong. "What?"

"I've been coming since high school, shit, I was married to Minerva eighteen years. I've never been upstairs. Didn't even know there were basements." Creases bracket Petersson's mouth. "Anyway, you're going upstairs later. Good for you."

A barefoot twentyish girl approaches, face painted green with yellow flowers. "You look sad. Don't be sad." She digs in pockets of short-shorts cut from camo pants. Grass-stained palms cup two red and white capsules.

"Tylenol?" Petersson asks.

She grins. "No, it's Molly." Her eyes widen, excited with a secret. "My uncle, he's a chemistry prof in Eugene."

"Why the hell not?" Petersson pops one. "Wipe the slate."

"Molly, that's X in kiddie-speak?" Bay swallows the other. "Terrible decisions are sometimes best."

The flower girl, fragrant of marijuana and pumpkin bread, kisses Bay's cheek. As she skips away, he feels a flutter of desire.

"Homebrew," Petersson says. "This place. One big experiment."

They circle the upper field, and at the top slip through a gap in the perimeter wall of blackberry vines. Crowd noise fades.

Bay stumbles over a hippy couple fucking in the grass.

Petersson laughs. "I don't think they want you joining in!"

Bay waits until the couple are well behind. "Tell me something about you and Minerva. So I'll feel better about my shit."

As he climbs, breathing hard, Petersson appears to be pondering the question, not ignoring it. "Turns out Minerva's poly."

"Polly what?"

"Polyamorous. Not the best thing to learn, post-marriage." Petersson gestures at thickening forest. "This goes miles. Doubt anyone's surveyed all ten thousand acres." He turns, walks backward. "Fuck, now you've got me remembering. At Minerva's place. On drugs."

"Right now, I don't feel so bad," Bay says. "But I keep feeling like I want to talk about it."

"No, don't talk. Just climb."

Steel blue sky deepens into evening. The tractor-notched trail arcs, old growth looming on the upper slope.

Petersson stops at a cultivated viewpoint, overlooking the house, surrounding fields full of vehicles and tents, and the river beyond.

"You can almost…" Bay steps out, compelled toward the edge.

How far would he fall? Vision flashes, inexplicable memories of motionlessness. A tar-stuck insect wriggling. A frozen moment. Inertia stored before a crash.

"All it would take…" Bay leans forward, starts to tip. Sickness rises in his gut. He reins himself in, starts to sit back. "I better sit."

"No, not here!" Petersson grabs Bay's arm. "This hill's one big ant colony."

Bay looks down, trying to figure. "Bullshit."

Petersson crouches, snatches something up. Grinning he pops the wriggling ant into his mouth.

5.

They descend to fields illuminated by flickering bonfires and the volleyball court's stand-mounted event lamps. Sludge metal slurs on the pavilion stage for an audience of bearded heavies in leather boots and vests.

Bay almost mentions the twitching, teeth-grinding tension, until he sees Petersson's shirt soaked, his forehead dripping sweat.

As they near the gravel lot, a girl with a black bob shouts. "Bayard Lane! Hey, fucker." She weaves side to side, blocking Bay from side-stepping to keep up with Petersson. "Don't fucking go past me."

He remembers: a long-ago ex, from college weekends visiting Roseburg with Petersson. "Sorry, didn't recognize you, Rachel. Someone gave us ecstasy."

"I used to love X. Definitely more fun. "She raises a bottle of lime snow cone syrup. "Had to quit vodka. Now I'm addicted to sugar." She drinks. "You're in Portland, right? What do you do in Portland?"

"Nothing." Bay looks for Petersson.

"Got to have a job, make money. Otherwise why go to college?"

The sky overhead churns, gray-winged outlines against black. Vast gaping mouths.

Bay slips hands into pockets. "I paint a little. It's just, there's no money in it."

"Creativity, that's awesome, you know I have my radio show, plus drive a cab. I had this idea, broadcast my show from the cab, kind of kill two birds. Also, did you know about my kid? I had this idea I could save on babysitters, take him with me. My fares get a kick out of it, watching me breastfeed, plus the radio audience calling in, wanting to ask him questions, saying are you really driving a cab around Roseburg, carrying your baby?"

"Shit, Rachel," Bay says. "I forgot you were crazy."

She smiles. "He's seventeen now. Not really a baby."

Bay doesn't really trust his own math. *Ninety-four? No, ninety-five?*

"I see you figuring. Not yours, not quite. Got kids, Bayard?" She points at his ring. "See you're married."

Clouds seethe, emitting sparks. The moon's potent gravity pulls. Invisible gasses drift.

"Don't know. Yeah."

"What's that mean?" She flashes white teeth. "Tell me something tasty."

"Yesterday, my wife emptied the house. Took all our stuff, all the money. Her money, really. Didn't have my own."

"Wow, truth. I don't drive a cab, that's stupid. I wait tables in Riddle Diner."

Down the hill, a bonfire roars. So huge, Bay wonders if it's hallucination.

"I need to look for Petersson."

He breaks away, drifts downhill, carried by a current. He looks back.

Rachel's eyes change. Black coal pits burn, glowing fire, spewing smoke.

6.

Nearer, Bay decides the fire near the pavilion is real. Several bikers chest-bump and gesture. It seems like posturing, until real fighting starts. Motorcycles circle, revving an overpowering roar.

A burly gray-beard intervenes, embracing one fighter, who pushes him away, then clutching the other. Knives appear. The peacemaker continues, heedless of swinging blades. Others rush in, some trying to keep peace, others bringing the fight. The swarm spills dangerously near the fire.

A biker lobs something sizzling, like a huge firecracker. It explodes. Bare-chested men scramble, fall, hands over ears.

The only sound, bright ringing.

A mirrorshaded Lemmy lookalike staggers, right eye streaming blood.

Knowing he should stay back, Bay approaches. Out of the flames, an arm extends, pulls Bay near. Radiant heat, so intense. Bay pulls back against the sweat-slick hand, breaks free. He runs clear, shirttail smoldering.

A wild-eyed tiger girl, naked body painted orange with black stripes, runs into the fight. Those nearest freeze.

"Stop, you assholes. They're about to start the firedancing!"

7.

Pavilion loudspeakers emit subtle percussive loops. The bonfire crowd quiets, listening. Sonic layers accumulate, suggestive of impending drama.

Onstage, Minerva Mallard leads the troupe of twelve women and men in loose white shirts and black short tights. They stride barefoot, confident, descend steps and slip through the crowd. They form a uniform line, impossibly near the flames. All are dark-haired, and even the Caucasians are so tanned, the troupe appears uniformly chestnut-skinned.

The dancers follow the music's lead, building a kinetic, multi-layered churn, a blending of world influences. Sweat glistens, despite seeming effortlessness. All appear ageless, though Minerva is Bay's age, nearly forty. Movements express natural joy, like a smile of the whole body. The pace quickens.

The fire wall flickers, coloring dancers and watchers red-orange. Even standing back, Bay feels a warm, luminous glow, a sensation of youthful energy and potential he can't explain. For the first time since Annie's note, he feels buoyed, capable of imagining a future. Life continues. He may encounter pain, but he'll survive.

Darkening music, a new dance. The horizon shifts. In the soundscape, crisp metallic ticking snare offsets a black sea. Clouds swirl, darkly churning. The ground rumbles. Flames leap and roar.

Thoughts veer sideways, out of control. What happened to possibility, to hope? Bay sees Annie, laughing. The bastard cinema owner flicks his tongue. Bay wants to kill. From self-pity to hope, sidelong to potent rage. He feels energized, lifted. An inward surge, a brew of anger and lust, propels him nearer the crowd. Strength surges in his muscles, a hot surging wave of testosterone. Vitality, danger. Bay wants to drink it in.

The throng moves in rhythm, rising, falling. Movement is handed off by touch. Each contact conveys from one to next the knowledge and timing of impending shifts.

Minerva's eyes are fierce, her body sweat-slick. She leads the dancers, pulling white shirts overhead to reveal naked torsos. Every body is tattooed on shoulders, arms or breasts. The tattoos themselves are alive, their flow distinct from the motions of bodies. Ink churns, spreading across hands, rising over faces like a devouring virus. As rhythm conveys from dancer to audience, lines of ink intertwine and extend, travel body to body. The audience nearest the troupe transforms, dark figures swimming outward in a wave of seeping black. Patterns move, carriers oblivious to their infection. The dance intensifies, quickens.

Bay wants to approach. Whatever this is, he'll surrender, let it take him. He's willing to forget, to wade in and submerge himself.

As he reaches the crowd's perimeter, those nearest the fire start to fall. They drop without protest, overcome. The troupe halts, motionless as mannequins, apparently unsurprised. The music continues, slowing. The audience's movements don't halt, but diminish with the rhythm. Those upright begin to disperse, sweat-drenched, murmuring satisfaction.

The collapsed are few. An opening widens around them. Others seem not to notice. Dark faceless figures in black hoods descend and drag away five motionless fallen.

Bay remains separate from the crowd, never quite joined.

Music stops. Bay wonders what he saw. Maybe he imagined black ciphers dragging bodies inked with contagion.

From the crowd, someone beckons. Minerva, in the white shirt again. She skips toward him, weightless. Her embrace is damp with the sweat of exertion. Her heart pounds against his chest.

"I'm so glad Petersson brought—" She backs up, pointing. "Oh, Bay, you're hurt."

The front of his shirt is cut, blood-soaked. "The fight."

Minerva pulls his hand. "Come in, I'll get you something."

8.

Inside the house, a tranquil oasis. Minerva vanishes into darkness behind the stairwell, returns holding a jar.

"Come up." She starts upstairs.

One hand pressing his wound, Bay follows into the dark void. Halfway, he bumps into Minerva.

"Hold still," she says. "I'll fix you."

His shirt lifts.

Minerva smears cold, astringent balm. "How's that feel?"

"No pain," Bay says.

"There's always pain." She turns, resumes climbing. "Old Mallard keeps asking about you."

The room is a broad, many-windowed hexagon packed with hand-built variants on musical instruments: a horizontal long-stringed harp like an oversized bodiless piano; squares of metal plate hung like gongs; panels of knobs, vacuum tubes and tangled wire.

"Welcome to Attainment." Old Mallard speaks without looking up from a tray of water-filled glass bowls. Delicately he strokes the rims, sounding vibrations which shimmer high and light.

A Miles Davis lookalike clad only in white tennis shorts perches on a piano stool before a plywood harpsichord beside a stand of DIY electronics, horned speakers and arcane analog circuitry. A microphone cable dead-ends in acid-smelling yellow liquid in a Pyrex dish from which a second cable-end emerges into a mixing board. Tall speakers emanate thrumming drone.

Minerva leads Bay to a pair of Mies van der Rohe lounge chairs. Both sit, listen.

Old Mallard and not-Miles improvise a slow-shifting ambience interspersed with rhythmic bursts verging on jazz. Patterns of insistent repetition underpin chiming drones. The mood tilts into a slant, euphoria fraught with digressions into panic.

Bay's stomach goes queasy. Nerves jitter. Maybe the pill he took?

"Ecstasy these days," Old Mallard intones, "mostly amphetamine, I'm afraid." He steps away from the bowls. The drone continues, sustained in feedback of loops overlapping. He slides a subwoofer across the floor, takes Bay's hand, places it flat upon the low bass cabinet. "You need to slow down. Feel this."

Old Mallard drifts away, turning knobs, tweaking circuits, plucking at hacked-together string instruments.

Bay's teeth ache, a taste like radio static. The bass makes his head wobble as if barely attached. Thoughts split into nonsense, then cohere again. He fears he's missing time, phasing in and out of reality, or consciousness.

In panic, realizing he's alone, Bay jolts upright. "Where is she?"

Minerva lies reclining beside him, eyes closed, face pleasantly relaxed.

Bay tries to stand.

Old Mallard approaches. "Stop looking. Close your eyes."

"You reminded me of The Necks," Bay says. "They're an Australian avant—"

"I know them," Old Mallard says. "They've performed in this room."

Bay wants to express what he imagines to be his own transformation. The walk in the trees, the firedancing, this world of sound. Something within feels loosened. "I need to…" He trails off, urgency extinguished.

"You've been imprinted, like lightstruck film." Old Mallard lifts an eyebrow. "Development awaits… some impetus."

"Why am I here? Bay asks. "Why not Petersson, or Erik?"

Old Mallard looks to Minerva. "The way is closed by default."

Minerva's eyes remain closed. "Even me, Grandfather only accepted me when I returned, already initiated. Many possibilities opened, but that ended things with Petersson."

At the same moment, both Minerva and Old Mallard turn, looking to a dark corner. There stands a figure, costumed and hooded in black, like those who retrieved the fallen firedancers.

"Soon." The figure turns, disappears.

Old Mallard stands. "To Lightpulse."

Bay expects Minerva to guide him downstairs. Old Mallard gives her a look.

"This way." Minerva leads Bay to another stairway, hidden in darkness.

9.

Lightpulse is smaller than Attainment, glass walls transparent to night. Hexagonal sides merge in steel pillars hung with massive photographs and dark paintings.

"Witkin, that photo. Joel-Peter Witkin." Bay turns, stops, unable to believe. "That's… you have a Francis Bacon!"

"Bacon created this," Old Mallard says calmly, "tormented at his love's dying."

Bay scans memory, trying to place the image. It resembles the Black Triptychs, brushwork looser, more organic. "Is that *Misper-*

ceptions of Broken Philosophers?" Immediately he regrets the suggestion. "It's considered lost."

"Lost?" Old Mallard shrugs, palms up. "Some may consider it so. Lost to the world of buyable critics, dollar-focused museums. But truly lost?" He points. "It's right there, on my wall."

Bay approaches the next pillar, hungry to discover new wonders. He stops.

In a window seat beyond the reach of halogen spotlights, a cloth-draped human shape reclines.

"Bayard," Old Mallard asks behind, "have you recently imagined dying?"

"I dreamed…." Bay backs up, turns. "Who is this?"

"Thoughts of death brought you here," Old Mallard insists. "Tolstoy said, Life is indestructible; it is beyond time and space, therefore death can only change its form, arrest its manifestation in this world."

Bay returns, scrutinizes the figure. Must be a sculpture. Some art piece, like a full-body death mask. "What did you say?"

"Death."

"I dreamed falling. The moment before the end extended forever."

Beneath the drapery, the figure moves.

"You want to postpone death." Old Mallard steps nearer.

The figure breathes. The head turns, the drapery slips. A woman's face, chalk white.

"Lightpulse is her favorite place. She chose to remain here tonight. Listening, waiting."

Bay doesn't realize he's reaching to touch the wrinkled face until Old Mallard stops his hand.

"My wife, Maia." Old Mallard turns her like an inanimate object. "She will be gone soon. Tonight."

Her eyes flick open, vibrantly alive. Such vivid green, Bay can't believe she's dying.

Old Mallard turns to Bay. "You're almost ready. But first…" He extends an open palm, offering a white flower petal, dry and powdery as Maia's face. "From Chile, in the Andes where I was initiated to the Six-Sided Circle. The wise have utilized it for millennia, perhaps eons. There hidden, sight turned inward, they shrug off our culture's pallid temptations for ancient truths. Such is only attainable..." He looks down, as if remembering. "...through deep time."

Bay accepts the flower, places it on his tongue.

Old Mallard's smile is so subtle, almost not a smile. "Tolstoy again, *The Death of Ivan Ilyich.* 'He sought his former accustomed fear of death and did not find it. Where is it? What death? There was no fear because there was no death. In place of death there was light.'"

He bends, lifts Maia as if she weighs nothing.

"Come." He carries his wife in his arms.

10.

Bay follows quietly, mind reeling in a way distinct from the afternoon's ecstasy trip. His vision brightens, even in the dark stairwells.

They pass Earthwide, the main floor, and continue down.

A room hexagonal like the others, but smaller. Dark stone floors. Around the perimeter, six classical statues, white marble figures.

"Subterrain," Minerva whispers.

Old Mallard places Maia, face uncovered, on a granite platform. He mutters words, like an incantation. Rhyme, poetic meter.

Time speeds past, a blur of obscure ceremony. From hallucination into clarity, back again.

Is it still night? Fear tickles the back of Bay's mind. What does Old Mallard want, and Minerva? It was her idea Petersson invite him. Now she leans against him, clutches his shoulder, his hand. So much is uncertain. Bay keeps expecting Old Mallard to reveal some surprise, or Maia to spring the joke. To sit up, laughing.

They're all looking at him. Even Maia's green eyes.

"The long view means watching many shorter lives end." Old Mallard's voice is steady, grave. He lifts his wife again. "Soon Maia will go. There will be no laughing."

"Down," Minerva whispers.

Bay follows through another doorway, hidden until it's seen.

11.

Strange atmosphere, basement smell. Floor of dusty, hard-packed earth, walls grown with fungus or ferment. Bay doesn't remember the bottommost level's name until Minerva speaks it.

"Blackshard."

Here, no artistic wonders to rival Lightpulse's Witkin and Bacon. None of Attainment's otherworldly sounds, Subterrain's statues. Colored lights shine on twelve books, ancient black leather, each displayed within locked glass cases.

Bay recalls the story Petersson told. Is this a burial chamber for ten previous wives?

"Nine," Old Mallard says. "Maia is ninth." He pulls back the cloth to fully reveal her body. Her face, hands and feet are perfectly white, strangely chalky, but the rest of her body is pink and vital, decades younger than Bay guessed.

"Her breasts, still round as the earth," Old Mallard says, "soft as clouds." Lightly he touches her nipple. The skin hardens. "You see, and her sex, still pink and moist." Gently, reverently, he touches the cleft between her legs. "Why should she die? Because she accepts this end. Cancer beckons, she follows."

Maia lets out a breath. Bay jumps, startled, then realizes it's an ordinary sigh.

"Teaching the Six-Sided Circle must wait. Maia won't last, nor the others. I offer this, to prepare you for what comes." Old Mallard's voice deepens. "The existence of *huitzitzili* is cyclical, like a tree. Vibrant and motile in summer, in winter motionless, shed of adornment. Waiting through cold for rebirth."

"What is?" Bay asks, breathless.

"*Huitzitzili*, the hummingbird. It defies physics, gravity, death. In winter it attaches to a tree trunk, remains frozen there, dry and featherless, lacking heartbeat. Spring thaw, it twitches to life, regrows feathers. It flies again, blue and weightless, a tiny god."

Minerva nods.

"I'm sorry for Maia," Bay says. "But what does this mean to me? And you, and Minerva?"

"I'm telling you there's no need to ride the train to the end of the line." He looks down, covers his wife in her wrap. "I will lie down with Maia, and others. I'll take from them, then wake strengthened."

"Even if that's possible, you can't live like that," Bay protests. "Always borrowing. There are only so many people…"

Old Mallard raises an eyebrow. "Such consumables are never in short supply." He bends, lifts Maia.

"Where next?" Bay asks. "We're at the bottom."

Minerva approaches his side, cautious, as if afraid he might spook.

"There's another, deeper, unnamed," Old Mallard says. "There had to be six."

12.

Through a curtain, down a sloping dirt ramp. Bay imagines the bottommost room a circle. Eyes adjust, discern flat walls. Six sides.

The floor slopes to a central pit, wider and shallower than a grave, moist soil crawling with worms. Five bodies are arrayed around the hollow, skin seething ink-black. All lie twitching, sweaty and open-eyed, life stories rewritten in creeping lines of ink.

This nameless room, so different from the rest. No art, no music or books. Just dying bodies and damp earth.

Old Mallard places Maia among the firedancing's fallen. She makes the sixth.

He turns, brushes Minerva's mouth with his thumb, then grasps Bay's elbow. "I'll take their deaths. I'll return. Distilled and clarified."

Bay realizes others are present, watching. Shrouded in black, they blend into walls. Bay recognizes the humming, throaty intonations, reminiscent of the music upstairs.

Old Mallard takes his place beside Maia.

Bay's mind spins, uncertain what he's seeing, what he's been offered. Membership in some circle? A creative life, empowered by agelessness. He can't imagine. The dead-end he fled already seems far away. Memory of Annie's face, the words in her note. All of it, another man's problem.

The tomb chills, the singing fades. The watchers vanish.

All that remains is the quiet stillness of death.

"Clarified," Bay whispers, sifting hints.

The emptiness of his life gives him freedom. If he found another Annie, he'd forget himself.

Minerva takes one step toward the bodies, then turns to Bay. He hopes she'll explain. She cut Petersson away, freed herself to enable her own pursuits. She knows how to live, unencumbered. Perfect, weightless freedom.

Bay remembers falling, stuck in black pitch. Extended anticipation of death. The agony of perpetual imminence.

Minerva's hand reaches.

Not a relationship beginning. Something else.

She glances to where her guardian lies clarifying in the shallow pit, then to Bay.

Her hand opens, reaching for his open shirt, grasping for his wound. Black lines on her palm elongate. Streaks of ink form vines and leaves, black fruit, wild faces. New forms creep outward, spreading to cover his chest, his arms.

Hot skin trembles. The bones of her hand reflect his heartbeat.

THE GOLDEN STARS AT NIGHT

Allyson Bird

Her name was Rawlie. She chose the name, obviously not at her birth but later—not gender specific and that empowered her for a good reason. She'd need to be strong. Rawlie had seen the world change. Sitting on the stile near the stream bank amongst the manuka trees she tied her brown hair back and shielded her grey eyes from the winter sun. It was still strong. All year round they had to be wary of it in New Zealand. It wasn't uncommon for many newcomers to fold with the heat and humidity. She was the first to rise too—just a quarter hour before the others but with enough time to grab a mug of coffee and wrap up warm against the cold. The mountains were visible today, still tipped with snow and rosy in the dawn light. Some days were better than others. The worst days started with her father sending a couple of ranch hands down to the main gate. They would wave a rifle in the air. Nobody set a foot on Campbell land without prior permission.

The day on the station would be a long one and she was always the first to go to bed each evening—exhausted from trying to be as good as or rather better than others. That was what she wanted. What she needed was to stay alive, eat, sleep and fuck. Her mind nowadays was closed off pretty much—kept apart from most others in some cosmic shadow of itself. She wondered what lay in—within the darkness whilst she tried to sleep. Not really of this world perhaps? Or a forgotten part of it? They seemed ever closer now.

Rawlie could shear two hundred sheep in a day, not bad as she wasn't greatly built and had small hands. But, she had determination, and that was what was needed. She was twenty-three, had been briefly married to a man long gone, and had an apprentice to look after named Mysel. He was five years her junior and was her responsibility. She had to keep him out of trouble and make sure he worked well. They were in fact bonded, not married—more like brother and sister but with less falling out, not that they didn't now and again when one or the other had too much to drink. Mysel liked his beer, and Rawlie loved her wine. Her father thought she would marry again but Rawlie didn't want that.

Recently there had been the storms. The two great and one lesser one—within a few months of each other. She recalled the first storm. The wooden chicken shed didn't stand a chance. The wind howled over the mountain, and smashed it to pieces, and the chickens sought refuge in a hollow in the far paddock. Rawlie had joked about the wailing banshee who had flown down as if to sweep the land clean of lies and corruption as well as the chicken shed. Rawlie didn't refer to her as the banshee for a long time after that. It seemed too familiar—too accurate.

The dreams came with the storms as the wind whipped the grass into waves along the paddock. A violent gust broke the large branch off the Old Man Pine in the paddock—the one which pointed directly west. The last dream she had was half remembered but there had been a man it. His face was unfamiliar. He nodded and said it had never been done before but then after a moment or two said yes—it had been. It was as if some magician had found the formulae. He had perfected the art again against an azure blue backdrop and golden stars at night. The stars inverted. Alien. Not like the ones in the northern hemisphere. Rawlie felt like an Alice and had tumbled into the South Pacific. And had been forgotten—legs and arms not fitting the house. She was an alien Alice on a torrid blue planet too small for her. And many could lose their heads when she fell. The rabbit was always looking at his watch, also. The dream made her wince and smile in turn.

An hour before the second storm which struck up out of nowhere there was the man again but not in dream this time. She saw him in the distance. Was it the same man—she wasn't sure? Halfway up the hill and sitting on a boulder. She had binoculars but couldn't quite see his face. The second storm was lesser than the first. But still lethal. She supposed the chickens dead this time. The arch of steel that formed the bulk of the chicken shed was torn from its mooring and flew across the field and hit a mound of soil. That sent the steel hurtling by her window. If she had gone to see to the chickens, which she had been thinking about doing a few minutes earlier, the steel would have taken her head off. Clean off. The chickens survived again.

After the storm she had gone with Mysel to the beach. The waves with still a rage of seaweed within began untangling in the foam. You could not swim in that sea. No way forward there. Poison in the sea. Way too wild. And the blue crab, a claw waving, as it fell into the tumbling wave. Waving good bye? A cry for help? Or come and join me?

That storm reminded her again she was only there by the tolerance of nature or something else. That could change.

There came a few days of calm. Nothing from dreams now—only no sleep and the grass shimmering in the darkness. During the day she saw the dark figure against the dry grass on the hillside.

In her own room at night she played Bowie loud. "Everyone Says 'Hi'" was put on repeat. It had been filed under "intermittent" in her collection. She smiled at that. She played OMD too with their rendition of "Pandora's Box" to the film of Louise Brooks playing the part of Lulu in THAT film. Rawlie felt the desperation at times but she tried to ground herself in her farm work and teach Mysel— the ever eager Mysel who soaked up stories like a sponge.

A brown parcel secured with string was left at the main gate of the ranch for her. Within was a leather-bound notebook and a silver pen with her name on it. She scribbled to see if the pen still worked—on the brown paper. The black ink. It always had to be black and not the blue. Another parcel arrived—this time with three books within.

Alberto Manguel. *A History of Reading*.

T. S. Elliot. *The Waste Land*.

Ovid. *Metamorphoses*.

There was little rebuff or criticism from the rest of the ranch hands on the station as Rawlie and Mysel sat around one of the few the campfires at night—he with his head in her lap when she read to him. The others didn't really bother at all and her father was never out at night but stayed in his bedroom looking through her mother's things perhaps. He sometimes did that.

The others thought them up to something else, too—but no. She stroked Mysel's dark hair and stared at any who came near to say anything. They soon turned away with a gentle gesture of contrition.

Rawlie read to him from Ovid of a girl who turned into a tree. And now and then Mysel would catch her arm and ask had she changed yet? Laughter from him. Rawlie smiled at that. The change—that was what it was all about wasn't it? The change from one time to another—from one being to another—one universe to another without losing anyone along the way—to anything. To madness. To isolation. To oblivion.

Rawlie thought about how the other someone she once knew who had given everything of himself to make things better for others—his hand always catching hold as they fell. He cared and it cost him. She wished they could bring him back. Or at least bring back what he stood for. Equality. Fairness for all.

She asked her father for the compound bow and quiver of arrows he had promised her a bit back. He nodded quietly and got on with getting them. They arrived within a few days and he patiently

set up a training area not far from the manuka trees. He got some
ranch hands to set up six large straw bales. He thought about a
target. So did Rawlie. In the end she sewed a blue jumper to some
old dark trousers and secured the ends of trouser legs and sleeves.
Then filled the whole thing with straw and attached it to the bales.
She placed a pumpkin which would suffice as a head on the level
top and even carved a face upon it.

At first she missed of course and hit a manuka with the first shot,
which caused her father to frown. But, from then on in she reached
her target time after time. Then she aimed for the heart of the guy.
She missed and hit the pumpkin head. Her father laughed. The
head or the heart. The heart or the head. What to do? she wondered. The quiver of arrows was fixed firmly on her back and as
she practised day after day the speed with which she could fire the
arrows increased and the guy was left in tatters. Different targets
were attached to the bales. The ranch hands came up with ever
more weird things to hang there. Some belonged to the insides of
animals. Once there was a sheep's head. It all became a running
joke. There was a possum one day. The targets became smaller. One
morning there was a heart of some animal or other. That was soon
reduced to almost nothing.

One night Rawlie sat on the floor and pulled out the wooden
chest from under the bed. There was a little silver plaque fixed to
the lid. The box had been put away since her mother's death a few
years ago with a note which said: "For Rawlie. A memory. Pandora's
box—to be opened only if and when." THAT had always puzzled
Rawlie. She hadn't wanted to open it until now. Her mother called
her Pandora now and again. Rawlie had joked that Hope could stay
out of the box forever. Her mother smiled but there was sadness in
her eyes.

Now was the time, thought Rawlie. She opened the lid. It was
empty except for one thing—a doll. A rag doll with scraggy blonde
hair, wearing a faded short blue dress trimmed with lace. The hem
was way above the knee. A goth lolly doll in fact but with cross-

stitches for a mouth. Rawlie got up from the floor and sat on her bed with the doll. Rawlie reached across to the small set of drawers by her bed, opened the top drawer, and found a pair of scissors which had been made in the shape of a stork. The cutting edges were the stork's sharp pointed beak. As a child she had made her hand bleed when she had tried to unpick some sewing with them. She hoped she could avoid doing that now. Rawlie used the stork scissors to take out the stitches that formed the mouth. She then threaded a needle with cotton and carefully made the doll a new mouth with neat backstitch. Once done she tied the doll's hair up as best she could and placed her upon the cream pillow.

Rawlie then picked up the notebook and ran her fingers across the leather. She opened it and on the first page she wrote the title—"The Keeper of Thoughts and Dreams." She wondered if that should be "The Keeper of Hopes and Dreams."

She glanced up at the hill that led to the mountain. There was nobody on the hill. But then she looked again—beyond the hill at the mountain. Almost at the top she thought she saw a tiny speck in the distance, and then saw it fall. It seemed to bounce off the large boulders.

Rawlie put a hand to her mouth to stifle a cry. She looked down at the words on the page; violently crossed out the title, and flung the book to one side—she then picked up her bow and went out into the paddock where as dusk fell the grass shimmered in waves towards her. She aimed and waited. Whatever was there could not be killed by a mere arrow but it was all she had now. Rawlie would not see the golden stars that night and she thought perhaps nobody else would again either.

THE LAST CROSSROADS ON A CALENDAR OF YESTERDAYS

Joseph S. Pulver, Sr.

Olympia was sunstroke hot on its way to inferno, day five. Even with frequent pulls on cans of slightly chilled soda, slow motion was all Chance and Ray could muster while moving Ray's baby-sister into her new walkup. The 25-each she'd given them was looking like tonight's *cold* beer money when they stopped at the traffic light and saw Pershing set the bulky crate of books at the curb.

"Might pick up a few more dineros for cerveza if we help him?" Ray said, pointing at the wall of crates and boxes Pershing had stacked at the mouth of the alley on the northside of the Broadsword Hotel.

"All fit in one load."

Ray lowered the window. "Hey, need help moving your stuff?"

Pershing was too wiped to glower. "They're junk. I'm just putting them out here for the garbage man."

"Lot of books by the look of it. One old classic can equal cha-ching," Chance whispered quickly to Ray. Gazing at fat leather spines, he grinned as a scene from *The Ninth Gate* glittered like cash-in-hand. *Collectors go for them old puppies.*

Ray smiled and nodded his yup. "Mind if we take 'em?"

"All yours."

It had taken Pershing three days of back-breaking labor to haul all the boxes down from the 6th floor to the curb. Chance and Ray had them loaded in the van in less than an hour. In the green patch with two wooden benches and a memorial plaque that passed for a park three blocks away they rifled through the boxes. There were skeletal pamphlets like *Magick in Theory, Will and the Cosmic Moment, Das Erdreich des Rundwurmes*, tucked between hefty volumes on psychic powers and séances, the use of poetics in the occult, arthropods in the supernatural, lycanthropy, demonology and the occult Reich.

"Now all we need is an obsessed follower of the dark side... With plenty cash."

"Gimme your cell, I have an idea."

Six hours later, Chance's old library connection, an ex that wished she hadn't dumped Chance for the Lying Asshole, had them hooked up and holding 725 dollars cashmoney. Showered and two rounds into killing the day's thirst, they were blasting rock-n-roll sexmusic from the jukebox in Guerlain's Boomtown. Ray was a Jack-double and a Lowenbrau (and a conditioned-with-vodka blonde) ahead and about to tell Chance they should have pushed for a few hundred more, when the blonde with the cleavage said, "My bedroom has a brand new A/C unit, but what it doesn't have, Ray, is a *stud* to regulate the room temperature." Any regret on parting with the books for less than a grand vaporized.

Ray informed Chance of his destination and was gone like a bullet-train.

Chance was traveling the wings and contours of the phone number his ex had given him... *Could... could. Maybe? Shit*. He took the slip of paper out of his wallet and placed it on the bar. For half a beer he stared at it. The razor chords of The Brandos' "Gettysburg" napalmed the bar and the pain-lyrics kicked in. Cold white moonlight on graves... mothers. Sons. Died... Her number and words in the song became a cascade of darkness, brought to mind the number tattooed on the old man's arm.

Ovens. "Fuck."

Following directions, they'd driven into the Black Hills and found the old man's house in a hollow that would have caused a surveyor to erase the word Boondocks from a map and replace it with PRIMAL. Kellerman came out to the van and looked at over two dozen books plucked from various crates; his hands trembled when he held Binsfeld's *Classification of Demons.* Chance clearly heard him say, "The Disputer." In a voice untouched by miracles or mercy or Heaven, Kellerman counted out the money and handed it to them. They carried the books inside for the old guy and piled them neatly in the center of a small, overfilled library. Chance read a few spines; they bore titles that alluded to obscene rites and dark subject matter. He also saw the numbers tattooed on the old man's arm and the traffic of pain and anger that made Kellerman's eyes and mouth terrible ground.

You survive the camps and when you come out the other side you're fucking interested in occult-shit. "Didn't you see enough monsters?"

Chance saw piles of bodies—shoeless, in rags, naked skeletons, belief and sense (every fact consulted) and miracles sliced away, broken… life sucked right out of them. Shivered. "Fuck." *Fuck.* He put the number written in blue ink back in his wallet and ordered another beer. "And give me a double-Jack back too, willya."

***

To and fro. Rocking. Slow.

Slow.

Measured, not sluggish. Predator readying true for ignorant prey.

To…

and back again. His grip not far from the shotgun.

The old man sipped his sweetened coffee from an old porcelain mug. From his hillside porch he stared into the night-darkened

forest toward what was no longer the Hambly property. Old dis-
comforts and slowmotion anger was a butchering quicksand that
was bringing on tears. Kellerman put the filtered-tip cigarette to his
lips and inhaled. Took the smoke deep. Held it. Exhaled. "Ruined,
Zina… Bastards have ruined it."

"—*against the horde of insidious parasites.*"

"You are the *White… American… Dream.* You are the defenders
of White European culture and heritage. Your commitment and
actions preserve what *Our* American Fathers—Benjamin Franklin,
George Washington, and John Adams—shed blood to establish and
protect… our Great White Nation. *You* are America's *true* patriots."

Pride-roasted cheers and a vigorous round of applause billow
through the compound carved-out of the darksome forest of rugged
pine.

"WAR DAY." The voice of the Allfather or a blood-and-fire Jeho-
vah at 110 decibels thunders from the loudspeakers and echoes in the
hills. "Is a HOLY DAY!"

Another explosive burst of applause followed by a chain reaction
of Nazi salutes expressing their pathological eagerness. Amens dash
like snarls. Three semiautomatic handguns bark and send their pay-
loads skyward. Two sisters, paleskinned twins married to paleskinned
brothers, rise from their seats and begin singing a bastardization of
"Onward, Christian Soldiers." Their enflamed voices are joined by
ten and ten and ten and ten. Fifty-strong becomes nearly one hundred.

Once Metzger disciple, before the riff became a chasm, Walter
Warren smiles on the crowd. "In a week this compound, the new
home of the White Liberation Alliance, will be completed. God is
pleased with *your* work, brothers and sisters. God is pleased."

Not enough miles away, or countries for that matter, Kellerman
caught the amplified words. He'd heard the raised voices sing and
the gunfire. Heard them last Saturday night, and too many times in
the last months.

"Nazis."

Zina sat up. Growled.

The old man shivered.

Zina stood, faced the black woods, offered the thunder her teeth and an unsheathed promise steeled with Till-Death-Do-Us-Part loyal.

Twenty years since he'd briefly lived in Olympia, in the distance below. Twenty years since he'd come west to these hills and hollows, hoping to find balm. There were small moments when he could pretend (if the sky was soft summer blue and the sun warm and the blooms gave off sweet scents) the beauty it held helped. Kellerman was an old man now, felt it when the cold ruled muscle and mind mercilessly, saw it sear the tired face the mirror slapped him with. The nightmares and wounds (still a bullet to heart and mind no prayer could moderate) of the small boy he'd been, the boy the Americans liberated from Buchenwald, now fully reawakened by the hate that had invaded his property, were, these last few months, as loud and haunting as the last breath of his cancer-ridden wife.

Kellerman's right hand stroked Zina between her ears. "Yes, girl, I know."

He stood and stubbed out his cigarette on the porch boards, picked up his mug, his shotgun, and turned to go inside. "Little good it will do, but we will try the Authorities again tomorrow, girl."

Zina, ninety pounds of unwavering attentiveness, settled at the foot of his bed. His Mossberg rested against the nightstand. Kellerman's hands were trembling fists as he fell asleep.

Blackboots half-dragging a teenage girl through the muddy filth in Buchenwald. She screams and pleads in Polish, as her terror-blasted eyes lock on the eyes of nine-year-old Samuel Kellerman. In her pupils the boy sees the abyss, not for the first time. He can feel as well as hear the sludge of hungry murmurs clinging to her. Her next scream pulls him back from the abyss.

Two SS officers drag her through the door Samuel holds open.

"You will take her in the other room and hose her off. When she is

dry, put her in a gown and bring her to me," Dr. Ernst Karl Strück spit.

"Samuel, clean that mud off my floor."

Samuel Kellerman stood on the other side of the door for two hours. His tears no armor against what he hears on the other side.

"Samuel. Komm' her."

Samuel tried not to look at the thing—maggot-ready wreckage scent of gut and fluids, innards observed by the medic of rooting hands, eyes missing from their sockets (and the room), hands and feet severed tossed in a metal medical tray, hours ago a young girl—on the floor. Tried not to look at the doctor.

Dr. Ernst Karl Strück walked to the boy, gripped his jaw with thumb and forefinger, raised his head. "Call the guards to remove this. And clean the blood from my floor."

The doctor, naked and still erect, was wearing the girl's skinned face. Samuel wet himself.

"When your task is complete, bring the Schwarze Führers *to my study. And Samuel, you will remember, do not look inside the books."*

Bolt upright. The dream-images deteriorating but the savage horrors the terrified child forever-bound inside Kellerman thunder from memory's tongue. Decades distant and still the frenzied riverbed of nightmares attack. Kellerman was quick to strip the sweat-soaked sheets. Lying there on dry sheets he did not sleep, but he cried, unconsciously scratching the inmate identification number tattooed on his left arm as he does every time he endures these night-terrors.

***

Sunrise and at times, quiet birds, outside the east window where his wife's crematory urn rested. A window once far away from what people are capable of. In May-June rose-purple rhododendron blooms softened the view. Morning coffee brewing, Kellerman lovingly dusted the urn.

"What thrived outside all rules, Raechel... it lives here now.

"I hope you can forgive me, but I do not think I can distance myself from the beast again... I'm too old. And where would we move?"

Kellerman poured coffee in the mug; he stopped when it was one inch below the rim of the mug. He measured one level teaspoon of sugar and stirred it, three times, into the coffee, then he measured one level tablespoon of whole milk and added it to the mug, stirring it exactly five times with the tablespoon. He set the mug on his small desk in his study. Then walked to the door. "Come, Zina." He looked at his wife's urn as he closed and locked the door to his library.

Half of the books Chance and Ray had sold to him were piled in a corner. They were too slight or redundant, and as they contained no pieces of his golem they were of no use to him. Seven volumes sat on his desk awaiting deeper scrutiny. He opened the next box and began looking at what he had purchased.

When the chimes of the anniversary clock on his desk announced the noontide hour he went into the kitchen and made a simple lunch, one slice of wheat bread, a thin layer of lightly salted butter evenly spread, and two slices of venison salami from Lundin's General Store. As he ate, he cut a four-inch hunk of the salami into eight pieces and slowly handfed them to his ninety-pound Rottie.

Thirty minutes later Kellerman was walking Zina on a curved, evergreen-hooded path that lead north; since Hambly's passing this had become his favorite walking track, in no small part due to the pink-bloom rhododendrons that were generously sprinkled along it. The boughs of ancient pines ringing the small clearing Kellerman liked to stop and take in moved in the breeze. This was a quiet place, undergrowth—that did not march to the rigor of any compass—threatened its unfilled, and thick hides of emerald moss covered the ten boulders that were scattered in the center of the clearing he believed Hambly would have found theatrical. Even with the fierce nature of a July sun lengthening above, it could be a lonely place; today it was gloomier without its usual birdsong.

Odd this. Unnaturally quiet. "Not a single bird." He did not think long on them being hunkered down or flown—

Gunfire. Automatic weapons. Close. Loud voices toasting in gutterwords between the bursts.

Kellerman repositioned his Mossberg. Should confrontation with his new neighbors suddenly bruise it would be no real defense, but...

"The demons came. They shattered the night. They butchered by daylight... Now their children unleash that hatred and bloodlust here. All they know is dismantle and decimate. This hostility must die."

Kellerman was not ready for the conflict he knew would come. He turned and walked home, the color of his step fueled by resolve.

***

Kellerman stepped away from the coal-dark window. There was no moon tonight and if and when the sun rose in the morning for him, any radiance it cared to extend would be stained by the blight of darkness that had applied its behavior and instruments on the quiet abundance his neighbor, and fellow refugee, Hambly had so loved.

Hambly was a good man. Kind and generous, a good neighbor. He was a poet, held in high regard and widely published. Soul-sore he fled the streets of illest-'cuz, nigga/drive-by L.A. to find roots, breathe stars and read the flux of seasons, and expand his craft.

Craig Hambly died, suddenly—unexpectedly—in his sleep, at fifty and his property was sold off.

Hambly and Kellerman had been out walking for the better part of an hour. Hambly stopped and sat on a fallen bole. He packed his pipe with a mild cherry-blend and after lighting it, said, "L.A. How long was a blues. Suddenly, a void. Same in Chicago. I couldn't breathe in waves of fine-print—gaps, junctures, last things, the vertigo of the turns and back that spoiled and slashed... it had become a harpoon, speed I kept stumbling over. I became a manifesto of excessive thinness... So I came here to wash off the stinging salt. To gaze at bowels and escape."

Hambly picked up a fallen leaf, twirled it between thumb and forefinger. "I have, as it were, my own sun and moon and stars, and a little world all to myself." His small smile seems to say he found his musing funny, but it faded quickly. He pointed along the shadowed deer runway they'd been following. "Nature's watchmen have told me this wood is a door, Sam. Behind this green curtain is another existence. One day I hope to find the truth there."

Kellerman hoped his friend would never come upon what he sought.

He didn't.

In Hambly's absence a different black kernel, a vulgar storm, stained the horizon.

Kellerman spent the night looking through the new boxes of books. He had black kernels of his own to seed.

**

Clouded in a whorl of cigarette smoke, Dr. Ernst Karl Strück read aloud from the dark books. Every night—displaying profoundly and black-flares of notions not-mastered. All day—all work. Samuel (statue, standing where instructed, awaiting instruction to do this, or fetch that) listened, didn't want to, but he did. Strück was a Nazi mystic, one of Hitler's occult seekers. When he was not carving his pleasures in adolescent flesh (which he ordered, almost nightly, from the women's camp) he was deep in the occult documents brought to him from every nook and crevasse in Europe.

His pencil, Strück could not abide pens, tapped steadily on the desk as he examined his copies of the *Black Guide*. Strück was in possession of three copies and aggressively in search of as many others as could be unearthed—"They assert there may be as many as fifty copies and all you can find is three? Your performance to date is wholly unacceptable. There are hells beneath the hells, Sturmbannführer, and if you do not find me other copies, you will find the ongoing agonies of the Jews in this facility are negligible in comparison to what you will endure." Tonight, warped by a foulsome mood, as a forth copy (acquired in a tiny village to the south and west of Kiev) had been held up by railway delays, Strück was seeking the key to his future in the copy that had been found in Barcelona.

"'There are wild places in nature where They reside, waiting for the door to be opened. They have always lived there. When the conditions are met the Thin People will come through.'

"'They will come for blood.'

"For *blood*."

Strück's head came up from the book. His eyes locked on Samuel. "Do you have the ability to understand, my little monkey? You see what I do here… but do you *see*?

"No. No, how could you? You are both child and Jew… you are merely another ant.

"A few of the sycophants who have his ear think my intellectual excursions and concepts are the products of mental illness… Mad!" Strück backhanded the telephone off his desk.

"My insights… *are wild claims?* I am no dolt. Make no mistake, boy; I am aware of which of them disparage me. When *I* summon the Children of the Black Sun they will understand. They seek the tools of Odin and the weapons of the Christ-father—there is no *Spear of Destiny*. *Gungnir* is a barbarian's myth. If there had been a Loki, he would have injured himself laughing at what they believe.

"If your people could have raised a golem, Samuel, would they be here now?

"Fools… man's gods have no power; they never did for the gods mankind's religions hold up never existed." Strück held up the *Black Guide*. "In this is the power that has been hidden in the mystic."

The doctor lighted an unfiltered cigarette and smoked it. "Their voices direct me. They will lead me to the broadsword that is hidden within these obscurities."

Nights Samuel stood on the other side of the door he heard voices, the doctor's, the pleas and screams of Strück's victims, and he heard unhuman amusement and the merciless and abrasive comments—bonfires of hungrily—of unseen *Others*. Yet he knew only two had entered the room, the room with no window or vent and only this bolted door.

Repeatedly, Strück tapped on the book's cover with his pencil. "One day soon. One day soon."

***

Two members of the W.L.A. (shaped like an explosion of blunt) thrust their neo-Nazi extremism—their flame (nothing concealed, nothing slight) could have broken rocks—through the door of Lundin's General Store, Isabella Gallo put the bottle of habañero pepper hot sauce and the cake mix back on the shelf and made a beeline for the door. Mary Caples scooped up her daughter, Nikki (and her red-horned/red-tailed unicorn plushy), and followed suit.

Had Lundin been at a party his scowl would have easily been awarded Best Eastwood Impression. *First we get the occasional asshole redneck coming in, now it's these assbags.*

"All set, Mr. Kellerman. Comes to $62.47 with tax. I'll have your girl's dog-food Tuesday afternoon."

"Kellerman?" Spit. "That a *Jew* name?" Roar.

"There are those of the Hebrew faith with the name, yes."

"Look like a *Jew* to me."

"I have heard it said everyone has an opinion."

"Old man" (spit) "and a *Jew*," (roar) "I'd be real fucking careful openin' my mouth. This country is going to get cleaned up real soon and a lot of trash ain't gonna do too well when Right and White reclaims its due."

"Yeah. War comin'"

The topography of detestation displayed gave Pete Lundin no pause. He'd been a nineteen-year-old grunt in The Nam and after taking two in the chest as his baptism of fire, kowtowing to hate-garbage wasn't in him. "It won't be today. And it won't be *in my store.*

"See that?" Lundin asked. "The guy I'm fishing with in that photo is my wife's brother, Mike. Folks around here know Mike as the county sheriff—been sheriff here for fifteen years. Him and me like to fish together and play horseshoes, or pool, together and we like to sit and have a beer or two… and we like to go hunting together. Bow, shotgun, or rifle all work great on *coyotes*. If you take my meaning? Now's a good time to git, Adolf."

Big hands (that wouldn't be slaying today), bodies (propped-up on rage), and hardened blackboots stomped out of Lundin's General Store, tails (and derogatory) not quite between their legs.

"This is America; good man's a good man no matter what god he thinks is best. Vermin and free-ranging predators… well, that's why we got guns. How you set for shells, Mr. Kellerman?"

"Very well, thank you."

"Lot of mouth, no backbone, Mr. Kellerman. I'll mention them and their mouths to Mike."

***

The fourth copy of the *Black Guide* had finally arrived. Strück's bursts and cascades were enormous, his eyes raced across the handwritten pages. His tongue and teeth and lips flared with every word he released into the room.

"'*They have existed long before humanity, and will continue to exist long after the human swarm has vanished.*'

"Listen, Samuel. It is written in this copy as well. '*The Children of the Black Sun, called by various adepts and seekers of arcane wisdom, the Thin People—"beings of fell potency that dwell between," live in dark forests, in places where the moon breathes. Inhabitants of the Dry*

Realms beneath the Black Sun they are called to blood.'

"When the moon colors the gate... their dance will break every wing. It will be my baton that conducts the currents they will ride.

"Night will come, Samuel. Even you must know it to be true. I am the hawk who has flown in shadows. I have been in the long, cold night, in the wounds that hold spooks to the Place of Skulls. My spade is the lightning that will learn their speech, the sounds and joy of it—how to hold it. I will open the way."

A year later, on the sunless day American soldiers from the 6th Armored Division (Third Army) took shoeless, in rags, Samuel from the camp (two days after a horrified, young American captain emptied his .45 in Strück's chest, an event Samuel was present for), the boy had all four copies in a cloth sack. From Buchenwald to a hospital (for nearly three weeks) to an autumn with shadows no music could climb, across Europe to the stamina of the American coast, no one thought to try to take the books from the boy.

***

Shots ring out.

The east window that brings sunrise into the room shattered. Cut, color, clarity, in the sunlight the pieces of the window cut mind and memory like diamonds.

Raechel Kellerman's urn in pieces on the table and hardwood floor. Her ashes scattered.

Outside, dead on the porch (where minutes before she dozed quietly), Zina. The first of the three rounds that cut her down struck below her left ear...

"You're next, JEW! Might come one night *and burn you out*—or alive!"

Tires on gravel, shitty-muffler noise.

No barking—old bones up off the kitchen floor, shotgun divining trouble, its able-bodied ready to address the visitation. Out the door.

Kellerman stood over Zina's body, his hands were quaking fists. "Yes to heat. The heat will come... very soon."

Kellerman was shattered but did not break. If there were a God he would have begged to be taken to some place of peace, but his task required him to bear the horror. He had. Had carried the moments. Took what was hard, what soaked and discolored every sky, what would not go away. Did when he was a boy. Did and did and did. This was harder, but he would do what was required, what he'd promised.

Kellerman took Zina's head in his hands and kissed her brow, another to have, now have not, and then he dragged her into the toolshed. Tied a rope around her back legs and hung her, head down, from a hook. He slit her throat with a hunting knife. Her blood, and Kellerman's tears, flowed into a washtub.

They will come for blood.

While Zina's blood dripped into the tub he went inside and swept up his wife's ashes.

For an hour he dug in a small flower bed that the morning sun kissed. Then he placed his wife's ashes on a comforter and wrapped Zina in it. Eyes stinging from an hour's worth of tears, he buried them together.

Over them no prayer, but his promise.

Back in the shed he stirred some of his wife's ashes into the blood before ladling the mixture into large pasta sauce jars. He took the jars inside the house and placed them in the refrigerator.

"If I need more... I have what flows in my veins."

***

Kellerman took down two ancient newspaper-boy canvas delivery bags from the hook in the bedroom closet and brought them into the kitchen. He slid the pages he'd removed from thirty-two of his rarest books into the first sack. He put a few hundred upholstery tacks and a tack-hammer in the second.

Ten days, night and day, napping when he had to, preparing the pages. Drop of Zina's blood and Rae's ashes smeared over a certain word on a certain page. Now all he had to do was post his handbills and wait.

Didn't lock his door on the way out. Might not get back.

If it was his time, it was.

Two hours of walking and selecting which trees on the east and north side of the compound to tack his handbills on. And another two as he repeated the process on the west and south sides.

After heating and consuming a small can of baked beans and a slice of wheat bread for his late dinner, Kellerman took his mug of coffee and his shotgun out to the porch and sat in his rocker.

He smoked and waited for the moon to rise.

A whisper after 10pm, moon on the day-maybe-two-till-were-wolf-full side and riding high. The fog had unspooled, stayed low, swelled and covered bushes and clumps of ferns, curled and moiled around the base of hardwood trunks and low pine branches, clung to the pages he'd tacked to the trees. Clung. The ministrations of the moon roosted on certain words smeared with Zina's blood and Raechel Kellerman's ashes. Fog and moon... blood and ashes...

His mug was empty. A breeze was in the pine branches. He stood. Looked east. It was quiet. Looked in his window at the coffeemaker on the kitchen counter. Walked inside.

Kellerman came back out and sat on his porch. Had his coffee in a mug and his shotgun resting across his thighs. He rocked slowly.

To...

and

back to the toil of waiting. Ears ready to read. Mind packed, attached to the landscape not weighted in occurring. Smoking a cigarette with hurts.

Slowly.

Measured, not sluggish. Predator readying true for ignorant prey.

Smoked his cigarette.

Sipped his coffee.

Rocked.

Smoked another cigarette.

Old man with the shape and size and weight of the memories of his heart. Looked east. Didn't smile. Didn't make a fist.

"War Day."

Heat, the dryness of an oven rising within the circular frame staked out by the pages. Leaves and needles and moss, brown, begin to wither.

"Blood." One judge—Death clings to The Enemy of His Kind. No jury. Stipulation: "Blood." Sentence pronounced.

The air is furnished with an unhurried, glimmering procession. They come, softly, like gargoyles not nailed to stone, smelling of tomb and the discolored bottom of roadside ditches. Float, glide, cloaked in misty nightclothes...

The human vessels that contain the blood are surrounded by the cold sound of fluttering.

What had yet to pale and brown in the branches and threaded undergrowth was visited by dry and shriveled in the strange heat the spectral consequences radiated.

Consequences visit human...

Blood... splatter and crackle. The roux thickens.

Soft white flesh... desperately alone, ripped open. Torn. Meat soft and gleaming, teeth in its flanks, at its throat. The clout of brutal teeth withholding nothing.

Cross-channels and torrents of pain. Panting. Sobs. Fractured arms. Pain, bewildering balloons of pain, and drop by drop. Eyes enlarged by suffering burst. No yes or no and few shocked outcries born in panic.

Heads are pulled off.

Meatfat dripping in the heat. Muscle stripped away, and bone, shattered, swallowed—no belching... mastered by beasts.

The strong cold moon shouting in the fog clutches. Blood.

The Thin People were called to it. Took laffs and its you again... Took dutifully... Took slower and praise and that's too much...

Took breath and all that was wet inside—

Soft flanks. Pain yes. Outcry and very little gunfire in response. Torn sinew. Stripped, unrecognizable. Swallowed in torrents. Bone gleaming.

No rowing away…

Spilled.

Cause of death: sentence pronounced.

{The Brandos "Gettysburg"; Steve Reich Different Trains for String Quartet and Tape—Europe—During the War (movement 2); Lena Griffin "The Ghosts of Pretty Cello Girls"; David Sylvian "Waterfront"}

THE WOMAN IN THE WOOD

Daniel Mills

From the diary of James Addison Thorndike II (1828–1843?)

14th July. Thursday.

Evening. I spent to-day with my Aunt while Uncle Timothy was at work in the fields. His farm is the largest for miles around with hundreds of acres of hilly pasture. There are few trees save for a solitary stand of pine at the edge of his property & the wind is strong & constant. It comes down from the bare mountains & crosses the open fields.

Aunt Sarah is not at all what I expected. She is only a little older than myself though Uncle Timothy is older even than Father. She is his second wife, the sister of a traveling preacher. She speaks plainly & with an accent & is fond of quoting Scripture, as is my Uncle, though she is superstitious as well & shivers to hear the whippoor-wills passing overhead.

The baby Mary is not yet two. Aunt Sarah dotes on her. She carries the child with her all about the house, though she is only a small woman & expecting another besides.

I arrived in the village last night.

It was well past suppertime when the coach reached town & my

Uncle was surprised to learn that my parents had permitted me to make the journey alone.

Later I heard them talking about me. My bedroom is next to theirs at the back of the house & I could hear them quite clearly.

A boy of his age? my Uncle asked. It isn't right.

Surely there's no harm in it, Aunt Sarah said. Traveling on his own.

He isn't yet fifteen.

Aunt Sarah laughed. She said: I weren't much older than that when you met me.

Yes, he said, a little sadly. I remember.

Then came a long pause before my Aunt spoke again. She asked: Is the boy truly ill? His father's letter says he does not sleep or eat—

Of course he isn't ill, my Uncle said. It's country air he needs, that's all.

***

[The following passage is the first of several written in a rushed and nearly illegible script as denoted here by the use of italics. It was subsequently crossed out by the diarist. —*ed.*]

& she's standing by the bed in her nightgown which she slides over her head, smiling as she reveals herself to me. She is white as milk & stinks of sin. Her belly bulges outward where the baby turns & kicks within her & below that the blackened mouth with its lips spread & dripping

***

15th July. Friday.

I found it in the fields near the pine-wood.

The beast was lying on its side & I thought perhaps it was sick. But I smelled the rot as I drew near & saw its blood splashed through the grass—

This morning it rained, though the skies were clear by noon. The day was hot so I wore my linen shirt & trousers. I ate sparingly of the dinner my Aunt had prepared (mutton roasted & charred) and afterward announced my intention to walk outside on my own as Father would never have permitted in Boston.

I walked the fields for the best part of an hour without seeing man or beast. Then I came over a rise & saw the great herd of them before me. They were grazing at the end of the stony pasture: dumb & grunting & caked in their own filth.

I went eastwards & climbed over a wall to the adjoining field where the land slopes down to the neighbors' property & the pine-wood, which lies in a depression between so that none know for certain who owns it (or so my Uncle says).

The grass is higher there & that is where I found the ewe.

Uncle Timothy was at work in the pastures to the south. I ran toward him, waving & shouting & he came to meet me at a sprint. I told him what I had found & he sent me back to the house. Then he called to Auguste, one of the hired men.

Come, he said. And bring your gun.

I went back to the house & told Aunt Sarah that I had found a dead sheep. She said it was probably dogs or a wolf, but Uncle Timothy returned to the house at dusk & said it was likely a wild-cat, though he hadn't heard of them coming so far south, especially in the summer.

Supper was strained & silent. Aunt Sarah was quiet where she sat opposite me & I could not meet her eye without thinking of the pasture & what I had found there.

I had no appetite. I asked my Uncle if I might be excused & he nodded.

So I came upstairs, thinking I might read *Wieland*, which had been Father's gift to me before leaving. But I could not touch my books & I passed the evening by the window, watching the clouds as they covered the moon & the stars.

***

~~without thinking of the beast where it lay in the grass with its mouth
forced open, the jaws broken & the organs wrenched from out the shat=
tered mouth: its heart & lungs & the ropes of its intestines, spread out
on a slick of blood & the stench of shit coming from the mass of them
where the sun's shone down through the day~~

***

There is something else.

After I found the ewe, I turned & ran to fetch my Uncle & nearly
collided with a woman in white who had, it seemed, emerged from
the pine-wood. She was of much an age with my Aunt, though her
dress & bonnet were as fine as anything Mother might wear to a
Society Ball.

She smiled & stepped aside to let me pass, though she did not
speak & appeared untroubled for all that she must have seen the
fallen beast behind me & the long streaks of its blood in the grass.

***

17th July. Sunday.
Church this morning—or "meeting," as they call it here. Uncle
Timothy is a Calvinist of a kind, as is most of the village. The
service lasted til well past noon with much of the town crowding
into the low meetinghouse, apart from my Uncle's hired men (who
are French-Canadian) and the woman I saw in the field, who was
absent.

My Uncle wore his Sunday suit while Aunt Sarah wrapped herself & the baby in a lacy shawl. There was little music but for some
hymns & these were unaccompanied with the preacher (a Mr Gale)
leading the congregation in a reedy voice.

He sang with great feeling of "the redeeming blood" & "the dear slaughtered lamb" & this though he is the town's butcher. I watched him. There was black grit under his fingernails & dark flecks about his beard & lashes. I tried to listen but could not concentrate for the force of the thing inside me & when the bread was passed I would not touch nor taste of it.

Afterward we had our dinner on the town green. Uncle Timothy introduced me to Mr Gale & to his wife (a shy, slight creature) as well as to our nearest neighbors Mr Batchelder & his son, whose farm borders ours along the pine-wood.

He's my brother's boy, my Uncle said. Up for a taste of country living.

No mention was made of my sickness.

Soon the baby coughed & started to cry & I gathered she was hungry. Aunt Sarah excused herself, but later I saw her gossiping with Mrs Gale. The two women huddled together beneath a spreading oak & spoke with lowered voices.

They fell quiet when I approached. Mrs Gale was pale & frightened & she brushed past me as though I weren't there.

I wandered down the green & paused by the gate to the churchyard. I went inside & came upon the place where my Uncle's first wife is buried. Someone (my Uncle?) had placed cut herbs & wildflowers at the base of the stone & these I cleared away to read the words inscribed there.

Martha Jane Thorndike
Who was once well belov'd & who
vanish'd into the wood
19th Aug 1838

No one else was about & I cannot say how long I lingered there. But the light was dimming as I walked up the green & when I reached the steps of the meetinghouse Uncle Timothy rose & said it was time for us to go.

***

watching as the blood seeped into it, turning the bread green & putrid. Corruption spilling from it, a dark fluid. The taste of it filling my mouth & nose & getting into my brain where the blood pulses, black & wild. Beating through the night so I do not sleep & then the woman comes for me, wearing her fine white dress with the skirts lifted up & the black mouth yawning beneath them, opening wide & then wider so her bones crack & break

***

19th July. Tuesday.

I saw her again, the woman in white.

After breakfast, I went with Auguste to the village & helped him unload the ox-cart. We returned to the farm around noon & took our dinner in the empty cart.

Auguste's English is better than that of the other hired men. As we ate, he told me stories of Quebec & of the Cree Indians & of an evil spirit called the Witiko, which possesses sinful men & fills them with unnatural desires.

Then he asked me not to repeat anything I had heard.

It is your Uncle, he explained. He would not like it.

In the afternoon, I crossed the low fields on my own & walked north & east til I reached the edge of the Batchelders' property then climbed uphill along the winding stonewall til I had a view of my Uncle's farm. From there I looked down toward the pine-wood & spied a flutter in the grass where the woman walked, moving away toward the trees.

She wore the same dress as on Friday & her hair, I saw, was long & black, for to-day she wore no bonnet. Her steps she took slowly & with one white hand extended as though to hold the hand of another.

She turned around. The distance between us was great, but I distinctly thought that she smiled at me.

***

Just now I heard them talking, my Aunt & Uncle. They were discussing the dead sheep which I had found near the pine-wood.

That were no wild cat what did it, Aunt Sarah said. No catamount could do as Auguste described to me.

My Uncle said: You've been speaking to Auguste.

I knew you weren't telling me the truth, not all of it. I saw the boy, the way he was shaking—and no wonder. To have seen that poor beast, with the insides sucked out of it—

Quiet yourself, said Uncle Timothy. We shall speak no more of this madness.

It is no madness, she said, to believe the evidence of your own eyes.

***

~~S's mouth clamped over my own. Her tongue pushes past my lips & wraps itself round mine, long & slick as an eel. I bite through it. I choke it down, the twitching weight of it. And then with the Witiko riding me devour her lips & nose, tearing the flesh from the skull til only those eyes remain, crusted round with blood & gazing into mine~~

***

20th July. Wednesday.

My Uncle will not speak of his first wife.

This evening at supper, I mentioned I had visited her grave & read the words carved upon the stone. He did not respond but proceeded to cut his lamb into dry strips, the knife scraping on his plate. Mary slurped & suckled at her mother's breast.

I said: I do not understand. Was she never found?

Uncle Timothy set down his knife. His hands folded themselves into fists & I knew he was angry, though he is not one to show it.

He said: You saw her grave. You know as much as anyone.

And here he stood & stalked away from the table. My Aunt turned in her chair, as though to call him back & the babe's mouth slipped free of her breast, exposing the nipple, which was red & inflamed & with a dribble of milk hanging from it.

She was not embarrassed by this. She shifted the babe against her breast & covered herself with its mouth once more.

She said: Martha went to meet someone. In the wood.

Oh, I said & was ashamed.

It's all right, she said. You weren't to know.

***

~~and felt my teeth bite through the teat, my mouth filling with milk. The foul taste of it, bitter as gall. I am~~

***

21st July. Thursday. Ninety degrees when I awoke. The barometer in the parlor read thirty & rising. Uncle Timothy feared a storm & left before dawn to fetch in the sheep.

In the kitchen Aunt Sarah floated between the counters & the table with her hands dusted in flour, singing to Mary in the cradle.

I went outside. Even with my books & journal I could not bear to be indoors. Again I walked to the edge of the Batchelders' property where it overlooks the pine-wood. The air was damp & sour & there were clouds blowing in so I knew I should turn back but didn't.

Then I smelled it: blood & rot & the odor of sheep's dung. There were five beasts this time, arranged in the grass in a circle with their heads pointing inward. ~~The jawbones were cracked to pieces as before & the steaming mess of their insides pulled out of them.~~

And I think I must have fainted because I remember nothing more until the storm broke & I felt the first of the rain on my face.

I opened my eyes & saw the woman standing over me. The sky sheared in two with a deafening roar. The storm was upon us but she appeared as serene as the angels & wore the lightning about her like a halo, though her lips were red where she had bit through them.

She gathered her skirts into her fingers & lifted them above her knees so I could see it all (*the black mouth yawning...*) and a drop of blood from her mouth spattered her breast.

She walked off toward the wood.

Somehow I made it back to the farm. Auguste met me at the gate. He sheltered me in his coat & ran with me to the house. By then Uncle Timothy had returned but he left again at once.

He was a long time in returning & would not speak of the matter until after supper when I had been sent to bed. I heard them arguing in the room next door: Aunt Sarah's voice shrill & stabbing while Uncle Timothy tried to shout her down.

She said: That devil has come among us again.

Do not speak such foolishness. You'll frighten the boy.

Good, she said. He ought to be scared.

How do you mean?

Those horrible things he reads. That little book he's always writing in. He's terrified of something. Surely you saw the way—

Hush, Sarah. He is ill.

Ill? You said it were country air he needed.

And so it is. We'll go for a walk to-morrow, the four of us. Up Bald Hill if the weather allows for it.

But the sheep—

Auguste can see to them.

I could not make out her response to this. For a time, they were quiet, their argument over & later I heard noises from their room.

***

S moaning as she rides me, her face looming over me, ringed with light like the woman's in the field. A skull with the flesh peeled back, the eyes white & wide. Her fattened belly swinging, slapping against me at every thrust as to smash the child inside, its bones breaking as the dark pours out of her to cover us both

***

22nd July. Friday.
Rain again this morning & lasting through the day. We did not go up Bald Hill. Uncle Timothy forbade me going out-of-doors & I spent the morning in this room, watching from the window as rainclouds drifted in the sky. I wanted to read but could scarcely touch the pages & found I could not concentrate for the images that crowded about me.

Around noon Aunt Sarah called me down for dinner. We ate together while Mary played beneath the table, murmuring to herself & ringing her bell. Presently she crawled away toward the parlor & my Aunt came to sit beside me. Her stomach bulged grossly beneath the plain dress she wore, but her voice was gentle & she did not try to touch me.

She said: The other night you asked us about Martha Thorndike. I told you she went to meet someone, a man. But that was only half the truth.

She leaned back against the chair & looked to the window. The world beyond had vanished into the haze of rain & wind & a long while passed before she continued.

There are things in this world, she said. Evil things, I suppose is what I mean. Timothy says I'm foolish to believe this but even the Word says it's so.

And here she quoted a line from Scripture: The Satyr shall cry to his fellow & the screech owl shall rest there & shall find for herself a quiet dwelling.

Five years ago (she continued), I was about your age. My brother Joshua was older than me by eight years & he used to take me with him when he traveled, preaching the Word to all with ears to hear. We arrived here in the summer, about this time, just before Martha Thorndike was taken. There were sheep-killings then, too.

My brother & I were in town three nights when Martha disappeared. Ran away with a man, Mr Batchelder said, a house-painter, but he was wrong. My brother was last to see her & it weren't a man she was with at all. Joshua was a holy man, God rest him, born with the Gift of Sight. Yet none believed him when he told what he had seen.

It was dusk & he saw Martha walking away toward the pine-wood with her hand out to one side as though it were being held by another though there were none walking beside her—only the old woman riding on her back.

Lilith. The screech owl, the woman in the wood. Old Virginia, I've heard her called, though she isn't always old, for she has such powers over the eyes of men. She sees into your heart, the sin what's written there, and she makes herself out of it. Those she chooses she calls to the woods & rides them down into hell. Those like Martha Thorndike.

Timothy doesn't like to think of it—or of Martha. He believes she deserted him & maybe she did in a way. But he won't visit her grave & it falls to me to keep it tended & clean.

Aunt Sarah fell silent. Her story was finished, but I could think of no response. I told her nothing of what I've seen & experienced since coming here. I think it might have given me some solace, the same as this diary, but words spoken aloud cannot be crossed out or blotted away.

She said: You're trembling.

I did not reply.

She went to the basin & washed her hands, scrubbing the skin raw.

***

~~She could not see the table-knife in my hand or feel the weight of it.
See me driving the tip through her belly again & again, though the
edge is dull & jerks like a saw for to cut the babe from inside her. Then
I hold the thing in my hands, still living: the slaughtered lamb, the
Body & the Blood. Take, he said, and eat of it~~

***

It is not yet dawn.

I slept poorly for dreams of the fields beneath the storm. Again
the sun beat down on me, wilting the grass & turning it yellow as I
approached the circle where the beasts lay slaughtered, their bodies
black & stinking in that heat.

The woman was there. The screech owl, Aunt Sarah called her.

She would not look at me but cradled something in her arms &
sang to it as to a small child. Her voice was low & pretty though I
did not recognize the melody & soon could hear nothing for the roar
of the storm around us.

I came nearer to her. I saw the thing she carried.

***

~~not a child but a lamb which she had pulled, half-formed, from its
mother's womb. The small bones were shattered & the face was missing,
eaten away, and the un-beating heart sucked out of it~~

***

23rd July. Saturday.

The house is quiet. My Aunt & Uncle have not yet returned & this
room is empty of all but my thoughts. Visions swim out of the dusk &
I can hear her calling, singing to me as to the lamb of which I dreamt—

The morning was clear, the barometer creeping up. Uncle Timothy worked through the morning & in the afternoon we went up Bald Hill. My Uncle was first up the path with Mary laughing on his shoulders while Aunt Sarah followed behind with a mildewed parasol.

The path bent sharply then followed the ridge over the valley. The slopes had been cleared of trees years ago but there were some berry bushes beside the path which blocked our view until we reached the summit. Then the bushes fell away with the landscape & the whole of the valley lay open before us, green & yellow & misted with heat.

Uncle Timothy stopped to admire the view. There was a cliff here & a long drop to the valley below, but Aunt Sarah joined him at the edge, quite un-frightened. My Uncle looked back at me with the wind rippling his beard & Mary's fingers twined in his hair.

Come & look, he said to me. But isn't this God's country?

Aunt Sarah asked if I might bring the picnic basket, which I did, though I stopped short of the edge & would not approach any closer. We sat in the grass. My Uncle said a grace. He thanked the Lord for the beauty of His creation & for His Son who saved us with His precious blood. We ate & afterward we lingered near the overlook.

Uncle Timothy produced a psalter from his pocket & proceeded to read some words of praise aloud. He meant them for his wife's ears, I think, though she wasn't listening. She stretched out alongside him with her eyes closed & the sweat glittering on her face.

And then I saw Mary. The child had made her way to the edge of the overlook. She stood there, swaying, about to fall & her curls blowing about in the wind.

I leapt up. I ran toward her.

My Uncle, alarmed, shouted for me to stop. I reached the child where she stood & gathered her into my arms even as Uncle Timothy came up behind me, his boots pounding in the grass. The child squirmed & kicked against me, crying out as I turned toward the valley—

***

And saw the whole of Creation awash in its impurity with man coupling with woman & child & beast & all while the sun poured down upon them, blisteringly hot, blackening the flesh & causing the fat to run, fusing all together in the moment of their ecstasy—a sea of open mouths—and still they did not cease from their depravities.

My parents were there & the Batchelders. My Aunt & Uncle & the baby Mary. And always the Woman passed among them, unnoticed, wearing white like the Lamb & making for the pine-wood. Once she looked back as to make sure I was following, and I was, and I saw the two of us as from a distance, walking hand-in-hand—

***

My Uncle was behind me.

I heard his breath come quick & gasping & glanced back over my shoulder. Aunt Sarah was on her knees, white with terror: the fear of what might happen, what I might do.

I tried to explain. I said: I wanted to save her.

I know, said Uncle Timothy.

She was going to fall, I said.

Please, James. Give her to me now.

***

I ran from him & from the sunlit fields & did not stop until I reached the farmhouse where I collapsed at last, hot & panting & dripping with the stink. That was nearly an hour ago.

Now it is nearly night. The cool of the pine-wood waits for me, the woman called Lilith, the screech owl. She knows the thing that is in me & still she beckons.

I think I will go to her.

BRUSHDOGS

Stephen Graham Jones

J unior wasn't even forty-five minutes into the trees when his son Denny called him on the walkie, to meet back at the truck. Denny was twelve, and Junior could tell he'd got spooked again.

He wasn't going to get any less spooked if Junior called him on it, though.

So, instead of staking out a north-facing meadow like he'd been intending, waiting for the sun to glint off some elk horn, Junior tracked himself back, stepping in his own boot prints when he could. And it's not that he didn't understand: coming out an hour before dawn, walking blind into the blue-black cold, some of the drifts swallowing you up to the hip, it wasn't the same as watching football on the couch.

The bear tracks they'd seen yesterday hadn't helped either, he supposed.

Since then, Junior was pretty sure Denny wasn't so much watching the trees for elk anymore, but for teeth.

He was right to be scared, too. Junior was pretty sure he had been, at that age. But at some point you have to just decide that if a bear's going to eat you, a bear's going to eat you, and then you go about your day.

One thing Junior knew for sure was that if he'd been in walkie contact with *his* dad, then there wouldn't have been any meets at the truck.

Junior was doing better, though. It was one of his promises.

So he eased up to the truck, waiting for Denny to spot him in the mirror. When Denny didn't, Junior knocked on the side window, and Denny led him fifteen minutes up a forgotten logging road to a thick patch of trees he'd probably stepped into for the windbreak, to pee.

"Whoah," Junior said.

It was a massacre. The bear's dining room. At least two winters of horse bones, some of them bleached white, some of them still stringy with black meat.

Junior had to admit it: this probably would have spooked him, twenty years ago.

Hell, it kind of did now.

"They're supposed to be asleep," Denny said. "Right?"

Junior nodded. It was his own words. The tracks they'd seen yesterday, he'd assured Denny, would lead them to a musty den if they followed them.

"Let's go work the Line," Junior said, and Denny was game.

The Line wasn't the one that separated the reservation from Canada, but from Glacier Park. It was just across the road from Chief Mountain.

Twenty-five years ago, Junior had popped his first buck there, across a clearing of stumps he'd been pretending just needed tabletops to make a proper restaurant. That had been his secret Indian trick to hunting, back then: to not hunt. The same way you never find your wallet when you're actually looking for it.

Just, keep a rifle with you.

Junior dropped Denny off right at the gate, told him to walk straight up the fence, and keep an eye out.

"Check?" Denny said into his walkie, stepping out, gearing up.

"Check," Junior said into his walkie, his own voice echoing him.

"Just walk back to Chief Mountain if you lose the fence," Junior told Denny. "You'll hit the road first. I'll be up at that other pull-out. Maybe you'll scare something my way, yeah?"

"Yeah," Denny said, looking at the tree line with pupils shaped like bears, Junior knew.

Junior left him there, pulled over a quarter mile or so up the road.

He hadn't been lying about them scaring elk or some whitetail into each other's paths, either. It was how he'd learned to hunt, his uncles pointing down this or that coulee, telling him to slip down there, make some noise, they'd shoot anything that spooked up.

Denny wasn't just a brushdog, though.

Really, Junior was half-hoping to scare something over to *him*. Every animal on the reservation, it knows to run for the Park when Bambi shooters are in the forest.

The kid deserved an elk this year, or a nice buck. Something to hook him into *this* way of doing things, instead of all the other ways there always were, in Browning.

Junior pulled his gloves on, locked the door, and beat his way through the brush, keeping his rifle high like he was a soldier fording a river, not a latterday Indian with a burned arm and forty-percent disability.

Maybe a half hour into it, half-convinced the world was *made* of trees all blown over into each other, the ground under his boots tilted up sharply. Junior followed, eager for an open space.

Like was supposed to happen, the trees thinned the windier it got—the *higher* Junior got—until he stepped out of the crunchy snow, then onto the blown-flat yellow grass of... not quite a meadow, but a bare knob, anyway. One of a hundred, surely, if you were flying above. But, standing on it, it was the only—no, it *wasn't* the only one: directly to the west of Junior, like a mirror image, like he'd walked up to his own reflection, was another bare knob.

Except this one, it had a little pyramid of black rocks right at the very crest.

Junior looked away to search his head for the word, finally dredged it up: *cairn.*

Like what you arrange over your favorite dog, when the ground's frozen and you can't cut into it with a shovel. Like what you put over your favorite dog for temporary, promising the whole while to come back in spring, do it right.

But you never do, Junior knew.

Because you don't want to have to see.

Except—who would bury a dog way the hell out here?

Maybe this was some super-old grave, some baby from the Lewis and Clark clown parade.

Or maybe it was older. Maybe it was real.

Junior brought his rifle up, leveled the scope on the *cairn* and steadied the crosshairs against the wind, gusting like it knew Junior was trying to draw a bead.

The rocks looked just the same, only closer up now, and trembling, the scope dialed up to 9.

Trembling until they smudged out, anyway.

Junior took an involuntary step back, pressing the scope harder into his right eye socket—*stupid, stupid,* he said to himself—and then got things focused again.

When there was just blackness again, a *fabric* texture to it, Junior lowered the scope, looked across with his real eyes.

Denny.

He'd lost the Line, it looked like, was falling up through the trees as well, his rifle slung over his shoulder.

Instead of doing it like Junior had taught—two steps, stop, listen, look, wait, then two more steps—Denny was just stumbling across the yellow grass, his face slack like he'd been out there for hours, not thirty minutes. One of his gloves was gone, Junior noted.

His first impulse was to put the scope on Denny, so he could give a report later. *Saw you out there, Cold Hand Luke. Didn't you see me?* Except, even if he drew the bolt back on his rifle, just the idea of putting his son in those crosshairs made him feel hollow under the jaw.

Saw you out there, son. By those black rocks.

Junior said it aloud, the wind pulling his words away.

And Denny *was* lost, Junior could tell. With Chief Mountain looming behind, the Park right there to the west, and Canada just a rifle shot to the north, if that, the kid had managed to get off-track somehow. Again. And in spite of how the Line was a three-strand *fence* for the first couple hundred yards. All you had to do then was walk where the fence would have been, if it went on. It didn't even take a sense of direction. The Park Service had come through with chainsaws back when, shaved a line through the woods, to tell the Indians what was America, what wasn't. Just follow the stumps, kid.

Junior *had* told him that at some point, hadn't he?

Now Denny was doing one thing Junior had taught, anyway: going up the closest hill to eyeball for a landmark. To find Chief Mountain, like Blackfeet had been doing since forever.

"Looking the wrong way there, son," Junior said, using his best John Wayne voice.

Soon enough, Denny was going to have to look over, see Junior waiting there for him. Even if he wasn't scoping for Chief Mountain or for the elk he was supposed to be after, then he would at least be checking for the bear he probably thought he was climbing away from. That he could probably hear huffing and grunting right behind him.

His knob of hill was steep enough now that he was having to reach ahead, touch the ground with his bare fingertips.

Junior took a step higher, his back straightening, some alarm ringing behind his eyes.

It was nothing. Stupid.

You're the one being stupid, Junior told himself, in his own dad's voice.

With his hands to the ground like that, Denny had looked like something else. Junior wasn't even sure what. A four-legged, as the old-time Blackfeet said it, in books written by white men.

And Denny *still* wasn't looking across.

"Hey!" Junior called, but didn't put any real force behind it.

Still, Denny's head rotated over at an angle Junior associated with owls more than people, his face snapping up perfectly level, his jaw hanging loose, mouth a skewed black oval, eyes vacant even at this distance, and Junior's breath caught hard enough in his throat that he had to cough.

By the time he was able to look back up, Denny's front hand was reaching forward delicately to the cairn, like warming his palm by a cast-iron stove. Junior brought the soft back of his glove to his face, to rub the blear and the heat from his eyes.

And Denny.

The bald knob across from him, it was just that again.

No rocks, no son. Nothing.

Junior lifted the walkie, said, "Den-man? You out there?"

Fifteen seconds later, the walkie crackled back in Junior's hand.

No words, just static. Open air.

Because of distance, he told himself.

Because these walkies had been clearance over in Cutbank, were pretty much line-of-sight pieces of crap.

When Junior stepped out of the tree line and into the ditch thirty minutes later, ready to tap the horn three times—their signal—there in the passenger seat of the truck was a shape that slowly assembled itself into Denny: hat, jacket, safety-orange gloves, frosted breath.

Behind the steamed-up window, he turned his head to Junior and watched.

***

Because Deezie was in Seattle sitting by her dad's hospital bed, Junior cracked open two cans of chili and poured them into a pan, shook their can shape away.

Denny was in his room, peeling out of his hunting gear. If Deezie were here, he'd have had to strip at the door.

Junior set the pan down into its ring of flame.

On the ride home he'd said the obvious aloud to Denny: that he'd found his other glove, yeah? Good thing they were orange, right?

Denny had looked at his hands in his lap, then out the window.

"I like hunting," he'd said.

They were picking up speed coming through Babb Flats.

Once Junior had seen a whole herd of elk there, pale in the moon-light like ghosts of themselves.

"How many horses do you think it was?" Denny asked then, and came around to face Junior. His face up-close was just normal.

"How many'd that bear eat, you mean?" Junior asked, changing hands on the wheel.

Denny nodded.

"We should have counted the skulls, I guess," Junior said, raising his eyebrows to Denny in halfway invitation.

Deezie wouldn't be home for two more days.

Maybe counting skulls would get Denny over the hump of his fear.

"Grub in ten," Junior called down the hall.

Denny's door was closed. No sounds from in there.

Junior knocked, said it again, about food.

"Check," Denny said, like they were still talking through the walk-ies.

Fifteen minutes later, the game was on and the couch was the couch and Junior was making his same joke to Denny about chili: that people shouldn't eat stuff that looks the same going in as it does coming out. Even Deezie would laugh at that one, some nights.

Like had been happening more and more lately, Junior fell asleep somewhere in the third quarter, woke to an empty room, a flatlined television.

And—an open front door?

"Den-man?" he said out loud, on the chance.

No answer.

Junior crossed to the door, hoisting his rifle up on the way. On *that* chance.

There was nothing, though. Nobody.

Junior had already closed the door when it registered, that something had been different outside. Not wrong, just... not the same.

Because he was the dad and couldn't afford to be scared, he hauled the door open and stepped out without looking first.

His eyes adjusted, fed him what was different.

Another cairn.

Out where the road to their house hooked over the creek.

Another cairn had been stacked out there.

Junior walked half the way there in sock feet, then looked back to the house, sure it was going to be surrounded now by ghost elk, or that there was going to be a figure in the doorway, watching him.

It was just the house. The same one he'd walked out from twenty seconds ago.

"Deezie," he said then, quiet, secret, because her name always reminded him who he was. And because maybe, six hundred miles away, she would hear, look his way, and that would be enough to keep him safe.

To show himself he could—because she might be watching—Junior walked all the way out to the cairn. With his heel, his gun in both hands, he dislodged the top rock, sent it clattering down the side, taking a couple of small pieces of slate with it.

Under that top rock was just another rock. Because it was rocks all the way down. That's all it *could* be.

Cairn was the wrong word, probably. *Pile* would have been better. Like what you end up with when you're trying to plow a field but keep snagging on rocks, keep having to carry them over to the one fence post left from when there were corrals here.

That's all it was.

Junior studied the trees all around, his rifle at port arms, and heard himself telling Denny again that he just had to walk toward Chief Mountain to find the road.

Chief was too far to even see from this side of Browning, though.

Junior shook his head and went inside without looking behind him even once.

Hours later in bed, his leg kicked deep into territory Deezie insisted was hers, Junior realized he was awake, and wasn't sure how long he had been.

After that came the realization that he'd been listening. With his whole body.

Something was moving down the hall, and Junior couldn't have said exactly why, but it was something big, something too big for the hall, but it was lumbering down it all the same.

"Six," he heard himself say, like an offering.

It was how many skulls there had been at the bear's dinner table.

He didn't know if that was a lucky number or not.

He rolled over, away from Deezie's side, and his burned arm crackled under him and he flinched, had to fumble for the light to see that he'd heard wrong. That his arm was just the same, that it wasn't on fire anymore. That all the therapy had worked.

Still, instead of sleeping, he rubbed the lotion into his scar tissue, into the moonscape of his melted skin, and then higher, into his shoulder as well. Just to be sure.

***

"But I want to see," Denny said.

The six skulls.

They were in the truck. The sun was just happening.

"Later," Junior said, and hated himself for it but did it anyway, again: glanced over at Denny's hands.

One of his gloves was safety-orange, but the other was Deezie's wool one. It was white with red-thread stripes that always looked like they were going to catch on something, tear away.

"What about that—that pyramid of rocks yesterday?" Junior said then just real casual, after running it through his head a dozen times, a dozen ways.

In reply Denny looked out his window.

He had no idea about the gloves.

Or the chili still crusted on his lips.

Junior swallowed. It was loud in his ears.

"Who won last night?" he asked.

"Patriots," Denny said.

"Good old Pilgrims," Junior said, leaning forward to rest his fore-arms on the steering wheel.

It was another one of his jokes: of course the Pilgrims won. Look around, right?

"I want to go to the skulls," Denny said, his voice flat.

"After this," Junior said.

"After what?"

"Chief Mountain."

"Chief Mountain," Denny repeated.

Junior moved his mouth in that way he used to do when his broth-er was torturing him and he was promising himself not to cry this time.

He cranked his window down.

"I saw a young bear here once," he said, hooking his chin down the road they weren't taking, the other way through Babb.

Denny looked down that road and Junior held his breath, waited for Denny to call him out: this wasn't Junior's story, it was one of his uncle's. Junior was stealing it.

Denny just looked over, waited for the rest.

"I had that little Toyota then, the hatchback. Jace drives it now. The one with the primered hood?"

Junior could feel his face heating up, even with the window down.

"You were, like, papoose size," he said, and waited for Denny to lodge his objection about that not being a Blackfeet word.

Instead, he just sat there with his one orange hand, his one white hand. Six skulls in his head.

"I was looking for this one old bull I knew had come over from the park," Junior said. "I was just married to your mom then, and we needed meat, yeah?"

No nod.

Just the eyes.

"So I was just cruising along, and this young bear he just comes trotting right up the yellow stripes, his feet flapping like flippers they were so big. Like he was a cartoon of himself. When he stopped beside me to put his paw print on the flank of my trusty steed"—not even a blink of disgust—"I could see his collar, the one that told he was crossing the Line here, that he was on *Indian* land now."

The rest of the story was his Aunt Lonnie, using her favorite nail polish to trace the bear's paw print in the Toyota, but Junior didn't have the heart, and Deezie didn't wear nail polish anyway.

This story had been doomed from the start.

"I miss that Toyota," he said. "It was one of the magic ones, I think."

"Papoose," Denny finally said.

Five minutes later Junior turned them up toward Chief Mountain.

The truck coughed like there was air in the line, but it caught, pulled them up the black ribbon of road, the clouds cold enough that they were skimming the trees.

There was nobody else.

In the summer, people would come up to tie ribbons to certain branches, to trunks that felt right, but in the winter those ribbons were all faded and frozen, their prayers trapped.

"There's where I came out," Junior said, slowing to show his tracks crunching through the crust of snow in the ditch.

Denny was looking higher, though.

Junior slowed to a stop two hundred yards farther up the road, where the next pair of boots had crossed the ditch. And the handprints beside the boots.

Because he'd *fallen*, Junior told himself.

Because he was *twelve*.

"This is you," he said, and Denny looked over to him, then back out into the trees.

"You don't remember, do you?" Junior said, the lump in his throat cracking his voice up.

"We were here yesterday," Denny said.

"We were here yesterday," Junior said, and, because that's what you do, Denny stepped down.

"It's loud in there," he said, pointing with his face into the trees.

"Scare something good my way," Junior told him, instead of everything else.

Denny kept looking.

"There's a restaurant out there somewhere," Junior said then, having to close his eyes to get it said, his chin trembling. "There's no tabletops, but it used to be a—a place."

"A restaurant," Denny said, looking back to Junior, not seeming to care he was sitting there behind the wheel crying.

"They served venison," Junior said, and looked hard the other way, toward Chief Mountain, stationed up in the clouds like a sentinel.

Junior prayed it was watching right now.

After a thirty-count, he looked back to the other side of the road.

Denny was gone, into the trees.

Junior turned around, pulled down to where he'd gone in yesterday—everything had to be the same—and stepped in all his same footprints as close as he could, and, crashing through the trees like he was, he could almost feel his uncles on the rise behind him, waiting for what he was about to flush out.

If they were still around, they could have told him what's buried in the cairns, he knew.

Or told him not to look.

But it was too late now. He was already doing it. *They* were already doing it, him and Denny, Den-man, father and son out in the woods, in the cold, trying to undo the day before, and Junior only realized it was too late when he opened his mouth to call to Denny and static from the walkie came out.

From deeper in the trees, his real son opened his mouth, answered with that same open-air hiss, and like that they felt toward each other in the new darkness.

YMIR

John Langan

I saw how the night came,
Came striding like the color of the heavy hemlocks
—Wallace Stevens

I

There was a child standing in the road.

Even as Marissa was jerking her foot from the gas, feathering the brake so as not to throw the Hummer into a skid, she was registering the child's threadbare clothes—rags, really—its bare arms and legs, its uncovered head, all impossible here, a hundred some miles south of the Arctic circle. The Hummer shimmied on the ice. From its back seat, Barret—Barry, he insisted she call him—said, "What is it?"

The child's hair was thick, black, long enough for a girl but not too long for a boy. Its wide eyes were brown; its exposed skin was an olive that had been sun-darkened. Although the Hummer was slowing, it was not doing so quickly enough to prevent it running over the child, the child who could not be here, in the middle of a road across a wide, frozen lake in northwestern Canada, twenty miles from the nearest human settlement.

"Marissa?" Barry said.

What else could it be but a hallucination, a manifestation of the PTSD she'd prided herself on managing so well since her return from the sand, from Iraq? "It's nothing," she said; though she did not return her foot to the gas, yet. "I thought I saw something in the road."

"Up here?" Barry said. "Not likely. At least, I don't think it is. Do they have caribou in these parts?"

"I don't know."

The child was ten yards in front of her. History prepared for its first, tragic repetition.

"It wasn't a polar bear?" Barry's voice betrayed his eagerness that it was.

"It wasn't."

She lost sight of the child beneath the hood. There was no thud of metal striking flesh, no barely perceptible tremor in the steering wheel. When she checked the rearview mirror, no small form lay crumpled and bloody on the ice. Her vision wobbled as her heart surged with relief. She let the Hummer coast until her pulse did not feel as if it were going to burst her throat, then put her foot back on the gas.

II

"You saw some crazy shit over there," Delaney said. They were on the beach, sitting on the lounge chairs the resort stationed there, passing a bottle of Kahlúa back and forth. Delaney had wrinkled his nose at the sight of the liquor, said he preferred his alcohol to taste like alcohol, not candy, but Marissa said it was what she had at hand, and if he didn't like it, he didn't have to drink it. After a night of screwing in her air-conditioned hotel room, they had ventured into the steaming air to watch the sun rise over the Gulf. A pleasant lassitude, yield of the last week's drunk and the last three nights' furious sex with Delaney, suffused her.

His words, however, curdled her satisfaction. She said, "Says who?"

"Says you." He drank from the Kahlúa, grimaced. "Jesus." He held the bottle out to her. "You talk in your sleep."

Marissa took the liquor. Across the Gulf, the line of the horizon was becoming more distinct, the sky fading from navy blue to pearl. "What did I say?"

Delaney shrugged. "Nothing too specific. You sounded pretty upset."

The drink was suddenly too sweet. She swallowed hard and returned the bottle to Delaney.

"I'm guessing you were Army," he said once it was clear she wasn't speaking. "I know women aren't supposed to be in combat roles; I also know things don't always work out that way. What was that girl's name? Jessica something."

"Lynch—Jessica Lynch."

"Right."

In the thickets to either side of the beach, songbirds were anticipating the dawn, their whistles long and liquid. She said, "I wasn't in the Army. I was a driver—private contractor for a group called Stillwater."

"Weren't they—"

"They did a lot of security work around Baghdad. But they had their fingers stuck in all flavors of pie. I was in West Virginia, Charleston, driving tankers full of you-don't-want-to-know-what from one coal plant to another. The money wasn't nearly as good as you would have expected. Stillwater put out the word they were looking to hire drivers to transport supplies from Baghdad to points all over. Starting pay was three times what I was making stateside, with gold-plated benefits, as well. It was no secret the situation over there wasn't nearly as rosy as the president and his cronies were claiming, but the Stillwater rep assured me we'd be using only secure roads. I knew it was a risk, but I figured I'd do it for a year, two at the outside—long enough to accumulate a nice little nest egg for myself. I thought I might be able to parley this position with Still-water into a better one, maybe driving a limo for some corporate bigwig. I had my livery license; just wasn't anyone interested in hiring me to use it in Charleston.

"Anyway, Iraq was a fucking disaster. Since the roads we were driving were supposed to be safe, they were lightly guarded, if at all. How long do you suppose it took the insurgents to figure that out? The second day I was in Baghdad, the guy who was in charge of my convoy, a big Texan named Shea, took me aside and handed me a duffle bag. Inside it was an AK-47, with half a dozen magazines. 'This'll come out of your first paycheck,' he told me. Called it a mandatory expense. He offered to show me how to use it, but I said I was fine. My daddy'd taught me how to rifle-hunt; I guessed I could work out this thing if I had to. Shea had no trouble with that. He insisted, on penalty of automatic dismissal, that I have the AK on the seat beside me for the duration of any and all runs I made as part of his team. If we stopped at any location that was not secure, which was everyplace between Baghdad and our destination, I was not to leave my cab without that weapon. Doing so was a fire-able offense.

"Intense, right? Most of the guys I drove with were like that. The Army said they'd do what they could for us, but they'd invaded with too few troops in the first place, far from enough to occupy the country, and with the insurgents popping up all over the place, there generally weren't enough of them available to accompany us. Once in a while, we'd luck into a couple of Humvees with .50 cals. They didn't do much to reassure me, themselves, but I assumed if we came under fire, we had a better chance of getting rescued with them than we did without them."

Above, clouds caught the light of the imminent sun and kindled white and gold. Below, the ocean went from slate to deep blue. Marissa held out her hand, and Delaney pressed the bottle into it. She raised it to inspect its contents, said, "When I started drinking alcohol, this was my drink of choice, this and Baileys. This was in high school, senior year. Girly drinks, the guys called them, but what the fuck did they know. Girly," she pfffed her disdain. "They'd stand around someone's car or pickup, drinking their cheap, crappy beer, showing off their varsity jackets like a bunch of goddamn peacocks flaunting their tails. One kick, and the biggest of them would've been down with a broken leg, a set of busted ribs."

"Tae kwon do?" Delaney said.

"Tang soo do," Marissa said. "Third degree black belt. *Sam Dan.*"

"Huh. You keep up with it?"

"Not formally. I train on my own, for what it's worth. What about you?"

"A little of this, a little of that. I'm more a learn-as-you-go kind of guy."

"Is that so?"

"It is."

The Kahlúa was still too sweet, but drinking it no longer made her feel as if she was going to vomit.

"I'm wondering," Delaney said, "if you'd be interested in a job."

III

The Eckhard Diamond Mine was a collection of Quonset huts set back from the rim of a titanic hole in the endless white. Barry leaned forward for a better view of it, whistling appreciatively. "Isn't that something? How far across would you say that is?"

"A quarter-mile," Marissa said.

"I expect you're right."

She stopped the Hummer at the front door of the metal shed closest to the pit. The light green paint that had coated the structure was visible only in scattered flakes and scabs. She left the motor running: the digital thermometer on the dash measured the outside temperature at forty below, and she didn't want to risk the engine not starting. For the same reason, she was carrying the heavily oiled .38 revolver in a shoulder holster under her coat. She zipped and buttoned the coat, pulled on the ski mask and shooting mittens lying on the passenger's seat, and tugged her hood up. She half-turned to the back seat. "You ready, Barry?"

He had encased his bulk in a coat made of a glossy black material that made her think of seal skin. The gloves on his large hands were of the same substance. He drew a ski mask in the gray and electric green of the Seattle Seahawks down over his broad, bland face. "Ready," he said. "Let's go look at my new investment."

Marissa had expected their arrival to draw some kind of reception from whoever was inside the hut. The moment she stepped outside, however, into cold that shocked the air from her lungs, that she felt crystallizing the surfaces of her eyes, she understood why those inside and warm might prefer to reserve their greetings for her and Barry joining them. The cold seemed to take her out of herself; it was all she could do to keep track of Barry as he lumbered the fifteen feet to the hut's entrance. Without bothering to knock, he wrenched the door open and squeezed through the frame. Marissa followed, giving the area surrounding this end of the building a quick once-over. She wasn't expecting to see anything besides the Hummer with its schoolbus yellow paint, a steady cloud of exhaust tumbling from its tailpipe, the great hole in the earth in the background. Nor did she.

IV

"His name is Barret Langan," Delaney said. "He was friends with a guy I used to work for."

"Why don't you take the job, then?"

"I'm happy where I am."

"What makes you think I'm not?"

"Maybe you are." Delaney accepted the bottle from her. The rising sun had ignited the sea to platinum brilliance.

She said, "What's the job?"

"He's looking for a driver, mainly. But it wouldn't hurt if you knew how to take care of yourself, which it sounds like you do."

"Why? What is this guy, some kind of gangster?"

"He's a man with a lot of money," Delaney said, "a little of which he inherited, more of which he married into, and most of which he made by taking the money that had come his way and investing it."

"So he needs, like, executive protection?"

"Not exactly. From what I understand, the guy spends maybe fifteen minutes a day working—talking to his investment manager, that kind of stuff. The rest of the day, he... wanders around."

"What do you mean?"

"I mean he wanders around. He's in Olympia, right? In Washington. Say he watches something on TV about a donut shop in Portland: he goes to Portland."

"In Oregon?"

"Yeah."

"Is that far?"

"For a fucking donut, it is."

"Is he married?"

"Macy, yeah."

"And she's okay with him taking off for Portland?"

"She's got her own things going, charities, mostly. She's out of the house as much as he is."

"Is this her idea? Get him a babysitter?"

"Don't know. From things I overheard him saying to Wallace— my old boss—he's walked into some pretty dodgy places. Bars so far off the beaten track, they aren't even a rumor. Ghost towns that were never on the map to begin with. Old industrial sites. I gather he's run into some less-than-wholesome characters. Could be he's just being prudent. Funny thing is, the guy's enormous, six eight, three-twenty, easy. Hands like canned hams. You'd think the sight of him would be enough to steer most trouble in the other direction."

"Size isn't everything."

"That's not what you said last night."

"Really?"

"Anyway," Delaney said, "the job's there if you want to look into it."

The sun had lifted over the horizon, lighting the landscape to gold-tinted colors. Marissa said, "If I were interested in this position, how much are we talking? Fifty? Sixty? I heard some of the guys who ferried around the Stillwater execs drew down as much as eighty."

"You'd have to do your own negotiating," Delaney said, "but I can guarantee you'd be making three times that, at least."

"Jesus," Marissa said. "Are you serious?"

He nodded. "Understand, you'd have to be available twenty-four/seven."

"For that kind of money, I'll sleep at the foot of his fucking bed."

"You want me to put you in touch with him?"

"Might as well. What's the worst that could happen?"

"Don't say that," Delaney said.

V

Inside, the Quonset hut was a poured concrete floor and metal ribs arching overhead. It had to be warmer than outside, but not by enough to matter. By what light the cloudy windows admitted, Marissa saw that, with the exception of a large, metal cage at its center, the structure was empty. Without hesitation, Barry strode to the cage, which appeared to contain another cage—an elevator, Marissa realized, it was an elevator. Barry swung open the cage door, and stepped into the car, which creaked with his bulk. A black box with a row of rectangular switches had been mounted to his right; he snapped all up at once. Within the elevator, a pair of halogen lights hung in opposite corners flared to life, while the air filled with the nasal hum of electricity. After making certain the door to the place was shut, Marissa crossed to the elevator. It shifted slightly with her weight. A narrow black box with two buttons set one below the other attached to the wire to her left. Barry nodded his ski-masked head at it. "If you would…"

She stabbed the lower button with a mittened finger. The car clattered, shook, and commenced a shuddering descent. Although her face was covered, she supposed her skepticism was evident. She said, "I was under the impression this place was more of a going concern. How long has it been since it was active?"

"As a diamond mine, thirty years, give or take. From the start, it was never as productive as its backers predicted. What diamonds were here were dug out almost immediately. The operation chugged on for a few more years, after which, it was leased to a pair of scientists."

"Scientists?"

"I met one of them; though I didn't know it at the time. At one of Manny and Liz Steiner's parties, a Dr. Ryoko. He and his colleague used the lower reaches of the mine for some type of subatomic research. Had to do with exploiting the layers of rock to slow down the speed of some exotic particles enough for them to be measured. After they left, the mine lay dormant for a decade and half, until a man named Tyler Choate paid a ridiculous sum of money to have the use of the location for three months."

The elevator lowered past an unlit tunnel. Marissa said, "What for?"

"That is a very interesting question. No one I talked to—and I spoke with a number of people—could answer it. I had to turn to a woman who's good with computers to find out exactly how much his rental cost Mr. Choate. I'm used to large amounts of money. This was enough to impress me.

"To make matters more perplexing," Barry said, "Tyler Choate undertook this course of action while an inmate at a maximum-security prison, where he was serving twenty-years-to-life for some especially nasty sex-crimes. Where, as far as I've been able to ascertain, he continues to pay his debt to society."

Marissa was about to ask him if he was sure, stopped herself. Of course he was. When Barry became interested in something—truly interested—he researched the subject as thoroughly as any scholar.

Instead, she said, "I'm guessing that Tyler Choate led you to this place, and not the other way around."

"That's right, Barry said. "You're wondering why."

"Yeah."

"When Delaney informed you I was looking to hire someone, he told you that he knew me through his employer, Wallace Smith. Did he tell you what happened to Wally?"

Another dark tunnel rose in front of the elevator door. "Just that he was dead. And," she added, "that Delaney had nothing to do with it. To be honest, he seemed kind of spooked by the whole thing."

"As well he should have been. No one has been able to say with any certainty what became of the man—of him and Helen, his wife. She had suffered a grievous injury and was being cared for at their house. One morning, she, Wally, and her nurse disappeared. Most of them did, anyway. There were… pieces of them left behind. Strictly speaking, there's no definite proof that Wally is dead—that any of them is. But it doesn't look good. The police were treating it as a probable multiple homicide."

"So Tyler Choate's some kind of crime boss, and your friend crossed him."

"That sounds as if it should be what occurred," Barry said. "I'm pretty sure it's the theory the cops are working from. From a distance—from what I've told you—it's the reasonable explanation. Wally's wife was injured in a barn that was connected to the Choates. This set him off in search of information about them. He hired a private detective, a man named Lance Pride; he was the one who located Tyler Choate."

"Wait," Marissa said, "the guy's wife was hurt in a barn? What happened?"

Barry considered the latest tunnel that had opened before them. "A horse kicked her in the head. Split her skull open. A freak accident, but it left her with massive brain damage."

"Ouch. I guess that explains why he was so keen to get hold of whoever owned the barn."

"The horse kicked Wally, too—ruined his hip, left him unable to walk without a cane. That didn't matter as much as the wound to Helen, though."

"What became of the horse?"

"Delaney shot it."

"Oh."

"Anyway—what I started to say was, when I began to poke around into Wally and Helen's disappearance, into the weeks leading up to it, what appeared to be the reasonable explanation fell apart right away. For one thing, the Choates weren't your typical crime family. Almost the opposite, in fact. Pig farmers and super-scientists. I know, it sounds bizarre, but several of the men in the family had careers of some note. In physics, mostly. They also raised pigs on their property, to no great profit, from what I could determine. Members of the family came and went from view. Sometimes this was because they were visiting universities, research labs, think tanks, consulting on theoretical problems and their practical applications. I'll be honest: I couldn't tell you what the hell they were studying, and I flatter myself I'm intelligent. Some of the projects had to do with fairly exotic subatomic particles, which may explain Tyler's interest in this mine."

"You said he was in prison," Marissa said, "Tyler."

The air had warmed sufficiently for them to remove their ski masks, which Barry did, leaving tufts of his fine hair half-raised. "He is. I gather he was as gifted as the rest of the family, but chose a career in law enforcement, instead. Presumably, to allow him a safe vantage point from which to pursue his less-wholesome activities."

"He was the bad apple," Marissa said. "The rest of the family was okay—weird, but okay—and he was into bad shit. Your friend messed with him, and Tyler had him taken care of. If he's important enough, then him being in prison doesn't matter. He wants to reach out and touch someone, he can do it."

"All very rational," Barry said, "except, there's no evidence linking him to any larger criminal network, not even in rumor. He appears to be a model inmate; at least, his warden thinks so."

Marissa pulled off her ski mask, stuffed it in her coat pocket. "Okay," she said. "I want to say maybe the Choates are a dead-end, but we're here, so I assume they're not."

They passed the entrance to a larger tunnel. "He called me," Barry said. "Tyler Choate. Last week. I've spent a lot of time and treasure on this matter. I've investigated the Choates as extensively as did Wally. Hell, I succeeded in laying hands on the transcript of a cassette tape Lance Pride sent to Wally about a supposed visit he paid to Tyler Choate in his prison cell. It's nonsense, but I read it half a dozen times. I've had Wally and Helen's histories put under the microscope, too. I've stood in the room where the pieces of them were found. It's been scrubbed clean, of course, but I swear, there is a feel to that space... It's as if, when you notice the walls and ceiling out of the corners of your eyes, they aren't meeting the way they should. But what other effect would you expect the site of such violence to have?

"The problem is, none of what I've found fits together. Despite my best efforts, I've been unable to arrange the information I've gathered into a coherent whole that will explain my friend's fate. From what I understand, the police have encountered the same difficulty. I've kept on searching—it was what led me here, to Eckhard. I did my homework; I knew that the mine was tapped out decades ago. I suspect the consortium who've purchased it intend to set it up as some type of tax dodge. I don't judge them; I've done the same thing, myself. What caused me to reach out to them was the fact that Tyler Choate had made use of the mine. In turn, this drew his attention to me."

"What did he say?"

"He asked me if I was a student of mythology."

The entrance to the next tunnel was smaller. "Mythology?"

"I said I'd read Bulfinch when I was younger, Edith Hamilton. Good, he said, I was familiar with the story of Ymir."

"Ymir."

"It's part of the Norse creation myth. Ymir is a giant, inconceivably huge. The god, Odin, together with his brothers Vili and Vé, kills Ymir, then uses the pieces of his corpse to build the world. His skull becomes the sky, his blood the sea—you get the idea."

"Lovely."

"These are the Vikings we're talking about. They weren't famed for their refined sensibilities."

"Okay—what does this have to do with anything?"

"Picture, Choate said, a being that size, vast enough that the inside of its skull could form the entire sky. How long did I suppose it would take for a creature that enormous to die? Eons as we measure time, even as our gods do. All the time Odin and his kin were carving up Ymir, tossing his brains up into the air to make the clouds, they were surrounded by his dying thoughts. When Ragnarok—their apocalypse—came, and everything went down in fire and ruin, it was only the last of those thoughts, coming to its end."

"That's pretty trippy," Marissa said, "but I don't—"

"Suppose," Barry went on, "you could drill into that giant skull, through to whatever remained of its brain. A sublime trepanation, he called it. Wouldn't you need a plane for that, I said, if we were inside the giant's head? That was taking the myth too literally, Choate said. What it described was the fall of a being—the catastrophic fall, the Big Bang as the original murder—in whose remains all of us were resident. We—everything was living inside this dying titan. Our solar system was a bacterium subsisting on its cooling flesh. Quite a hopeless situation, he said, no less for him and his family. The Choates had scaled the evolutionary ladder, climbed so high above their fellow apes they could no longer see them below, but for all that, they were little better than tapeworms gorging themselves in the loops of the giant's rotting intestines."

How many tunnels had they passed? All full of darkness that had a curiously flat quality, as if it had been painted on the rock face. Barry said, "There are points, however, where the tractability of the quantum foam might permit you to pierce the giant's forehead, to expose the surface of that great brain. You might stand at one end of an unbelievably long tunnel and watch thoughts light Ymir's cerebrum like chains of bursting suns. If you could decode those lights, who could say what you might learn?"

"All right," Marissa said, with sufficient force to interrupt Barry's reverie. "We've moved from trippy to batshit insane."

"I know, I know." Barry shook his head. "The man's voice… it was as refined, as precise, as an Oxford don's. It seemed to surround me. I wanted to ask him about Wally, say, How are you connected to my friend's death? But as long as he was speaking, I couldn't force the words out. They were trapped by Choate's voice. I had the sense that he knew exactly what my question was, but he never answered it. Instead, he invited me to meet him here, today. I agreed. I knew he was still in prison—and I double-checked, after the call ended—but I also knew I would keep our appointment. And," Barry opened his hands to take in the elevator, the surrounding rock, "here we are."

Half a dozen comments competed for Marissa to voice them, ranging from piteous ("Oh, Barry.") to scornful ("Seriously? This is why we drove to the ass-end of nowhere?"). All were choked off when movement to her left drew her eyes to that corner of the elevator, where she saw the same child who had stood in front of her on the ice road. Its eyes were wide, its mouth open.

VI

After her breathing had returned to normal, Marissa rose from the bed, pulled off the baseball cap and sunglasses Delaney had asked her to wear, and tugged on a t-shirt. Rather than returning to the king-sized bed, she settled in one of the chairs beside the small table that served as her personal bar. Most of the bottles ranged on it were down to a film tinting their glass bottoms, but the Baileys sloshed when she hefted it by the neck, and that was fine. She wasn't certain Delaney was awake; she didn't bother checking before she started to speak.

"On the beach," she said, "earlier, I never finished what I was saying to you."

He mumbled what could have been, "Doesn't matter," his words
already half a snore.

She swallowed a mouthful of Baileys. It had been a week since she
had not been drunk. Each day's biggest challenge lay in consuming
enough alcohol to maintain the pleasant version of the state, without tipping over into anger and self-pity. She said, "This one day,
my convoy was caught in an ambush. Textbook example of how to
spring one. There were eight of us, traveling west to one of the bases,
there. I was third in line. The country was flat, which somehow registered in how big the sky felt. We stuck to the middle of the road,
which ran through neighborhoods of squat, sand-colored houses,
past palm trees and these big bushes whose name I couldn't remember. The ground was dry; the rigs pulled up rooster-tails of dust as
they went. There wasn't any speed limit—well, none that we kept to.
In front of some of the houses, groups of men in white robes and red
headscarves watched us pass. A few of them threw rocks; although it
was more the kids, teenagers and younger, who did that. They had
a pretty good aim, too. I'd adjusted to the crack of a rock striking
the windshield, the bang when it struck the door. We hadn't been
driving that long when the guys ahead of me slowed, fast. Over the
radio, I heard Grant, in the lead truck, say, '—in front of me,' and
then the IED detonated.

"I saw the explosion, the jet of smoke; I heard the boom, like one
of those big fireworks they set off towards the end of Fourth of July
displays, the kind of sound you feel deep in your chest. It blew out
Grant's windows, shredded his tires, tore the shit out of his engine.
Probably concussed Grant, too; although, the insurgents shot him,
so who knows? Everything came to a halt. I knew we'd been hit, and
when the shooting started, I knew it wasn't over. After the bomb,
the gun sounded almost tiny, like strings of firecrackers. I wasn't
sure, but I thought we were being targeted from the windows of a
couple of houses on either side of the street. Crossfire, right? Most

of the fire concentrated on the first truck, but I heard McVey, who was in the second truck, screaming that his windshield was full of holes, and he was pretty sure they'd hit his engine, too, because it was dead.

"Everyone was on the radio at the same time. Shea, the head driver, who was fifth in line, kept trying to raise Grant. 'Grant,' he said, 'move ahead.' Finally, McVey told him Grant was dead, and things weren't looking too good for him, either. 'All right,' Shea said, 'you're going to have to pull around him.' 'No can do,' McVey said, his rig was not moving. Shea couldn't—this was the guy who'd come off as such a badass the first time I met him. Now that the shit was burying the fan, he couldn't process what was happening. He must've told McVey to drive around Grant half a dozen times. McVey said he would love to, but his truck wouldn't move.

"The whole time, the insurgents kept firing, pop pop pop. A bullet punched through the top of my windshield. My AK was on the passenger's seat; I was waiting for Shea to tell us we were going to have to leave our trucks and take the fight to our attackers. At the very least, I was expecting him to direct us to rescue McVey. Because it would have to be us. Someone had radioed the Army for assistance—it must have been Shea—and the woman on the other end told him to wait for an answer that still hadn't come. My heart had shrunk somewhere deep down in my gut. The base of my throat hurt. I was wearing the flak jacket and helmet the company had issued us, but I didn't rate its chances of stopping a bullet from an AK too high. Any minute, I expected the insurgents to leave their windows, or start targeting the rest of us. But all they did was empty magazine after magazine into Grant and McVey's rigs. McVey had gone from demanding help to repeating this kind of prayer, 'Jesus, Jesus Christ, oh Jesus, save me, Jesus Christ.' There was room to the right of his truck, maybe enough for me to squeeze through. I thought I might be able to roll up beside him, use my truck as a shield to let him escape from his and climb in beside me. I could picture myself doing this, but I couldn't do anything to make it happen. My left hand was on the wheel, my right was on the gearshift; my left foot had the clutch pressed in, my right was over the gas— and I sat where I was. Shea was speaking to me, had caught up with the situation and was saying I had to pull around McVey and lead the group out of there. I didn't."

Her throat was dry. She took a generous pull on the bottle. "They had started kidnapping contractors, the insurgents. They were posting videos to YouTube of these guys sitting cross-legged on the floor, their hands tied behind their backs, surrounded by men in black ski masks. All of them denounced the occupation, a few made requests for ransoms. One guy was murdered, there, on camera, his throat slashed and his head cut off while he was dying. Afterwards, the murdering fuck who'd done it held up the poor guy's head like it was some kind of trophy. There was this expression on the dead man's face... I don't know how to describe it. He looked sick, as if he'd been choking on his own death. I want to say that this was what was keeping me from moving. Maybe it was. Shea was telling me to put the truck in gear and step on the gas. McVey was crying, 'Jesus,' over and over again. My nostrils were full of the burnt stink of gunpowder. The insurgents' guns rattled on, blowing out another of McVey's tires. 'Move,' Shea was saying. I couldn't believe how level his voice was. 'You have to move.'

"Then I was. I can't say what happened. One moment, I was paralyzed; the next, I had the truck in first and was spinning the wheel to the right. It was a tight fit between McVey's truck and a couple of those heavy bushes, but I cleared it. Bullets smacked the passenger door. One punched through and drilled the seat beside me. I didn't slow beside McVey's cab. I didn't look over at it, or at Grant's rig, still burning. I focused on the road before me, and that allowed me to see the child standing in the middle of it in plenty of time. I couldn't say if it was a boy or a girl. It was young—six, seven—dressed in rags. Barefoot. I thought about Grant's sudden stop. There had been reports of insurgents putting children in the way of approaching convoys and, when the trucks slowed, hitting them. I hadn't believed the stories—hadn't wanted to—but it appeared that was precisely what had occurred, here.

"Passing Grant's truck, I steered left, in an effort to avoid the remains of the IED scattered across the road. This set me straight towards the child. I wanted to turn right, but I had to wait for the truck's back wheels to clear the bomb wreckage, and by the time they did, I was already too close. I pulled the wheel around, anyway, shouting at the kid to get out of the way, but even if it had heard me over the roar of the engine and the popping of the guns, I doubt it understood English. It stood there, its eyes wide, its mouth open, its arms hanging at its sides. I could have stomped the brake and done what I could to miss the child, but I didn't. It was like, now that I had put myself in motion, I wasn't about to stop.

"There should have been no way for me to feel the truck striking something that small. Yet I'm positive a slight tremor ran though the steering wheel as I sped past the place where the child was standing. I didn't check my mirrors for anything lying in the road.

"Later, after we'd pulled into our destination and were sitting around the mess hall, I asked Shea if he'd noticed a child's body a little way past Grant's truck. Yeah, he said, he'd seen a body there that must have been a kid's. Motherfuckers must have stationed it there to stop Grant, then, when they set off the IED, it was killed in the blast. 'Savages,' he said. 'Motherfucking savages.' I said nothing to contradict his version of events."

The bottle of Baileys was empty. Marissa turned it in her hands. She thought Delaney was asleep, but she wasn't certain. She sat where she was, and did not say anything else.

VII

With a shuddering clash, the elevator came to a halt.

"End of the line," Barry said, and slid back the door.

The child was still in the car, its expression of horror unchanged.

Barry stepped out into darkness. For a moment, Marissa was alone in the car with the child. *Not real*, she thought. *It's not real. There is nothing standing there.* Then the tunnel at whose end they had arrived filled with pale, flickering light as Barry flipped the switch that turned on the fluorescent lights set in its ceiling. "It's this way," he said and, without waiting for her, set off.

Pulse thudding, she fled the elevator, rushing ahead of Barry. She swallowed, said, "You should let me go first."

He grunted.

To give her hands something to do, she unsnapped the row of buttons fastening her jacket over top of its zipper, pinched the zipper's tongue, and eased it down far enough at allow her access to her pistol in its shoulder-holster. She considered tugging off her mittens, but decided that the air, while warmer than it was at the surface, was not that warm. Although she could sense the child at her back, she did not turn her heard. Instead, she said, "This Wallace—you guys must have been pretty close."

"Oh?" Barry said. "What makes you say that?"

The tunnel was surprisingly finished, its floor and rounded walls concrete. The lights buzzed. "Well," she said, "I mean, here we are, right? I'd have to check the odometer for the exact mileage, but we've come pretty far. Not to mention, all the other stuff you've been up to. You don't do that for just anyone."

"I suppose not," Barry said, though the tone of his voice was threaded with doubt. "Wally was a friend, of course. We certainly drank enough of one another's Scotch. There wasn't a function amongst our set that the two of us didn't attend, and exchange a few words at. He'd traveled quite a bit, and if we were stuck for conversation, we would compare notes on Finland, or Egypt, or Mongolia. We were forever going to do something together, plan a return trip to one of those countries, take our wives someplace new. We got along all right. I had the sense that, wherever we went, we'd have a fine time, together."

The tunnel curved to the left. Marissa wondered how far down the pit—or beneath it—their ride had taken them. She did not look behind her.

"I'm sorry," Barry said. "'A fine time together:' sounds like something out of bloody F. Scott Fitzgerald, doesn't it? Chin chin, old boy, jolly good. Or maybe Wodehouse. The fact is, we weren't especially close. After he died—disappeared, but who is anyone kidding?—afterwards, I was waiting for one of Wally's other friends, the fellows I considered his close friends, Skip Arden or Randy Freeman, to step forward, keep up with the police investigation, ensure that everything that could be done was being done to locate whoever was responsible and bring them to account. No one took that step—Skip and Randy seemed to have fallen off the face of the earth—so eventually, I did. I picked up the phone and dialed the police because I could, because it was necessary that someone should do so and I was available. You could call it loyalty, I suppose. It's difficult to speak about without sounding ridiculous to yourself."

"It's okay," Marissa said, "I understand loyalty."

In front of her, the tunnel dead-ended in a concrete wall in which a flat, gray metal door was centered. Marissa said, "Through here?"

"I assume so."

She pulled off her right mitten and reached inside her coat for the pistol. She withdrew it from its holster, and let it hang muzzle-down in her hand as she approached the door.

"What is it?" Barry said.

"Just being cautious."

A simple doorknob swung the door in. A wave of warm, humid air spilled over her. A rough, unlit corridor stretched maybe fifty feet to a doorway full of soft, yellow light.

"Well?" Barry said.

Before she could answer, the silhouette of an enormous man occulted the doorway. Marissa raised the .38. Mouth dry, she called, "Hello?"

The voice that answered made her want to scream. "Is that Barret Langan?" it called.

"It is," Barry said. "Is that Tyler Choate?"

"The very same," the voice said. "And you brought a little friend."

"Ms. Osterhoudt sees to my well-being," Barry said. "I'm sure you have employees who do the same for you."

"Not employees, no," Tyler Choate said. "I prefer to think of them as associates, fellow-travelers who have not progressed as far along the particular road we walk. Nonetheless, your point is taken. I would consider it a favor, though, if she would lower her pistol. Good manners, you know."

"Go ahead," Barry said, "but keep it handy."

Whatever rock the corridor had been carved from was full of tiny crystals that caught the lights shining at either end of the passageway and glowed like stars. Some peculiarity of the walls' contours leant the crystals the impression of depth, so that, in walking the passageway, Marissa had the impression of crossing a bridge spanning the stars. The sensation received a boost when she noticed that certain groupings of the lights seemed to align into patterns, constellations; albeit, none of them familiar. She could not hear her boots scraping the floor. She glanced down, and saw a ball of light streak from left to right, apparently far below her. *Shooting star*, she thought, then, *That's ridiculous.* All the same, the relief that suffused her on reaching the other end of the corridor—from which Tyler Choate had withdrawn—was palpable.

She stepped out onto a white marble floor. Directly in front of her, plush leather seats ringed the base of a sizable marble column. A newspaper lay folded on one of them. A mural whose brightly costumed figures suggested Renaissance Italy decorated the walls before and to either side of her. On her right, a rectangle of black marble, set lengthwise, formed a counter atop which sat a gold pen in a polished wood holder and a small crystal bowl full of candies in gold wrappers. The entire space was suffused with the buttery glow of the sun descending the sky, which appeared to originate from the wall in which the doorway was set. Marissa leaned forward, and saw rows of tall windows bracketing the entrance, each one brimming with daylight. "What the fuck?"

Barry had followed her into the room. "Why," he said, "this is the Broadsword. What are we doing here?"

"This is the Broadsword," Tyler Choate said. He was standing to the right of the marble column. How, Marissa thought, could she possibly have missed him? The man was a giant, easily eight feet tall, five hundred pounds at minimum. A sleeveless white robe draped him to the tops of his thighs; the garment looked to be a sheet in whose center a hole had been cut for Choate's outsized head. An assortment of astronomical symbols—stylized suns, moons, stars, planets, comets—had been written on the material in what appeared to be black magic marker. The body under the robe was exaggerated, swollen with muscles traversed by rigid veins. Nor was the face any better, the almost-delicate features situated in an expanse of flesh bordered by glossy black hair that draped Choate's shoulders. What Marissa took to be a white dunce cap rose from his head—a wizard's hat, she realized, to match the robe. A single symbol was inscribed on its front, a circle, its circumference broken at about the three o'clock mark.

There was no way for Marissa to have missed him, and yet, she had. It was as if he'd stepped out from behind the creamy light. His voice something with too many legs skittering over her, he said, "To be precise, this is Olympia's famous hotel as it was mid-afternoon on March 5, 1927."

"It's an excellent reproduction," Barry said. "I could almost believe I'm standing in the Broadsword at that exact moment."

"You are," Choate said, "although, the moment has been sliced from its context and slotted here."

Wonderful, Marissa thought, *guy thinks he's a supervillain. Must be all the steroids he took to get this big.*

"Why?" Barry said.

"My father was very fond of the Broadsword," Choate said. "His father took him to dine at it when he was a boy, and he retained a lifelong affection for the establishment. Call this an act of filial piety."

"All right," Barry said. "Why are we meeting you here? What does this location have to do with what happened to Wallace and Helen Smith?"

"Truthfully, not much," Choate said, "although, given its association with my father, it is not completely inappropriate."

"Wallace ran afoul of your father?" Barry said.

"Father developed an unusually... *intimate* relationship with Helen Smith," Choate said. "In the end it tore her—and her husband—apart." He grinned at the obvious pun.

"I was hoping for a more detailed explanation," Barry said.

"He split her head open," Choate said. "He crushed her husband between his teeth. Is that detailed enough for you?"

"Where is he, now?"

Choate waved his enormous hands to take in the surrounding luxury. "Father was much further along in his development than either me or my brother, Joshua. While he could still appreciate the immediate pleasures of your friend and his wife, his form had become more subtle in nature. It was an ideal substance for the process I described to you in our chat. You remember: the sublime trepanation."

"Drilling a hole in the skull of a dead god," Barry said.

"It's a metaphor, of course; except, it's also true. You can imagine, an enterprise of this magnitude requires unprecedented tools. Together, my brother and I were able to fashion such a device from our sire's form."

Great, Marissa thought. *We're in the underground lair of a crazy, giant sex-offender who, from the sound of it, is also a patricide. And who knows? He's probably a cannibal, too.*

As if reading her mind, Barry said, "You killed him? Your father?"

A look of almost comic frustration twisted Choate's features. "Come in," he said, beckoning them toward him. "Come in, and have a look out the windows."

Marissa glanced back at Barry. He nodded. She advanced three steps across the floor, and half-turned to view the wall in which the door opened. There were seven to eight windows to either side of the entrance. Tall, wide, arched at the top, they shone as if their very glass had been ground from light. It was a good trick, but not nearly as good as what she saw through the shining panes. A cratered plane of black sand stretched away to blackness. The sky was black, too, with the exception of a scattering of stars, several of them much larger and brighter than any she knew from the night sky. While she watched, one of the stars swelled, two, three times its diameter, more, before contracting to half its original size, then bursting in a phosphorous-flare that jerked her hand in front of her eyes. "Jesus!" she shouted. Behind and to her left, she heard Barry murmur, "Fuck!" Vision bleached, lids fluttering, she pivoted towards Choate. If he wanted to make a move, now was the time. She raised the .38 in his general direction.

Someone was standing next to him, equally tall, wearing a plain robe whose hood had been raised. *This must be the brother*, she thought, *Joshua*. When he lifted his hands and drew back the hood, she saw that she was right; although this sibling seemed much thinner, the skin shrunken around the contours of his enlarged skull. "Can you see anything?" Barry said. She could. She could see Joshua Choate reach his right hand into the left sleeve of his robe and withdraw a knife that was more a machete, a sinister bit of slight-of-hand. He exchanged a nod with his brother, and started towards her and Barry.

Marissa shot him five times, centering on his chest and tracking up to his head. The first two shots cracked the air and puckered the tops of Joshua's robe. The third shot rung in Marissa's ears like a hammer striking an actual bell; she didn't hear the fourth and fifth shots, only felt the revolver buck in her hand. Holes opened in Joshua's throat, his right cheek, his forehead. His knife bounced on the marble floor where he dropped it; he collapsed next to it and did not move. Marissa swung the gun at Tyler Choate, who had not strayed from his position. His lips were moving, but whatever words were leaving them were kept from her by the ringing in her ears. She shook her head. "I can't hear you."

Tyler nodded, held up one paw with all five fingers extended.

"That leaves me one," she said, "and I'm betting I can put it some-place that will hurt."

A hand pressed her shoulder: Barry, his cell phone out in his other hand. She did not need to hear what he was saying to know the threat in it.

Choate, however, grinned and gestured at the windows with their special-effects scene. Marissa looked at Barry, who was frowning at his phone. Were they too deep underground? Speaking in the too-loud voice of someone whose hearing was still stunned, Barry uttered a retort that was on the verge of being audible. Marissa thought he was accusing Choate and his brother of luring him here to murder him, to put an end to his investigation into Wallace and Helen Smith's deaths.

That she could see, Choate did nothing. But the roof, the walls, the furniture of the room in which they were standing flew off in different directions, as if yanked away on enormous strings. Now nothing separated them from the desolate plane she had viewed through the windows. In the blackness overhead, a trio of stars flashed one-two-three, strobing the black sand with silent light. Joshua Choate lay where he had fallen; though his knife had been swept away in the disassembling of the room. Tyler Choate also remained in place. Marissa had the impression of something vast looming in the dark landscape behind him, a great, tumorous mass to which he was teth-ered by a fine thread that floated up from the back of his head and corkscrewed over what she judged a considerable distance.

This time, when Choate spoke, it was as if he was whispering in her ear. "You?" he said. "Barry, my friend, you're incidental. Your companion is the reason you're here."

It was perhaps more shocking than anything Marissa had wit-nessed. "Me?"

"I required someone to kill my brother." He tilted his head at Joshua's remains.

His words still half-shouted, Barry said, "What?"

"This was a hit?" Marissa said. The notion was laughable, completely out-of-keeping with the madness surrounding them.

"A sacrifice," Choate said, "of himself to himself. Like Odin on Yggdrasil's branch. The only way out of this festering cosmos, this heaving meatwheel. My brother underwent a *kenosis*, an emptying; he divested himself of all he had become. He learned, you understand. From the vantage point we established, here, my brother taught himself to decipher Ymir's dying thoughts. Spelled out in a language of dying suns, he found the key that unlocked the exit to this cadaver universe. That key was nothing, the place that is not a place, the state that is not a state. There, where all things are equally nonexistent, he would have parity with Ymir, and might discover what the ancients called the *Ginnungagap*, the breach that birthed the giant.

"Funny," Choate said, "it all sounds rather Eastern, doesn't it? The renunciation of everything and all that. I had always dismissed such notions as so much hippie nonsense. According to my brother, though, those fellows were onto something.

"I helped him to expunge the more… developed aspects of his self. But when it came to helping him out of that most fundamental encumbrance, his life, I could not bring myself to offer him that assistance." Choate smiled tightly. "I will admit, of the multitude of vices I might have numbered amongst my practice, sentimentality, family-feeling, would not have been one of them. Well. I could not take my brother's life; any more, I suspect, than Joshua could have taken mine. I searched for a suitable vehicle to deliver my brother's death to him. You may imagine, I have a substantial list of potential names. By this time, however, Barret's interest in me and mine had drawn my attention, and after I conducted an inquiry into him, I discovered Ms. Osterhoudt in his employ. Further research into the particulars of her history convinced me that she was the person for the job. It seems I was correct."

"All right," Barry said, "all right." The words quivered with strain.

"We've done what you brought us here for. It's time for us to go."

The great, dark shape behind Tyler Choate rushed forward, as if the distance between it and him had collapsed. His body rippled, the skin tearing up and down his arms and legs. His mouth split at the corners, widening across his considerable face. Curved teeth that would have been at home in a tiger's jaws burst from his gums. A hellish light ignited within his eyes. "Go?" he said, and the single syllable contained a brief monologue's worth of sinister statements. *My brother may have believed in renunciation, but as far as I'm concerned, the jury's still out. He may have wanted it, but you killed my brother. We haven't had anything to eat, and I'm* starving. Blood streamed from his body, steaming with whatever energy was burning through it. He stepped towards them.

Would the single bullet remaining in her pistol be any use against whatever vision of raw appetite Tyler Choate was becoming? Even allowing for a miraculous shot to the eye or forehead, she doubted it. She raised the pistol, turned, and shot Barry in the head. His expression blank, he fell dead. She tossed the gun down beside him.

Choate's face was mostly a gaping maw; the look on what was visible of the rest of it was unreadable. Marissa said, "Loyalty."

He gave a wet, barking cough she realized was a laugh.

"Fuck you," she said.

And he was gone. In his place was the child, the one who had traveled with her in the elevator, the one who had been standing on the ice in front of the Hummer, the one whose death she had felt tremble the steering wheel of her truck. Its mouth was open, alight with unearthly fire.

"You," she said. "Okay. I'm ready for this. Okay. Let's go. I'm ready."

As it turned out, she was not.

For Fiona, and for Laird, amigo

OF A THOUSAND CUTS

Cody Goodfellow

Only in the final, volatile moments of the ludus, when vows made by will are broken by flesh, does the Samurai forget himself and mar his hitherto flawless performance by trying to die.

Dragging his left leg, javelin jutting from butchered knee, hastily resected bowel waving like a gory pennant, yet the Samurai circles his remaining opponent with calculated poise, herding him downwind into the black, creamy smoke wafting from the pyre of his identical twin.

Frenzy and fatigue vie to take the Roman even before the Samurai can close with him. Plunging his broken *katana* into the smoldering corpse to goad his enemy, the Samurai presents his *wakizashi* like a gift and settles into a waiting pose.

The Roman has abandoned all technique. Draws a whickering, whooping breath into the broken basket of his ribs, roars hollow blood-flecked hate and charges through charnel smoke, gladius swinging in a blind woodsman's coup de grace.

And then the moment that puts the lie to perfection, proclaims it the act not of a masterful athlete, but of a slumming, drunken god, or a troubled automaton. Samurai bows his head, arms out in supplication. Throws up an arm, not in defense, but to tear off his helmet. Impossible, of course…

The Roman's chopping stroke shears an antler from the Samurai's helmet and glances off his leather cuirass. Overextended, he tramples his opponent and lands among his brother's blazing remains. Before any outside his inner cadre have noticed his deathwish, the Samurai recovers and hamstrings the Roman. Wakizashi eagerly swims up hyperextended calf muscle, flensing meat catbox-bitter with lactic acid from spiral-fractured bones.

The Roman turns, seemingly revived by blood loss. Brings the gladius down on the Samurai's shoulder, splitting the torso down to the solar plexus. What little blood comes out at all is almost black.

The wakizashi quivers, sheathed to the hilt in the Roman's kidney. Samurai's hand touches but can't grasp it. The Roman's spade-shaped sword twisting in the burst balloon of his lung. With his other hand, Samurai draws the javelin from his knee. Nearly faints, but somehow he drives the long spike up through the corded muscles of the Roman's neck, penetrates the ribbed vault of the hard palate and into the cavernous echo chamber of the gladiator's brain.

It takes nearly another minute for the Roman's body to get the message.

It takes the surgical team another seven minutes to separate the bodies and check vital signs to certify the winner. The Roman called Pollux, though stabbed in nine places and burned to the third or fourth degree over ninety percent of his body, almost survives the night.

Shot up with painkillers and adrenochrome, the Samurai lurches out of the arena using the Roman's enormous gladius as a crutch, to the muted cheers of the small, select audience.

***

In the time after a battle is when it gets worst. He can almost remember who he is.

He knows he had a name.

Before this.

His name.

It was... something.

But in the Pageant...

Now... again and forever... he is the Samurai.

Rumors swirl about the champion few choose to fight, relegated to sideshow matches in pariah state circuses. All but destroyed in six of fifteen matches in nine years, but undefeated, and none have ever seen his face. Even in the pitch-black demimonde of the Pageant, the Samurai is a cipher, his identity insignificant next to the paradox of his survival. Students of the art point to the many awful injuries sustained; not even the Pageant's surgeons could rebuild such terrible carnage. Indeed, from one match to the next, the Samurai gains or sheds weight and height. Lord Sun makes no promises regarding the identity of the Samurai. Only the masked helmet and the mated swords and the implacable, elegant butchery remain the same.

And yet, the obligatory devil's advocates must insist, compare the perfect discipline, the rigor of technique maintained even unto dismemberment, the reflexive disdain for mere mortal injury, the true absence of fear of death or pain. No matter how many bodies he's gone through, it could only be the same man.

***

After Lord Sun has viewed his champion and given his orders, the surgeons take Salazar off life support. From behind his mask, he can see the locker room and the masked doctors slick with his blood, drugged with his secrets.

"We've learned so much from him, but all of it useless." Tsukue, the surgeon, changes his gloves while his nurse fills a styrofoam cooler with ice. "A doctor is wasted on this one. He only needs a seamstress."

He knows he is a freak. No other bodies share his readiness for transplants. He knows they've tried to make a transplant enzyme agent from his blood.

When he can remember, he tries to spare his opponents' limbs so he'll have a ready spare-parts bank in the locker room. Two out of three donors are compatible with any body with his blood flowing through its veins, and anything that can be laser-stitched together can be walked out in, and might not be rejected for weeks.

Dr. Balance wears no blood, but Salazar's stink is all over him, oozes out his ears. The hypnotist is as responsible as the surgeons for the miracle of the Samurai. He smiles and dangles a pendant that swings and makes fiery mandalas of the light. Tsukue catches himself staring at it and curses. He takes a phone call and immediately waves to the hypnotist, pointing at Salazar as if he can't see.

Salazar tries to talk around the tubes down his throat. "I can... come back..."

They cannot fix him in time for the next ludus. Even if the bowel could be bypassed, the torso is cracked. *Look down, boy. That blue shirttail... That's your lung, the one that still works.*

"I can't feel it..."

The hypnotist bows. He must prepare Salazar.

"You can replace everything. They know I won't reject it... He just wants to send me... back there..."

Holding up the pendant, he sighs. They have a comprehensive donor. Perfect match, and as he understands, a young Caucasian, and even uncircumcised. Congratulations are in order. Salazar is going home, after a fashion.

Salazar reaches out, twisting the hypnotist's wrist. He could break it and do many terrible things with a greenstick fracture before the hypnotist could even scream.

But Dr. Balance would not scream. He would have only to utter a control word and all the memories Salazar has carefully buried, which should have killed him by now, would rise up to crush him.

"Set me free."

The hypnotist shakes his head. "I have tried to teach you..."

Breathing exercises. Counting sheep. "I can't... Go back, I... Won't..."

"Please." Red hands free, the hypnotist waves away the surgeons and the bodyguard. "Now, are you an enthusiast of haiku?"

"I hate poetry."

"The perfect haiku is a perfect translation of a dream of a moment. But a moment, as you must know, may contain lifetimes..."

Salazar begs. "Just let me loose... His own people despise him. They won't kick once he's put down. I don't want anything but that. You can have it all..."

"I am so sorry not to oblige, but I already have so much more than I want in this life."

"I can't go out and come back, again... all over again. I can't..."

"But you can. You have and you will. This is your seventh body, after all. What a wonder you are! You have cheated death, but who would share your secret?"

"Fuck you... Set me free. Kill me...!"

"Matsuo Bashō's haiku lose nearly all their potency in English, but listen carefully." Swinging the pendant in front of Salazar's remaining eye until it defocuses, he recites,

"A cuckoo cries,
And through a thicket of bamboo,
The late moon shines."

Salazar's agitated, bubbling wheeze subsides to a soft, circular rasp.

"Did you hear the cuckoo?"

Salazar nods.

"Did you see the moon shining through the bamboo?"

Choking, he trembles and says, "Yes."

"Then you are free." Pocketing the pendant, he nods to the surgeons, who winch Salazar down and pump him full of a cocktail of drugs similar to that used on California's Death Row while a third technician enters with a portable guillotine.

***

The Dark would be nothing to fear, if only it were empty.

His Darkness is an invisible orgy of bodiless abominations. Hardboiled horrors within soft-boiled eggs. Cracked and showed him unbearable visions, the worst of all possible worlds…

His.

Amerasian war-trash, street-raised in Saigon after Papasan went home with Uncle Sam and killed himself without producing a legitimate male heir. Suddenly, the family came looking, and eventually got Salazar immigrated to the United States.

He made them pay, though whether for neglecting him so long or for dragging him into a world he could never understand, even he never knew.

Boxing cultivated his skill for inflicting harm into a genius. He acquired a rep for cracking skulls with his fists. Bad temper got him blackballed, sold downriver. Gray-market cage-fighting. After he killed an opponent in a practice bout, he was jailed and forgotten.

Salazar in Folsom lockdown, a walking death penalty. Gladiator school. Shivved seven times; disciplined for nine jailhouse murders, thirty assaults. Recruited into the Pageant at twenty-two. For nostalgic value, he is christened the Cong.

His signature move: crack the chest and cut out the beating heart. Fuck Vietnam. Fuck America and absentee Papasan.

Call me the Aztec.

Twelve main events… and then a brutal, pyrrhic championship that left him unable to defend his title until a tissue donor could be found to give him new hands. When his cumulative injuries couldn't be repaired for competition, he was retired.

Burning with bitterness, denied a glorious exit, circling a funeral pyre. Out of his search for the ideal death, he found the cult of the samurai. He acquired a sword and a book of Mishima and a promise of inner peace.

It didn't last. Lord Sun's people found him in a Myanmar prison that had exploited his talents to relieve overcrowding. Lord Sun bought Salazar from the prison and took him in as a bodyguard for his family.

Under Lord Sun's wide, shadowy wing, he trained fighters and courted wisdom, but when he expected it least, his anger was abruptly snuffed out.

All his life, he had paid for the damage inflicted by his anger. But it was his first true act of love that condemned him to *ling chi*, the Hell of Slow Slicing.

***

Just like his father, the new dictator has his guests waited upon by starving, malnourished servants. Jaundiced eyes slather every sumptuously overloaded platter with longing and loathing like an exquisite condiment, complimenting the savory spice of terror infused into every dish by the slaves in the kitchen.

Salazar eats with his handlers in a bunker beneath the arena in a subterranean athletic complex that could adequately host the Olympic games, if it were not in an insane dictator's pariah state, and if the Olympic committee was more receptive to bloodsports.

At least twice that Salazar knows of, he has been served human flesh, this time in some weird approximation of beef bourguignon with plum sauce. He recalls a period when gray, freezer-burned pork was a daily staple. Rancid, but he devoured it grimly and doesn't remember why it was so important to have it inside him…

Tsukue worries that Salazar shouldn't try to eat, that intubation is the only sure way to stave off infection of the ridiculously elaborate tapestry of microsutures and meat-glue holding together his new head. But tonight, Lord Sun has made an exception and provided every comfort. Even his owner expects him to get demolished by whatever's ripping the plumbing out of the concrete walls of the adjoining bunker.

Only two days in the Dark this time, they told him. Only two eternities. After the third transplant, he has never come all the way back. The surgeons tirelessly recorded his impressions. He no longer registers colors, except in sporadic, terrifying bursts. Pain is a capricious and fickle liar; sometimes a grievous wound goes unnoticed until he slips in his own blood, but phantom agonies like being burned alive suddenly assail him in his sleep, as if his well-traveled nerves had become some sort of shortwave for picking up distant pain. His motor skills, however, have become uncannily refined. Dr. Tsukue credits his revolutionary dendrite braiding technique, which might've rendered spinal injuries curable, if anyone in his peer review group thought cripples were worth saving.

Salazar wants to stab someone. Something in a time-release drip makes him drop his fork. His hands slur across the table like drunken crabs. Dr. Balance comes in and the food is taken away. The hypnotist gives him another haiku, repeats it until Salazar can see the moon and his breath as crystals…

While he is distracted, they put the helmet on. An authentic but heavily rebuilt Edo Era helmet of bronze, steel and lacquered wood sheathed in a carbon fiber mesh, with a bronze facemask. Lord Sun's engineers reinforced the dome of the helmet to stop anything short of a sniper's bullet.

Lord Sun has invested more in Salazar than in the rest of his stable combined, but not to bring victory in the Pageant. Lord Sun would give his whole fortune to insure that Salazar will continue to survive and suffer forever.

The technician takes the surgical steel screws out of his breast pocket and closes his eyes to fight down panic. The gong has sounded and it'll be his ears if the Samurai misses his entrance. He fits the first screw on the 1/16" Phillips driver of a two-speed cordless drill and sets it into the recessed guide over the insulated hole in Salazar's left occipital bone.

The senior engineer usually uses an ordinary manual screwdriver to remove and attach the Samurai's helmet. His trainers use a pen-light-sized screwdriver.

Though Salazar is heavily sedated, he jerks as if stabbed in the face just as the technician applies the screw.

The spinning steel screw sinks up to the hilt in Salazar's left eye. Already grimacing with phantom pain, his face freezes, set in concrete.

The technician drops the drill. The surgeons fulminate but immediately take X-rays. Lord Sun's staffer orders the orderlies to seize the technician, and reluctantly picks up the phone.

Dr. Balance seems amused. Dangling his pendant, he asks the technician if he has ever been hypnotized.

"You can't take it out on me… you can fix him, you fix anything!"

"We *will* fix him," Tsukue says. "He is most important. While you…"

"Please, I didn't mean to… Just fix it, it's just one eye…"

Somewhere overhead, a deranged marching band strikes up nobody's national anthem. Salazar will be the opening event.

"Indeed," says Tsukue. "Only one eye…"

Dimly, he recalls his last North Korean ludus. As an environmental hazard, the match took place amongst twenty blind men with chainsaws. Political prisoners, eyes burned out with lye. The chugging Honda saws drowned out all sound and choked the air with smoke and gasoline vapor.

Balance whispers something to the technician, who relaxes into the chair and lets himself be restrained. Tsukue selects a tool like a notched melon baller. If Salazar's vaunted immune system will cooperate, he observes, this should not delay the ludus at all.

***

A nerve is just a wire made of conductive organic cells. A conduit for binary electrical signals that aggregate to form the touch of a lover's skin or the impulse to smash an enemy's face.

Just as wires can be spliced together, severed nerves may be introduced to other nerves and new synaptic chains induced. While no mortal surgeon could manually join every nervous chain in a severed spinal cord, the doctors of the Pageant have found it quite easy to mesh them together with an enzyme derived from nameless Amazonian botanical products and animal donors like Salazar. Gradually over successive transplants, the surgeons have rebuilt Salazar's skull with steel reinforcements and lead shielding, and made it into a module as easily plugged into a new network as any portable hard drive.

Replacing an eye in this improved cranium is as simple, then, as swapping out a burned out headlight. Before the local anesthetic has entirely worn off, Salazar begins to see through the technician's eye.

At first, white flashes and stabs of neuralgic fire, but a psychoactive cocktail of neurotransmitters and mescaline induces a kaleidoscopic optical storm and then a disturbing razor clarity.

After the initial shock wears off, he insists the eye is working properly and takes up his swords, eager to enter the arena.

Only the hypnotist notices something furtive in his manner. After every transplant, he has warned Lord Sun to expect the Samurai to wither and die. The experience of a brain finding itself in a new body dwarfs even the upheaval caused by a massive stroke. The surgeons themselves predicted years of rehabilitation before he could perform even the most rudimentary physical routines. But always, the Samurai rose from his bed and took up his swords with new hands. Even if the brain could not always feel pain or recall itself, no matter if those strange hands had never hefted a weapon, he made them his own in less time than another man might break in a pair of shoes.

Though he is too stricken to betray any sign of it, the first things Salazar sees with his new eye make him try to claw it out.

He sees...

Ghosts—the dead serve the living—Lord Sun drinks with the dictator—parades of zombie military slaves, peasant serfs and at his side— Her.

His hands claw at his face, but with his gauntlets on, he can't get through the mesh screen joining his snarling demon mask with the brim of his helmet. He tosses his head as if the helmet is full of hornets, but after a shaky moment, the Samurai rolls his shoulders, bows his head and strides up the corridor toward the blinding lights and the flatulent blasting of a blind marching band.

***

Nothing in this life was his, but his body and his hatred.

With her, he lost even those.

An impromptu ludus resulting from an awkward ejection of a boorish houseguest. Her face, painted white geisha accessory, carved with tears at first sight of him. Red with blood shed defending her honor. Alone in a sea of howling mouths.

Always, he'd felt as if his nerves extended out of his body. All the world too bright, too loud, in need of a beating. At last he knew where his nerves ended.

Where his true, secret heart had always been.

With his master's wife.

Lord Sun, bastard offspring of a Manchurian "Daughter of Joy" and an anonymous Japanese officer. Master of Hong Kong's black market and a ferocious opponent of Nippon. Builder and destroyer of fortunes, with a stable of gladiators unequalled in the eastern hemisphere and a harem culled from the world's nightclubs and brothels and nunneries with a zookeeper's methodical thoroughness. All but forgotten among the graveyard of discarded human toys and trophies, the Lady Sun.

Assigned to guard her wing of the palace, Salazar did not see her again for the first year of his service. He stood watch outside her garden. He heard her sing. He fell in love with her before they had spoken, before he knew anything about her but that she was also American, and the father of Lord Sun's only children.

Like the birth of a cold, sorrowful star in the void of Salazar's heart, his love for her transmuted his nature. But almost before it was conceived, his new universe began to collapse under its own unstable gravity.

He could not resist her. She seduced him with horrors. Lord Sun was a cannibal who ate his own unborn children. She had become his lawful wife because she bore him two male heirs. When the boys came of age, he would make them fight to the death, and he would have his brain transplanted into the body of the victor.

They waited until his indenture to Lord Sun was paid off before he betrayed his master.

***

The Mongolian storms the arena like a minotaur on ketamine. Trainers remotely spike his adrenaline drip and drive him through the gate with cattle prods, dropping the portcullis behind him. With a seven-foot axe, he splits a peasant retainer to the waist, kicks the underfed kindling off the blade and basks in outrage. The audience of local Party elect shriek like electrified lab rats. In an imperial box fortified by ballistic glass, Lord Sun sits with their host and the other patrons and a group of bored, constipated old men who can only be Chinese dignitaries.

When the Samurai enters, the crowd settles into an unsettling hush, as if refrigerated narcotic gas has filled the vast underground arena. Like something frozen, limbs tightly coiled, he pads into the murkily lit center. Shivering, staggering. Stripped of poetry, of technique, he advances like a praying mantis intent upon mating.

Obscured behind a veil of chainmail, the Mongolian's welcoming grin is almost audible as he beckons. Nearly twice the Samurai's weight and with a good eighteen-inch height advantage, he is a bear to Samurai's skinned rabbit.

A few desultory swings of his axe and jerky feints with a steel net fail to draw any notice from the Samurai. A fusillade of fireworks spray the field. A rocket vomiting green phosphorus sparks cuts between them. The Mongolian must expect the Samurai to be blinded, for he avalanches the smaller man.

This is where the battle typically becomes a dance, where the Samurai's elegant minimalism seeks parity with the Mongolian's barbaric onslaught, and a whole new art form is invented.

Even the Mongolian must realize that something is wrong. What he lacks in tactical skill, he more than compensates with his apparent knowledge of Samurai's eye injury. Circling clockwise, trying to get outside the vaunted reach of Samurai's infamous sword, he drives to get into Samurai's blind spot.

Instead of his customary dual-wielding *nitoken* technique, the Samurai has forsaken his *daisho*, holds the 74cm katana close to his chest like a precious thing sure to be shattered. Samurai circles the Mongolian several times, then a bloodcurdling scream rips out of him and he flings himself, swinging the katana like a baseball bat, headfirst into the heel of the oncoming axe.

The audience leaps to its collective feet. Shock quickly sours into outrage. This isn't what they came to see.

Samurai reels backwards and falls like a doll to the ground, still holding his sword in the same awkward two-handed grip. Mask split wide open, revealing a one-eyed, slack-jawed Asian face. Drooling, tripping his head off on ketamine administered directly into his surviving eye, the technician doesn't even know he's losing a fight. Arms flopping frenziedly, trying to drop the weapon glued to his gauntleted hands when the Mongolian tramples him. Katana snared in steel net and he's slung into the air and slammed into a stone column but still he won't, he can't let go—

Irate Lord Sun calls his trainers, surgeons, hypnotist, security staff.

Message center.

Calls up security camera view of Salazar's bunker on a laptop.

Red.

The hypnotist calls back. He's left the compound for the night, and when he left, everything was as it should have been—

The doors slam open to make way for a headless bodyguard. Screaming like sheep downwind from the slaughterhouse, patrons on their feet amid bodyguards and concubines.

Salazar slides into the box and moves through them like a gardener among windswept trees, artfully pruning limbs with his short sword. Through the boiling crowd he cuts a path to the front row and a phalanx of Triad soldiers backing Lord Sun into a corner. One of them tries to shoot down the glass. The bullets bounce off the walls until they hit one body or shatter and maim several.

One far more astute bodyguard, using two ceramic-silicon automatics the size of credit cards, pump sixty-eight .12 caliber rounds into Salazar. Half of them glance off his naked steel and bone cranium, trailing drug drip tubes and leaking exotic fluids. His new left eye is so dilated that it looks like a black coin, a mouth overflowing with the Dark.

The host disregards his own prohibition on firearms and draws a massive Glock with a laser sight, shaky with the prospect of firing a shot in anger. He shoots two of his own bodyguards before the survivors sweep him out of the box.

Salazar chops down the last Triad guards and lays bare his nemesis.

Here, some small demonstration of his humanity, of the tenderness that cost him everything, would vouchsafe him the role of hero in this confrontation. And if there were gods who cared not for morality plays but only fed greedily upon empty human trauma, then Salazar's sacrifice would be accepted and miracles would abound.

Lord Sun, a sickly ancient, bald as an egg, blue veins bulging with sluggish blood, clutching his chest with one palpitating claw, takes out his phone with the other. A vile, boneless creature shucked out of its shell of mercenaries and unmasked at last for a coward, squirming behind the last living body left in the box.

Salazar does not act. Less a warrior in repose than a machine with its gears stripped, arm raised above the last one blocking Lord Sun, cowering against starred glass...

It's her...

But how long has it been? How many fights, how many bodies, how many seasons of rehab and torture...

Ash-blonde hair and honey-gold eyes and her face unpainted unwrinkled uncreased by the sorrows that drove her mad...

She sobs and the musical sound of it undoes him.

"Ka... Ka... Ka... ren..." He reaches out to her. "Is... it is... you...?"

She lifts up a hand to take his. No, she holds out something.

She presses a button.

Salazar's heart explodes.

***

Death is emptiness.

Death is the void.

Death is easy.

Where Salazar goes, the nothingness itself is alive. Emptiness infested with itself.

When you have nothing left, no *you*, no *I*, the Dark gets inside you and you remake yourself out of it until you're at one with Nature's other face. In the Dark, you become everything eating everything else, eating fucking killing dying in the Dark forever and ever.

In here, forever is a breath.

To keep from going mad, you make something. You build a memory palace and fashion the Dark into an infinity of gloomy rooms filled with shadowy impressions. You move from room to room to keep the lustful turgidity of darkness out. You unpack your memories and burn them for warmth, for light.

Until you only have one memory left.

***

Lord Sun's wife leaves Hong Kong only twice annually, once to shop in Paris and for once the family trip to the seashore.

Lord Sun predictably abstains, but insists they get off the continent and buries them with extra security. A surge in threats from various Triad factions with the imminent handover of Hong Kong, so Salazar accompanies her and the boys to Brunei. He bought her a private island in the Maldives, but she won't go. Just once a year, the children will at least see normal people, and play with children whose parents don't aspire to be gods.

A terrorist bomb in the lobby of the Hilton Darussalam kills twenty-two, including the entire family party. None of Indonesia's menagerie of Islamic terror groups step in to take credit for breaking the unprecedented truce, but it fits the profile of past bombings almost perfectly.

Even in the midst of such a devastating tragedy, Lord Sun is not without suspicions. Allowing for the possibility of his having lost his entire family—wife, sons—and several of his most trusted staff in a tragic accident, he cannot help but look to his enemies. Within hours, a team of private operators is dispatched to Indonesia to meet with the Royal Brunei Police Force, insurance investigators and the Sultan's security staff, and repeat the same message: Deliver them.

The heat, the humidity, it's like breathing steam. On a rundown former plantation in the jungle above Sipitang, Salazar hides with his bride-to-be. They make plans, they fuck and they fight. Did so many have to die? Stand-ins for each of them accompanied the party into the hotel. The device planted in her luggage. The children and their nanny, the security detail, all expendable. It shocks him that he mourns more for her sons than she does. She rakes his face with her nails, tries to slash him with the neck of a two-thousand dollar bottle of champagne. "He made them," she screams. "He took them out of me and he made them dirty and they... as soon as they were old enough... they tried..."

What she tells him then about her boys makes him sick up the last of his remorse.

Before dawn, a truck driver smuggles them out of Brunei on mountain forest roads for ten thousand dollars. From Tarakan, a fisherman is to take them across the Celebes Sea to Sulawesi, but Salazar plans to hijack him to the Philippines, where they will use new passports to fly to Mexico City and vanish in South America. Even if their scheme unravels and the authorities prematurely discover the truth, Karen tells him, they'll never be caught. She knows of plastic surgeons in Mexico; she has the numbers for holding accounts into which she's siphoned petty household cash for years. Millions. Enough to hide for a long time, or live well for a while.

They're going to get away because they are young and in love, and they are going to grow old together and the story of their romance and heroic escape and flight will become a fairytale, and innocent bystanders never die in fairytales.

She says it again and again, and when he goes out to the beach to signal the fisherman, he believes it. If there is any balance, any order, any meaning to the universe, his life has been darkness and blood, a slow whittling away of all that he called himself. He believes now that the dawn must come, for he has earned it.

And he thinks this right up until he goes back into the beachside hut to find not Karen, but only the bloody obsidian knife that was the Aztec's chosen tool, the shard of volcanic glass with which he cut more throats than he cared to count. It drips fresh red on the grass mats, still damp with their sweat.

He takes the knife and runs from the hut, through the village and into the mountainous rain forests of Kalimantan.

Lord Sun discovered the whole architecture of their ruse before they got out of Brunei, and identified his wife's location by the GPS chip implanted in her skull.

Lord Sun's hunger for vengeance is no less than any reasonable man's would be under the circumstances, but he gives Salazar eight hours to go to ground in the trackless highlands before he and his operators come searching. After all he's invested in Salazar, he might as well get one last bit of sport out of him.

***

The body on the steel slab quivers. Salazar opens his eyes and weeps
with joy at the revelation of having eyes again, before he even realizes he's on fire.

His screams only suck the flames down his throat. Choking,
gasping for air—

Drowning, thrashing for the surface but unable to find which
way is up, and the cold and the pressure crushing him—

The hypnotist smiles. "What news from beyond the veil?"

Salazar chokes on air, gags out noises that no one else would
recognize as words.

"You were in transit for nearly eighteen months. Much has
changed while you were away."

His arms are lead with rubber bones. Try to strangle Balance, they
roll off his torso to hit the steel like shit in a bedpan. More noises.

"You are in no condition to fight. That part of your life is behind
you. As punishment for your actions, Lord Sun has elected to subject you to the most terrible suffering which he could imagine."

Salazar's eyes nearly roll out of their petrified sockets when the
hypnotist shows him a hand mirror.

His face is sunken, jaundiced, withered, wreathed in yellow-
white beard like dead roots from an uprooted onion. It is the most
hateful face he has ever seen.

He is Lord Sun.

"The old coward finally took the plunge," Balance says, smiling.
"You gave him a reason."

Make him grimace and shake. Make his jaw drop like he is trying
to throw up. His hands try to crawl away.

"His son, the one who survived the bomb... His father let the
world suppose he was dead, and raised him for this. I never believed he would go through with it, frankly..."

Salazar wonders what he should feel. Nausea, exhaustion, the gravity of despair crushing this ruined, used-up vessel… Still, does it lighten his load to know the boy survived his mother's murder attempt? Perhaps he yet lives. The son's brain could be living in his old suitcase. Meanwhile…

"Where…? Let me…" Stick out his tongue. Swallow it. Choke on it.

"It is impossible. You will have no chance. We have worked for months to resuscitate you after the operation. It was nearly a failure, but no one was surprised you pulled through. Some part of you, at least, clings to life. But now you are alert and in full possession of your faculties, you will finally be executed…"

A spray of spit. Black spots swarming over Dr. Balance's sad smile. Salazar clings, mind and soul, to this rotten raft until the Dark subsides.

"Of course, at the moment of expiration, every effort will be made to recover your brain and transplant it again and… well, it is obvious. If he has his way, you will never stop dying."

Bow his head. Try to gouge out his eyes. "Ssssaaaaaw… errrrrrr…."

Balance touches his widow's peak, dabbing at his nose. "That is too bad, my friend. She… is not the one… but the resemblance *is* remarkable, no? That is no doubt why he took an interest."

Make him shed tears. "Ssssssshhhhh…"

"She… is her mother's daughter. And the father… it's complicated, but… biologically speaking…"

MAKE HIM BREAK FREE MAKE HIM STRANGLE—

Balance easily pushes him back and cinches the straps around his concave chest. He's not going anywhere.

Lord Sun lives to inflict pain. Why would he throw her away? Especially when he learned she was ripe with a seed he could nurture and nourish to become what he'd always wanted…

"Put all dreams of vengeance out of your mind. They are worlds away from this one. Now begins as many lifetimes of suffering as your soul can withstand… but you need not suffer any more than you wish to."

The hypnotist draws close and recites the haiku that he taught Salazar.

Eyes gleam. Pupils dilate. Breathing subsides to a tidal purr. Make his ears *listen*.

"You have learned at great cost that you are not your body. How much less difficult, indeed how liberating, to grasp that you are also not your brain?

"You are a dream your brain has always dreamt, a story it tells itself. But a tale once told does not belong to the teller, but to the reader, the world. Compose your story, and you may not only withstand the pain and the darkness, but you may escape your body altogether…"

Make him look again at the face in the mirror. Salazar tries to tear it off his skull and eat it.

***

The ancient Chinese practice of *ling chi* or "slow slicing"—more popularly known as the Death of a Thousand Cuts—in the Western imagination grew into a nightmarish ordeal of precision torture which dragged on for days or even weeks. Like the infamous, equally exaggerated "water torture" and similar techniques involving ants or swiftly growing bamboo, it fueled Western paranoia about the inscrutable patience and eerie cruelty of the Oriental mind long after it was banned under British colonial pressure in 1905.

In reality, *ling chi* was reserved only for the worst criminals—traitors, fratricides—and even the most skilled Chinese executioner could not stave off death beyond a few hours.

Dr. Tsukue tells Salazar right away that he's going for a record. Perhaps never in history has such painstaking care been taken to preserve the life of a patient slated to die by torture.

Two pit crews of three caring professionals will see to his dismantling. Dr. Tsukue conducts the primary excruciation, while his apprentices follow along, debriding and dismantling tissue, cauterizing or clamping critical blood vessels until the maximum amount of agony has been milked from each limb and amputation can proceed; and an antianesthetist with two nurses are charged with keeping Salazar paralyzed with suxamethonium chloride in an intratracheal drip along with epinephrine and acetylcholine to keep him exquisitely alert, yet just below the threshold for shock and cardiac arrest. The pain manager has the most difficult job. Lord Sun abused his body as if certain he would someday get a new one, but in his new incarnation, he is equally adamant that his discarded body survive long enough to satisfy an impossible grievance.

Traditional *ling chi* customarily opens by dramatically mortifying the pectoral muscles and the fronts of the thighs in shallow, gaping wounds that bare the ribcage and straps of skeletal muscle. Tsukue is wary of blood loss and premature myocardial trauma. Still, this is an operating *theater*, and just as in the Pageant, all must perform here for a demanding audience. Using a Blumlein ablation knife, he digs into the chilled, rubbery flesh of the chest like a pudding, plowing out jaundiced scoops of skin backed by pale adipose jelly and dropping them in a steel bowl.

Fully alive to all that is inflicted on him yet unable to move beyond the feeblest galvanic twitch, Salazar seems to slip immediately into shock. The pain manager calls for a recess. Observing from his own hermetically sealed recovery ward, Lord Sun demands escalation. Burn his genitalia off with a laser to wake him up, or better yet, peel and invulse them, making a woman of him. But only after coming within a hair's breadth of triggering a heart attack does the pain manager recognize that Salazar is quite awake, yet in a meditative trance.

The next incisions begin at the fingertips and the soles of his feet, long, sweeping slices with a fluted scalpel that turns up the lips of the wounds like furrows of tilled soil. A few nicked capillaries add only stray trickles to the slime of cold sweat beading on Lord Sun's mortified castoff body. Nerves assaulted, outraged, jolted to twitching overload, but never severed. Exhausted parchment skin peels away from flaccid fascia, livid and throbbing with the terminal arousal of amputation.

Goosepimpled flesh shivers in restraints as slices become slashes, as digits in all four extremities are systematically degloved and filleted. So adept is Dr. Tsukue with scalpels, lasers and forceps that even when he strips muscle and sinew from the nerve-rich fingertips, exposed nerves linger on clinging to barren bone, still aquiver with microscopic messages of apocalyptic pain.

The medics constantly check Salazar's mental acuity. He remains lucid throughout, gritting his teeth whenever he is queried, but more with the air of a man upset at a distraction, than one in the throes of shock.

While they flay him, he loses himself in words, recalled to the torments of his body only long enough to stretch out to pick up several larger scraps of his own skin on his outthrust tongue and ball them up in his mouth. Dr. Tsukue notes this gravely, but says nothing to the pain manager. If he is not truly paralyzed, so be it. In the longest recorded executions of *ling chi*, the victim would be allowed only his own discarded flesh for sustenance.

But Salazar does not swallow.

After sixteen hours, a recess is called for Tsukue's sake. While he rests and self-administers extensive acupuncture, Salazar is wheeled into his closet-sized cell, suspended supine on a trolley, slathered in ferric acid and industrial Neosporin, to rest.

Before Tsukue's hands have stopped shaking, he returns to the theater. Lord Sun is most unimpressed so far, but even his most aesthetically drastic efforts fail to arouse any perceptible reaction from Salazar.

Waves of pain pass far above his head, but he barely notices them now, like distant traffic through a sealed window.

Salazar is making a new body, a new palace in the Dark, out of words. Literally, he composes himself, weighing words, images, snapshot reminiscences that well up from the seemingly emptied void of his memory. Paring away fat and redundant and flat impressions to vivisect the image, the idea, of himself. Within the rigorous latticework of the haiku, he distills himself into a flow of words and images that set him free and bind him in the surge of red darkness to an anchor. Reciting the words, he holds the walls against the deeper darkness that hungers to reclaim him.

With only three recesses, the *ling chi* of the gladiator Salazar lasts six days and three hours. Dr. Tsukue has his record, but he hardly seems proud of it, now.

Salazar's brain is pitted with lesions and dull, partially decayed parts, but still emits a stable comatose EEG when reconnected to the monitor and nutrient feeds of his second home, the suitcase.

Only Dr. Balance examines Salazar's cell with any diligence once the last remnants of Lord Sun's corpse are vacuumed away. At first, he mistakes it for a bit of misplaced gore, even as he searches for just such an artifact as it turns out, upon further inspection, to be.

Opening it, he closes his eyes at the first glimpse of its contents.

Salazar has transcended himself. No longer merely a gladiator, now a poet.

***

The elite box of Hong Kong's Kuan Yin Arena more closely resembles a parliament conference room, with sensibly upholstered chairs arranged within horseshoe tables on a steeply tiered gallery with scarlet porphyry floors and columns.

The reincarnated Lord Sun sulks with his retinue, alone. Less than a year after the operation, he is still a hostile occupier at war with his son's unconquered body. His lipless rictus and incessant stammer freely betray the deranged ancient hiding inside the teen-aged body, but the fault lies with all the immunosuppressors and hormones and the many arcane drugs required to maintain even infantile control over the body's basic motor functions. Frustrated with the headset he uses to communicate with the servants waiting outside his inflated plastic hyperbaric bubble, Lord Sun raps angrily on the interior wall, demanding to see the hypnotist. His servants hardly hide their sneering expressions. They think him weak. They see his imminent demise and their greedy enrichment. He's surprised them before.

Dr. Balance finally arrives, looking uncharacteristically excited. "Your new Samurai is prepared for battle. I think today my Lord will enjoy a most interesting match."

At last, Lord Sun recalls some spark of vitality. "The odds. What odds does she command?" A string of drool wiped away by rash-ravaged hands.

"Twelve to one, my Lord."

A young man's lungs vapor-lock on old man's laughter. "She will... destroy... them all..."

Dr. Balance locks eyes with Lord Sun, guides him to a relaxed state. By his own insistence, Lord Sun is immune to hypnosis, but Balance's relaxing influence has made him the only one he can trust with the care and feeding of his most prized possession.

"They underestimate you at their peril, my Lord. But not entirely without cause. For far too long, you have pursued your vengeance to the detriment of your business pursuits and your stable. You've become known for vulgar exhibition matches. But your reinvention as a patron shall be as dramatic as your physical reincarnation."

Nodding until he swoons with dizziness, Lord Sun breathlessly agrees. "If he knew... it would destroy him utterly. He should have been revived in time to witness this moment."

Around them, the crowd thickens, patrons and prostitutes take their seats as the lights over the arena brighten. The first event is hardly a title match, but it marks the first appearance of a female gladiator in the history of the Pageant.

"I know you have misgivings, my Lord, but it is best that you not allow yourself to become... compromised again. She is her mother's daughter, full of defiance, but also her father's, and so a formidable contender in the games. Her natural anger channeled in that direction will yield you great benefits, instead of bringing further trouble to your house."

Lord Sun's mouth says something Balance misses because his hand moves to cover it and slap it repeatedly.

Best get this over with. "As luck would have it, I have uncovered a token which was no doubt meant for you. Whether an act of surrender or a last gesture of defiance I leave to you, but I think that once you hold it in your hands, you may find the contentment to leave the issue to the past."

Knowing he treads on rice paper, Balance quickly proffers the tiny pillow book.

He has trimmed its chewed borders and replaced the haphazard binding of hair and detached ligaments and perfected the botched curing which Salazar attempted with his own urine. In spite of some shrinkage, the painstakingly inked words are still clearly legible when he holds it up to the convex belly of Lord Sun's bubble.

赤い風泣くこと

Trembling, Lord Sun reads, unblinking.

私の体は本です

Eyes screwed shut, Balance turns the pages as Lord Sun consumes each inhumanly compressed line.

私の名前は剣です

Eyes riveted upon the unwritten *kereji*—the "cutting word" upon which the last line turns, he says the Samurai's true name aloud, curse turned into prayer.

His eyes go on roving behind closed lids, as if in deep REM sleep. His lips go on reciting the haiku.

"*Akai kaze ga naku...*"

Repeating the mantra until its resonance overlaps with the endless repetition out of the Dark behind every closed eyelid...

"*Watashi no karada wa hondesu...*"

The cutting word picks the neural locks of the door at the back of every brain, the door that drums, drugs and blood alone can open.

"*Ken wa kotobadesu.*"

The crowd rises to its feet at the first sounds of the ludus... not the expected horns or strident martial music, but a piercing black static scream of inhuman desolation that rebounds through the cavernous arena.

Lai's opponent enters the arena to distracted applause, but some of the more astute patrons turn to the back door when they notice that the screaming is getting louder, and it's not coming from down on the dirt floor, but from somewhere much closer. From down in the catacombs where Dr. Balance only minutes ago placed Lai Salazar in a deep trance before showing her the Samurai's pillow book.

Only the hypnotist can recognize the name the newly resuscitated ghost is trying to speak with both Lord Sun and Lai's lips.

Before any can react, the screaming becomes a chorus. Lord Sun claws at the walls of his bubble. His screams tear the microsutures in his scalp, man becoming madman becoming God.

Even Dr. Balance cannot tell, looking into those streaming, alien eyes, whether he is observing his favorite patient in the ecstasy of his hideous miracle—the impossible, the unspeakable, coming true twice—or the Darkness, incarnate at last and utterly devastated to find out how incredibly overrated being alive is...

Yes, he thinks as the doors fly open to admit a chill steel wind, *it promises to be a most interesting match.*

TENEBRIONIDAE

Scott Nicolay & Jesse James Douthit-Nicolay

...and the red light was my mind.
—Robert Johnson

Dumont wriggled his shoulders, shoved from his feet and twisted at the hips to inch himself further up the back of the fox hole. Not so cold yet and it was hell for comfortable but he wanted to keep as much off the gritty metal floor as he could. You weren't careful in a cold train car, metal would suck the heat out of you like *nuthin*. Without a sleeping bag best he only touched bare metal at his shoulders boots and butt.

Missy lifted her head from his chest to wedge a wet nose against his chin and neck, lick up at his cheek. Dumont wrapped his left arm around her and winced. He hadn't peeked yet to see how deep the cut ran. He was gonna have to look soon. Last he could see, the dirty bandanna he tied round it was soaked a darker red all cross the top. Not enough light to check it now anyway.

Least he managed to score a good ridable from NOLA on a grainer porch. Damn lucky but that didn't change how fucked his situation was overall. He thought about his pack. Fucking Shadow Riders had it, together with his sleeping bag and most of the rest of his shit. Who knew what they were doing to it? Trashing it all, dividing it up… most likely some black magic bullshit. And his last pint of whiskey was in there too. With time to grab one thing only he went for his guitar, the scratched up acoustic Susie True-Bright gave him at Eufaula Lake two Novembers back. He was probably going to regret that choice. With neither whiskey nor water left, he knew he was going to regret it *soon*. He craned forward to check he at least hadn't lost the guitar, right now riding by the bottom of the grainer's ladder since it wouldn't fit with him in the hole. The bottom edge of the case cut a thin arc from what light the moon still dribbled down. The case seemed steady, moving only in time with the slow swaying rhythms of the train.

He let the back of his head rest against the chill rusty wall and tuned in to the trainsong, hoping it would lull him to sleep.

Only five things could steady him, still the deep waters of his chaos. Whiskey. Missy. Playin'. Fuckin'. And the sound train wheels made over steel rails. *Rat ta tat tat rat ta tat tat*. Best lullaby ever. Better than any his foster parents ever sang him, that was fersure…

Fersure.

He couldn't catch the rhythm tonight though, ride it into sleep. Not yet. Too much rage and anger ran still through his veins, the gin in a cocktail spiked with confusion and fear.

That was *some* fucked up shit there at the squat, Shadow Riders comin' in like they did… Yeah sure, Bald Jonny Ben warned him 'bout them way back when, first time he came through NOLA, but that time Dumont only nodded, passing the stories off as fairy tales in his mind. Occultist train riders? Seriously? Only they *were* real and they were *very* serious. So was their black magic. 'Course Tigger tried to tell him the same but he tuned her out too. Now he could tell his own story about them if he wanted. If he ever got the chance…

What he'd seen at the squat twisted in his brain like a wind whipped plastic bag snagged on a barbed wire fence. He'd been chilling there waiting for Tigger. They were s'posed to meet up, hitch out of NOLA, take their love on the road. Maybe not love exactly, but close enough. She was good for him and she said *he* made her feel safe.

First though she was gonna try to get this money some other ex owed her while he was supposed to go busk it in the Quarter. Only he drank a little whiskey to get his nerve up, then a little more and a little more after that and ended not leaving the squat.

Tigger said meet her 'round 7:00 but she never showed. Best he could estimate she was already an hour late. Still, everything was copacetic till right before the Shadow Riders appeared.

He had a seat up against one wall, a flipped over five-gallon plastic bucket, bright orange once, writing under all the scuffs and scratches said it came from Home Depot long time ago. Missy lay on his right, tongue out and panting softly, his battered pack, packed and ready, propped against the wall on his left. He was thinking about breaking out the guitar, maybe tuning it or working on a song. Then things twisted up, got all strange.

The smell hit him first, a bitter edge coming on beneath the general mist of wet plaster, rust and mildew and his own unwashed body. Missy must've caught it before him 'cause she sat up and growled, her growl becoming a whine before it choked off in silent tension. Right as his nose registered it too a thin ripple rode over every horizontal line, kinked level architecture downward a moment before pulsing on and out the corners. Shit might make sense if he were shrooming but he only had whiskey in him, and he knew that drink's distortions full well as a sea captain knows the waves and the sky or whatever. He sat up and was still watching for a repeat when the graffiti went wrong.

That came instant, a spasm. The lines of spraypainted scrawl across all four walls, the artful head high plaques of balloon letters, the smallest penciled scribbles… it all became ugly, rough, illegible. All at once every letter was an affront in both texture and intent though he could no longer read a one. There'd been names before, bands as well as individual punks, some with tiny train tracks and an X for the crossing to show they were riders. Scraps of lyrics and fragmented rants, the ubiquitous anarchy symbol… All gone. Incomprehensible hieroglyphs swirled out at him now.

The whole room pulsed next and… altered, made no architectural sense. Missy barked and twitched her tail against the bucket and Dumont placed a hand on her back. He felt dizzy and fought the urge to puke. The doorway spun around him several times—round and round and round she goes, and where she stops—Ratch and Worm and Marlo stood. The two sidekicks drifted into place behind Marlo right away, assuming generic bully positions so fast Dumont was tempted to laugh. But Marlo had his K-Bar out beside his thigh and the other two each wore their general bulk as a weapon so no way was it time for wisecracks or laughter. The room no longer spun, only rocked a bit side to side in a seasick way as if whatever whirlwind torqued it had settled in overhead for now.

—*Lookit the schwag bitch*, Marlo sneered at him, spoke the words as a slow smoldering threat. His voice oscillated in tempo as if the distance between them were stretching and receding. Dumont felt another twinge of nausea and struggled to suppress it. Ratch and Worm sneered in their special fleshy ways but said nothing. Missy pressed closer against his thigh, hindquarters stiff with tension as she barked in bursts. He stroked her head to calm her.

—Are you *sad* because your girl ain't here? Well you can go ahead an' cry now 'cause she ain't comin'. Little Miss *Tigger*. Turns out she don't bounce too well.

Dumont didn't much care to hear what he was hearing but he knew Marlo was s'posed to be big on head games. Didn't mean any of it counted for a damn thing. If it did then he failed her just like he failed Hector, the kid younger than him at the foster home, what they'd done to him.

He could stand—he was taller than all but Worm—only that would likely take things physical quick, and they were three on one. Maybe they only came to threaten him, scare him into leaving town. They could threaten away. He'd been ready to leave anyway, only *with* Tigger. But what had they done to Tigger?

She told him about the Shadow Riders almost at the start, how she hooked up with Marlo till someone tipped her off he only wanted her for some kind of sacrifice. How she found it out Dumont didn't know but the whole story confused him anyway. Tigger was holding some big pieces back, he could tell that easy. Made it all hard to follow but main thing was he could see she was scared. Way shit scared. Now she was missing maybe worse and the Shadow Riders were all up in his face.

He never dealt with Marlo or his crew himself before, only saw them from a distance and Tigger would whisper *that's them* or sometimes their names. There were others, Crunch and Skurd, Arkansas Jason and Jimmy Whip, more whose names he could not recall. But Marlo was supposed to be their king or ruler or some shit like that, Ratch and Worm his left hand and right.

—*Du*-mont. That girl took something from me, Du-mont. Something she shouldn'a took. Did she give it to *you*, *Du*-mont? I think she did. Hey, we understand how these things can happen. It's *na-chur-al*. Why don't you just let us take a look in your pack Du-mont? We'll take what's ours and leave you with your mutt. No harm no foul, whadda you say?

Ratch stepped hands out toward Dumont's pack. Although he seemed to move in slow motion Dumont didn't try to block him, but he teetered sideways away from the Rider, his bucket seat tilting almost toppling.

Marlo started to say something like *That's it*—and nod before he saw how Dumont slid himself several inches along the wall, bent to grab the bucket handle, then pushed up the wall all the way and with his sea legs at least half back beneath him swung the bottom of the bucket at Worm. Ratch was closest but Worm was the tallest so Dumont went for him first. The bucket with its half dozen rough crusted inches of lumpy concrete at the bottom took Worm full on the side of the head and he. Went. Down.

Missy lunged for Ratch and her teeth sank into his left calf above his boot so he cursed and stumbled back a step. Marlo jerked to his right, brought the K-Bar full up just as Dumont yanked back hard on the bucket only to feel the wire handle tear free from plastic. The battered orange cylinder tumbled away into the shadows and slammed loud against a wall somewhere off in the dark. Everyone looked surprised. Everyone except Worm, who lay staring at the dirt floor. Staring at it real close, like point blank close. Staring at his blood pouring on the dirt.

Dumont yelled to Missy and grabbed the guitar case, booked it for the exit. He felt a tug on his arm as if someone grabbed him and he yanked hard to get free. He heard Ratch pound after him several steps till Marlo shouted —Leave him, asshole! Get the pack! The pack!

Missy hit the doorless doorway ahead of him and staggered as she went. As he trucked through he felt himself swing up sideways on an incline a second, the whole room pitched over the major part of 90 degrees. His applicable senses all told him brace for the fall but he did not fall. Missy yelped ahead so he knew she felt the same still they both pressed on and came level again in three more steps. His stomach prepared to purge but he fought it down one last time, staggered forward anyway. Not now. Not here.

Marlo called from behind —Run sad punk. We'll see you again. Run run run and we'll all have some fun. Later on down the line.

Dumont ran. At least half a dozen blocks, Missy skittering always several feet ahead before Dumont felt the warm wetness on the fingers of his left hand and held it up to see first the blood dripping off them, then the red-streaked facing crescents of pink white muscle revealed in the deep slash across his forearm. He was leaving a trail but he didn't stop to bandage himself till he reached the yard.

***

He was pissed he left his pack. *Pissed to leave the squat.* Pissed most of all he had to leave without Tigger. Sick over Tigger and whether she was okay. Tigger mighta helped him keep it together but even that hope was gone now.

He actually liked that squat. Better than the Pink House, which most everyone said was haunted by ghosts of all the junkies who ODed there. His squat was a derelicted grain and feed store in the 8th Ward, right up close to the decommissioned levy that carried freights along the border strip between the 8th and 9th. The hobos hippies train kids and gutterpunks who came and went there called the location Ward 8 and ¾. The drunker Dumont got the better he liked the joke. He wasn't stupid. He read those books when he was a kid. Some of them anyway, the ones he could find at the school library because his foster parents never bought them. Those books were Satan's work. If wizard books were Satan's work then what were the things they did to their foster children? Dumont had his own ideas about Satan's work in this world.

The squat itself they called Viking House for the inked and bearded white boys who came and went there in this mostly Black and Latin town. Dumont himself bore the nickname *The Norse* for his dirty blond and tangled beard.

He found family at the Viking House. Better and truer than his birth family. Better fersure than his fosters and their own two sons. Folks came and went but they were mostly *real* people, *good* people. His people. Fucking Shadow Riders made him leave too early. Made him leave without Tigger. Tigger, mellow and quiet in spite of her name. How she held so tight to him not only when they fucked, and how she cried softly with him in her but laughed when she came. The eye of his own private hurricane. Tigger with him this shit would not be so bad. But Tigger was gone for now. Only how gone? Was Marlo for real or talking shit?

The farther he rode this freight, the less likely she'd ever find him, or he her. Her pale blue eyes. Her streaky blonde bowl cut, overgrown and combed crossways above her face. Her super old school Navajo rug poncho they used for a fuck blanket. The accustomed tang of her unwashed bod, and the way it blended with his own aromas.

In time he'd reach another yard. Once there he could aim for a freight headed back to NOLA. Back to Tigger. Yeah, and back to the Shadow Riders. Maybe. If they were even still there. If Tigger was...

Or he could strike out alone for... what did those old time writers call it? *Terro incognito? The Territories?* He didn't much like to ride further east or north than NOLA. His winter home for three years running. He had only a vague sense of this freight's next destination. Mississippi somewhere maybe. Or Alabama. He felt the train was headed either north or east. Maybe northeast. When it came to a yard he'd get off, try to find where he was, maybe ask the crew if they seemed cool. Good as lost for now with only vague ideas where to go next. If Marlo and his crew were coming behind him, it might be best to switch up, hitch to the next city, get away from the freight lines a while.

***

Dumont and Missy both slept in fits. He shielded her short fur from the cold metal but it bit him where it could. His ass caught it worst, gone all numb. Legs barely responding, hard to bend. Too low to stand in the fox hole so he flexed his painful frozen legs inside, kicked numbly at the scoured wall.

The brakes screeched and he realized the train was slowing. Soon it shunted onto another track. He could tell they weren't coming into a freight yard yet. He'd see other trains if they were in a yard. The only shapes he saw in the night were trees. The junker he was riding was just siding out to let a faster train pass.

He couldn't see the sky much but where he could it was taking on pink. As he watched the voices came.

So faint at first he pegged the sounds as his imagination. Then he thought *bulls*, but bulls didn't ride the trains. Mostly lazy they patrolled their yards from trucks or golf carts, checked inside cars at stations only.

Not till the volume of the voices rose did he recognize Marlo. Coming from somewhere above. Ahead or behind he could not tell, but close. No words came clear but Dumont knew. He *knew*. And somehow *they* knew. *They knew he was on this train.* They hopped out too and now they were hunting him. Coming over the tops of the cars like some idiots in a western movie. One of the craziest things you could do in real life whether the train was rolling or not.

The guitar. They'd spot it from above. Fersure. The case was too big to squeeze into the hole with him. Aw fuck. But maybe not the guitar.

He set Missy on her feet and flopped on his front. His legs remained unresponsive. Wriggling half out the hole he tugged the case close and popped the snaps. And got another surprise. Atop the soundboard was a kind of book. A grubby thing bound with crooked staples, big crude letter C backward on the cover in Sharpie. He knew it at once: a *Crew Change*. The hobo bible to hop outs. What Marlo must be hunting. When had Tigger stashed it in his case? And why? Fuck. Was that what this was all about? But a *Crew Change* was not all that hard to get. Not *easy*—he never had one himself before—but not something you followed someone over the tops of cars for. Not something you killed over...

The freight they sided out for came on now, an almost endless intermodal stacked double deep with shipping containers. Dumont tugged the book in with him, hefted the guitar by the neck and with its body pushed the case over the edge. Any sound it made was lost in the clamor of the passing train. Fucking Shadow Riders. First his pack and now his case, all his favorite stickers on it best of all the Hank III.

After forever the IM was past and his train lurched forward a few feet forcing Dumont to grip the rim of the fox hole. As they moved he heard the case crunch under the wheels of the next car back and right away Marlo called out. Dumont hoped the sound would draw them away. He hoped Marlo and his crew fell off, broke their fucking necks. Not likely he'd be so lucky though. Another halting advance and they pulled back onto the main track, picked up speed. He withdrew into the grainer's next interior compartment, wiggled the guitar in after him. Missy hopped through and sidestepped a bit before she huddled with him as far from sight as they could get.

He was trapped now if they found him, no weapon in this confined space. Fists and feet, what he was best with anyhow. Missy would bite, though if he hadn't lost her leash he would hold her back. No room to swing his smiley. Forget the guitar he couldn't swing it in here either. He waited, listening for the sounds of their feet or Marlo's voice above, or worse on the platform outside. Meanwhile he curled the *Crew Change* into a slit tube, slid it up his right sleeve then redid the buttons at his wrist. This might prove useful, if not for its content then as armor up his sleeve. It might save that arm from getting cut like the other. Like the padding folks wore to train guard dogs.

In his hidey hole he stayed on alert despite the sleep he needed. But the voices did not return. No voices, no footsteps above. Had they given up? Found their own car to wait out the ride? Too much to hope they'd jumped or fallen off. Most likely they'd be waiting to grab him when the train stopped and he got off.

Missy also kept alert, body tensed, ears up, but she didn't bark or growl. He massaged the tips of her ears to calm her and whispered —Smart girl, yes you're a smart girl—then smiled and nodded as he waved a finger before her face. She licked his hand once then paused and began to bathe it.

She curled against him next almost the same as when he met her, hiding in a shed in El Paso with another gutterpunk named Clutch, waiting for a hop out on a freight to Houston. Clutch stepped out to take a leak and came back 10 minutes later tugging Missy by the scruff, his hand streaked with blood. —Look what I found. Bitch bit me too! He dropped her and she trotted right up to Dumont, curled in his lap. The three of them hopped out right after that but Clutch parted ways at the next yard. Missy stayed with Dumont. He got her cleaned up, groomed and dewormed. Whenever they got to a field or park they played for an hour or more, her puppy energy inexhaustible.

Missy slept now, head tucked within Dumont's secondhand army jacket. Slowly a dim pink glow began to ooze through the opening of the fox hole. The train blew its whistle more often which meant it was coming to a town or city with roads and crossings. Somewhere ahead it'd stop. They couldn't stay on long then—they needed to get off quick but not get caught. Run like hell was not an option—no matter how he shifted his legs stayed half numb from the cold. He'd be stumbling when he hit the ground. But he couldn't stay. If the Shadow Riders didn't find him the bulls probably would.

He jostled Missy gently to wake her and she raised her head, rolled to one side and stood as he began wriggling back to the outer compartment. He had to be ready when the train stopped. His legs remained a mix of numb and pain. Not good. He stretched and flexed them best he could. It didn't do much.

Outside the portal was near full light now though the sky he saw was filmed with haze and white. Beyond the tall grass he saw ranks of pine interspersed with random spreading magnolias. A highway paced them on one flank a bit, though traffic was scant. Dumont guessed westbound. The train began to slow, tempo of the trainsong diminishing. Before long they slowed to a crawl as stilled trains slipped around them right and left. A yard. Soon their train would stop and he and Missy would need to make their move. Hop out on another freight or hoof it to the highway and hitch a ride from there. No matter what, they needed to *move*. Bulls and Shadow Riders would be checking the cars.

He scrambled out stiff legged and caught Missy in his arms, almost tripping before he set her on the ground. No one else in sight, but the voices came again, close, only from behind the train. He rolled under an old coaler on the next track, Missy dodging ahead than looking back. Circulation was returning in his lower half, and quick as he could he cut across two more parked freights. Let the

Riders check the train he rode in on first. One more train traversed and they reached the edge of the yard. A dismal section of town extended before them.

Whatever the station, Hattiesburg or Meridian or who knew where, the stop came near the obligatory industrial park. Factories, warehouses, a few wholesale operations. Yet Dumont saw no activity. Was it Sunday? He'd lost track of days. Or had the shit economy stifled enterprise here? No matter. He'd have to hoof it through this part of town till he came out on a residential or commercial zone. Then he could make his way to an intersection and hitch to the next big town or city, find a hop out on a line the Riders hadn't infested. Mobile seemed like a good destination. Someplace he and Missy could maybe sleep on the beach.

He figured 10 blocks at most till he came out in a more congenial neighborhood but he had to hurry 'cause he had to take a dump now. He needed a convenience store or a library, someplace with an open restroom but where they wouldn't call the cops.

He made his best guess as to where the long buildings gave way and struck crosswise toward what he thought might be north. Missy's nails clicked on the pavement behind him. He needed to clip her, that was overdue. But not right now. Not today.

Something struck him funny about the factories and warehouses in this district. They were the usual colors, gray and brown, white and blue. But their paint seemed more washed out faded than those he'd seen elsewhere. And the signs... the letters on some swam in his vision, impossible to read. Did he have a concussion? But he hadn't taken a hit on the head. Could blood loss cause this all alone?

The few he could read made little sense. *Tortoise Stapling. Kabinet el Sand. Plumb Coriolism. Carpenter Carpenter...* The address numbers on the buildings were lost on him altogether. Each time he tried to focus on a sign either it or his vision shifted to one side so he found himself staring at blank wall.

He saw no workers. Few cars in the lots, and none on the roads. No traffic at all. No trees, no grass. Just pavement, asphalt roads and concrete walks, flat tarry tendrils patching networks of cracks. Sky overcast gray. No wind. No birds. No sound. Some of these buildings shoulda hummed. Buzzed. But nuthin. Obvious Missy disliked the whole area. She stuck close to Dumont, sniffing the ground, her ears down and tense.

The humped cracked sidewalk led him past one building with glass front doors hanging open. All he could make out of its name was *AZOTY*. There seemed to be more letters but the rest defied his vision, their rusted outlines blurred and swimming. Missy stopped, lifted her leg in that halfhearted girl dog way she sometimes did and let loose on something. Possibly a fire hydrant, possibly a tree stump. Whichever, it was painted white. Or gray. He knew he had to let it out soon too.

Dumont peered inside the open doors and saw no receptionist's desk, only a wide empty room. Further down the opposite wall he saw the windowless cabin of a probable restroom. One, two steps inside yet still no workers. To his left the manufacturing floor stretched to an uncertain horizon, bare but for a few shrouded hulks in the middle distance, tarp-covered machinery of unknown function. No one was visible. No activity. Why not? He scuttled all the way in, made his way to what he thought was the men's room. Both the lettering and the icon were uncertain to his eyes, but the simplified woman in a dress on the opposite door showed clear so he knew he had the men's by process of elimination...

He wanted to get in and out quick so he whistled Missy along in case any workers arrived. The things she'd seen for lack of space...

Inside all was normal, even clean. Until he opened the only stall and looked in the commode. Though no foul splatter marked its rim or lid a burnt orange haze hung still within, at its center a denser clot, sunk and obscured. The murk was the hue of blood diffused in water, the clot some unseen discarded hunk of flesh or gland. Dumont had his zipper half down when something splashed and the water in the toilet rippled as if whatever was hidden beneath the diffused blood within got restless of a sudden. Oh *fuck* this! Dumont staggered out of the restroom in reverse yanking up his zipper as he went, and Missy followed close, growling but not barking yet. He'd shit in an alley if he had to, if he could find a safe one. Wouldn't be the first time. He'd shit in all kinds of crazy places and was not picky but shitting on whatever was in that toilet was not in the plan. He would have to hold it, clench his bowels till the next opportunity.

The long floor remained empty. Still no workers. He shuffled toward the front doors, Missy hugging his thigh. She knew something was off with the place same as he did. Strange thing though, she wasn't sniffing. There were always smells.

Outside things were even stranger now. Not only the signs but the buildings themselves seemed ill defined, their shapes distorted, lines gone off plumb, sides and facades fuzzed and blurred as if through TV interference. The lump Missy pissed on before, hydrant or stump, nothing but a fizzing gray puddle now. As he and Missy passed it the mass oozed flat viscous tendrils toward them, impossibilities they had to dodge. Dumont cursed softly as they hurried along their path back to the yard.

Missy meanwhile whimpered and hugged his leg, sleek flank pressing against his calf. The structures around them lost definition and stretched like taffy, flattened in the air. Had he really lost enough blood to cause these distortions? Or had Marlo dipped his K-Bar in some hallucinogenic poison only kicking in now. Not like shrooms or acid or even K. Real ugly stuff. But Missy wasn't cut and she was seeing something wrong too, same as back at the squat. She bit Ratch though—could his blood have dosed her?

He backtracked best he could. Back to the yard to try for another hop out. This town was major fucked up. He hoped the yard wasn't fading into static too. He hoped they could make it back before it did. He hoped he wasn't dying or going insane.

Even the sidewalk felt wrong beneath his feet, giving softly as if cut from tough rubber. The clicks of Missy's nails were muffled.

Around him the buildings shifted into forms he could no longer pick out yet he pressed on in the direction he thought took him back.

What was left of his luck held and the yard reappeared, if not quite where he remembered. The trains were still trains though veiled in a vague gray shimmer. Then another break came his way. One of the freights had begun to roll, slow.

The last half dozen cars were all coalers, no good for riders unless already filled. They'd cover your clothes and flesh with black dust, make you cough and burn your eyes, but worst of all was if they got filled while you were inside. Then you got crushed and buried. Behind the coalers though was another engine facing back. Empty engines were excellent rides. This one was a blue and yellow CSX, what they called the *Dark Future* paint scheme. What coked up corporate dickhead came up with a name like that?

Bald Jonny Ben taught him early on the basic rule for hopping freights on the fly. If you could count the nuts on a turning hub, you were good. He could.

He cut across the yard, paced the engine's inching crawl. First he raised the guitar and slid it onto the unit's outer catwalk. He hefted Missy up the first stair next, cut left arm protesting, and she scrabbled up the rest on her own. With his right he pulled himself up the rail to the little walkway and yanked on the door, yellow with a bold blue C dead center. It was like cracking the hatch on a ship. He watched Missy perk up as the warmth of the heated cab wafted out. She slipped around him to get inside where she turned and looked back, wagging her tail and waiting for him to join her. He swept up the guitar by its neck and ducked in after her.

Inside the engine were leather seats. A little fridge. And a *restroom*, oh thank you Jesus!

He took care of the most important business first then shut the door so Missy wouldn't try to drink from the squat chemical toilet. They still needed water though. Both of them.

He tried the miniature metal fountain but nuthin. Out of order no doubt. He checked the fridge, Missy peering in hopefully beside him, but they found no food, only five pint water bottles. He took two out and closed the door. Missy stared up at him in expectation. With his left forearm he pressed one bottle against his side while he used both hands to unscrew the lid from the other. Missy wagged tail and tongue together. —You want some water, don't you girl? Problem was the dinged up little aluminum bowl he carried for her was lost like so much else with his pack.

Fuck it. He tipped the water bottle slowly above her nose. She craned her neck and lapped at the water as it dribbled down. Over half dripped onto the floor. He tilted the bottle up again and after an expectant moment Missy bent to lick the water from the floor. He hated for her to have to do it this way, but better than the toilet. Three rounds of this left the bottle drained and the floor almost dry. He drew the second bottle from beneath his arm and drank.

Dumont knew to take it slow. He'd eaten nothing for over a day and now he felt the chill water settle in his empty stomach. It hurt at first, a dull cramping ache in the depths of his abdomen. He spasmed, bent over, pressed his right forearm into his guts, but didn't puke. The pain faded in increments and once it was mostly gone he sank back into the right hand engineer's seat, cradled the half empty bottle at his crotch. Sleep took him quick though it did not hold him well.

He rose and fell from the depths of his rest on and off for hours, Missy curled and sleeping at his feet. Dreams visited him, vivid and important, but he remembered none on the waking side. Outside the windows day grew dim again in time as a divided forest receded in his sight.

He went to the fridge and got another water bottle for Missy, poured it out as before and drank the fourth himself. Stuffed the fifth and final in a pocket of his jacket. He knew he could no longer put off inspecting his cut—but what was he gonna do for it anyway? He had nothing to sew it up with and only their last pint of water to clean it. Maybe he could drain it if he had to at least.

Slowly he unwrapped the blood crusted bandanna he wore around it. He expected the cloth to stick, to cling, to pull painfully at his flesh, but it came off easy. The wound beneath was like nothing he'd seen, not the expected narrow cañon of maroon surrounding a canal of pus, but a charcoal swath of desiccated black.

Puffs of dust rose up from the cut and he whiffed the same bitter undercurrent he caught at the squat, initial herald of the Riders' approach. Probably he needed this slice seen to and soon... which meant he was gonna have to tough it out. The idea of doctors was a joke in his world. Nuthin else for it now so he wrapped the bandana back around. It didn't hurt all that bad anymore. Kind of numb around the cut, the numbness maybe spreading, but he was gonna be all right. He'd find some iodine, figure something out.

Dumont settled again into the engineer's chair. If all he did today on this ride was snooze his time would be well spent. He wished for some whiskey... but if he wished in one hand and shit in the other he knew which would fill up first. His foster father used to say that, and who ever gave Dumont more shit than him? Damn those Shadow Riders, takin' his fuckin' whiskey... farther this train carried him away from them the more he liked it. He slipped back into sleep until...

Missy tugged his right hand with her teeth, her grip nowhere near so soft as their normal play. He cursed then saw how she sought to drag him toward the short stair back down to the hatch. And saw now what she must've heard. Someone turning the door handle. Could it be one of the Riders? No way they could've tracked him here, not this time. Probably bulls. But the train was moving, far from any yard. Bulls stayed each in their own yard, checked the trains there. So couldn't be bulls then. Couldn't be good, whoever it was.

Whoever wanted to open the door was doing it with painstaking slowness, which meant they knew he was in there. Probably saw him through the windows, asleep in the chair. Dumont tried to rise but his arms had gone to tingling jelly, effect of poor circulation and his position in the seat. He leapt to shaky feet, wobbling, unsteady, flapping his arms to get the blood back in them fast. The door latch opened with a muffled click. Without further thought he dove down the stairs toward the door itself right as it began to ease open, leading with his left shoulder. He stumbled on the steps but traded equilibrium for momentum, slammed the part open door hard and into whoever was outside. He felt first metal crack against skull then connect with padded flesh as the door flung the other back onto the railing and Dumont tumbled out on top.

Dumont shoved himself away from the hulking figure on the catwalk. He saw black leather a pale blocky head and gray fuzz for hair. Ratch. And he recognized the jagged C on the shoulder of Ratch's jacket as *the same sign on the Crew Change what the fuck?* Ratch caught the cold steel rail with his right hand to keep from going over. Dumont drove forward kicked the Rider hard in the crotch with booted foot while he was still off balance then struck twice again quickly at Ratch's hand on the rail. The Shadow Rider gasped a muffled —*Fuck* and sought to pull back but he had nowhere to go. Dumont kept a loose grip on the flapping hatch door with his numb left hand as he kicked Ratch in the shoulder the ribs the side of his head. Dumont knew he had only this moment's advantage and had to press it, his leg pumping at the knee aiming striking in vicious reflex. He could no way let Ratch draw in, grapple with him, drag him down on the catwalk or back into the cab. The guy was a fuckin' tank. His only hope was to finish it here, now. Most of all if Marlo or any others were coming. He had no chance if he had to take on more than one. Adrenalin powered his attack.

Ratch's right hand was blood and pulp, shreds of muscle showing and even bone at a couple knuckles but he still found strength enough to throw his left into Dumont's own crotch and drive him back against the cab though the shot missed hitting his balls dead on and took him more on the upper right thigh. Dumont gasped and spun but kept his grip on the door even as it swung to on his fingers and gouged them. Crotch and cut arm shooting pain, he drove two more quick kicks at Ratch's wrist before the other fumbled for the rail with his free left. Bone cracked and Ratch's bloody ruined right grip slipped and he tumbled backward from the platform, flopping left to keep from falling off and thrusting himself instead half over the righthand stairs. Dumont rained kicks against his feet and crotch and thighs, anything to propel him further... and *off this fucking train.*

Ratch struggled to rise but this only cost him further traction and dragged him down. He bumped flailing over the stairs, skull grinding a second in the right of way gravel before he slipped off the ramp altogether, whipped away quick in the outside wind. He didn't cry out or scream and the trainsong covered any thump he might've made as he struck.

Oh fuck oh shitfuck had he just killed a man? Dumont fought near as often as he ate—sometimes more—but he never sought to kill, only to defend himself a friend or a dog, only to protect, only to survive. True he might've done for Worm already but he had no way to be sure so he wasn't going to count it. Not just yet at least. Dumont leaned panting on the rail, wounds and bruised scrotum still screaming with dull aching pain, and looked into the night along the route they left behind. He saw Ratch's crumpled form beside the tracks receding at twenty plus miles an hour... then rising. First the Rider was on his feet again then he was running down the tracks after them in ever lengthening strides, right arm flopping loose at his side. Coming closer.

With no time and still too pumped to reflect on this latest madness Dumont glanced around the platform for something to throw and so missed the moment a vast blot of blackness shuffled out of the night on the left, a thing impossible in size, larger than an elephant though smaller than a house, stumpy limbs visible only as hints. It bent over the running Rider and dipped, engulfing him to the waist and hefting him up. Ratch's legs kicked half a minute then the top part of whatever... clenched. Or something. Ratch's lower half tumbled back to the tracks in a dark spray. Dumont turned away. He'd seen enough. This time Ratch was dead. No question. Those legs would not be running after him all on their own.

He stared and the mass astride the tracks cocked the hump he took for its top as if to watch him but it did not pursue, halting there instead above Ratch's bottom half, disappearing back into the dark in the wake of the train. Missy barked from between his ankles but he shushed her, herded her back inside the hatch door and relatched it.

Inside Dumont pressed his hands to the chill trembling walls for balance, stability, tried to process what he'd seen. Shit had gone from crazy to what he couldn't even say. And yet he'd taken out two of the Riders, if Worm was truly down for the count and he included Ratch in his tally. He had a little help on that one. Somehow he got the jump on each of those guys though. They were as big or bigger than him and experienced brawlers both. But they hadn't shown it and he had. They'd been slow. Could be Marlo doped them with something to guarantee obedience, but Dumont never heard of any such drug. And what about Marlo? Was he somewhere on this train too? How often did he rely on his flunkies? Or could it be he and Ratch split up to hunt for Dumont on separate trains? Or did he send Ratch ahead alone because he himself was a coward? He had that coward stink, big talk but bigger buddies. Could be Marlo had his whole cult or crew with him now, scouring the train for Dumont from front to back and Ratch was only the first to arrive. Two more Shadow Riders might show up next. Maybe three or four or five, Marlo with them. Dumont could make his way back up the train but he was probably gonna run right into them like that. Getting Missy over the tops of cars wasn't likely either, and he wasn't going anywhere without her. He could hide with her in the engine's restroom but he knew Marlo would look there and he and Missy would be trapped. In the end he slumped back in the leather seat, determined to stay more alert for the next attack or the end of the line, whichever came first. He slid into sleep again almost at once.

***

When he woke a gray fingered light reached in for him through the windows and his balls still ached. The train was slowing though. Fersure.

Missy remained on guard at his feet, lying on her side but head still up, her vigilance more consistent than his. Must be she'd been like that all along. He slid down, crouched beside her, scratched behind her ears. Oh you're a smart girl, yes you are. You done good. *Way good.* She saved his life already once this ride. Both their lives. He stroked her sleek black fur and she rolled on her back, offered her belly, legs quivering with unrestrained joy while he scratched her. He knew they could go on like this forever but it was time to hop off so he stopped. She arched to lick his hand and he leaned over, hugged her once quick tight. She licked his cheek, his ear. His intended laugh emerged as a grunt and he released her after a final squeeze.

He felt their pace slow further, the trainsong tempo extending in an exhausted drawl. They were moving slower now than when they hopped on. —Time to go, he whispered in Missy's ear. She seemed to understand, rolled to her feet, watched him expectantly.

He led her down the steps to the hatch, opened it slowly this time and peeked around. No more Shadow Riders, no Marlo, no bulls, no one at all. No monstrous globs of night behind them either. He supposed some Riders might be out of sight on the roof, approaching like spiders or ants, but he and Missy would have to risk it.

They worked their way down the stairs, Missy turning her nose up at streaks of Ratch's blood on the steel. She leapt from the still moving engine then paced the train till he stepped off behind her toting the caseless guitar with a hand around its neck.

***

They'd got off before the yard this time, though they could see it ahead. He had no clue where they were. To their left the backs of shops butted up all but on the railroad's right of way. Retail stores, not the sort of industrial stuff they'd waded into before. At least now he could hitch out of a proper town, shake whatever scent Marlo and his crew somehow followed on the freights. Might be he'd head up north where he was supposed to have family. Real family, blood family. He knew he had cousins he never met somewhere. Jersey, he was pretty sure. Yeah. Jersey fersure.

He called to Missy and they set off toward the shops, crossing several empty tracks and crawling under a chain link fence before reaching the back street. He wished he could clip a leash on her but that was lost with his pack. He'd keep his eye out for a scrap of rope that might do the trick. She still wore her collar at least.

From there they took an intersecting side and a short block later came out on what had to be Main. The sidewalks remained empty of pedestrian traffic this early in the day and the only cars were parked, but it seemed otherwise solid and real, not like the industrial park in Meridian or wherever. He could read the signs on the stores even, across the street a Rexall Drugs beside an antique shop, display window crowded with old clothes and ottomans and a faded red Radio Flyer sled. A grubby dive bar that hadn't opened yet two doors down. Everything closed but otherwise normal.

He took off with Missy in a direction he thought perpendicular to the now obscured yard, hoping to spot the red and blue shield of an interstate on-ramp or at least a local highway or truck route. They passed more restaurants and stores and bars, everything closed. Even this early something ought to be open, a lunch counter serving breakfast maybe, not like he had the cash, or that they wouldn't throw him out 'cause he was dirty and he smelled.

At least the stores were normal and he could read the signs. This wasn't another mindfuck trap like the last stop. Just an uptight southern town where they rolled up the sidewalks at night and put them back out late in the morning and... he spotted *them* ahead, four or

five all scrunched up together near the next corner, a bunch of gutterpunks same as him.

Okay… if they were cool they would help him, tell him where to
find food, water, where to catch a ride. Maybe share some whiskey.
Best to come up slow though, be all nonthreatening, most of all not
look like he planned to stay any while. Talking up his search for a
ride out ought to help that.

Closer in he saw four dudes and a girl, backs to him all, mix of
leather jackets with Carhartt overalls, hoodies, flannels, camo. All
with their heads down and angled away from him.

About 10 feet out he stopped and called to them —Wassup dudes?
No response. He came forward a few more steps, spoke again —Hey,
no hassles you know. All I'm lookin' for is the best place to hitch a
ride on to F.L.A., maybe some water and some dumpster pizza. Then
I'm outta here, fersure. Can you be cool with that?

None of them turned but at last the girl began to speak, a blunt
susurrus Dumont could not understand. The first phrase he could
pick out came across as —Along alas alack a leak…

Followed by the boy in leather…

—Tracks leak to the dark star call for a bite of blood bad bitter or
better.

Had leather boy said leak or *lead*? No way to tell. And the girl—
what the fuck, were these kids talking French? Could be they were
Cajun, but all the way out here? Wherever here was… 'Bama, Georgia maybe…

—Hey guys, we're just looking for a good spot to hitch out from,
head north maybe, you know?

He paused so they could respond. They said nothing but one began to turn, a boy with ragged dreads wearing filthy Carharrts over a
torn green Army jacket.

The boy had no face. Beneath his dreads and a bare inch of greasy
forehead the front of his head was a round dark hole. Other than the
teeth that lined it Dumont saw nothing inside. The blank aperture
contracted slightly in an irregular quivering rhythm, pulsing to nar-

row its diameter just barely then expanding again, all as if with some unseen breath.

The faceless boy began to chitter and hiss. The other four turned and Dumont saw the same impossible lamprey faces gaping each in dark lopsided holes rimmed with rough and irregular teeth, each with its singular rhythm of expansion and contraction, each hissing or even screeching at him now in its own particular pitch. Some spoke in broken words others simply chittered or moaned and one cried —*Dumont Dumont Dumont…* but he couldn't tell which.

He staggered back feeling Missy dodging and feinting around his calves. She didn't bark though. She really was one smart girl. She knew when to sound the alarm and when not to push it. Was he hallucinating? If Marlo's blade dosed him there should be other effects… there was that last town of course—that and the thing that bit Ratch clean through.

He saw the worst then. The five faceless punks were not just scrunched together—they had only one body below the waist, cloaked beneath folds of filthy cloth. The heads all twisted toward him now, necks extending to impossible lengths and writhing like flower stalks in the wind, like baby birds begging for puked up food from their mom. They chittered or chanted nonsense except for the one repeating his name.

He backed away two more steps as the whole distorted distended mass began to advance his way, crawling heavily over the concrete sidewalk same way as a slug—a slug the size of a rhinoceros. He turned and ran, Missy pacing ahead but glancing back every few feet. The punk glob came on only at a slow and plodding pace and he soon opened up a lead, the better part of a block. He turned the corner and… there they were ahead. Crawling toward him again from the end of the block. Same overlapping clothes, same many headed configuration reaching toward him like an enormous hand.

Dumont turned back, saw them still there advancing as if in a mirror. He ran with Missy back to Main… and there they were as well, crossing toward him from in front of the Rexall. He found a side street leading away from Main and it was empty. He and Missy hustled down it and came out close to the yard. No one blocked their path, no mass of toothed blind heads, no Riders, no bulls.

In the yard itself he found an open corrugated aluminum shed and crouched beside a stack of rusted parts. Missy paced before him and he stroked her back each time as she passed. Dogs were a big part of this life but he never saw any of the Shadow Riders with one. Another reason to give them space, keep away. Never trust anyone who rode the rails without a dog.

A sketchy rain began falling, fat scattered drops plink plopping over the rippled roof and puffing small tired question marks of dust from the ground outside. Dumont thought about plucking out a song on the guitar, practicing one of his originals, but he had to remain vigilant, couldn't risk it. Bulls, Riders, those freaky gape mouthed kid things… all might be hunting him. Best not to call their attention down. Seemed like they were safe here at least for now.

He dozed in fits. At some point the rain stopped. A bit later he woke. The rain began again. It didn't last this time, ten minutes tops. As it faded he heard train wheels beginning to roll.

Gripping his guitar he made his way into the yard, Missy close behind. Rounding three trains he found a fourth pulling out, a row of rust hued boxcars passing close. He eyed one of only two still open and as it came close he trotted to pace it, shoved the guitar across its floor, lifted Missy inside, then followed along till he could clamber up to join her, his cut arm almost altogether numb.

Boxcars. The classic hobo ride still good after all these years. Dumont rested on his back several minutes as the train picked up speed. But he could not ignore the door for long. Another of Jonny Ben's basics was when riding in a boxcar always wedge the door open with a spike in its track. If the door slid shut on a slope somewhere it might be months before anybody opened it again and found the withered mummy of your corpse.

Problem was the rusty spike he carried for just this purpose was in the pack he lost. He had nothing but the book and the guitar and neither seemed right for the job. The floor of the boxcar around him was all bare, but in the shadowed rear he saw a dark mound of lumps and sticks. Might be something there he could use. If not, he had major problems.

He rolled onto his right side, rose and shuffled toward the neglected heap. He had to hold his lighter down close but he saw quick it wasn't sticks.

The mound of rags and bones rose two feet high, all dismal black and tarry. A scatter of broken skulls made it clear at least the majority were human. He saw a dogskull too and something else he couldn't identify, a skull with five eyeholes, incomprehensible in shape and over three feet long.

Repressing his first impulse to retreat yet again, he scraped out a dehydrated thought and nodded, bent to tug loose a knob ended long bone from the general mass. A black tarry nastiness coated it all over and it stuck a couple seconds in the rags of the pile before it came free.

Prize in his hand he bopped for the side of the train, set the bone at an angle between wall and floor then stomped it hard with booted heel, once, twice. On the second shot it shattered along a long jagged angle though the two pieces hung together. Dumont took the broken bone in hand and slammed it against the boxcar's wall till one half fell free. He soccer kicked the fragment out the door and jammed the piece he held point end first into the track, stamping his heel down on the joint end once, twice, three times so it was good and set.

That done he stepped to the side opposite the door, dipping to retrieve his guitar, and slid down against the wall where he could stare out the open door. He hadn't even reached the floor before it hit him just how beat he was, how whipped and weak and worst of all dehydrated. Hungry too but he could handle that. At least for now. All the crazy shit he'd scene, monsters, slug punks, whole fake towns… was it all just poison or dehydration? Could any of this craziness be real?

Missy walked over and laid her head in his lap. Poor girl. She had to be as bad off as he. Her food had all been lost with his pack. He dug the remaining bottle of water from his pants and dribbled it into her mouth in fits till it was gone, saving only the final sip for himself.

Outside a wooded landscape rolled on by. Engines and even grainer foxholes might be more comfortable, but an open boxcar really was the way to ride. Dumont felt connected to the old time 'bos of the depression in a boxcar, back when riding freights was almost respectable. He loved the scenery he could see like this. Trains were a different world. They moved through night and day, they were neither here nor there, they traveled forgotten parts of the country. Once crossing Georgia he swore he saw a Civil War battle out the door of a boxcar just like the one he rode now, the blue and the gray, bloodied bodies, cannons firing and the low fog of smoke from ordinance everywhere just overhead.

The wall of trees on this route stretched on for miles, something he never saw riding out from Albuquerque and El Paso, where empty spaces came in a thousand shapes, sometimes trucks or trailers or dim toiling figures in the distance but little else to mark. Here the trees approached dense and sudden just outside the right of way, interrupted only as the train passed nameless towns where the backs of buildings displayed elaborate graffiti as they faced the tracks. Slowly wisps of smoke threaded in, outliers of some forest fire or perhaps simply fog.

The scenery revived memories from when he counted his age in single digits, how he'd take his temporary escape from his foster brothers into the undeveloped country west of their rundown neighborhood on the seedy south Cerrillos side of Santa Fe. He would run out and into the pink-brown sand and scattered sage till the houses behind were the dimmest strip then crouch behind bushes or in a shallow arroyo, sometimes bruised and bleeding still, crying and poking in the sand with a branch. He never drew anything, but he watched the large dark beetles that came and went, occupied on cryptic errands known only to themselves. No matter how far he followed them he never saw them eat or sneak down any holes. They just walked and walked—unless he got too close and they hiked up their butts, extruded bits of foul orange tube. If you tried to pick them up and they rubbed that nasty odor onto you it took several days to wash it off.

He had his own idea about where to go next. He was still heading east, he was pretty sure of that much, and would have to hit the coast or Florida soon. If Missy and he could make their way to Tampa they could catch a juice train. Word was Tropicana ran *three* juice trains a day, one to Jersey, one to Ohio, and one all the way to L.A. Fastest things on rails, right of way all the way and forcing even the fastest freights to side out. He'd never ridden one and he heard from Jonny Ben they were hard as hell to hop, with Missy most of all, but if they could, any of the three would carry them far beyond the Riders' reach. Despite whatever fam he might have in Jersey, Cali seemed the best bet, a straight shot back across the country in only two days and far far away from Marlo and his crew. Dumont was sure he could shake the Shadow Riders then.

A thick fog ruled beyond the doors. He stepped closer to the opening so he could inspect it. The mist looked close enough he could run his fingers through it if he only leaned out but he felt somehow that would be unhealthy. Instead he withdrew, positioned himself half behind the boxcar's door as if it could shield him. Light flashed at intervals inside the smoky curtain, red and pink and without visible source. With each pulse something like veins lit within the vapor, red branching networks glimpsed for a moment and lingering briefly as afterimages, seeming to follow the direction of their travel. Down below the tie ends blurred by, the gravel bed beneath them an uncertain blur. The train swept on through this medium for hours, the better part of a day perhaps. Dumont strode across the car, far away from the tarry tangle of bones and clothes, curled up best he could and slept. Twice he awoke and each time still saw the same weird fog outside. He wondered if it was just him or the engineers saw it too. What they made of it if they did. He wondered if this train even had engineers anymore…

He unbuttoned his sleeve and slipped out the *Crew Change* figuring to see what it said about the juice trains and the Tampa yard, at least get some guidance from this thing that caused him so much grief and cost maybe three lives already. Only when he opened it the lines seesawed left and right and the size of the type itself shrank and swelled in his tired and crusty eyes. He tossed it down beside him in disgust and saw Missy shy away from it. Fuck it. He got on fine without a Crew Change all this time. He didn't need one now.

He lifted the guitar instead, propped it on his thigh, drew the last pick from his pocket—at least he hadn't lost that—began to strum out some chords. The thing was way out of tune—carrying it by the neck hadn't helped no doubt. He powered through the song anyway. One of his own. No title 'cause he hated titles. Titles were labels and he had enough of labels already. No chorus either. Fuckin' knowitalls always asked him where was the chorus, where was the bridge, and he'd say why do I need a chorus if I'm all alone, why do I need a bridge if I ain't goin' nowhere?

Freight trains and whiskey is all that I need
Cause I'm far away from my home
Whiskey keep me warm train roll me along
I'm all alone right now
Spare some fuckin' change right now
Cause I'm hoppin' on and I ain't comin' back
I'm hellbound for the devil's plains
I'm just a loner who's gone insane
I just watch those wheels spin as I'm carried to my grave
I live for the moment I live for today
Salvation is a thousand miles away
Knowin' me I'm not gonna stop
I just keep on rollin' on
Freight trains and whiskey is all that I need

He wrote that a year or so back after finding this bullshit Christian tract called *The Hellbound Train* in another boxcar he rode. He did not miss out though on how the lyrics suddenly became more true. He understood irony and it seemed to be gunning for him most of the time.

Missy perked up as he played. He could never decide whether she liked his playing, but she always listened at least.

—You like that girl? He half expected her to nod but she didn't.

—Anyway, I'm not really alone so long as I got you. He shrugged.

—It's just a song.

Dumont set the guitar beside him. He knew before he looked up Marlo was in the doorway. He hung there, same way a spider hangs from a strand of web. Except Dumont couldn't see any web, no rope, no wire, no line.

—Listen to the schwag bitch.

Dumont didn't reply, didn't move. He calculated distances, angles, steps and times. He peered beyond Marlo, alert for the appearance of other Shadow Riders.

—*You* were just s'posed to be meat, you and your little girlfriend, just another delivery. Now you've got *their* attention. They've gone back to watch you. Forward and back. You're starting to grow on them. They want to meet you. I say fuck that, you're not growing on *me*, and I still call my own shots on this side.

Marlo slid all the way to the floor, took two steps toward Dumont. The Rider had his K-Bar out again, obscure hieroglyphs etched into the blade of the old military knife.

Missy growled. Marlo advanced. Missy barked.

Marlo paused. —You should get your bitch on a leash, *bitch*. They want her too you know. But I say no. You know that's not happening either. I'll take care of her when I'm done with you.

Dumont hissed —No, Missy. He didn't want her running at Marlo, getting cut. He was gonna handle this himself. Dumont did not rise however, hardly moved. Marlo took three more steps and scoped the *Crew Change* on the floor at last.

—Fuckin' bitch I knew you had it all along. Well, time—

Though his angle sucked Dumont arched up and swung the guitar hard as he could, took Marlo just below the left knee. The soundbody crunched and crumpled as the Rider went to his knees. Dumont got full on his feet then, striking down at Marlo with the shattered body first then just the neck when the rest fell loose. *This machine kills fascists.* Right? Missy barked and lunged but held from attack. Marlo scrambled back on buttocks, hands and feet, crab-walking away from this onslaught of wrecked lacquered wood, the guitar itself dying by crunches and groans till even the flat-pegged head dropped from Dumont's hand.

Almost to the door, Marlo rose and shook himself free of shattered fragments, smiled at Dumont, brought the K-Bar to the level of his hip, advanced.

Hands empty, Dumont still held his ground, Missy barking but keeping back of his knees. —All this for a *Crew Change*, Marlo? Can't be that hard to get another...

Marlo paused a second and laughed —Bitch, you think that's a *Crew Change*? Ha!

Dumont bent to lift the rough bound book in his left, fixed his gaze on Marlo's face, targeting the raw red scar that crept up his chest and neck to twist along beside his nose.

—Giving it back is not enough now Du-mont. You and that mutt are gonna—

Dumont flung the book toward the door to Marlo's left, flat like a frisbee, hard as he could. The Rider batted at it with one hand and managed to knock it back to the floor. Dumont rushed forward tugging the tail of the faded blue bandanna that hung from the chest pocket of his weathered jacket, dragging free his smiley, a plated steel padlock tied at the end of the cloth. As Marlo groped on the floor for the book Dumont swung the smiley at the back of his head.

The makeshift weapon's impact felt oddly blunted, dragging across the Rider's skull instead of rebounding with a crack. Marlo spun and shrieked at Dumont, his mouth grown impossibly wide though not round like the slug punks in the town behind them. Instead his whole face split along the scar that ran from his neck to create an irregular quavering gash.

Fixed on that mouth Dumont failed to block the K-Bar when Marlo brought it up and slid it into his guts. Despite the instant waves of pain he struck Marlo's knife wrist with the smiley and heard bone crack like the Rider's skull had not. Marlo lost his grip on the knife though his mouth had grown gigantic now, big as the bell of a tuba. He leaned toward Dumont as if to engulf him as Dumont himself collapsed to his knees.

Marlo's mouth spread like smoke, filling over half of the doorway now and expanding. Dumont felt his hand on the book, dropped the Smiley and yelled —Marlo, here goes your fuckin' book! and lobbed it low off the train. It struck the veiny mist beyond and hung there, shot away with their passage. Marlo spun the meaty bloom of his face to follow it and overbalanced as the book zipped from sight. Dumont flopped back, cocked both feet from the knees and slammed them straight against the pockets of Marlo's Levis even as he gasped at the pain from the blade embedded below his ribs.

Marlo seemed to vault from the boxcar almost on his own and struck the oppressive soup outside, embedding himself instantly like an insect in amber and shooting away in their wake. Dumont was certain he saw his adversary begin to dissolve before their passage removed him entirely from sight.

Dumont collapsed on his back before the boxcar's open door and laughed. It hurt to laugh but he could not keep it in. —Fucker, he called softly after the vanished Rider. —Fuck you, fucker. You're fucking done now.

He made no attempt to rise. Meanwhile outside he witnessed a genuine surprise. The fog began to thin in patches, whole stretches next, and where it did thin he saw the scenery of the south once more. Green again, a vast unbroken curtain of high dark pines. Georgia somewhere most likely. For the barest intervals at first then several seconds at a time.

The old world showed through only to a point though. As Dumont lay panting, Missy licking his face, the intervals of normal began to diminish again.

He knew it was the worst thing to do in his case but he tugged the knife free and flung it aside. Black dust puffed from the wound, followed by slow-pumping gouts of thickened blood, the anticipated crimson streaked with swirling interwoven threads of pitch.

His good arm began to grow numb.

Dumont drew Missy to him, wrapped both arms awkwardly round her. He rolled on his left side, slid toward the door, limbs he could barely feel loose around her sleek black fur.

He timed it, waiting for the world he was leaving behind to flash beyond the open door again. Missy wriggled in his grip, suspecting his plan, not wanting to leave him. The train was moving slower now, not much more than 10-15 mph. Trees reappeared. A sky of blue and white. He saw genuine birds, dark streaks and flapping eyebrows, probably crows. Standing water even, a pond or small lake. He tried to lean over far as he could, drop Missy not throw her, but he was weak from blood loss and dehydration and who knew what else so in the end she simply slipped to the gravel from his unsteady hands. She rolled, resilient as ever and back on her feet in a flash, running after him barking, chasing this strange damned train but dropping fast behind. She was a survivor though. His hopes all hung on that. He had time to gasp —I love you girl, and then the red veined haze returned and he knew he'd be alone on the other side. Fuck it. Let this place cope with his chaos. Fersure the other world never could.

AFTERWORD

Ross E. Lockhart

One of my first gigs in this crazy business we call publishing was writing the flap copy for the hardcover edition of Laird Barron's first collection, *The Imago Sequence*. As I recall, I got paid in books for this, which is fine because I'd likely have spent any monetary compensation on books anyhow.

The Imago Sequence blew me away. I was already fairly well versed in the weird tale, and in the typical tropes associated with Lovecraftian pastiche, but Barron's approach did something unexpected with the form, fusing the strangeness of supernatural horror with the stark naturalism of Jack London (whose "To Build a Fire" Barron himself classifies as Cosmic Horror), daring to deliver something different, a high-stakes carnivorous cosmos populated with tough, rugged protagonists more accustomed to inhabiting hard-boiled tales of crime or espionage than Lovecraft's prone-to-fainting academics. Through this (at the time) unlikely combination, Barron managed to, in the words Ezra Pound once pinched from a Chinese emperor's bathtub, "make it new."

One does not read a Laird Barron story so much as one experiences it in a visceral manner. A tale like "Shiva, Open Your Eye" strips away a reader's reason, flaying him, leaving him floating in the primordial jelly, innocent of coherent thought. "Hallucigenia" is, quite literally, a kick in the head. The painstaking noirish layering to be found in "The Imago Sequence" culminates in a ghastly, shuddering reveal of staggering proportions. And it is that sense of culmination one finds echoing throughout Laird Barron's work, binding the whole together into a Pacific Northwest Mythos reminiscent of, but cut from another cloth entirely from, Lovecraft's witch-haunted New England.

A handful of one-off copywriting gigs led to greater opportunities, and soon, I found myself working full-time for the publisher of *The Imago Sequence*, which led to my meeting Laird in the flesh at the World Fantasy Convention in Saratoga, NY. I found we shared a kindred spirit… and a taste for rare spirits and supernatural tales. Upon my return, I worked on the trade paperback edition of *The Imago Sequence*, and on Laird's next collection, *Occultation*, where I not only wrote the jacket copy, but laid out the book, coordinated the production team working on it, supervised copyedits, approved those edits with Laird, and corrected the book (as a nod to Robert Bloch, I suppose you could refer to me as "The Man Who Corrected Laird Barron.").

Shortly after *Occultation* landed, my wife and I embarked on a road trip up the West Coast, a drive where the scenery—stark mountains, tall trees, steep costal drop-offs—constantly reminded me of one Laird Barron story or another. Our journey brought us to Olympia, where we met Laird for lunch, talked martial arts and American literature, and I snapped a few photographs of Laird playing with our little dog, Maddie.

Somewhere along the line, both *The Imago Sequence* and *Occultation* managed to win Laird his first and second Shirley Jackson Awards, and I began working with Laird as editor of his first novel, *The Croning*, which he sent to me in bits and pieces over the course of a tough year, building it like a wall, brick by brick and layer by layer. With *The Croning*, Laird metaphorically opened a vein and bled words onto the page, and while a casual reader might not spot the author's open wounds, the emotional wallop delivered by the book more than assures you that those wounds are not only there, but that they are raw.

I published Laird's novella "The Men from Porlock" in my first anthology, *The Book of Cthulhu*, and his "Hand of Glory" in my second, *The Book of Cthulhu II*. And over the course of 2012, I worked on Laird's third collection, *The Beautiful Thing that Awaits Us All*, reading stories as Laird finished them and sent them along. One of my favorites in the collection, the wickedly sardonic "More Dark," managed to get me in trouble when I read it on my phone during a baseball game, prompting my wife to elbow me as I laughed— then shivered—at a situation that rode the train from bad to weird to worse to a downright Barronic level of darkness. *The Beautiful Thing that Awaits Us All* was the final project I worked on for its publisher, which might bring us full circle, were it not for the fact that this circle, like the sigil marking *Moderor de Caliginis*, is an open—and hungry—curve.

In 2013, I started my own publishing company, Word Horde, launching the press with *Tales of Jack the Ripper*, an anthology that included Laird Barron's tour-de-force "Termination Dust," a fractured narrative not only providing the thrills and chills expected from Barron's oeuvre, but marking a new venue for his brand of cosmicism, a strange, savage, and sanguine land that Laird knows quite well… Alaska.

Not long after the publication of *Tales of Jack the Ripper*, Justin Steele, who had reviewed *The Book(s) of Cthulhu* and *Tales of Jack the Ripper* at his weird fiction website, *The Arkham Digest*, approached me suggesting this anthology. I receive—and say no to—a lot of anthology pitches, many of which are suggested as possible co-editorial projects, but I found the idea of honoring Laird, an author whose work has influenced and intersected with much of my professional career, irresistible. I approached Laird, asking for permission to let other authors play in his sandbox, and to my delight, Laird said yes. For that, Justin and I owe Laird a lifetime of gratitude. We immediately set to building a roster of our favorite authors, authors who we felt shared Laird's vision of a ravenous universe, and an understanding of that terrible, beautiful thing that awaits us all.

There are no accidents 'round here. The editors of, and the authors included in, this volume have been inspired and affected by Laird Barron's carnivorous cosmos. We've all gazed at mysterious holes, wondering where they lead. We've all found ourselves in conversation with a stranger, staring at a scar and wondering if it is, instead, a seam. We've all heard the voices whispering in the night, praising Belphegor, and saying, "We, the Children of Old Leech, have always been here. And we love you."

Copyright Acknowledgments

ABOUT THE EDITORS

ROSS E. LOCKHART is an author, anthologist, editor, and publisher. A lifelong fan of supernatural, fantastic, speculative, and weird fiction, Lockhart is a veteran of small-press publishing, having edited scores of well-regarded novels of horror, fantasy, and science fiction.

Lockhart edited the anthologies *The Book of Cthulhu I* and *II* and *Tales of Jack the Ripper*. He is the author of *Chick Bassist*. Lockhart lives in an old church in Petaluma, California, with his wife Jennifer, hundreds of books, and Elinor Phantom, a Shih Tzu moonlighting as his editorial assistant.

Visit him online at www.haresrocklots.com

JUSTIN STEELE spends his days counseling high school students and his nights reading as much dark fiction as he can. He is a resident of Delaware, where he also obtained a Bachelor's in English Literature and a Master's in School Counseling.

In 2012 Steele started his blog, *The Arkham Digest*, where he writes about horror and weird fiction. When he's not working with students or reading he can usually be found playing with his dogs, Watson and Bella, or cheering on the Baltimore Ravens. *The Children of Old Leech* is Steele's first published anthology.

Visit him online at www.arkhamdigest.com